Praise for COLUMBIA ROAD

'Big Brother meets Bonnie and Clyde – the results are fast, exceptionally funny, and surprisingly touching' Stella Duffy

'An interesting take on the London flatshare genre and a serious, if funny, comment on the downside of webcam mania' Heat

'If you were a Big Brother addict, this is the book for you' Company

Praise for MAN OR MOUSE

'A funny read . . . puns in every paragraph, and the author makes mischief with computer-speak by relating it to the lexicon of love' The Times

'Hilarious tale of online fun and offline frolics . . . Cyrano for the internet generation' Glamour

'Pacy, racy and cyberspacey' Mirror

Also by Matt Whyman

Man or Mouse

About the author

Matt Whyman is a popular internet and magazine agony uncle. He has a Master of Arts degree in Creative Writing from the University of East Anglia, and lives in East London with his wife and two daughters. He is the author of the state-of-the-art, highly-acclaimed romantic comedy *Man or Mouse*.

MATT WHYMAN

COLUMBIA
ROAD

FLAME
Hodder & Stoughton

Grateful acknowledgement is made to HarperCollins Publishers Ltd for permission to
reprint an excerpt from *Trigger Happy* by Steven Poole © 2000

First published in Great Britain in 2002 by Hodder and Stoughton
A division of Hodder Headline

A Flame paperback

1 3 5 7 9 10 8 6 4 2

A CIP catalogue record for this title is available from the British Library

ISBN 0 340 76905 x

Typeset by Palimpsest Book Production Limited,
Polmont, Stirlingshire

Printed and bound in Great Britain by
Mackays of Chatham plc, Chatham, Kent

Hodder and Stoughton
A division of Hodder Headline
338 Euston Road
London NW1 3BH

In memory of my mother and my sister.

Acknowledgements

Thanks to: Philippa Pride and the Hodder clan; David Godwin and all at DGA; Nick Duerden; David Kirkup; Serena Mackesy; Adrian Taylor; G-Stone for the vibe; Unreal for the action; G&B for ever; Emma for everything and more.

'We don't want absolutely real situations in
videogames. We can get that at home.'
Trigger Happy: The Inner Life of Videogames,
Steven Poole, 2000

'You might think you know each other intimately,
but moving in together can open up a whole
new world of surprises.'

Ask Patrick
Sparkle!, 1998

Get Cartier. That was the plan. To profit from him as he had from us. An eye for an eye, that sort of thing, but with damages tacked on too. We saw it as compensation. Payback for the grief and indignity suffered as his tenants. I might have been feeling a bit biblical when I set my sights on retribution, but the only good book in this girl's life was one with cheques in it.

Things weren't so desperate to begin, far from it. My name was written all over the place when I first moved in – a two-storey set-up overlooking a unique street scene, with windows that sucked in the sun from dawn to dusk. What more could a graduate want? OK, so a decent job was on my wish list, along with a late growing spurt so I didn't have to kiss on tiptoe, but that was about ambition and dreams. What this house appeared to offer was a little bit of security and warmth, a roof over my head until I started going places. What failed us were the fixtures and fittings. That's what persuaded my housemates and me to recoup the cost of living here.

Emotionally speaking, my stay has left me close to bankruptcy. You only have to look at me now to realise my balance sheet doesn't quite tally. I mean, I'm hardly dressed for the occasion: barefoot in the yard at daybreak in a candy pink slip and no face on. Think bombshell blonde, before the clear-up operation. Twenty-two going on forty, the way I feel right now. It's chilly outside, as well. Way too early in the day for the barbecue I've built, but at least it keeps me warm while I contemplate the cooking. Armed with the bare necessities, it doesn't take much to get the charcoal started. A cigarette lighter, an incendiary blast of hair spray and *whoosh*! Within seconds the flames are springing up and down like hatchling birds, desperate to be fed. And what a treat I've got for you, kids. Look what Momma has clutched to her breast. Bundles of notes! Bloody great bricks of cash! A six-figure treat, I'd say. In easily digestible denominations, too. The fruits of our earlier foray and money to burn, if I can just stoke my courage to see the job through.

When you rent a shared house at this level, you expect a little grief: damp in the bathroom, maybe, washing-up wars and fiercely protected fridge space. Even buckled bedsprings from the previous occupants that you try not to think about when you turn over at night. Even so, nothing should push you to this kind of extreme. Here in Columbia Road, for that matter, *everyone* ought to come up smelling of roses. You want local colour in the East End of London? Hey, you're in the right place. Come in daylight hours, for that's when you'll find the flower market. It's always packed, and in full bloom. Festooned with flora from every nation, the perfume can be as overwhelming as the traders who vie for your custom. Sometimes people turn up just to stop, look and listen, or pass through on their way to dates, weddings and wakes. It's the place to come when words are not enough, when only the freshest, finest bouquets will do. By sundown, as ever, the stalls will be gone. You might see a sprig of heather bowling along like tumbleweed, but the peace and quiet is something special. More so, I imagine, after the great upheaval we've just come through.

For a street with such different sides to it, the houses themselves are almost identical. On first moving here, ours seemed like one more desirable residence. By which I mean every residence except the place next door. Aren't all Victorian terraces let down by at least one like this, some miserable, Munsteresque joint with a rate of decay that exceeds all others? You know the type, all blackened bricks and peeling paintwork. A gaff that garners more shadows at dusk, and *always* has a light on through the night. We live at number 664. Across the road stands 665, which makes us 'the neighbour of the beast', as some people have been drawn to say. We never saw an old goat coming or going, of course, but whoever did live there had to be wise to us. Everyone else was familiar with our daily domestics, and it sure as hell feels like we've been living lately with the devil in our midst.

So what could have possessed me to take things so far? Even to *contemplate* flinging a fortune into the flames.

Because I know what it bought, is why. And I know what it cost me.

We're talking about an abuse of rights here, and not just our rights as tenants. This involves broadcast rights, even basic human rights. In my book, that makes this money dirty. The fruits of a Frank Cartier Production. I may have been part of the main attraction, but I wasn't his damn property. I just lived in it, along with the other two members of the cast. My housemates, in fact, are still on show right now, living at large behind closed doors, in full view of the world around.

Let's start with Slim Jim. The love interest. Not just for me but many others. I only say this because the click count soars when he lopes out of the shower each morning. I'd like to think most people see through his vest. The one with 'BORN HUNG' emblazoned boldly across the chest. It's the dressing-gown I hold responsible for his reputation, some adolescent synthetic affair with a scuffed Manga print on the back. One so shrunken from a decade of washing-machine misuse that it barely brushes his thighs. All part of the appeal, so they say. Personally, Slim has to work on me before I'll admit that he's a sweetie underneath. I am, after all, the one who has to live with him for real. Everyone else can switch off whenever they like, take a break, get on with their own lives. Which leaves me to kick-start his. My long-limbed loafer with the hippie-hair history and the Roman nose. An emperor of slack who's happy to slip a ring through his eyebrow but would wince at the idea of slipping one on my finger. Not that I've ever asked, of course: having only just regained my freedom, I've no plans to sign any other contract for some time.

Besides, Slim's virtually wed as it is, to his online gaming console.

It's an open affair, but he's committed. Right now, in fact, I imagine anyone monitoring the front room should see him saunter in, stoop to pick up the joypad and then settle into the sofa, there in front of the screen. It gives him Internet access, this console of his, but the keyboard that came with it doesn't get a look in when Slim's at the controls. I know for a fact that he could play games from it just fine, but apparently the keys 'aren't designed to be manhandled'.

I suspect it's an image thing. Maybe if it was called a pleasure deck or some such he might be inclined to get to grips with it more often. As it is, the joypad is what he uses once he's logged into the gaming arena. A zone out there in cyberspace, where Slim can go head to head with Slims from all over the world. In direct contrast to his philosophy in life, my boyfriend's gaming tactics are always about seizing the initiative. Don't wait to defend. Hit all opponents hard and with whatever comes to hand. In other words, *kill everything that moves.* Even if it is just a round of virtual golf. That's how it is with him. Unless, of course, he calls an amnesty to roll a joint, or a member of the viewing public alerts him to the fact that his penis is peeping out of his dressing-gown. More often than not it's a combination of the two that persuades him to press pause and shuffle back to the bedroom to throw some clothes over his frame, stopping only to deliver a half-smoked spliff to the third occupant in this very public house of ours. 'Room service,' he'll call at the door, and tighten his sash before going in, not wanting to frighten the horses.

If you're among the numbers who have visited us to date, you'll be fondly familiar with Pavlov. My older brother, the comic relief. A mess of a man in a room so retentively tidy that Slim instinctively cups his palm under the spliff to catch any ash. He's been up for no more than half an hour, but already his futon's back in the sofa position. Even the sheets have been folded away for the day, replaced with cushions so plumped they defy you to sit down. Pavlov works from home, claims he needs an uncluttered environment to counter the chaos of his writing. It's a rule that extends to his desktop computer, where the screensaver constructs random mathematical patterns that most probably trigger tidal waves out in the Pacific. Appearance-wise he seems amazingly together, too: close crop, close shave, pressed shirt, fresh pants and socks. You can be sure the trousers will have killer creases too, once he's finished ironing them. Anyone watching him align the folds with such confidence and ease could be forgiven for thinking this was one together dude. It's only when people choose to zoom in on his heart-shaped face that Pavlov gets twitchy. For that's when the cracks start to show, fanning from the corners of his eyes and stacked across his brow. An expression that comes to the fore if he chooses this moment, for example, to look up from his labours.

'This isn't a good time,' he tells Slim, shaking his head as the spliff comes his way. 'It doesn't fit into my schedule right now.'

'That's why I'm offering it to you, so you stop using words like *schedule* and loosen up a little. Come on, Pav. If any man can smoke and iron at the same time, it's you.'

In a hiss of steam, Pavlov stops to level his gaze at the offering. 'Is that a compliment, or am I going to have to ask you to leave?'

'First of the day,' Slim reminds him. 'Always the finest.'

My brother palms the back of his head, as if he needs to ask an audience for advice.

'Just say yes, Pavlov.'

'There's no shame in knowing how to iron properly.'

'Look, do you want this or not?'

'Unfortunately I don't have a girlfriend who I can appeal to whenever I need a shirt doing.'

'True,' Slim agrees. 'But, then, who do you appeal to whenever you need a joint rolling?'

A tic flutters across Pavlov's face, his pursed expression threatening to fall apart like his spliffs. He glances at his wristwatch. Accurate to the nanosecond, as ever. 'Come on, then. Just quickly.'

My brother pulls hard through the roach, and comes across like an asthmatic with an inhaler.

'So what've you got lined up today?' Slim enquires. 'Anything glamorous?'

My brother nods affirmatively and, without exhaling, squeaks that it's possibly the most important day of his career.

Slim steps back a pace. 'I'd go easy on that, then. It's red skunk.'

'Bastard!' coughs Pavlov, smoke pouring forth. 'I thought it was pungent.'

Slim turns his attention to the ironing-board. 'Actually, I would say that'll be your trousers.'

'Fuck!'

Pavlov grabs the iron, grimaces at the scorched imprint underneath.

'Careful,' warns Slim, and points to the joint pinched between his fingers. 'You might drop a blim. Burn a hole or something.'

In a moment, Slim will reclaim the spliff and continue his tour of duty. Assuming he had even granted my brother a hit in the first place, that is, for I am busking this particular exchange. With no access to a screen I can only guess at what's going on inside the house, but you get the drift. We're talking about two very different boys here: one born to burn out; the other still waiting for the spark.

Unlike Slim, Pavlov attracts as many male eyeballs as female. The figures certainly indicate that my brother's appeal swings both ways, though he really wouldn't thank me for saying so. 'I'm not *gaaay*!' he always protests, in that scared-of-his-own-sexuality kind of way. He's not, but it's still guaranteed to wind him up. Calling him by his nickname once had the same effect, but it's become second nature to him now. *Pavlov*, as in the man who discovered dogs could be trained to salivate at the tinkling of a bell. Except in my brother's case it isn't a bell that triggers an involuntary response but the call of nature.

Unusually for a guy, Pavlov isn't ruled by his prick, his head or even his heart. It's his bladder who's boss. Honestly, his need to pee can be triggered by the slightest stimulus – as Slim and I know to our advantage, not to mention those visitors who seek out every opportunity to watch him run for the closest convenience: running taps, prising off beer caps, the squeak of a balloon. You only have to look at him questioningly and he'll excuse himself. Poor old Pav blames the pressure of his chosen profession, but take it from me, the seeds had been sown a long time ago. As kids we owned a hamster each. Mine perished between the paws of the cat one night after I forgot to shut its cage. His contracted pneumonia, having gone fatally bald due to overbrushing. Died of the indignity, I shouldn't wonder. A fate I imagine Pavlov fears for himself now he's knackered his lucky trousers.

'You can always borrow a pair from me,' Slim suggests, and finds himself the subject of a withering glare.

From Pavlov's point of view, this man is standing in front of his bookshelves, shoulders slightly sloped to one side, messing up the symmetry of his surroundings. It's all becoming too much, so he says. 'Bespoke moleskin jacket and saggy-ass combats? I don't think so.'

'I do own a pair of suit trousers,' Slim counters.

'Yeah, and you cut them down at the knee last summer.'

'So wear big socks—'

'*Forget* it,' snaps Pavlov. 'Even if you did have a decent pair, I wouldn't touch them with gloves on.'

'Why not?'

'Because I know for a fact you dress commando.'

'Going without underpants is a liberation. The male equivalent of burning bras.'

'Slim, I can only compare it to a dog without a collar.'

My boyfriend takes this as a compliment. 'You're right. There is something wild and untamed about it.'

'No, it's just scary. Period. Come across a dog with no collar, most people cross the road. You just don't know where it's been or what it might do.'

Slim shrugs. Mumbles something about less washing. Whatever, is Pavlov's response. Thanks for the offer, but pants are a point of principle with him.

'You should at least try it once.' Slim scoops at his own crotch. 'Might help you feel less uptight.'

'Leave me alone,' my brother retorts, and turns to work through his colour-banded clothes rail. 'I'm going to have to rethink my whole outfit.'

'All right,' says Slim, prickling now. 'No need to get so *pissy*.'

Pavlov freezes in the wake of this word. Those watching my brother's face should see his nostrils flare and his lips compress. Anyone watching Slim should see him attempt to suppress a sly grin. In the next frame my brother will be gone, and if you really want to follow the action then toggle along to the toilet. Alternatively, follow my boyfriend and the stubby remains of his spliff back to our bedroom, though you may want to hang back in the landing. For in a second or so he'll be out again.

Looking for me.

Ten minutes earlier I had been spooned up beside Slim, wondering how he always managed to doze so effortlessly. When he closed his eyes the world around him ceased to exist, but for me it just closed in. At the time, I'd had my fingers in the space between his ribs. Toes barely touching his calves. Tickling him towards the edge of the bed as I did every day until he fell out and gave me some space. It was one of those rituals all couples rely upon to bind them. A shared moment that signposted the start of each day. Except this morning Slim would return to find a change to the published programme. Due to circumstances beyond his control, I would not now be turning down the daily dog end for the simple fact that I had vanished.

The sound of flushing water now. Out on the landing, Pavlov emerges from the toilet with both arms crooked up at the elbows, his hands rendered out of action until he can get into the bathroom and scrub them in the sink. Cranky, I know, but when it comes to sharing a house with two different males, anal counters animal, and that makes room for me.

'Do us a favour.' My brother tips his head at the door beside the toilet.

'Can't,' says Slim. 'Your sister must be in there.'

Pavlov's expression darkens a watt. Already? he thinks. At this time?

Slim taps the door with his knuckle, turns to hear a bit better. 'Baby, there's a joint out here with your name on it.'

Whether he would dare to call me 'baby' is debatable. All I can do is stab a guess at the scene inside as the boys wise up to the fact that I'm missing. Their suspicions are confirmed when Slim finds the door is unlocked. 'Did she say she was going anywhere?'

Pavlov shakes his head, slips in, spins the hot tap, then spins himself around with the same dawning horror mirrored in his housemate: *'The money!'*

You can trust me when I say they both sounded freaked. I imagine the traders in the market could testify to the panic spilling from our house. The scramble to prise off the bath panel. More crowing when they find the haul gone. Going by the slamming doors and fast-descending footfalls that I really do hear from the yard, I guess there's little time left to act in their best interest. So let me just complete the picture by telling you a bit about *moi*.

I'm Cisco. Yeah, I know, my dad's brainchild, and one that just kind of stuck a bit faster than my real name. It's not exactly Cathy or Claire, but at least if we were ever introduced at a party the conversation wouldn't fall at the first hurdle. Anyway, I imagine you've seen a thumbnail of me. Reduced to fit on a monitor screen, I could pass as a perfect size ten. There's a little more of me in the flesh, however, as some of my truly dedicated followers can vouch. Not that I'm an attention-seeker by nature, just design. Slim and Pavlov loathed this constant scrutiny as much as I did. We stopped being individuals and became objects of desire, even derision. That's why we took action. Turned against the man who made it happen. Our landlord and entrepreneur, impresario, and imagineer, Svengali, showman, *swindler*, Mr Frank Cartier. And yet, despite walking away with a handsome settlement, I've come to the conclusion it'll never be enough. Nothing could buy back all the things we've lost. That's what I realised when I woke up this morning, and that's why I came out here to start the fire. Because if we're going to move on we have to burn this bridge. The one supported by the money in my arms.

'Cisco! Don't do it! *Stop!*'

I turn to see Slim bowl into the yard. Pavlov hurtles out in his wake. Trouserless, as I had imagined, but just as desperate to stop me from feeding the flames.

'*No—*'

2

Money wasn't an issue when I first came to town. It wasn't an issue because I didn't have any. Not a bean. I was young, gifted and skint, as any good graduate should be. A mistress in the art of trashing trust funds, buttering up the bank manager then wondering where it had all gone when the party finally finished. It was a lack of cash, in fact, that persuaded me to seek my fortune in the capital. Which was how Pavlov came to find me on his doorstep, earlier that summer. Shrinking under a sudden downpour with two stuffed suitcases and a cabbie who needed paying.

'Cisco!' he declared, and faltered there. Once upon a time we hooked up every holiday, but lately that had been confined to Christmas, and so the surprise was kind of mutual. Not least because I was so used to seeing him with a scarf knotted round his neck to keep out the chill. Regaining his composure, Pavlov looked at me quizzically. 'What are you doing here?'

I clutched at the fake-fur collar of my coat, said, 'Lend us sixteen quid and I'll tell you.'

'Are you in trouble?'

'Not yet,' I replied, aware that the taxi driver behind me still had my luggage. Okay, so it wasn't exactly a bundle on a stick and a cat called Socks, but I came with a Dick-like charm that surprised even me when a figure appeared behind my brother. 'Oooh, hello.'

Jesus Christ with a jester's nose. That was my first impression of Slim. Dreadlocks on a white boy was the second. A firm handshake was the next. The fact that I couldn't take my eyes off him probably featured in there somewhere too. He had a bad Hawaiian shirt on his back, one that hung wide open like the wallet he produced.

'Pavlov doesn't carry cash.' He grinned, and handed a twenty to the driver. 'Covered in germs, he reckons.'

'Damn right.' My brother shuffled aside for me. I stepped in from the rain. Music drifted from the kitchen at the end of the hall, a lazy, looping groove. Someone had been roasting peppers in there too. It smelt fantastic: woody and warming. At the top of the stairs was a stained-glass window. I wondered if I would still be here to see the afternoon light swing through it. 'Just ask yourself how many people have touched that twenty.' This was Pavlov, still pressing his point. 'I imagine a fair percentage have also rolled it into a tube and inserted it up one nostril.'

I turned back to see that the cabbie was checking the note against the rainclouds. Then he gave it a tug as if to test its strength, and reminded my brother that money was money.

'In terms of bacterial transmission,' said Pavlov, 'it's second only to the sneeze.'

Slim looked embarrassed, and invited the man to keep the change.

'Bless you.' The cabbie released the suitcases, scorn and pity in his eyes as Pavlov dragged them both inside. But then he jabbed a thumb at the market behind him, and his expression brightened. 'Maybe I'll buy the wife some flowers.'

'Money well spent,' said Slim. 'You can always get a good deal round here.'

I watched him direct the cabbie to a stall at the end of the street, and couldn't help but glow inside. Strictly speaking, he wasn't my type. I placed him in his mid-twenties, which was in my league, but that beach-lizard image was a world removed from my own. The suntan, the sinews and the potential for sand in the pants, it was all just a bit too untamed for me. Too itinerant. Like you might get a night of wild, indecent sex, only to find it wasn't just the man who was missing when you regained consciousness but all your valuables as well. And yet despite the hustler shirt and the gym-rope tresses, there was something decent about him. Honourable, almost. The thing with the wallet, coupled with his easy smile, told me a caring, sharing young man was in there just busting to break out. He didn't exactly look like a guy who could afford to drop twenty pounds after all. Going by his appearance, I was a little worried that he had just blown a sizeable chunk of his dole money for the week.

'You're very kind,' I said. 'What would my brother do without you?'

Slim switched his attention to Pavlov, his eyebrows lifting sharply. 'This is your *sister*?'

'Afraid so.'

'Pav, she's nothing like you.'

'Is that good?' I asked, and was pleased to hear that it was.

Pavlov closed the door. Reluctantly, he made our introduction. We shook hands, my brother like a referee between us, watching for signs of foul play. I gave Slim my best smile, and saw him pick up on the space between my teeth.

'Cisco's just graduated.'

'Nothing to write home about,' I pointed out. 'A degree in Media Production.'

'Wow!' said Slim. 'Was it all "lights, camera, action"?'

'It might've been,' I said reluctantly, conscious not to come across like the laziest student alive. Lying in through lectures had been my specialist subject, but I really wanted to make the right impression here so I flagged up the fact that I had knuckled down at the last minute. Scraped myself a 2:1.

'You must know how to put on a show, then?'

'Not at all,' I told him, with absolute honesty, and figured I should come clean. 'Actually I know nothing about the nuts and bolts. I guess you could say I'm just qualified to blag my way on to the credits.'

That smile again. If this Slim was mine, I remember thinking, then the goatee would have to go. I could live with the dreads, providing there was nothing else lodging in there. For a moment we shared the same doormat, the three of us uncomfortably close, so it was a relief when Slim prompted Pavlov to put the kettle on. I followed my brother through the hall, looking up and around all the way. The white walls were scuffed by the passing of time and bicycles brought in from the street, while the carpet had been worn into a spine of sorts. Nevertheless, the place felt lived in for all the right reasons. Sauntering behind me, Slim said, 'So what do you want to be now you're ready to take on the world?'

'Well, whatever I do mustn't feel like work,' I told him, pausing to peer into the front room on our way through. As all the furniture seemed oriented towards the box, I suspected hard labour wasn't a priority in this household either. I took in the lampstand first, the shade cocked artfully to spotlight the screen, then marvelled at all the space behind the sofa. An unlit expanse that extended to the bay window, where the curtains had been clothes-pegged shut for good measure. All in all, the place looked more like a *viewing* room than a front room. The TV was quite literally on a pedestal, with all kinds of gizmos underneath it, and as for the kitsch prints of doe-eyed dogs on the wall . . . I wondered if either of them had ever really taken stock of their surroundings. Moving on now, I said, 'As I see things, the only way to avoid work feeling like work is by making a success of something I enjoy.'

'My kind of philosophy,' Slim agreed.

'Slim's a millionaire.'

Pavlov's deadpan delivery made me chuckle, until I turned at the threshold to the kitchen and saw that Slim wouldn't meet my eye. 'Seriously?'

'Only on paper,' he said shyly. 'I had an offer on my e-zine.'

'Your what?'

'It's just a website, really.'

'Yeah? What's it about?'

'Online gaming, basically. News. Downloads. Message boards. Reviews.'

'Geek stuff,' said Pavlov, as if summing up.

Slim ignored my brother. 'I just got lucky,' he continued modestly.

'There must be more to it than that,' I said. 'I didn't think any business made money from the Internet.'

'I'm not a business,' said Slim, and for a moment I thought I had insulted him. 'I never set out to get rich, either. I'm amateur and proud of it, true to the spirit of the web.'

'Slim is what's known as an early adopter,' Pavlov cut in, 'which means if you weren't online by 'ninety-four then you just weren't *there*.'

'Tell me about your website,' I said, and I was genuinely interested. Not least because it meant I could lose myself in that languid gaze of his.

'Before cyberspace went commercial,' he started, 'I built a lo-fi site as a way of connecting with other players. The beautiful thing about game-heads is their enthusiasm. It's a pursuit some take very seriously. They go *insane* for the latest online action, so when the virtual big bang happened that kind of passion attracted investors.'

'But so did lots of sites,' I said.

'Yeah, but unlike the start-ups that tried to cash in, I had a loyal user base. More so now the gaming industry is hot to trot. Some suits in the City see things getting madder still on that front, which is how they proposed the million deal.' Slim tossed this out like he was talking beer money. 'The less I took up-front for the site, the more I get in shares I can cash if the company floats. So I accepted a grand, and hedged my bets on a mill.'

'Is that good?' I asked. 'It sounds good.'

'Good in that I won't have to lean on your brother to cover the rent for a while, like I normally do. *Great* in that I could buck the trend and make a bunch from the stock market. Bad in that it's left me feeling like a sell-out.'

'So give it to charity,' suggested Pavlov, who had just filled the kettle.

'I'll take care of you,' said Slim, mischievously. 'Don't worry.'

'Does Pavlov contribute to your site?'

My brother's derisory snort informed me that he didn't. 'Any nutter can get published on the Internet. All you need is a keyboard, a modem and a probe strapped to your forehead.'

I looked at my mules and wished I'd been born an only child. Instead, I was saddled with an older sibling who could act like one. It wasn't as if Pavlov even had much reason to resent success in others. As a journalist, my brother was a household name. Not the whole house, I should say. Just certain bedrooms, really. The ones where pony posters jockeyed with boy-band centrefolds. Where teddy-bear hot-water bottles hid half-drunk bottles of Bacardi. The place where teen girls took their magazines and pored over other people's problems, which was where the Pavster came in, and which was perhaps why he got a bit touchy when people talked shop. My brother being an agony uncle. *Sparkle!*'s very own Love Surgeon, to give his full credit. Cool in adolescent quarters, maybe, but not the sort of thing you'd include on a passport. Unless you were begging for a strip-search.

'Are you okay with instant?' my brother asked, holding a teaspoon of the stuff over the first of three cups. 'I have to be out of here in ten minutes.'

With my suitcases standing sentry just inside the door, I was hoping he might have realised I was in no hurry to leave. As it was, I said instant would be fine. Figured I should buy some more time before making my pitch. 'Where you going?' I asked him instead.

'Photo-shoot. The editor wants a fresh picture of me for the problem page.'

Pavlov finished scooping from the jar, and glanced sideways to gauge my reaction. I tried to look impressed. Unlike Slim, who came into the kitchen with me now and said, 'In that shirt?'

My brother was wearing a vibrant orange button-down. Hesitantly, he confirmed that this was his outfit of choice. Slim sucked in air between his teeth. Pavlov gritted his. I couldn't help thinking he was clashing badly with the green chequered lino under his feet. Even the back door that framed him couldn't quite contain the glow.

'For a man with a penchant for palm trees and pelican prints,' my brother complained, 'I hardly think you're in a position to criticise.' Slim shrugged, said it was his call.

'So you have a problem with this shirt?'

'Not personally, but I can't speak for your readers.'

'How so?' asked Pavlov uncertainly.

'I'm thinking what you really need is a smoking jacket.'

'Huh?'

'A velvet smoking jacket and an outsize glass of brandy you can slop all over your slippers.'

Slim knocked me a wink on the sly, which only served to make me go a bit red. Not as red as Pavlov, however, who tossed his teaspoon into the sink and asked him to explain.

'It's about the vibes you should be giving out,' said Slim. 'You're supposed to be a master in the art of love, right?'

'I'm hired to provide insight into how guys handle relationships, yes.'

'The voice of experience and expertise.'

My brother sank his hands into his pockets. Modestly, he accepted the point.

'Well, couldn't you at least try to look like a sack artist? A serial shagger who's in between beds?' I stifled a smile when Slim hit him with this. Hoped it wasn't going to put Pavlov in a mood. 'Mark my words,' Slim finished, 'if you have your picture taken in that tangerine effort, the ladies are going to question your credentials.'

'It's not tangerine.'

'To me, it *screams* Outspan.'

'I think you'll find it's peach, actually.'

'Either way,' said Slim. 'A fruit's a fruit.'

My brother asked if I took sugar, clearly stung despite making

17

every effort to pretend Slim was no longer with us. I told him just milk, and prayed my voice didn't waver when I added that he looked fine. It was only when he turned for the fridge that I shared a look with his housemate. 'How he got that job beats me,' I said, under my breath.

Pavlov had held the post for half a decade, landing on his feet like this within weeks of moving to London. No counselling qualifications or anything like that, he just happened to have been in the middle of an interview for a copy sub job when the editor burst into tears. Some kind of personal love crisis, apparently, and Pavlov was there with the sympathy and the shoulder to cry on. Even if it had meant spoiling a good shirt.

'In magazines,' explained Slim, 'it's all about who you sleep with.'

My brother turned from the worktop, handed me a steaming mug and said, 'My editor's a guy, actually.'

'I know,' replied Slim, reaching for his own.

I liked Slim, but not just because he could keep my brother in check. As we sat around the kitchen table with our drinks, he wheeled out a miniature skateboard, no more than three inches long, and rode it with two fingers. It was one of those boys' toys for guys who were old and wise enough to know that they'd look a total arse on the real thing. Still, the way he whipped it this way and that told me he was skilful with his hands. I liked him even more when he backed up my bid to stay a while. A week or so was all I wanted, and that was all I asked for. Without an address I couldn't get work, I explained. Without work I couldn't get a place to live. After that, I'd have no option but to sell my body. O and A levels, just like it said on those cards in the phone box. Pavlov listened without once blinking, but to my surprise he declined my appeal to his protective nature: 'Sorry, Cisco. There are only two bedrooms here. I'd love to help out, but what can I say?'

Slim stopped flipping the fingerboard, just stared across the table at him. 'Say yes. Say we'd be delighted. Say the front room's hers for as long as she likes.'

'We'd be in breach of contract,' countered Pavlov. 'You know the rules about subletting. If Cartier found out we'd all be on the streets.'

'Please, Pav, I don't have anywhere else to go.'

'Cisco, it's not my problem.'

'Great advice from an agony uncle,' muttered Slim, then assured me I was welcome to the sofa. 'The landlord lives way out by the coast. He's not even going to know you're staying.'

'Sofa's no good,' said Pavlov.

We both turned his way.

'Why not?' asked Slim, his digits dismounting for a moment.

My brother looked at the dregs in his cup, as if seeking his response from there, then revealed that a couple of the springs were bust.

'Fine by me,' I said. 'I don't mind getting poked a bit.'

Across the table, Pavlov seemed deeply troubled. His gaze turned inwards quite suddenly, uneasy with what he saw, and that was when I understood his reluctance to let me stay.

'Chill out.' I levelled my gaze at him, mostly because I couldn't bring myself to look at Slim. 'I can handle it.'

'Cisco, it's not on.'

'Since when was the sofa sprung?'

Ignoring Slim, my brother suggested I could put my stuff in his room. 'I'll sleep on the floor,' he said. 'You can take my bed.'

'There's nothing wrong with the sofa,' Slim persisted.

'It's just not a good idea, okay.'

'Did you break the sofa and not tell me?' The little skateboard whizzed across the table, as if to deliver the accusation, and dropped on to Pavlov's lap. 'If you've broken it you'll pay, my friend. That's my sofa.'

Angrily, Pavlov flicked it back at him. 'I'm talking to Cisco,' he said, 'and quit fooling with that board.'

'I'm very fond of that sofa. Reclaimed it from the skip myself, remember? I have a right to know if you've broken it.'

'All right, shut up,' said my brother, and surrendered just there. 'It's not broke.'

'So why can't she kip there?'

'Because.'

'What because?'

'Because she's my little sister is why!'

Pavlov stood up smartly. Slim muttered something final about the sofa, and withdrew his toy from the table.

I said, 'I'll sleep in your room, if it makes you feel better.'

My brother held my attention for a second, and then all the air left his lungs in a sigh of resignation. 'Take the front room,' he said. 'You can lock it from the inside at night.'

'What are you suggesting?' asked Slim.

'I thought she might appreciate the privacy,' said Pavlov, who consulted his watch just then and left his seat with a bitter curse. 'Now you've made me late for the shoot.'

'Good luck,' I said, as he circled behind us, heading for the door.

'What time do you plan to be back?' asked Slim, sulkily.

My brother's shoes ceased creaking. Next thing he was leaning in low between our chairs. 'Any time,' he growled. 'You get me?'

3

Three days. That's what it took for me to find work. A time spent turning up at temp agencies and playing down my qualifications. It was something I learned to do after my first couple of interviews. Sitting opposite whoever, with the name badge that should have read 'bored', I would mention that I was a graduate and suddenly it was like I had a criminal record.

'Can you use a phone?' was the kind of thing they would go on to enquire cautiously. Meaning was I prepared to switch off my brain five days a week, and which ultimately persuaded me to quit plugging my degree in favour of my practical assets.

Three years. That's how long I'd spent in higher education, and what got me the job was a posh sexy accent pushed to the fore and the ability to differentiate between a cappuccino and a latte. It wasn't work I enjoyed, but it would at least afford me a room of my own. A room in a hovel, it was that kind of wage, but I couldn't let that dampen my spirits when I came back to Columbia Road. Even if it was a half-way house I had really grown to like.

'What a result!' beamed Slim Jim, when I told him my good news. 'Girl comes to town, gets a modelling gig just like that. Mind you, I'm not surprised.'

The boys were preparing supper at the time. My brother wore a pinny over his shirt, and was sitting at the table slicing pepperoni into tissue-thin wafers. His flatmate stood at the worktop, stacking a pizza base with what appeared to be the contents of the fridge: cheese, tomato, mushrooms, peanut butter and popcorn. Slim had his dreads pulled back with a black velvet scrunchy. I owned one just like it, but didn't like to ask about that either.

'If it's glamour modelling,' my brother said, turning from his chopping board now, 'you'll have to think again.'

'It's not modelling as such.' I wished I had been a little clearer with my job description, just as I wished Pavlov would put down the knife when he addressed me.

'A top agency, that's what you said.'

'It *is* a top agency. I'm their new receptionist.'

Slim turned to scoop up the pepperoni slices from the board, and said it was still worth celebrating. 'We should go out,' he suggested. 'Anywhere you like, Cisco. My treat.'

'Really?'

'Sure. Anything so long as it's salsa.'

'*Salsa?*' my brother and I said together.

Slim shrugged, said he'd always fancied it, just not with Pavlov as a dancing partner. Even if he did dance like a girl.

'No, I don't,' my brother squeaked. 'I'm very uninhibited with music.'

'That's why we should go salsa with your sister. It's a forgiving kind of rhythm.'

I folded my arms, unsure if he was serious. 'Don't you need to be the same height for that sort of dancing?' I asked.

'Who knows,' he said, 'until we try?'

I was about to agree to give it a go, when Pavlov turned our attention back to supper.

'What the hell is *that?*'

My brother was looking at Slim's creation, one hand on his hip, the heel of the other pressed to the side of his head. For a moment I thought he might wilt.

'Pizza,' said Slim, a little wounded.

'It looks like a Petri dish.'

'At least you know what's in it,' Slim said, 'which is more than can be said for the takeaway deliveries.'

'Peanut butter might be okay,' I cut in, thinking perhaps he had been preparing something special on my behalf. 'It tastes good with jam, and you'd never expect the two to go well together.'

'Exactly,' said Slim. 'Sometimes the most unlikely combinations bring out the best in each other.'

I sensed my face warming and quickly looked away. When I glanced up again, Pavlov was untying his pinny. 'I know you've just got in,' he said, 'but it's time we went out.'

'Already?' Slim picked up a bit now, and did a kind of hands-in-the-air, hip-swing thing round Pavlov. 'Baby, there's no *stoppin'* the music in you.'

'Consider me the chaperone.' My brother took off the pinny and folded it neatly into a drawer. 'But first we have to eat.'

Slim stood tall again, said the pizza would take twenty minutes. Pavlov said we could be seated and served in the tapas bar at the top of the road in half that time.

'I'm not sure I can afford to eat out just yet,' I said diplomatically.

'Don't you worry,' said Pavlov, with one last disparaging glance at the pizza. 'Slim will be paying for the food too.'

Salsa night at the Pandemonium. A cavernous club complete with alabaster columns and an upper gallery we stood no chance of reaching. The floor was packed, people from all over, mostly dressed in vests and sweat and easy grins. If I closed my eyes I might have been on the other side of the world, lost to myself in a sea of drums, bells, whistles and lights. Then I'd open them again, and the boys would bring me right back to reality: Slim with his feel for the sound, a laid-back style I could relate to. My brother with his head tossed back and his hands held high, moving like he had a hula-hoop orbiting his hips. It was Pavlov who persuaded me to keep closing my eyes, Pavlov who was first to thumb upstairs and suggest a break, and Pavlov who got as far as the spiral staircase when the bouncer came down like two different people. A tank on top with little scuttling legs underneath.

'Do you know who I am?' my brother asked, leaning in to make himself heard.

The bouncer consulted his clipboard, his five o'clock dome gleaming under the droplight. Then his brow went up and his fat face followed. 'You the one been dancing like a dick?'

Pavlov didn't answer either way. Just stood there panting, his pastel shirt spread open to the waist.

Cautiously, Slim said, 'Does that mean he's on the list?'

'It does,' the man growled, without looking up. 'But not this one.'

'If you had *any* idea who you were talking to,' said Pavlov, fired right up now, 'you'd step aside and spend the rest of the night worrying about whether you still had a job!'

It was then that the bouncer appealed for help here. Advising us both to look after our friend before someone got hurt, and then settling his gaze on Slim, who said, 'I just live with him. Don't hit me.'

The heavy came closer, squaring up to him, I thought, until his scowl softened into something less scary. 'Are you the guy with the gaming website?' he asked, and a smile like you'd see on a baby eased across his face. 'I read about you.'

It was me who encouraged Pavlov towards the cheaper-looking bar under the gallery. Tucked away from the sound system, we could at least hear ourselves speak without yelling. Indeed, my brother's mutterings were frighteningly audible as we watched Slim sign the bouncer's clipboard for him.

'What's with you?' I asked. 'Does he look like a *Sparkle!* reader?'

My brother rested his forearms on the zinc and appeared to address his own reflection. 'Slim's had his picture in print one time. *One time* in some minor gaming magazine and suddenly everyone knows him as "The Dot Com Dread". I've been fronting up a whole page every *week* for the last five years. Is it unreasonable to expect just a little recognition and respect?'

Slim had rejoined us by now. He flipped open his wallet like he was going to talk into it, but then slipped a business card inside. 'You're a teen agony uncle,' he reminded him. 'At the very least you're a familiar face to underage girls, but that's not something to shout about. People might get the wrong idea. Now, what are you both drinking?'

Pavlov asked for a vodka and tonic. I said I'd like the same. Slim ordered three, ice in them all, extra lemon for my brother, then raised his glass to toast me. 'Here's to your modelling career.'

'Hardly,' I said. 'Models don't wear headsets all day.'

Slim took a slug, swallowed it down. 'Uhuru did.'

My brother groaned. 'Lieutenant Uhuru from *Star Trek*,' he said, as if I didn't know already. 'Reference points for geeks don't stretch beyond *Star Trek* or *Star Wars*. It's like their Bible. *Star Trek* is the Old Testament, *Star Wars*, the new. You could argue that *The Simpsons* rather fucks things up, but there's always room for a third way in any religion.'

'Heretic.' Slim looked down his nose at him, which was a long way to look but gave him the air of some higher being passing judgement. Then he turned my way, softened into something more benign. 'Uhuru, as everyone knows, was the looker on the bridge who took all the calls.'

'You make her sound like the secretary.'

Slim stopped to think about this, as if I had just made a valid point. 'It would've been one hell of a rewarding temp job,' he suggested, and looked up at the skywriting he went on to envisage for us. '"College leaver required for Federation flagship. Intergalactic communication skills essential. Must be prepared to travel. High-cut uniform and fancy earpiece provided."'

'Oh, please,' said Pavlov sourly.

'I bet she had some breathers in her time too.'

'Don't embarrass yourself any more,' he pleaded. 'Cisco's already got to deal with the fact that it was your decision to salsa.'

'I'm not embarrassed.' I showed them my near empty glass. 'But I might embarrass myself if I drink any more.'

'That would be embarrassing,' my brother agreed. 'The last time you got drunk in a club with me you started dancing on the tabletops.'

'We were in Ibiza,' I reminded him. 'That's what tabletops are for out there. If you want to eat you get take-out after the clubs have shut.'

'The place was full of loved-up teenagers,' he grumbled.

'Did any of them recognise you?'

'Not that I could tell.' Despite himself Pavlov grinned at Slim. 'They were all up there with Cisco. Hugging each other like you can when you're that age without it looking a little bit desperate.'

'If I remember rightly, you were the only person who stayed at ground level.'

'How embarrassing,' said Slim. 'Is there a history of embarrassing moments with your brother?'

I looked at Pavlov.

'No,' he said quickly.

'That's not strictly true—'

'*Cisco!*'

'What?' Slim switched his attention between us. 'Do tell.'

Pavlov held out for as long as he could, but it wasn't his gaze that gave in on him. 'I need a wee,' he grumbled. 'Just keep it short, eh? I really don't want to hear you still telling it when I get back. In fact,' he finished, directing this at Slim, 'I expect to hear about *your* most embarrassing moment.'

We watched my brother circle away, skirting the dance floor on his way to the gents.

'It happened a long time ago,' I told Slim, reluctant to go into detail now I'd thought ahead.

'There's no shelf life with embarrassment.'

'On holiday in Italy.'

'Shame is a universal language,' he said determinedly. 'Give it up, girl.'

So I did. Right there and then. As Slim ordered one last round of drinks, I took him back to the time when my parents had gone on a vacation of their own – some safari deemed too dangerous for us. 'We were staying in Italy with friends of the family,' I began. 'They had a villa on the shores of Lake Como. You could look out across the water at these lush wooded mountains with villages tucked into pockets of rock. The fact that they also owned a mirror dinghy made it all the more special.'

'Sounds beautiful.'

'She was.'

'The boat?'

'The daughter. Only child of the family. Same age as Pavlov, but way beyond him in every other sense. She was all long limbs and lashes. A mass of black hair and eyes like chocolates. That was her unique selling point, these eyes. They melted my brother's heart whenever she looked his way. Which she did, quite a lot, but I think mostly because she was a little unsettled by the way he behaved around her. It must have been like a ghost had taken up residence, the vibes he gave off in her presence. He'd try to communicate, of course, but it was never going to happen for him. Let's just say there was more than a language barrier between them.'

'This is going to be embarrassing.' As he spoke, Slim clawed the scrunchy from his dreads then shook his head like a dog in the wake of a downpour. 'I can feel it in my bones.'

'Her father had promised us this sailing trip for the last day, and I just knew Pavlov saw it as his final chance to win her over. The night before, he couldn't sleep he was so uptight about the prospect of a day on the lake with her. The poor lad was white as the snow-caps before he'd even climbed on deck.'

'Don't tell me, he was seasick down her dress.'

'Worse,' I said. 'Midway across the lake, on this little boat with no facilities, Pavlov had an urge.'

'He *peed* down her dress?'

'It wasn't a pee he needed.'

Slim pulled back a pace, and looked at me with some alarm. 'Couldn't he hold on?'

'Pavlov had to go,' I said. 'It was a slow build-up, I think, but by the time he reached the point of no return the shore was way beyond reach. I could tell he was in real distress. He went so quiet. So *clenched*. Now obviously there was no way he was going to squat over the side in front of this girl, so I took it upon myself to have a quiet word with her father. He suggested Pavlov could go out in the inflatable and "make the *merdaio*" from there. They had it tied to the back of the yacht for emergencies.'

'Which this was.'

'So we all had to look the other way while Pavlov clambered across with some tissues, let out enough rope to hide his modesty, and set about doing his business without falling in. The father tried to distract his daughter and me by getting us to pull in the sail and start lunch, but it was impossible to relax, knowing what was going on to our aft. By the time we got round to breaking our baguettes this unnatural silence had settled over us. Even the wind seemed to die. Nothing but the sound of water lapping against the hull, and then a distant . . . well, y'know.'

'Oh, my God.' Slim had one hand on the crown of his head now, his eyes locked on to mine.

'We all heard it, and I forced myself to kick start a conversation. Anything to move on from that terrible moment, even if I had to push my Italian to the limit. But I knew my efforts would come to nothing when they both began to steer their gaze around me. I could see it in their eyes, almost. A vision of this turd coming round the portside, bobbing in the water behind me. Pavlov was a little reluctant to get back on board after that. He even asked to stay in the dinghy but apparently it would've been a hazard.'

I reached for my drink, watched Slim as I took a sip and wondered what it would take to break the spell. He was just standing there with his mouth open, still staring at the imaginary picture I had painted. I debated telling him that our folks never made it home from their own holiday, but that was a traumatic tale of tigers and tour guides without tranquilliser guns. Besides, I figured Pavlov must have told him all about that, and I didn't want to darken this moment with Slim. Even if I had already left the poor guy lost for words, it was good just being in his company.

'You wanted to know about his most embarrassing moment,' I reminded him instead, and watched him pull focus with a shiver. 'Plus you'll never need to ask him when his hygiene habits became an obsession.'

'That boy so badly needs a girlfriend.'

'Has he ever been on a date since you've known him?'

'Once,' said Slim, 'but I think the problem now is his job. As a Love Surgeon, it must be like taking work home with him. He's trained to pick up on the problems.'

'So this date of his, what was wrong with her?'

'Pavlov felt her eyeballs were too big.' Slim shrugged, as if to say he couldn't work that one out either. 'Between you and me, I think he's just freaked by the whole idea of getting physical. All those body fluids mingling don't sit too comfortably with his outlook on life.'

'It's easy to see why people think he's gay.'

'Genetically straight, culturally screaming, that's how your brother seems to me. If he could decide which camp he really belonged in I feel sure he wouldn't be such an embarrassment to himself.'

'Either way,' I said, 'it would do him good to find someone special.'

Behind us, a shrill of whistles greeted the next DJ in the box, and when the drums rolled in, Slim said, 'What's your worst moment?'

'I just told you.' I paused for him to appreciate how bad that episode on the boat had been for me. 'Pavlov wasn't the only one who got left with a thing about deep water. It was so humiliating I sometimes think I'll never sail again. Anyway, what's yours?'

'Me? I haven't got one.'

'Play the game,' I said, laughing now. 'Come on, everyone has a time in their life when they wished the ground could open up beneath their feet.'

He consulted his thoughts for a beat. 'You really want to know?'

'Of course.'

'Well, it depends on you, really. How you react.'

'I'm not easily shocked,' I said, but I was when he closed in and kissed me. Slim coming down like a kingfisher, his lips connecting with mine, then a blink and he was back at the bar. Standing there uncertainly, awaiting my reaction.

'There are a lot of people here in this club,' he said next, and invited me to look around. 'Should you go ahead and empty your drink over my head I would look upon it as my most embarrassing moment ever. If it stays in your glass, however, it might just be one of the best.'

After what had just happened, I wasn't aware that I was even *in* a club. The salsa sounds just fading away as the spotlight came down on me. I opened my mouth, began falling in and out of words, then abandoned that response for something better. As it was, my mouth never quite found his because Pavlov found us first.

'Tell me it's over,' he said, and the pair of us stepped back smartly. Pavlov leaned in and collected his drink from the bar. Probably wondering what was with the huge space we had just given him to do this, but missing the glance we exchanged that would have brought him up to speed. 'So now you know our most embarrassing moment,' my brother continued, addressing his housemate now, 'it's only right that you tell us yours.'

'He doesn't have one,' I said, before Slim could draw breath, and batted a glance up at him. 'Not yet.'

4

What Slim did have was front, more than I imagined, but not in the way most men might express it. That kiss of his had taken guts, but I could tell by the way he came away that it was a genuine gamble. Had he looked at me like I should have been grateful it would have been a case of wet dreads. As it was, I left the club with a man who had risked it all, who knew what he wanted but wasn't confident he could get it – not while his flatmate was around, at any rate. Pavlov walking between us all the way home, then spreading out on the sofa before either of us had a chance to lay claim to it.

'So you're staying up, then?' Slim watched my brother make himself comfortable. 'Isn't it late for you?'

'It is for me,' I said. 'I really ought to be turning in soon. It's bad enough having to face natural-born beauties in my new job, I don't want to make it any worse by showing up for my first day looking as rough as I'm bound to feel.'

'Why don't you sleep in my bed?' Slim suggested, then braced himself for the inevitable growl of disapproval. 'And I'll take the sofa once your brother's turned in. That was what I was going to say. Cisco needs a decent kip, Pavlov, and that's not going to happen if you're in here watching late-night movies.'

'She'll be fine right here.' Pavlov was still bristling about being tested like this. 'As soon as *you* hit the sack,' he told him, 'Cisco can have the sofa.'

Slim's expression darkened. 'Don't spoil a good evening,' he said. 'You're my friend as well as her brother.'

An awkward pause followed, and all because of me. Which was why I assured them both that I would start looking for a place of my own just as soon as I got my first pay cheque. 'I'm really grateful you guys let me stay here,' I sighed, 'but the truth is I'm busting to unpack my bags properly.'

Since my arrival I had gathered up my stuff every morning and stowed it all behind the sofa: my sheets and pillow, my jimmy-jams, my wash-bag, clothes and cleansers. I had virtually removed all evidence of my existence for them. For the sake of my own identity, it was probably time I found a room where I could make my mark. It was Pavlov who quit the face-off, and agreed that moving out might be a good thing. Slim nodded once, like he would deal with him later, then suggested a nightcap before we all turned in. I took him up on the offer, if only so I could have a word with my self-appointed chaperone.

'Stop this,' I hissed, once Slim had slipped into the kitchen. Pavlov checked his palms, and ran a thumb down one of his lifelines. 'I appreciate your concern,' I said, 'but you have to let me breathe a little while I'm here.'

'I'm not so concerned about Slim.' My brother looked up finally. 'It's the landlord who keeps me awake at night.'

'I'm sure he'd understand. It's not like I'm staying on a permanent basis.'

'The only thing Frank Cartier understands is the stuff that folds away inside his wallet. He only puts up with a scruff like Slim because he knows he's about to come into a lot of money. You don't want to mess with him, Cisco. Our landlord has a lot of connections.'

'So does the gas man,' I said. 'He's still just a service provider.'

A faint smile, and then Pavlov tucked his legs in so I could sit beside him. 'I know I can be a little protective,' he conceded. 'It's just that now you're here and not at university I feel duty-bound to watch out for you. At least if you had your own place I wouldn't get on your nerves, but I'll always worry. It's what I do best.'

'You do more than that.' I patted his ankle, and said I was grateful for the sofa. Pavlov didn't answer. He was too busy feeling down the back of it all of a sudden, quietly cursing his housemate. I sensed he was reluctant to talk about himself any more, and half wondered if he had opened up on a couch like this before. 'Have you seen the remote?' he asked. 'Ever since Slim got his online gaming console I've never been able to find it.'

I glanced at the unit under the TV set, a brushed-steel box sporting an entire life-support system of cables. Both the keyboard and the joypad came with wires so long you could have opened up the bay windows and let the florists have a go from the street. Then I felt Pavlov rooting round behind me, and suggested he give up the search.

'Can't you just get up and change channels by hand?'

My brother regarded me as if I had suggested the unthinkable. At the same time, he extended a damning finger towards the keyboard on the carpet. 'He keeps telling me to use *that* for changing channels, but I refuse on principle. The telly will only get ideas above its station if I start using a keyboard. It'll throw up error messages if I turn to Channel Five, or warn me that *my* memory is running dangerously low when *it's* the one with the problem. At least with a remote you're in charge.'

I was going to ask why they needed a keyboard under the telly at all. Slim had his laptop, after all, and my brother had his own computer. Was it really necessary to surf the net from the sofa? Then I considered the online shopping potential, and said, 'I'm sure the remote will turn up.'

'Mark my words,' my brother said, 'if you get rid of your basic control unit there'll come a day when the machines will have one for *us*.'

'Or a joypad.'

'Imagine.'

My hand closed round the object of his search as Pavlov made his point. It was tucked down my side of the sofa. Part of me wished I could use it to switch him off. Aim between the eyes and close him down for the night. At least that way I could spend some time alone with his housemate, and find out if we played well together. But as he was up and running, and looked set to remain that way, I figured I should at least press him for details about Slim while I had the chance. Which was why I reclaimed the conversation in exchange for his control of the television.

'This thing about the landlord,' I said, 'you two must've had people back to the house in the past.' I looked away before he could read me properly, then tentatively dropped the bait. 'Surely Slim's had a girl stay overnight?'

'Put it this way,' he said, 'when the rent is due, there's nobody here but us.'

I focused on the blank TV screen, wondering whether my brother was implying that Slim couldn't commit. Worse, was he a trophy hunter? I had been with guys like that before, the kind who could conceal their true intentions until they had got what they wanted – who could be everything you wished for and more until the big moment came for them, upon which it was like watching a light go out in their eyes. I couldn't believe Slim was made in that mould, but the fact that I had panicked about it told me more about my growing feelings for him. No, I told myself, he wasn't that sort. Slim was like no other man I had met, in fact. His lifestyle was unique to me, but I was drawn to him by something deeper. Not his looks, or his penchant for salsa, cyberspace and scrunchies, but the way his heart seemed to beat in time with my own. It was a rhythm that had started from the moment I arrived here, but which had taken a kiss before I could truly hear it. And now I knew that it was him I wanted, and I guess my brother did too.

'Slim is a good lad,' he conceded, though I didn't push him about it any further. Not because he had just switched on the telly, but because he seemed so resigned in his observation. 'It's all just a bit close to home for me.' From the kitchen came the sound of ice gliding around a glass. I pictured Slim stirring something into my drink so he could have his wicked way, but opted not to share it with Pavlov. He was in no mood for jokes and, besides, the man himself returned to the room just then with a tray and three whiskies. I stood up to give him a hand, and was somewhat startled to see the tumbler on the right seemed a little cloudier than the other two. I looked up at him in alarm, caught his little brow ring twinkling. 'That's not yours,' he said, under his breath, but saved his smile for the individual now surfing through the channels. Looking for something suitable for us all, I imagined. No easy task at that time of night, when the schedules are dominated by just one thing.

5

I awoke the next morning with the looming sense that somebody was observing me. I opened my eyes a little, dazzled by the sudden intrusion of light, and slowly he came into focus.

My very own big brother.

I winced. Pressed a finger to my temple, and wished I had declined that final drink. For a man who had also consumed 25 ml of homeopathic sedative with his own final shot, Pavlov looked frighteningly together. At the time, he had slugged it down then wobbled off to the toilet with the promise that he would be back. Minutes later, he honoured his word, and for the next half-hour it was just a constant shuttle between the two rooms for him. For Slim and me it was a chance to exchange smiles then longer, lingering looks. A process that turned all the more intense when my brother conceded that he felt a bit woozy and wobbled off to bed. Who knows? Maybe he had figured Slim was just as trolleyed, that it was safe to leave a damsel in the company of an incapable. As it turned out his housemate had hardly started.

Which was how I had ended up sharing Slim's bed, and where my brother went on to find me.

I sat up gingerly, gathering my wits with the sheets. Slim didn't even stir. Too spent, I reflected. That or Pavlov had already dealt with him.

'I should go,' I croaked, wishing I had insisted that Slim leave my bags behind the sofa. I had only mumbled something about needing to hang my suit trousers so I wouldn't have to iron them, and suddenly all my stuff was in with me, Slim padding around naked in the moonlight, unpacking my things and insisting that

I feel at home. I glanced at all the clothes he had hung from the wardrobe door, and quickly shooed away the flashback of him reaching up to stow away the empty bag. Still, he had really gone to town, even shifting his laptop off the little corner table to create some space for my makeup. In daylight, the room looked more mine than his.

'I don't want to be an issue here,' I said.

'Too late, Cisco. We have a visitor.'

'Who?' I asked, upon which Pavlov stepped back and a little gasp stopped dead in my throat. Even Slim snapped upright, eyes locked open as if he'd just escaped some dreadful nightmare. He should have stayed asleep.

'Knock-knock,' grinned the meaty-looking man now filling the frame. 'Am I disturbing?'

Frank Cartier wore a tan greatcoat draped over his shoulders, his thinning white hair pulled into a stub. He was handsome in a battered way. The Ronnie Biggs of the rental sector. That's how Slim would later describe him, and a man on the make for sure: gold nuts for finger rings, chunky bracelet and cufflinks. Always on the lookout for another property to add to his portfolio, as I would discover. Indeed, the most obvious thing about him was the nature of his gaze: clear blue eyes under two heavy hoods, eyes that seemed too small, too recessed, too penetrating.

'Boys,' he said expectantly, just standing there like it was the front door and not Slim's personal space, 'where are your manners?'

Slim cleared his throat. 'Uh, this is Cisco.'

'My sister,' Pavlov added quietly, shadowing him like a dignitary's interpreter. 'And this is just a temporary arrangement.'

'Seems so.'

'Pleased to meet you,' I said weakly, and looked at Slim for support.

'Cisco's just here until she finds a place of her own.'

As if he hadn't heard us, Frank Cartier leaned back and enquired if I had a job. He spoke with a clipped Cockney accent. Cheeky, was how I might have described it, had his presence not left me so cold. Pavlov confirmed that I had just started a new job. In modelling, he said.

'In that case,' Cartier turned his attention right back at me, 'the pleasure's all mine.' I drew breath to point out that I was only a temp, that all I did was work reception at a booking agency in town, but by now he was beaming so brightly it didn't matter that the bedroom blinds were still closed. The way Cartier's gaze lingered, however, it appeared that his mind was on my other assets. 'A pretty girl like you probably doesn't get up for less than a thousand,' he ventured. 'Am I right?'

I looked to the foot of the bed, told him it was a bit less than that. Slim cleared his throat. 'Mr Cartier, do you think we could discuss this once we're dressed?'

'Sure,' he said, and felt for something in his coat pocket. A pistachio, as it turned out. 'Be my guest.' He popped it into his mouth, and rolled it to his rear molars. All of us watching him in silence, until Slim sought to clarify things.

'I was thinking maybe with the door shut?'

I clutched the sheets tighter. Wished this man would quit looking at me as he made that crunching sound. Which he did, quite suddenly. He swallowed the nut, stepped right into the room then turned to address Pavlov. 'You heard him. Shut the door and put the kettle on. We'll be out in a minute.'

'But, Mr Cartier—'

'Coffee would be quality. Just what I need.'

I turned to Slim and matched his shocked expression. My brother, meantime, actually reached for the bloody door. Only stopping short from swinging it shut when Cartier came out with a pair of imaginary pistols and aimed them right at us.

'Just kidding!' He fired off both chambers, one after the other. 'Jesus, your faces!'

'Very good, Mr Cartier.' Slim exhaled hard, and slid back down the headboard. 'You got us there.'

'Didn't I just?' he said. 'What a picture.'

I glowered at Pavlov. His hand shrank from the handle.

'Maybe we should just give them a minute,' he suggested, belatedly. 'I think they deserve a bit of privacy.'

Cartier insisted there was no need. He wasn't stopping. 'I've seen enough,' he finished, and turned for the door.

'Enough of what?' I asked.

Slim flinched at the question, but now it was my turn to stare as the man in the coat turned back to face me.

'Enough to know the rent has got to rise.'

The boys groaned. Cartier spread his hands. 'Take it or leave it,' he said.

'How much?' Slim asked.

'A little.'

'Meaning?'

'Nothing to worry a mover and shaker like you.' Cartier directed this at me, making out that he wasn't talking about Slim's professional performance. 'What's a hundred to a millionaire in the making?'

'You're joking,' Slim protested. 'Another hundred a month?'

'A week is what I have in mind.'

'That's *outrageous*,' wailed Pavlov, and broke off to do his sums. 'You're taking us up to nearly a thousand pounds a month.'

Cartier began to button up his camel. 'It's not so bad with a third person. Very reasonable, in fact.'

A moment passed before I realised he was talking about me. 'I don't know—'

'Sleep on it.' Frank Cartier took another nut from his pocket, the conversation closed. He shelled this one with his thumb, in the same way show-offs pop the cap off a beer bottle. Before the husk hit the carpet, he had turned to leave the room. 'Maybe I'll see you end of the month.'

'This place isn't big enough for three of us!' My brother squeezed back against the jamb to let Cartier pass, then flinched when he pulled up just an inch from his face.

'You managed fine so far.'

It was only after my new landlord had cleared the stairs that Pavlov dared to move. 'That went well,' he said to himself, then to us: 'Do you think it could have gone *any* better?'

I glanced at Slim. He looked a little overwhelmed, had the sheets bunched higher round his chest than I did.

'Do you want me to get out of bed?' I asked, and braced myself for bad news. When Slim didn't answer I twisted round to find one, and saw warmth come into his face.

'Don't I get a say, too?' We both turned back to the foot of the bed, found Pavlov with his hands held wide. 'My best friend and my little sister, going against me like this.'

Slim reminded Pavlov that he had almost shut the door on us back then. My brother opened his mouth to defend himself, only for his presence to be eclipsed once more. Cartier. Back in the frame. This time clutching two business envelopes like they were a pair of aces.

'Looky here what I found on the mat.' He tossed them both on to the bed. 'You have mail.'

6

There are a few things I'd like to point out here, just to set the record straight. First, I don't make a habit of sleeping with men too quickly – certainly not a man I go on to move in with. If I'm looking for a fling, then fine. Hell, twenty-four hours is probably too long to leave things. But a serious commitment? I didn't need Pavlov to tell me I might have been courting disaster, or anything else for that matter. Pavlov being the second issue I want to straighten out, not his sexuality, but our own relationship. All that crap with the sofa? About not letting me sleep out of his sight? Much as I loved him as a brother, he was more like an overprotective father to me. Which is where the problem came into focus for us. Our parents being past tense, and Pavlov being, well . . . just tense. I couldn't lose sight of the fact that ultimately he was like this with me because we only had each other. Which was why I joined him in the kitchen after Frank Cartier finally left us alone, dressed for the day in my proverbial hair shirt.

'Look on the bright side,' I proffered. 'At least you can keep tabs on me here. I'm sorry I've upset you, I really am, but it's good to see you again, Pavlov, and I promise I'll work hard to fit in. We can make this a happy family, you'll see.' My brother had his back to me. He didn't appear to register my presence, let alone my olive branch. Great, I thought. Travel to London, get sent direct to Coventry. I tried a different approach. 'Slim told me you guys have been sharing this place for a while.' I took a breath, hoping my breeziness would clear the air. 'At least I know now why you never invited me to stay.'

Pavlov remained unmoved, shoulders slumped, head bowed, mumbling now as if I wasn't worth turning round for. 'You can't do this to me,' he said.

'Do what?' I asked, prickling now. 'What exactly is the issue here?' I could see a fight was in the offing, and felt compelled to stand my ground.

'It's outrageous,' he said next. 'Bang out of order.'

'I can't keep apologising,' I told him. 'And neither can I pretend that I'm an innocent virgin so you can justify fussing over me. Pavlov, I've probably done things you've only seen on the *Internet*!' Still nothing. Not even the hairs on the back of his neck stood on end. Impulsively, I said: 'A threesome once. How about that, eh?'

That got him, or so I thought. Pavlov faced me, pale and tense, and that's when I became aware of the letter clutched in his hands.

'How about what?' he asked absently, and I could see he hadn't heard a word.

'Nothing,' I said hurriedly. 'Forget I said anything.'

He glanced back at the letter. 'Can they do this to me?'

'What?'

'It's from my editor at *Sparkle!*. He's cutting my fee by half.'

'Half? That's not on. He can't do that, can he?'

'He just has. The magazine's being revamped, cuts have got to be made.'

'Resign,' I instructed him. 'Walk away with your honour intact.'

'Where would I go? The dole office?'

'You'll land another advice column. Easy.'

'Cisco, I'm too old.'

'You're thirty!'

'I'm also an agony uncle for teenage girls, adolescents half my age at least. No new magazine will want to take me on. Readers will take one look, think, Fuck it, might as well be asking my dad.'

'No, they won't,' I said dismissively.

'They will. You burn bright in this job, not fade away.'

'Come off it, Pav. You're overreacting, surely?'

He handed me the letter. Clipped to it was a mock-up of his next page. 'Look at the new picture of me,' he said. 'When I started out my page featured a natural close-up, but every year they take a new shot, and every year I'm a little further back in the frame. More airbrushing too. I stopped recognising my own teeth a long time ago.'

It was some smile, I had to agree. 'Still,' I said, hoping to lift his spirits, 'the orange shirt works well with the white background.'

'That's not the point,' he said. 'Cisco, I can't go any further back. Do you see what I'm saying? They can't hide the fact that I'm getting older. Any further back I'd have to step out of the studio and on to the street.'

It was then that Slim ducked into the kitchen. Hands on my shoulders from behind, a kiss to the crown of my head. I should have felt like a princess.

'What's up?'

'Pavlov's had a pay cut.'

'Oh, man,' he said, 'that's a bitch.'

'Yeah, and he won't quit.'

'How can he, at his time of life?'

'Oh, don't you start,' I sighed. 'Thirty's not too old for an agony uncle.'

'It is in teen mags,' lamented Pavlov.

'What about the women's monthlies?' asked Slim. I looked across at him and frowned. Slim cleared his throat, and rephrased the suggestion. 'I mean, the magazines for women that come out every four weeks.'

Pavlov shook his head, said he was way too young. 'You need the silver hair, the bad bow-tie and a port-drinker's complexion to get a gig with those titles.'

'I can't believe what I'm hearing,' I said. 'You're too old for one market, too young for another.'

'Agony limbo.' Slim studied my brother's picture. 'What you going to do?'

'Accept the cut. Worry about how I'm going to cover the rent.'

'Leave that to me,' said Slim quickly. 'I can take care of any

45

shortfall. With the money my backers are promising I can probably buy this place outright.'

My brother smiled grimly. He was probably thinking what it would be like to see Cartier's face when Slim put in an offer. I gave his arm a little squeeze. 'It'll be all right,' I told him. 'I can pay my way with the temp job, plus I'm a damn good cook on a tight budget. So long as you like a lot of tuna bake.'

Slim handed back the letter with the mock-up, and attempted to bolster his spirits further. 'What I said about the shirt,' he offered, 'I was wrong. You look good.'

Pavlov took another look, then crumpled the letter into his fist. 'I look like a fruit,' he muttered, then promptly excused himself.

Slim and I watched him head for the stairs. It was only after he had locked himself in the loo that Slim faced me directly. 'That thing you said back then.'

'What thing?'

'The three-way thing.' He grinned wolfishly.

'You were *listening*?'

'Not exactly. It's just that guys are primed to pick up on certain words from a thousand paces.'

'How so?'

Slim shrugged. 'Some sort of heterosexual gaydar, I guess. Girl mentions that she's got it on with more than one person at the same time, our ears just swivel right round.'

'Pavlov's didn't.'

'An exception to the rule. So how did it work out?'

'What?'

'You know? What was the combo? Boy, girl, boy? Two girls, one lucky guy? *All* girls?'

'That's my business,' I replied, incredulous but enjoying the exchange none the less. 'I'm sure there's plenty I don't know about you.'

Slim considered this for a beat, then silently conceded the point. 'Where would a relationship be without its secrets, eh?'

46

'Exactly,' I agreed, sitting at the table now. Slim plucked his envelope from the pocket of his drawstring pants, and set about tearing it open.

'From the suits,' he informed me. Taking the chair opposite, he unfolded the letter. 'At least one of us is on a roll.'

I watched his eyes scan to the bottom of the page, then stay there. He looked like he was trying to decipher the signature. 'Something you want to share?' I asked eventually.

Slim looked up, pale and tense as Pavlov had been, and immediately I sensed my morning start over.

'They can't do this to me,' he said weakly. 'Can they?'

7

So I'm like the bad penny. Through one day into the next, and on into the rest of the week, that's exactly how I felt around the boys. Pavlov took refuge in his room, brooding over his own problems more than those of lovelorn adolescents, while Slim continued to assure me that none of this was my fault. How I couldn't be to blame for my brother's agony crisis, or for the fact that he had just been digitally downsized. Stocks went up, he said, stocks went down.

'Except yours sank like a stone,' I pointed out. 'Slim, this company didn't even get as far as floating before it went under. They still managed to take your e-zine with it.'

'People say never trust a hippie. I say never trust a suit – especially suits that came off the peg.'

'What were they doing, thinking they could profit from you when their own business was so close to bankruptcy?'

'Last-ditch effort, I guess, but it doesn't matter now. I'm just another net casualty.'

'No, you're not. You'll bounce back.'

'Face it, I'm a dot bum.'

'Dot bomb,' I corrected him.

'Dot bum is more romantic,' he said. 'I'm a moon-in-the-gutter type of geek.'

We were lying in bed, staring at the ceiling, and for a moment it served as a blank canvas for our thoughts. I couldn't speak for Slim, but I was trying hard not to imagine what his paper million looked like pulped. A share option turned to sod-all now that the receivers had been called in. The company responsible for breaking up Slim's business had itself been smashed to smithereens. I must say he had taken the news well. Had it been my website sucked down the virtual drain, I would've taken out *windows*. Namely those belonging to the suit behind the suits. Maybe burst into tears before and after, too. Slim couldn't be said to have taken it like a girl, however. If anything, he regarded it like the end of his turn on a game, a chance to sit back and let someone else have a go. I guess I should've been the one to spur him on, adopting responsibility for the upkeep of his ambitions. As it was, I just felt responsible. I couldn't help it: no matter which way I looked at the situation, my arrival here had seen the boys' prosperity pack its bags and head elsewhere. Which was why I turned my head on the pillow and said that I was sorry. I'd lost count of the number of times I had apologised to Slim since Cartier had caught us together, but it seemed the only way I could face him when I awoke each morning.

'Cisco, will you stop it?' he said this time. 'You're not cursed. You haven't brought bad luck into the house. There's no hex going on here. Shit happens, especially when you're thinking life is starting to look good.' I listened to him and I listened to the sound of rain drifting against the window. It hadn't stopped since the day I came to stay. If anything, the weather had just got worse. I let out a long, despondent sigh. 'Knowing my luck you'll turn out to be everything I could hope for,' I said next, 'but I'll do something dumb and screw it up for the both of us.'

Slim glanced sideways at me, then looked back up at the ceiling. 'Optimism. That's what I like in my women.'

'So what do you see in me?'

After a moment, Slim freed his hands from behind his head and worked a bracelet from his wrist. It was woven from coloured strings, and tied off with frayed ends. 'Try this on for size,' he said.

'What is it?'

'Call it a good-luck charm. I've had it for years. Picked it up in Thailand.'

Not quite the same as picking it up in Tiffany, I know, but that wasn't the point. In some ways it was worth a whole lot more. 'I can't,' I said, returning his smile. Slim leaned on his side, encouraging me to slip it on. 'I'll probably break it before lunchtime.'

'I'm in bed with a girl I click with completely,' he replied, 'and she sure as hell doesn't want me for my money. I don't call that bad luck. I call everything else that's happened a small price to pay.'

I rolled closer to Slim, tucked my head under his chin, then groaned when the weatherman joined the moment, courtesy of the clock-radio. The forecaster promising a warm front, if not today then maybe tomorrow. Either way, it was time to get up, get out, get behind that reception desk and start earning some cash for the coffers. As the main breadwinner in the house now, I had a responsibility to work, work, *work*, and that meant overtime too, putting together portfolios out of hours for girls who were on their way up. It was far from glamorous, but at least it stoked my determination to follow in their footsteps.

'You've worked late for days,' said Slim, watching me climb into my clothes. 'I miss you.'

The way he lay shrouded in the sheet, with his ankles and feet poking free at the far end, it seemed that the only thing Slim missed right now was a toe tag. 'So what are your plans for the day?' I asked, straightening the straps of my dress.

'*Global Takeover*, most probably.'

'No, seriously.'

Slim looked confused, like he'd missed his own joke, then informed me it was a classic strategy game you played online. And a wicked one at that. 'Especially if you go with the Russians,' he said, suddenly animated, and sat up straight in the bed. 'You might start off with less money when you take their side but you get the meaner gangs. Nasty mothers who can take care of anything.'

I did my hair as Slim continued to enthuse, and concluded that if a woman could be a cook in the kitchen, a whore in the bedroom and a realistic opponent on the PlayStation, she would truly be a goddess. Sex and gaming. That was where it was with men right now. Honestly, I had never seen him so turned on. Not since his Internet bubble burst anyway. And although I figured it was probably good catharsis for him, I also resolved that I should be the one to bring sunshine back into this house. Whatever the weatherman said.

'D'you want to play me?' asked Slim, hopefully.

'Let me take care of the rent,' I smiled, 'then I'll take care of you.'

8

Late that evening, mindful not to snag Slim's bracelet, I returned home bearing gifts – nothing extravagant, more bric-à-brac tat than Bond Street boutique. Despite all my overtime, the modelling agency didn't net me much. I'd say even the cycle couriers trousered more than me: whenever they strode through the double doors, it was compulsory to look up and concede these guys were *loaded*. But despite such perks, being a temp meant I was at the very bottom of the professional food chain. A position reflected by my measly wage and the presents slung in my carrier-bag. With my limited budget, I had deliberately gone for boys' toys. Something spot on for Slim, I hoped, and a nice surprise for Pavlov. I just prayed it would be enough to bring a little light into the house.

It was only as I hurried home from the tube, cursing the relentless drizzle, that I decided I deserved a present too. It was dark. It was wet. It was windy. I wanted to get home, but if I was to feel I belonged then the place required some kind of feminine touch. By the time I reached Columbia Road, where all but one of the stalls had packed up for the day, I realised I should say it to myself with flowers. Even if the florist did make it his mission to identify my sentiments first.

'You want a bunch?' he asked, then motioned me under the awning. 'Or is it some kinda pot you're after?'

I looked up at him, this brawny ox in a puffa, and wondered what was with the conspiracy. The stall was illuminated by torch lamps. They were clamped to the crossbar at the back, with only a string of fairy lights tucked under the awning. The effect was unusual, and somewhat intimidating, for this strong backlight made it hard to view the stock on display, while throwing the florist into silhouette.

'Some kind of pot, I suppose. Anything that lasts a month would be great.'

He beamed at me like I'd given the right answer, whatever that was. I cupped my brow against the light, but saw nothing but bunches in the buckets and the racks. There were no begonias, no violets, no potted plants of any description. 'Weed is good right now,' he said, squeezing behind the counter. The man was built like a bullet, I thought, a bullet with a belly and a mile-wide smile. 'Premium shit guaranteed to take the strain outta your day.'

'Eh?'

'You want a sample?'

I wasn't sure, and it left me a little unsettled when he unzipped his money pouch and began picking through the coins. Cautiously I pointed out that I didn't have much to spend. The florist glanced up, said, 'Gimme a reference, you can pay me later if it suits.'

'Pardon me?'

He leaned over the counter, rocking forward on his knuckles. 'Honey, you look like an honest fox, but if I'm going to give you credit I gotta know you're good for business. Know what I mean?'

'Not really,' I confessed. 'I just want some petunias or something. I wasn't planning on buying the whole stall.'

He stood tall once more, eyes narrowed, and zipped his puffa to the first of his chins. 'You do know what I'm selling here, don't you?'

'At a guess I would say flowers.'

'Yeah,' he said slowly. 'I do that too.'

A drop of rain found one of the bulbs just then, sizzling sharply. I took a step away from the counter, distancing myself from this looming figure with the sandpaper stubble and the strange-sounding subtext. 'I only live up the road,' I said, and half wondered if I should just keep backing into the night. 'Maybe I'll try another stall when the market opens in the morning.'

'You live in Columbia Road?' he declared. 'Why didn't you

say you were local?' Out of nowhere, a wrapped bunch of roses came over the counter at me. I threw out my hands, mostly to protect myself, and found myself in possession of a dozen long-stemmed reds.

'So where you based? You must be new, I haven't seen you before and I know everyone.' A look of concern crossed his face just then. 'Stone me, you're not the niece of the beast, are you?'

A little stunned by all this, and aware that he was talking about that stupid coincidence with the house number, I told him no. Just the neighbour.

'With Slim Jim and the panty-waist? The boy who's always disappearing to powder his nose?'

'Pavlov,' I informed him, hugging the bunch now. 'My brother.'

'You're *related*? Get outta here! Pavlov always struck me as an only child.'

'He doesn't talk about me much. Certainly not in the company of men.'

'I can see why. Sort like you.'

I wondered whether that was a compliment. Going by the way he had suddenly warmed to me, I took it as a good thing. Still, I was keen to find a decent home for the flowers. Having stepped away from the shelter of his stall, out into the rain, I sensed the roses offer up a rich and heady bouquet. 'How much do I owe you?'

He waved away the question, told me nothing. 'Call it a house-warming present.'

'Thanks,' I said, smiling now. 'I'm Cisco, by the way.'

'Cisco as in the kid?'

'As in the city.'

'Far out. Were you born there?'

'No,' I said, a bit embarrassed. 'My dad was just a huge fan of the TV show.'

'*The Streets of San Francisco*?' he said, to clarify, and when I nodded he did that finger-snap thing with a twist of his wrist. 'Your old man had taste.'

'Actually, my real name's Fran, but Dad thought Cisco sounded like a girl going places.'

'It does,' agreed the florist. 'I can see you're one to watch.'

I grinned at him, but said I'd better get home nevertheless.

'You do that,' he said. 'Anything you want in future, just ask for me.'

'Who shall I ask for?' I called back, now leaving the light from his stall. 'I don't know your name.'

'You will,' he replied, and gave me one of those winks that saw his whole head twitch right round. 'Everyone knows who I am.'

9

I dropped my stuff in the hall, found the boys around the kitchen table. My brother was consulting Slim's laptop, chewing a pen. Slim was poring over a notepad beside him, toking on a toothpick joint. Neither of them appeared very enthusiastic about what they were doing. In fact, they both seemed far too pleased to see me.

'Cisco,' said Pavlov first, and made a vague effort to stand. He was wearing his little round writing glasses, though he peeled them off to focus on me, and turned them in his hands. 'Why do men find bottle blondes hornier when their roots are showing?'

I glowered darkly at Slim. The last thing I'd done before moving to London was my hair. I had intended to make an impression. Obviously I would have to wait a couple more weeks. 'Is this your way of getting me to grow it out?'

'Your brother asked the question,' he protested. 'What do I know?'

'It's a letter to my problem page.' Pavlov angled the laptop for me to see. 'This girl suspects that guys find roots a huge turn-on. She wants to know what I think.'

'So why you asking me?'

Slim braved the moment to look me in the eye. 'Pavlov's had a bit of a crisis of confidence. He's lost faith in his own advice. Got a bit blocked, so to speak.'

My brother looked at me imploringly.

'Since when?' I asked.

'Since his editor decided he didn't love him any more.'

'So?' asked Pavlov. 'Are roots erotic?'

I told my brother that collectively women spent millions of pounds each year on making their hair colour look convincing.

Any man who claimed trailer trash was more of a turn-on might be right, but he wouldn't be popular.

'Is that a "no" then?' he asked. 'Could you elaborate, perhaps?'

I sat down opposite the boys. 'What do you want me to say?'

Slim glanced at Pavlov, as if they were talking telepathically. 'It's not what he wants you to say,' revealed Slim, 'it's what he wants you to write.'

I assumed he was joking, but when neither of them showed signs of cracking I targeted Pavlov directly. 'You want *me* to write *your* column?'

'That's about the size of it.'

'Offering a male view on female relationship problems?'

'Please, Cis. It's really important that I deliver genuine insight and analysis this time round. I have to prove I'm indispensable.'

'Which is why you're asking a woman?'

'You'll do a great job,' he said. 'I know you will.'

'Even better than the real thing,' Slim added, beaming at me now.

I declined the spliff when it came my way, electing to keep a clear head while I addressed the problems Pavlov had selected for his column. Four in all: the roots issue, followed by a couple more from girls who had each found themselves on the bum end of different relationships. One was all about being dumped by the boy next door, but mostly about receiving the bad news by email. Another concerned a kissing crisis, this poor thing having been accused by her ex of 'going at it like a guppy fish', while the final problem came from a girl whose boyfriend had turned his bedroom into a Jennifer Lopez shrine. Why? they all asked. How could they be so unfeeling? *What makes men tick?*

The answers took about five minutes. I punched them out on the keyboard while Slim fixed some coffee and Pavlov looked on edgily. I didn't feel the need to check my work, just hit the final full stop and pushed the laptop back across the table. My brother snapped his glasses back on. Hungrily, he read what I had written, his lips twitching as he scrolled down the screen. Finally he looked up at me, blinking behind those little lenses of his. I couldn't decide if it was confusion in his face, or disbelief. 'Because they're bastards at heart,' he said. 'Even the nice ones.'

It was a bit of a summary, but he'd understood me right. 'What about it?' I asked him.

'That's the gist of your answer.'

'Uh-huh.'

'For *every* question?'

'Why not?'

'Cisco, this isn't advice. Coming from a bloke, it's treachery. I could get lynched!'

'If you ask me,' I said, 'you should go further and feature the full names of these sad lads. Go on. Out them in your column. Chuck in their addresses too. Damn it, publish *mugshots*! That would really give your readers something to talk about.'

Pavlov seemed a little overwhelmed, his glasses fogging as his face began to heat.

'What have you got to lose?' Slim shrugged. 'Between us we just came up with apologies, and that took us half the afternoon.'

'Is that your attempt there?'

Pavlov said, 'Actually, it's his list of career options.'

'That's great,' I offered, pleased by his initiative. 'What have you got?'

'Well,' Slim said shyly, like a schoolboy asked to present his project to class, 'like you, I want to make a success of something I enjoy ...'

'So you don't have to work again,' I finished. 'Good start.'

'But I'm finding it hard to come up with practical suggestions.'

'Can I see?' I ripped off the sheet before he could object. 'Number one,' I read out, 'sperm donor.'

Pavlov coughed into his coffee. 'I guess it's a golden handshake of sorts,' he said, recovering, 'but it won't pay the rent.'

'I was brainstorming,' Slim countered, 'it's the first thing that came into my head.'

'Number two,' I pressed on, 'become famous.' I lowered the pad, narrowed my eyes at Slim. 'And that's it.'

'If you got rich from sperm donation, my friend, I guarantee you'd be a superstar.' Pavlov was leaning right back in his chair now, gloating at his housemate. 'Men around the world would gladly pay a fortune for the secret behind your potency. You could even give master classes. Imagine!'

'All right, easy,' said Slim. 'The fact is, I've tried to be a success at something I enjoyed, but look what a mess I made of that.'

'So it isn't just Pavlov who's lost his confidence, then.' A moment's silence followed before I invited the boys to look at themselves. 'If we're going to sort our lives out, at least let's be united.'

'Not sure there's much point,' my brother muttered. 'Cartier's going to be wanting his rent money in a couple of days. If we don't get it covered we'll all be going our separate ways.'

'Okay,' I said. 'I have some presents.' Sure enough, that shut them up. The pair of them uncertain of the occasion as I left my seat for the hallway. 'But what I didn't buy is parting gifts.'

'Nice bunch,' said Slim, when I returned with the bag over my shoulder and the roses in my hand. 'For me?'

'For me, actually. Got them from a bloke who says he knows you.'

Slim looked back at Pavlov. My brother closed his laptop.

'The big man outside,' I continued, 'like Desperate Dan on drugs.'

'That'd be right,' murmured Slim.

'Sweet William,' my brother said.

'Our florist and dealer.'

'*Dealer?*' My mind raced back over the encounter, filling in the holes.

'Sweet can get anything you want,' said Pavlov, 'fen violets, snow-drops, even in summer, Moroccan blonde at any time, honeysuckle, sensimilia, whatever.'

'Except crack,' Slim put in. 'Willie got out of that game a while back. Attracted the wrong kind of customer. The man always was a recreational at heart.'

I asked why he hadn't just come right out with it and said what he was really selling. 'Had he talked sense,' I argued, 'I would've clicked that he was a dealer straight away.'

'Since when did a dealer ever talk sense?' Slim crumpled the remains of his economy spliff into the ashtray. 'If a dealer talks sense it's a sign his drugs don't work. If you want to understand him, you have to learn the code.'

Pavlov pointed his pen at the flowers. 'I see you have some roses.'

'How much did you pay for them?' asked Slim.

'I didn't. They're a present.'

'Even better,' he said, smiling. 'We've just finished the last of our stash.'

'Clearly Sweet took a shine to you,' my brother added, then cautioned me not to get too friendly.

All this time I was looking from the flowers to Slim, from Slim to Pavlov, from my brother back to the bunch. They were roses, fresh cut too, but where did the dope come into it? I'd had a hard day at work, I told the boys. I was tired and in need of a hot bath. A stitch-up like this was the last thing I needed, please. Slim took the flowers from me, felt his way up the wrap and, midway, smiled victoriously.

'In Sweet's world there are roses,' he broke off to tip the bunch upside down – a liquorice-black, stock cube-size lump, fell on to the table, 'and there are roses.' I picked up the hash, squished it a little between my thumb and forefinger. 'Now there's a stroke of luck,' he said. 'Maybe things are looking up.'

'There's more,' I said, surprising Slim this time as I reached down for my bag. 'I know you're going to love this.'

10

I had bought Slim a game for his console, from a stall in Brick Lane market. You could get anything there. Even if you had to ask, they could find it for you.

'*The Money Shot*!' Suddenly I was the recipient of a sloppy kiss from Slim. 'I can't believe you got this!'

'I'm just relieved you like it,' I said. It was the stallholder who had offered it to me, in fact. He'd had masses of games on display, but I was worried Slim would be familiar with them all. As soon as I mentioned that my boyfriend was on the cutting edge of game play, he had brought out this one especially for me.

'Cisco, it's perfect!' Slim continued to stare at the jewel box. 'I didn't even realise it had been *released* in this country.'

My brother returned from the sink just then, the roses in a carafe of water. 'Unless it features weapons of mass destruction on the sleeve,' he said to Slim, 'chances are you just didn't notice it.'

Slim flipped the box face out, showed him the graphic image of the angular blonde with the perky ponytail. She was wearing a pair of big boots, black Lycra shorts, cute-looking backpack and a cross-your-heart bullet belt. The picture had her leaning against a giant globe like it was her best mate or something. I doubted Slim would have missed this one. Even Pavlov bobbed his head appreciatively. 'Who's the honey?'

'Misty Ventura,' Slim answered. 'Female leads are compulsory in gaming, ever since men went out of fashion, really. Nowadays you want brains with your brawn and a little beauty too. But the best thing about Misty is that you get to customise her first – change the way she looks, and select from certain skills, like martial arts or mountaineering. Basically, you're making her unique, so when you take her online no two competitors are the same.'

'Yeah? Can you make yours naked?'

Slim looked disapprovingly at Pavlov, as if he was a throwback to some earlier age. 'This is a state-of-the-art multiplayer adventure game,' he said, 'not a skin flick. It's designed to test your stamina and dexterity.'

'So are dirty movies.'

'Behave.'

'I'm serious,' Pavlov insisted. 'Watching porn demands a degree of eye-to-hand co-ordination.'

'Yeah, but you don't get to control the action.' Slim popped the CD from the jewel box, turned it so the light slid around the surface. 'Thanks to this disk, there's only one thing in your hands, and that's Misty's destiny.'

'But I heard somewhere you can get her shorts off,' my brother insisted, taking the box for a better look. 'Some of these games you can do all kinds of things you wouldn't believe.'

'Only if you know the cheats,' said Slim, his patience thinning.

'What's that, then?' I asked. 'It doesn't sound very sporting.'

'Most games come with cheats programmed into them,' he said. 'It lets you skip a level or awards you extra lives. Sometimes more.' He waited for Pavlov to put down the jewel box. 'But you're stuffed unless you know which buttons to push.'

'Sounds like sex,' I said.

'Easy there,' my brother conceded. 'All I'm saying is, if you find out how to get Misty in the buff, call me.'

'Pavlov, will you shut up?' I said. 'I bought something for you too.' I reached into the plastic bag and found the Sea Maidens.

'What is it?' he asked. I handed him the box. For a moment I thought he was going to sniff it. Instead, he held it close to his ear and gave it a little shake. Something rattled inside. On the front was a picture – an illustration of some underwater boudoir with lots of little nymph things reclining about the place, flipper-footed sea creatures with big eyes and bigger smiles. Some were waving too.

'They're brine shrimp,' I said. '*Artemia salina*, only Sea Maidens sounds cuter. Apparently you just add water to the eggs, a little food concoction, and bang! You're the proud owner of a whole family.'

Under his breath, Slim said, 'Can you make them naked?'

With a cautious look in his eye, Pavlov opened the pack and pulled out a plastic aquarium. It was about the size of a disk box and contained two plastic tubs, like film canisters, along with a banded roll of instructions. He left the lid on the aquarium but I could tell, because he was struggling to find the right words, that I had definitely struck a chord. 'You really bought this for me?' he asked.

'I was hoping it would take your mind off things. Maybe you could put them on your desk beside the computer. A distraction like this might be just the thing to clear that block of yours, start building up your confidence again.' Pavlov didn't appear to register anything I had said, just kept turning the aquarium in his hands. 'What do they look like?'

'Shrimp,' I said. 'I think.'

'How big do they get?'

'If you look after them right, half an inch, maybe.'

'Look after them?' Pavlov seemed a bit shocked. 'Like *pets*?'

'You'll make a great mummy,' said Slim. 'Now, what do you say to your sister?'

Reluctantly, Pavlov thanked me for the gift. Slim broke off from building his first proper spliff of the evening. 'What's with you? Cisco's making a real effort here.'

After a moment, Pavlov stood up, said, 'Today is Thursday. On Monday, Cartier will be here to collect. Presents are lovely. Really. Slim and I never do this kind of thing, and it's nice. Cisco, I'm even starting to like the idea of the three of us living here, but presents won't pay the rent.'

I glanced at Slim. Like me, he didn't have a response, and in that silence I think we all felt bound by the same sense of isolation. The whole house opening out, so it seemed, reminding me of the night. I pictured all the other residents in the terrace, bound up in their own problems. Here in a city so big it could have been a forest at times, all you could do was look up to find some space. My brother picked up his laptop. 'If you'll excuse me,' he said, 'I have an agony column to check.'

Another two hours passed before the toilet became vacant again, for that's where Pavlov chose to make his corrections. Slim reckoned it saved him the effort of travelling from his bedroom and back. By the time he came out, we had turned in for the night. I had work in the morning, after all. I heard the water flush and the bolt shoot free, but by then we were otherwise engaged. I only hoped he had worked off his stress as well as Slim was working on mine.

'How's that?' he asked, straddling my back in bed, kneading the heel of each hand across my shoulder-blades.

'Not bad,' I said, between moans. 'Bliss, in fact.'

It was rare to find a guy who could massage – properly, at any rate. Normally, an offer of a rub-down was just a covert way of pressing for sex. From behind. That sudden introduction of a third hand never came as much of a surprise. Slim was different, however. He actually *volunteered* to use my essential oils, but even more surprisingly he had started as far up as my scalp. His fingertips making gentle circle motions in all the right places. I felt as if I was melting into the pillow, and for once I welcomed the slow slide south. 'Maybe I should hire you out,' I suggested. 'If other girls knew about your hidden talents you'd be in hot demand.'

'Thanks,' he said. 'I think.'

'But first we have to tackle that foot problem of yours.'

I felt his hands draw still. 'What foot problem?'

'The fungal thing,' I said, turning my head so I could see him. 'Don't say you haven't noticed.'

66

Slim reached back to grab his ankle, and fanned his toes. I had noticed the flaky skin some time ago, but now that I was beginning to find some in the bed I decided to pipe up.

Slim said, 'I heard if you pee on your feet it can clear up most things down there.'

'So what does that tell me? You have an aiming problem too?'

His foot fell back, but Slim came round to find me smiling to myself.

'Actually I was hoping it would sort itself out.'

'How long have they been that way?'

'Not long,' he said, after a short pause.

'A month?'

'I believe I picked it up in Thailand. It was the rainy season.'

'Which was when?'

'Several summers ago.'

'Right,' I said, and lifted my cheek from the pillow so I could see him even better. He wore a mystified frown behind his dangling dreads, that smile of his held in check. 'You haven't been in a relationship for a while, have you?' The massage resumed. A silent confirmation of sorts, which pleased me. More so as he worked his way across my shoulders, brushing the edges of my breasts. Finally, Slim said, 'So why the unhealthy interest?'

'All men need cleaning up here and there when we first start dating them,' I told him. 'Medically speaking, there's always something unsightly they've got tucked away. Something that's been neglected and thrived as a result. Spots on the back are usually what we're braced for. And I must say, Slim, I'm slightly disappointed that your skin is in such reasonable condition. A good squeezing session can be very therapeutic. It's a bonding opportunity, in some ways, but I'll settle for sorting out your athlete's foot. We'll get some powder in the morning, start the treatment right away—'

All the air left my lungs just then, pushed out with one heavenly sweep. Next Slim floated his hands down my spine, spreading slowly across my ass to form little erotic eddies on each cheek.

67

'So you're my girlfriend now?' he asked, matter-of-factly.

I rocked my hips from the sheets in response, pushing against his slow-turning touch. 'Did I say that?' I bit into my lower lip. 'In this state I can't be responsible for anything I say or do.'

'Then forget about my feet and go with the flow.'

'You should consider yourself lucky. Girls have been known to withhold sex until problems like yours have been sorted.'

The way his palms kept forming circle after circle told me this wouldn't be an issue here. I relaxed my hips for him, the sheet underneath compounding the heat coming off me. Here I was, with someone I hardly knew, I realised, and yet we seemed to read each other perfectly. Pressing Pavlov for insight into his housemate's life hadn't offered up much but, then, Slim knew little about mine. The more time we spent together, the less that seemed to matter. It was just one of those relationships that worked on its own terms, whatever anyone said. As Slim broke off to reach for a little more oil I thought back to how natural it had been to wind up in his bedroom. Then I considered the possibility that we would soon have to find another. 'Would Cartier really kick us out?'

Slim rubbed his palms together, bringing the oil to body temperature. 'Put it this way,' he said, 'Frank owns a string of properties. He's a self-made man. A millionaire, perhaps. Anyone who gets that far without signing away their lives to the suits in the city has to be ruthless in my view.'

'But it wouldn't be the end of the world,' I said, as Slim's handiwork resumed. 'There are other places, other landlords.'

'Not round here,' Slim said, talking as he turned me on. 'You want to rent a half-decent house around the flower market, there's only one man you see. Cartier is to property what Sweet William is to pleasure.'

'So move someplace else. Go west.'

'I'd sooner go six feet under. If you live in the East End, Cisco, you can't move west. Can't move south or north either.'

'Why not?' I asked, spreading my legs a little as his hands travelled up the inside of my thighs.

'It would be unthinkable! Mutual contempt is what binds the four quarters of this city.'

'Just say we did have to move,' I ventured, 'would you want to find somewhere else with me?'

It was there that he said no, that wasn't something he would consider. I twisted round from the waist, a half-corkscrew that Slim completed by swinging my leg right over his head. 'I'm not going to consider it,' he said, hovering now between my knees, 'because we won't be leaving here.'

'Slim, we can't afford it.'

'Oh, I think we will.'

'How?'

'Trust me,' he said, and sank away like a setting sun. 'You're in capable hands.'

'That's not your hand,' I moaned, as the world went molten from the inside up, but I trusted him all the way.

11

Slim was slim, but not flat, which was how he felt to me when I awoke early the next morning, stirred by the sound of a modem warbling downstairs. It took me a minute or so to unstick my eyes and confirm that I was alone in bed. I lifted my arm from the crumpled sheet and rolled to face the blinds. Things were certainly looking brighter, in a grey-dawn kind of way, but at least it wasn't raining.

I glanced at the clock-radio. It would be a long while before the weatherman joined me, so I figured I should seize the day before it had even started. After his pep talk the night before, I assumed that Slim had got in ahead of me. The modem fell silent just then, and I pictured him in front of the telly, dressed for a hard day's work with the keyboard on his lap. Such was the effect of his chat that I had him constructing another e-zine before lunchtime, and securing more investment by tea. Even if he was just laying the foundations, his enterprise meant a great deal to me. Personally, I wasn't due at work until ten – the modelling world depended on its beauty sleep, after all – but when I stepped behind that reception desk I planned to put my heart and soul into the job. All I had to do was keep smiling. It wasn't hard. I threw on a jumper and jeans, unwilling to dress up for the part just yet, and shuffled out to find Slim. Half-way across the landing, however, I heard Pavlov muttering to himself in his room. The door was ajar, so I just said, 'knock-knock', and walked in anyway. 'What's with the early start?'

My brother was at his desk, dressed and distressed already. He had one hand on his mouse and both eyes pinned to the screen. It smelt of lavender in here, but although the market started before sun-up his window was closed to the fragrances that often laced the air at this time. Then I noticed the candle burning on his bookshelf. Aromatherapy of some sort. 'Bloody teenagers,' he said.

'Sorry?'

'If you have problems, there are people out there who can help, right?'

'I suppose so.'

'Teachers, friends, counsellors, helplines. Youth workers and drop-in centres.'

'Family are good too, sometimes.'

The agony uncle swivelled round, ripping off his glasses at the same time. 'So why don't they turn to them instead of bleating to me?'

It was then I realised he was still wearing the same clothes as he had been in the night before. I decided it was probably best not to ask if he'd been to bed, and looked at his screen instead. 'Isn't this the column I wrote for you?'

My brother turned full circle and confirmed that it was.

'So send it. Get it out your system.'

'I wish I could, but I've been looking at it so long now I can't even make sense of the questions.'

I skim-read it again, saw that nothing had been changed, and assured him it was fine. 'Go deliver,' I said.

'You don't think it needs watering down a little?'

'Nope.'

'But it says "bastard" in it so many times I lose count. I'm not sure teen mags can print that kind of thing.'

I told him to go with the courage of my convictions. Pulling back from the monitor, I noticed he had filled the aquarium. It was sitting at the back of his desk, next to the Anglepoise lamp.

'You made the Sea Maidens come alive!' I moved round him for a closer look. 'Is that them?' I turned on his lamp. Light flared through the water, picking out a dozen tiny specks. All of them were motoring in different directions, spiralling here and there. 'Wow! I can't wait to see what they look like fully grown.'

Pavlov didn't appear to share my enthusiasm. 'I'm not sure they're such a good idea, actually.'

'Why not?'

'Well, I was hoping you'd be right, that maybe watching them would clear my head, but to be honest they make me feel a bit queasy.'

'How can you say that? They're cute.'

'They look like fish poo, Cisco.'

'Oh, come on.'

'Stringy bits of fish poo with eyes.'

Pavlov took a magnifying-glass from his drawer and invited me to look closer. I found a Sea Maiden with it, and instinctively pulled back. My brother was right. This wasn't the waterborne harem that the picture on the packet had promised. I patted his shoulder, then backed towards the door. 'Give them names,' I said thinking perhaps they improved with age. 'You'll bond in no time.'

Where my brother had lost his confidence, I found Slim had regained his in spades. I should have been relieved when I found him in the front room, just as I had hoped. That he was wearing his Manga gown and hairclips was understandable as he operated alone. When it came to the freelance life, I had come to realise, every day was Dress-down Friday. What troubled me was the direction of this new drive, for what I saw left me feeling even more uncertain about our future here in this house.

'As soon as I get a feel for this baby,' he said, 'we'll all be winners.' Slim was sitting on the edge of the sofa. He had two hands on his joypad and both eyes on the screen. It smelt stuffy in here, the curtains behind him begging to be unplugged and the windows thrown open for a change.

'What do you mean winners?' I asked. 'Is this *The Money Shot*?'

Slim confirmed that it was. 'The controls are a bitch to master, though. I can make her move OK, but I'm having a directional problem.'

I gave the screen my full attention, and took in the customised behind of Misty Ventura for the first time. Two eggs in a black handkerchief sprang to mind – that is, if ostrich eggs could be squeezed inside such a tight space. Honestly, what he had done to her was ridiculous. Compared to the image on the sleeve, Slim appeared to have tied off Misty at the neck, limbs and waist, then inflated the rest of her anatomy.

'Nice job,' I said, 'for an adolescent.'

'Thanks.'

I thought he might at least look up at me when I took the piss. On the screen, his pixellated heroine was advancing across a jungle clearing in a strange sideways fashion. The whole place was tangled with vines and strewn with boulders and bolt-holes, while unseen wildlife whooped and wittered. Jungle drums were out there too. Misty looked so unprepared for the occasion I was amazed she could move at all. The cycling shorts and the bullet-bra thing were functional enough in this fantasy world, but her boots had heels, and that was just silly in these circumstances.

'I thought this was a game for everyone.'

'It is,' he said. 'Boy to man, they love this stuff.'

'So what's in it for the female players?'

'Oh, well, there are lots of puzzles to do along the way. It's seriously stimulating. A real teaser.'

I didn't disagree. Watching Slim attempt to stop Misty moving like a crab, it was clearly a challenge to some. 'Those thighs are ridiculous,' I pointed out. 'You could fit a stack of two-pence pieces between them.'

'I know.' There was a hint of pride in his voice when he said this. Worrying, what seemed to please him most was that I had recognised his attention to detail.

'Slim, the gold standard is a fifty-pence piece. That's if you're going to be idiot enough to start measuring in the first place.'

For the first time since I had walked into the room, Slim turned his attention from the screen. 'A fifty-pence piece? Is that all?'

'I believe so, but don't you dare ask me to try it.'

'Shit,' he said, returning to the game. 'Pavlov said it was fifty pence *worth* of two-pence pieces.'

I was about to suggest that a little recalibration might make her walk more comfortably, but a patter of footfalls sent Slim into a state of alert. Something was closing in on his Misty, and fast. Punching wildly at the buttons, he managed to make her twitch in a slightly spastic way, only for another Misty to zoom past his own creation. Hurtling across the clearing so swiftly she actually put my boyfriend's effort into a spin. I couldn't even see how her legs measured up, they were just a blur.

'Running is something I need to work on,' he said, a little tight-lipped.

'What's the objective here?' I asked, wondering if I should have raised a few more questions myself back at the market. I had always assumed that games like this were for all the family and, though I could see the appeal, this one didn't quite scrub up so cleanly.

Having picked Misty off the jungle floor, Slim paused the game and pointed to the jewel case on the carpet. 'The creators have been trumpeting it for months. Apparently there's a vault hidden somewhere.'

'Uh-huh,' I said, unimpressed. 'Containing what?'

'Bank details, basically. An account containing a million bucks.' Slim turned to check my reaction, his eyebrows hoisted high, which was when I realised he wasn't talking play money.

'Are you serious? A *million*?'

'For real,' he said, and demonstrated his intentions by having Misty break into a fit of some kind. 'Once you find the vault with the digits inside, you call up the hotline and never work again.'

'Okay, so what are the chances of finding this vault?'

'I'm working on it,' replied Slim. 'It's on limited release to stop the world and his mouse from getting online to find it, which means this game here is gold dust in more ways than one.' Another fumble with the joypad and, without warning, his heroine was off. I didn't think her arms needed to flap like that, but she was running nevertheless. 'Go, Misty,' crowed Slim, upon which the ground gave way beneath her feet and the poor girl fell headlong into a pit full of snakes.

'Encouraging,' I said, after a moment to reflect. 'She looks a little dead, there.'

Slim slumped back on to the sofa, tossed the controls to one side. 'It's a minor setback. I'm only on level one.'

'How many are there?'

'Approximately one hundred and seven.'

'Right,' I said. 'Value for money, then.'

'Still, I'm half-way through the first level. The trouble is each level has its own unique hazards.'

'Like snakepits.'

'Snakepits can be jumped, once I learn how. What I need is firepower. Until I come across some it's the other players I should be worried about. I was lucky just then. Maybe she didn't think I was worth wasting.'

'Eh?'

'Most of the Mistys I've come across are more tooled up than Carol Smillie,' he revealed. 'Only we're not talking glue guns here, far from it.'

'I know that, but it doesn't take much intelligence to pull a trigger. Where are the puzzles you mentioned?'

'Well,' he said, after a moment, 'every weapon is different, so you have to suss out how to fire them effectively. Random shooting is fine, but the instant kill is where it's at, and that takes a few brain cells, I can tell you.'

'I'm not sure I approve,' I said, sitting beside him now. 'Give us a go, then.'

Slim snatched the controls to his chest, then looked at me like I'd just asked for his babies. 'I'm sorry?' he said. 'Do *what*?'

'I thought you could show me how to play.'

Slim, mouthing the word, seemingly astonished. 'Cisco, I'm doing this for you. For all of us. We haven't got time to *play*! I have until Monday to find the vault and make a million. Once I've found it and paid off Cartier, you can play it all you like. Until then, I have work to do.'

12

So each of my presents served a purpose, neither of which I intended. One had left my brother creatively constipated, the other luring my boyfriend on a run to nothing. As for my own little pick-me-up, the flowers looked fine on the kitchen table, brightening up my morning as I got ready for work. As did the greeting I received from the florist himself as I wove my way through the market crowd. Normally, catcalls left me cold, but having been sidelined by the boys I found myself enjoying the attention. More so when Sweet William persisted and the other traders turned to look.

'Check it out, fellas.' The big man grinned mischievously at me. In daylight, his puffa looked so padded out it could have been cut from a duvet. 'There's a girl going places.'

'If only,' I called across to him, flushing a little as I moved along.

'Cisco, can I ask you something?'

It was the sudden change in tone that made me stop and glance back at him. Through the throng I saw his expression had retracted into something altogether more serious. I cut across to his stall. 'What's the matter?'

He beckoned me closer, looking one way then the other before showing me his nails. 'Would I benefit from buffing?'

The first thing I did was smile, unsure if he was joking. Here was a man as wide as a sideboard, asking me for beauty tips. Sweet straightened out his fingers some more, and when he turned them in the light, I knew that he was being serious. Even so, I could've answered him from across the street: anyone who works with flowers wasn't likely to be in possession of a perfect ten. But was it soil or resin encrusted under there? 'I think they need scrubbing before I can say for sure,' I offered tactfully.

'But should a man have a shine to his nails?' he persisted sounding anxious now. 'What does it say to a fox such as yourself?'

I tried to recall how Slim's looked. They were trimmed, if I remembered rightly, not bitten. That I couldn't say much more about their condition seemed to answer the question. 'Nails on a man shouldn't be something you notice,' I decided. 'Ultimately, you don't want us thinking you might invade our space on the bathroom shelf.' It was then I looked up at him. 'Who are you trying to impress, Willie?'

'No one special.' In the same breath, his hand pulled away from mine and plunged inside his puffa pocket. 'Just curious.'

I smiled wryly. That was fine, then. 'If you want I can give them a manicure.'

'Yeah? Would it hurt?'

'Only if I told everyone.'

Sweet William smiled philosophically. 'But you could shine them up so it looks like I don't give a shit?'

'Naturally immaculate,' I promised. 'But it takes a little effort to get right.'

'I'll pay for your time,' he said, 'and buy your silence, if I have to.'

'Doing it for you would be a pleasure,' I told him, 'though, God knows, I could use some proper money.'

Sweet pulled his whole self away from me this time, and reminded me that I was dressed in a business suit. 'Work is money,' he said.

'Not when you're a temp –'

'Ouch.'

'– with a rent demand I can't meet without losing sleep at night.'

'A double blow. How about your boyfriend? Word is he's loaded.' I told him the City deal had collapsed, taking his website venture too. Willie said, 'Man, that's too bad. How's he taken the news?'

'Let's just say Slim's gone underground for a while.'

'The retentive, then. Is he good for a touch?'

I explained that my brother was feeling unwell right now, which wasn't far from the truth, and that it was basically down to me to cover the shortfall on their behalf.

'Who's your landlord?'

'Frank Cartier. D'you know him?'

He winced at the name, and I wondered whether he had experienced some kind of bad deal with him, too. I looked up into his face, hoping to find a solution in that street-smart look of his, and in a way I did. 'Maybe I should work for you,' I suggested, half joking. 'There must be fast money to be made in your kind of business.'

He shrugged, and focused on a point way behind me. 'Depends on the season,' he said. 'Summer's all right, but nothing compares to spring. When the daffodils first come in, you know it's time to party.'

A moment passed before I said I wasn't talking about his flower stock. Sweet seemed not to register, and I took it as a sign to back off. Learn the code, like Slim had said. Maybe try again when I talked the same language. 'I'd better get going,' I said. 'I thought I'd pitch up early at work and use the phone to do a little job-hunting. I need something better, Willie. We're desperate.'

'Are you going past the hospital?'

'Sure. It's on my way.'

The florist turned to the racks and withdrew a bunch of Oriental poppies like a scimitar from its sheath. 'Could you deliver these to a friend?'

I glanced at the blowsy pink offering, a little shocked at being asked. I know I had said I should work for him, but now he was giving me a chance I felt a sense of hesitation. 'What kind of delivery is it?' I asked.

'A "get well soon",' he said. Was that a code, I wondered. He appeared to read my mind: 'What else do you give someone in traction?' Right then, I was too intimidated to think about it. I didn't dare check to see what else was in there with the stems, or even question why someone known to this man would wind up requiring that kind of treatment. It occurred to me that maybe whoever it was had refused a delivery job like this one. Cautiously, I accepted the flowers. 'Good girl,' he said, and patted my cheek. 'Ward G. Ask for Rose.'

'A *woman*?' Sweet William dipped his eyes from mine when I said this, and pinked around the jowls. I didn't need to crack a code to understand him this time. Suddenly the flowers felt a lot more comfortable in my grasp. 'Shall I send her your fondest regards?'

'No need.' He retreated behind his counter. 'Bleeding Rose knows the score.'

'What kind of name is Bleeding Rose?' I asked.

'My friend is a little accident prone,' he said, and swept away a litter of petals with one hand. 'Always cutting herself on the job.'

I breathed easier, deciding that she had to be a fellow florist, and said I really had to get going. 'Next time,' I promised him, 'let's do nails.'

'Cisco, you're a star. I'm indebted.'

'And I'm just in debt,' I said, sotto, turning to leave now.

'*Hey*,' said Sweet abruptly. I looked around. 'It's only money.'

13

Hospitals freak me out. Always have. I'm not scared of surgeons. I quite like the smell of antiseptic, and I can just about stomach the food. What I find so hard to deal with is the leaving bit: the moment I arrive back in the street, it always feels like the world has moved on without me. The sunshine seems brighter, car fumes more noxious and even the taxis strike me as more expensive. Somehow time inside those whitewashed walls just isn't the same as time outside. Whether you're a patient or a visitor, you can't get *on*. All you can do is take stock of where you've come from, and consider where to go when you get out.

My first time through the exit doors didn't count, because being a newborn things weren't different but utterly new. Eleven years later, I was wheeled out with a cast on my ankle and a renewed respect for ponies. At fifteen I left minus my appendix and a boyfriend who hadn't bothered to visit, while a year later I stumbled from the hospital mortuary minus my parents. Every time, I rejoined the world with a different perspective on it, and the morning I met Bleeding Rose was no exception: delivering a bouquet to the ward as requested, receiving a lesson in life in return.

The first thing she did, she stopped reading and said: 'Are you a nice cop or a nasty cop? Even with flowers I can never be sure.'

This was in a private room that smelt of Chanel with base notes of bleach. The patient was dressed in red satin pyjamas, her left leg plastered, pinned and raised in traction. She had one wrist in a bandage, Jackie Collins splayed across her bosom and suspicion all over her face. I had only just walked in, but her question stopped me short of the chair beside her bed. Rose looked like the kind of woman who had a husband doing time. For life. She was old enough to be my mother, but with the features of a Barbie gone bad. I told her I wasn't a cop, that my name was Cisco and we had a mutual friend.

'Sweet William?' she said, with a bead on the bouquet I had with me. Her accent placed her east of here, Essex some place, in a manor house probably, one of those modern red-brick jobs with big gates and Doberman Pinschers and unspoken question marks about where the funds had come from.

'Sweet William, the florist,' I added, just in case she was in any doubt about the purpose of my visit.

Bleeding Rose had blonde hair with roots so black she must have dyed them that way. As for the top-knot, it almost doubled as a face-lift. Without the slightest crack in her complexion, she narrowed her eyes at me. 'You sure you're not a cop?'

'Even in heels,' I told her, standing back so that she could appreciate what little height I had. 'In uniform I command all the authority of a stripper.'

She conceded my point with a smile. One that spread out and softened her expression into something less like a prison widow. I was busting to ask what had happened to her, what her problem was with the law, but as I sought to summon the courage her attention returned to the flowers. Beckoning me closer, she asked how much was owed. 'Nothing,' I said, but it sounded unconvincing. For both our sakes, I turned the bunch upside down and tapped it against my thigh. The poppies came up clean. Rose tutted to herself and, strangely enough, I felt a little let down too, as if the absence of any narcotics meant I couldn't cut it as a courier. I circled round to the sink, found a jug to fill.

'Either it slipped his mind,' she said ruefully, 'or it slipped out on the way here.'

I shook my head. 'Maybe he was just hoping this would be enough to cheer you up.'

'That's Willie.' She sighed. 'Always there when you need him.'

A silence opened up between us, which I should have broached by just agreeing. Instead, I turned to face her again. 'Actually, I think he's sweet on you.'

'Sweet?' she remarked, surprised. 'On me?'

'Is that so bad?' I set the flowers on her bedside table, then pulled up the chair to find out more.

'I'm not sure Willie sees women in that way,' said Rose. 'Flowers are his big passion in life. That's what turns him on. You only have to look at his nails to see where his heart lies.'

'Oh, I don't know,' I said, but held back on his manicure anxieties. Instead, I gestured at the blooms I had brought on his behalf. 'These flowers say a great deal.'

'A deal is what's missing,' Rose cut back. She grinned briefly, then resumed her cautious air as she studied my face. Looking to see if she could trust me, so it seemed. 'Willie and me go way back,' she said next. 'He's always picking up the pieces.'

'Yeah?'

'*Always*, honey. Every time.'

Her reluctance to go any further was enough to persuade me to stay. I had another half-hour before I was due behind the desk, and the prospect of sneaking in early to blag the phone didn't seem so pressing now that I was here. I just couldn't leave without knowing the bigger picture. I had to find out for my own peace of mind. 'So,' I said, eyeing the framework of pulleys and wire that caged her bed, 'what the hell happened to you?'

'Nothing much.' Rose batted away the question as if being trussed up like this was only a minor inconvenience. 'I had a fall in an art gallery.'

'God, you must've landed badly.'

'The marble floor didn't help.'

'Sounds like a posh gallery,' I said. 'Can't you sue? Get compensation?'

She smiled to herself. 'That would be a problem.'

'Why?'

85

'I was robbing the place at the time,' she said. 'But I'm only telling you this because I know that any friend of Willie's won't take it any further.'

I opened my mouth, then closed it again, stunned by what I had heard. Rose mentioned something about a glass roof giving way, but I didn't take it in. Instead, I was struck by the thought that her confession made me party to the crime. In my world, an accessory was something I bought from Top Shop, not an offence that could send me directly to jail. Aware that she was watching me closely now, testing my response, I recovered my composure and said, 'Did you get caught?'

Bleeding Rose swung her bad arm in the direction of the door. 'Without Willie, I'd have a police guard out there right now.'

'He was *in on it*?'

She laughed. 'He doesn't approve of my profession,' she said, 'but he'll always make it right for me when things go wrong.'

'You make it sound like a regular occurrence,' I replied. 'Actually, Willie did let slip that you're always cutting yourself on the job.'

'He told you that?' I noticed Rose flush through her foundation and looked away, embarrassed for her. When I glanced up again she said, 'Okay, so I have a DNA problem.'

'How so?'

'I keep leaving it behind at the scene of the crime.' She showed me her wrist, gave me time to work it out for myself. 'Almost severed an artery this time. Glass shards followed me down on to the marble.'

'Messy.'

'The place was a state, but Willie takes care of all that. I only have to call him out on the mobile and he'll come to my rescue, even if it is usually the middle of the night.'

'He never does!' I said, incredulous, though I had to concede that he looked like the type of bloke for whom friends were family.

'You should see the face on him whenever he finds me,' Rose continued. 'He turns up with his cleaning gear, puffing and cursing and swearing blind it's the last time he'll do it, but I know deep down. I know.' She broke off there, most probably revisiting a memory that should have been sealed off with police tape.

I said, 'You make him sound like a guardian angel.'

'If Willie didn't mop up, Forensics would have a field day.'

'What about the hospital?' I asked. 'Don't they suspect?'

'Look at all the pretty flowers they got round this place,' she suggested. 'Who do you think keeps the wards in bloom?'

I sat back in the chair, reeling in the light of all this. 'Can I ask you something?'

'Feel free. This is more fun than medication time.'

'I just want to know if it pays.'

'What?'

'Crime.'

I'm not sure who took longer to register the question, Rose or me. What am I like? I thought suddenly. I always had myself down as one of the good guys, and yet here I was in conversation with a cat burglar. One who had lost a few lives, by the look of her. I should have changed the subject, backtracked from the conversation, but times were just too tough. Which was why her reply would come to stake out my thoughts for the rest of the day. So did it pay? I asked her again. Breaking the law like she did?

'That depends,' said Bleeding Rose, choosing her words carefully, 'on how badly you need the loot.'

At work that morning, every face floating into the lobby masked a criminal past. At least, they did through my eyes. Not the fresh young faces with portfolios under their arms, but the people behind them, the ones who made all the money out of modelling: the agents and scouts, the clients and chaperones. Quite suddenly, every move they made looked shifty – the hushed request to see someone, the way they fidgeted in their seats, muttering into their mobiles, waiting to be ushered upstairs. All of them were on the take, weren't they? Until my audience with Bleeding Rose I had never looked a thief in the eye, or considered moving in such circles. Now it seemed that *I* was the odd one out, Miss Muggins, the temporary, fighting to cover her costs legitimately.

Come lunchtime, I directed my questioning closer to home. 'Have you ever committed a crime?'

It was the first thing Slim heard on picking up the telephone. No 'Hello' or 'Are you dressed yet?' Still, he considered my question calmly enough. I could even hear him chewing something as he thought about it. Despite the time, I had a horrible feeling that whatever it was he probably regarded it as breakfast.

'Cisco,' he said eventually, 'we're all criminals.'

I glanced at the only person in the lobby. He was standing by the revolving doors, where the sunlight flared through the glass whenever someone came in or out. The guy had been there for some time, which wasn't unusual in a business that seemed to make it compulsory for people to be kept waiting. I half wondered if I had missed him on the way in that morning, because he was reading a broadsheet from the day before. That he sported the kind of buzz-cut you needed for the police was what really persuaded me to speak low into the phone.

'I'm no criminal,' I told Slim, addressing the memo-pad in front of me. 'I've never broken the law in my whole life.'

'Yes, you have. This week, in fact.'

'So I used up the water for a bath,' I said, but stopped short of pointing out that half the tank had gone on cleaning the tidemark off the tub before I dared use it. 'That's no offence, Slim, not like leaving a pool of pee behind the loo seat.'

A pause came down the line. Then, 'How did you manage that?'

'Not me, *one of you guys!*'

'Believe me,' he insisted. 'You're a law-breaker too.'

'Some of the things I dragged from the plug-hole. You and Pavlov could do time for crimes against humanity.'

'I refer to Exhibit A,' he went on, like a cheap barrister. 'Not the suspect butts in the ashtray at home, because you could always claim you didn't inhale, but the game you bought me. Irrefutable proof that you're no angel, Cisco.'

'*The Money Shot*? What about it?'

'You got it on the black market.'

'You sound very sure.' I switched the phone from one ear to the other, just as a bar of sunshine whipped across the walls. I looked up with a start, and saw that the guy with the buzz-cut and the paper had just left. I wasn't sure if I should be relieved, but stood tall anyhow. 'Just because I bought local,' I continued, 'that doesn't mean it's dodgy.'

'The sleeve's a colour photocopy, Cisco. It's so obviously a pirate copy, the guy who flogged it must've had a peg leg and a foul-mouthed parrot. Check your change if you don't believe me. Look for pieces of eight.'

'All right,' I conceded. 'But I hardly think it makes me party to a major crime.'

'No?' he said. 'Right now, the cash you coughed up is probably being used to finance some international drug-smuggling operation.'

'It only cost me a couple of quid,' I reasoned. 'What'll that buy? A packet of paracetamol and a bus fare into town?'

'All I'm saying is you broke the law. You bought an unlicensed copy, but it makes no odds because my console's chipped.'

'What happened? Did you drop something on it?'

Slim informed me that it was chipped in the technological sense, so that the processor inside could no longer scramble the snide games like the one I had bought him. Thus freeing him from the obligation to buy the more expensive, official versions.

'So you're as guilty as me,' I cut in, doodling furiously now.

'Like I said, we're all criminals.'

'And you don't feel bad?'

'Hell, no! Why should I?'

'You're ripping off the makers. Stealing their profits.'

89

'At their prices? If I bought legit, they'd be ripping *me* off. That's why I got my console chipped, so I could buy bootleg disks and play the makers at their own game. It makes you feel like a winner before you've even started.'

'Okay,' I said, with a sigh. 'How about Pavlov?'

'What about him?'

'I don't think he's capable of seriously breaking the law.'

'Cisco, the man wears peach. Peach is a crime against fashion.'

'I mean it.'

'Why?' he said next. 'What's on your mind, all these questions?'

Suddenly I had to ask myself the same thing. 'It doesn't matter,' I told him, as the sunlight went into a spin once again – people coming into the lobby this time. 'I'd better get back to work.'

'Me too.' Slim said this as if he had deals to close, not buttons to push on his joypad.

'So how's it going, anyway?' I asked him quickly, wondering at the same time whether Misty Ventura would perform any better if *she* was under pressure to find the rent.

'Good,' said Slim. 'Great.'

'Yeah?'

'Well, okay. I haven't quite cracked forward motion. But I learned how to make her duck, which might be handy.'

'Good,' I said, less convincingly. 'Great.'

A brief silence followed, and when Slim spoke again it was as if he had tuned right into my thoughts. 'I won't let you down, Cisco. I'm going to find this million, you'll see.'

I smiled to myself. Maybe I was dating a dreamer, but at least I could be sure that I figured in this fantasy world of his.

'So will you be late?'

I looked at my watch. Time was money. Overtime was more. 'Can't say for sure just yet,' I replied, 'though we badly need the loot.'

14

It was my conversation with Bleeding Rose that helped make up my mind, not during the first visit but the second, when I returned to her bedside later that day. As the afternoon wore on the prospect of overtime had lost its appeal, and my receptionist's smile reflected that. Come six o'clock, it had all but disappeared and, indeed, that's what I did too. Racing across town to the temp agency so that I could collect my wage packet and plead for more lucrative employment. It was the outcome of that brief meeting that had persuaded me to stop off at the hospital on my way home. It wasn't a crime to reconsider my career options with a cat burglar, even if it did take me one step closer to trying my hand at something you wouldn't feature on a job application.

'You must be desperate, honey.'

I pitched my shoulder-bag under the bed and pulled up a chair. 'I guess I am.'

'Cisco, there are less hazardous ways of making money.'

'In a weekend?'

Bleeding Rose inched herself up the pillow and invited me to tell her all about it, so I did, from the rent demand to the fact that our landlord would surely evict us unless we found the cash by Monday. I told her about the bad luck I seemed to have brought to the house, and my pledge to bring us all back into the black. At any cost, as I finished defiantly.

Rose heard me out, and responded with a question: 'Ever been naughty before?'

'Haven't we all?'

'I mean it,' she said, and I realised she wasn't talking about breaking bathroom rules, 'because I'm only prepared to help if you have a clean sheet.'

Quietly I admitted that I was clean, that I had never been in trouble with the law in my life. So clean, in fact, that I virtually squeaked in my seat as I leaned forward and said, 'Isn't that a disadvantage?'

'Quite the opposite,' said Rose. 'As long as you don't get caught at the scene, there's no way the law will come looking for you. They have no record of your prints, after all, no previous form that'll give them a clue it was you. *Nothing.*'

I tried to imagine a photofit of my face in three sections, and figured it would bring me in midway between Christina Ricci and Cruella de Vil. Not a bad combo, but I could see how countless blondes would fit the same description. 'So, will you help?' I asked.

'Depends what kind of job you have in mind.'

I sat back to think: I hadn't given this bit any consideration. It was the end result that had consumed my thoughts all day, not the act of pulling it off. 'What would you recommend,' I asked awkwardly, 'for a first-timer?'

A slow-burning smile came from the cat burglar, and I just knew Rose had realised what a novice she had on her hands. 'This isn't about bunking a bus fare to save a few pennies,' she said.

'I know that.'

'You seem very sure.'

It was then that I showed her the fruits of my first ever theft. Back in the temp agency, as my boss attempted to justify the massive percentage he was creaming from my wages, I had been overwhelmed by the desire to claim something back. It wasn't much, but to me it represented a willingness to take control of my finances.

'It's a paperweight,' I said, watching Rose heft the big glass pebble in her good hand. 'The agency must've had them made up as corporate gifts because there were boxes of them all over the office. Anyway, the boss took this call, pretending it was work not personal, so I just took the one he had on his desk. He was looking straight at me, too. Giving me this blank gaze as he struggled to explain why he hadn't gone home the night before. I felt compelled to get one over on him, if not for me then for his wife or whoever was on the other end of that line.'

Rose tipped the paperweight back into my upturned palm. 'So how do you feel now?'

'Good,' I said. 'Like I've achieved something today.'

'And what if it had been his wallet you stole? Something of value to him.'

I closed my fingers over my trophy, and suddenly felt stupid. 'That would be different,' I admitted. 'I'm not cut out for that sort of crime.' I pocketed the paperweight, wishing I'd never taken it.

Then, out of nowhere, Rose said, 'Cisco, you're my kind of criminal.'

'I am?'

'Not taking money from the man direct, that shows you have a conscience. It means deep down, you gave it some thought.'

'I'm flattered, I think.'

'Don't be,' she said. 'Women always make better criminals.'

I liked Bleeding Rose. I liked her front. I liked her outlook on life. Even if I didn't buy it all at first. 'Okay,' I said. 'I'm listening.'

'Doing a job is like having an affair,' she began, and waited for my smile to shrink. 'Unlike the men, who steam in waving their tools and hoping for the best, we consider the bigger picture. We're smart. We use our heads. We study the layout back to front before we go in. We work out the exit routes in case things turn nasty, but ultimately we're less likely to get reckless and go back for more.'

I didn't like to point out that she was arguing her case from a hospital bed. As a serial offender, a cat burglar who persistently came a cropper playing away, I could only conclude that Rose had a one in a million man in her life. I was going to press her about the nature of her relationship with Sweet William, but she

93

stole in first with a question of her own. 'So how do you feel about a bank?'

'*What?*'

'You heard.' Rose's eyes narrowed as my own opened wide, and I realised she had planned this moment, had waited until my guard was down so that I would give her an honest response. After everything she had just said about women and crime, this seemed to back it up. 'Everyone loves a bank robber,' she insisted. 'If you rip off innocent people, they hate you. Do an institution and all of a sudden you're a folk hero.'

'But a *bank*! I only want to pay the rent, not retire to Rio.'

'A rural branch is best,' Rose pressed on. 'They recognise good manners in the countryside. Rob them with respect and they'll only recall the decent things about you. Makes it a bitch for the officer in charge of statements.'

'But don't you think I should start with a fruit machine or something?'

'Aim high,' she said, 'else you'll be tempted to go back for more, and that's when your face gets familiar. This is a one-off, okay? Something so far removed from your everyday life that you'll look back and wonder if you went there at all.'

'Yeah, but—'

'Trust me,' she said. 'Just go up to the counter and ask for all the cash. Be firm but be courteous, then fill your boots.'

'What if they refuse?' I asked. 'I don't suppose bursting into tears would earn me a reprieve.'

'That you've had the front to take this to the till will be enough to persuade them not to mess. The threat is implied, which is way more effective than all that twitchy trigger-finger stuff you get with the meatheads. Why use a gun when good manners will get you what you want?'

'You make it sound like a movie.'

'So it should. You're not the only one who's going to question if it's really happening. Coming from a nice girl like you, the clerks will be stunned into submission. And when it does sink in you'll be long gone. End of story. Pay the man his money.'

All this, I thought, for a greedy landlord. It just didn't add up, and I told Rose exactly that. 'It's too crazy for words,' I scoffed. 'Way over the top.'

'Only way to live,' agreed the cat burglar.

I stood up to leave, my feet on the ground once more. It was out of the question, a robbery. To think I was close to entertaining the idea left me reeling. I mumbled an apology for wasting her time, turned to leave, and came right back again when Bleeding Rose said, 'Don't forget your bag.' I reached under the bed, and promptly picked up on why she had said it with such glee. 'There are thieves in here, y'know.'

I couldn't shake the idea. To think I could be capable of committing a Class A crime was ridiculous. It was the kind of thing everyone fantasised about, but nobody actually *went* there. And yet, from the moment I left the hospital, I considered nothing else. I felt as if I had been set a stupid dare. I didn't want to do it, wasn't even sure that I could see it through successfully, but backing down was just as bad. A submission, it seemed, to the standard slide through life. I was a graduate, a temp, a career girl in waiting with a husband in time and a family to follow. Did I really want to head towards my grave without straying once? It would certainly be something to tell the grandchildren, I thought. Nan with her stick-'em-up story.

The dilemma stayed on my tail all the way home, stalking my thoughts like I was easy pickings. A tourist on the wrong side of town. That was how I felt as I hurried towards Columbia Road: a little lost and vulnerable, wearing my worries like a brightly coloured backpack. Arriving back on familiar territory didn't make me feel any better. I even wondered if someone had slipped into the house ahead of me. All I did was push the key into the lock to find the front door hadn't even been closed properly.

'Slim? Pavlov? Anyone in?'

I glanced both ways up the street, wondering if one of them had just popped out for a moment and left it open like this. It was hard to get a clear view – the sun may have been winding down, but the flower market showed little sign of following suit. With perishable stock to shift, the place was ablaze with activity. All I could hear was florists trading discounts, and the scent of lilies on the turn was almost overpowering. I hovered on the doorstep, pondering how bad it would be to ask Sweet William to come with me at this busy time, before concluding that I had to get a grip. I was being paranoid, nothing more. Willie might have owed me for delivering to Rose, but I figured that if I acted on her advice I might really need his help one day. Squaring up to the door now, I took a tentative step inside.

'Guys? Who's here?'

I was relieved to find that the lock hadn't been forced and I felt much better for being inside. The place looked a bit trashed, of course, but that was down to us – also Poppa Italiano. We were responsible for the jackets that had missed the hooks, but the pizza flyers under my feet were beyond our control. A few days before I had been clearing the mat when another sheaf had fallen through the letterbox. Some days they arrived so frequently it seemed that the house itself depended on them for sustenance.

'Come out, come out, wherever you are,' I called next, although I sensed I was entertaining myself. Shrugging off my raincoat, but mindful to hang it properly, I moved through the hall and blamed Pavlov for the door. My brother had been living in another world lately, drifting in and out of the house as if he was the only one with problems. I found his note to me in the kitchen. The tiny, perfectly sculpted handwriting was unmistakable, but I didn't have to read it to confirm that both he and Slim were out.

'They're with the bank manager.'

I whirled round, a cry dying in my throat when I saw him there, inches away, deftly shelling nuts without once taking his eyes off me.

'No financial problems, I trust?' Frank Cartier chewed in double time, his mouth popping open every upswing, not giving a damn about his manners. The man exuded so much confidence just then, anyone would've thought he owned the place. Which, I guess, he did. Even so, I wasn't sure that any landlord could let himself in without warning.

'We weren't expecting you until Monday.' A tense smile masked my shock at seeing him like this. I didn't feel threatened by his presence, more a sense of being entirely invaded. 'The rent's not due until then,' I reminded him.

Cartier tossed another pistachio into his mouth, said he knew that. 'But I'm delighted to hear you're staying, Cisco. Letting this house to a pair of boys, it was starting to smell like a locker room.'

'Mr Cartier,' I said, gathering my wits now, thinking it was better to play along with him at this stage rather than piss him off, 'is there something you wanted?'

Our landlord arched his snowy eyebrows, indicating that he wanted to finish what was in his mouth before putting me in the picture. I looked at my feet, feeling awkward and unsettled. More so when two discarded husks hit the lino. Bouncing apart like dice.

'That's a nice T-shirt,' he said suddenly, stepping back to take in the space between my crop top and jeans. 'Ever think about getting your belly-button pierced?' I crossed my arms and scowled, which only seemed to fuel his interest. 'Don't cover up on my account,' he insisted. 'You're killing me, but it's good a girl makes the most of herself.'

'You know, I have a feeling the boys will be back any second.' I slipped to one side as I said this, anxious to reclaim some space.

He sighed heavily. 'I've got other properties to check up on right now. I was hoping to talk to you all together.'

'We're busy people.' I shrugged. 'Always the rent to pay.'

'You're telling me,' he said, and settled on a chair at the table.

I hadn't said this to start a conversation. I had said it so that he would leave. He gestured at the adjacent seat, with those big pasty fingers of his, inviting me to sit. I folded my arms a little tighter, stayed right where I was. 'You can't do too badly,' I said, as a concession. 'Property is a licence to make money, I hear.'

Cartier chuckled, and rested his shoe on the edge of the chair I had just refused. 'Not with the overheads on my own place,' he said. 'Keeping the wolves from my door is murder.'

Didn't I know it, I thought, watching him tilt the seat now so it balanced on two legs. 'Slim said you live on the coast. Nice place?'

'Formidable,' he said. 'A regular playboy mansion.'

'Seriously?'

'Would be if it wasn't falling into the fucking sea.' Cartier took his foot away from the chair. It balanced on two legs for a moment, then tipped back into place. 'Built on a cliff edge, isn't it? Every day I wake up to find the grounds have got a little smaller, while the bill for reinforcement grows.'

'At least you have people like us to cover your costs,' I said, feeling even more animosity towards him now that I knew where our money would be going. 'Unless, of course, we can't afford it any more.'

'That's what I'm here to discuss.' Climbing off his chair now, Cartier invited me into my own front room to hear his proposition. 'Whenever you're most comfortable, I'll move there.'

'What kind of proposition?' I asked, returning to his point.

He said one that would be to our advantage and his, and politely insisted I lead the way. Mindful of our financial situation, I figured a minute of my time would cost about as much as it did to power the light-bulb out in the hallway. 'I'd offer you coffee,' I said, on my way through, 'but the milk's gone sour.'

'How about something stronger?' I glanced back over my shoulder, and was sure I caught him checking me out. 'Believe me, Cisco, this is one offer I just know you'll want to toast.'

16

'No way. Forget it!'

That was how Pavlov responded later, when I tabled our land-lord's offer.

'My words exactly,' I followed up. 'I told Cartier he could double his ridiculous rent increase and even then we'd never get into that kind of arrangement.'

Where my brother and I shared the same sentiment, Slim adopted a more practical perspective. He pointed out that we hadn't had the money to cover the rent even *before* Cartier blew it sky high, which was why we were having this conversation in front of the screen. I was slumped on one side of the sofa, hoping the spliff that had just come round would help me forget about the day. Pavlov was slouched at the other end with the ashtray, while Slim sat bolt upright between us with the joypad in his hands, directing Misty Ventura on her mission to save us all.

In terms of progress, which was a generous way to describe things, Slim had directed Misty into the catacombs beneath the jungle floor and was looking for a way back up. He had managed to get her jogging at last, even if she did go into a pissed sort of wobble every now and then, cracking her head against the low beams or tripping up on tree roots. It was a small achievement on his part, but it certainly outshone the outcome of their meeting with the bank manager. I decided it was too late to ask Slim whether the Alice band holding back his dreadlocks had gone along too. It had been missing from my make-up table that morning. I only hoped the manager's response would persuade him to leave the hair accessories at home next time. That was if he wanted to create an impression that worked in his favour. I watched him follow Misty for a moment, then broke the spell by waving the spliff in front of him.

'Okay, let me hear it again before I get too wasted.' Slim halted the game to address us both. 'Cartier offered us the chance to live here rent free in exchange for putting a few webcams around the place?'

'That's what the man said,' I confirmed. 'A virtual show home for prospective tenants. They log on, look around, and sign up for details of his other properties.'

'Sounds like our landlord's been watching way too much reality TV,' my brother suggested. 'Next thing, he'll be suggesting we look after a bunch of chickens while we're at it. What is he like?'

Slim guffawed, expelling the smoke in one breath. 'TV is precisely what he hasn't been watching,' he said. 'On the box, what you see is all you get. Sound and vision filtered down like water through rock. It's clean. It's palatable. Pure entertainment for a mass audience, maybe, but not reality, just the highlights. If you want to see life as it happens, and even call the shots, you have to look online. The catch is, you can't have a life away from your computer if you want to see it all.'

'You're not exactly selling it to us,' said Pavlov, appealing to me at the same time with a faintly offended look.

'Cartier wants a webcam in the kitchen, one in the hall, one here in the front room and also upon the landing.' I stopped there to give them both a moment. It had taken me until now to accept that our landlord wasn't joking. 'But get this,' I finished, 'one in every *bedroom*, too! Can you imagine?'

Slim released the pause feature and suggested to me that he could.

'What are you?' asked Pavlov. 'Some kind of exhibitionist?'

'Says the *inhibitionist*.'

'But how does it pay the rent?' I asked quickly, anxious that we remained focused on the fact that we had no cash to cover it ourselves.

Hunkering over the controls again, Slim said, 'There's always money to be made from people watching people.'

'Especially when they're naked,' Pavlov muttered.

I looked at Slim, aghast. 'This is a *sex* thing he's proposing?'

'It's the *real* thing,' he said, directing Misty towards a pipe outlet that jutted from the rockface ahead. 'The best dot coms are about community, right? Sites that help people connect with one another so they can talk and gossip, rant and rave. Now webcams are taking things a step further and allowing us to *see* each other too. They're literally breaking down barriers, turning bricks to glass. It means we can look in on complete strangers without being obliged to view their holiday snaps or run the risk of getting murdered.'

'Well, that's a relief,' I said icily. 'Cartier even promised to do the place up a bit if we agreed. He was talking about redecorating the main living areas downstairs, so I guess he must be expecting visitors.'

'Of course,' Slim continued. 'Prospective tenants get to view the kind of house they're after without actually having to visit. For a landlord with a property portfolio that makes sound business sense. He's on to a good thing.'

'If you want my opinion,' came the voice from the other end of the sofa, 'it's a geek thing.'

'We're all geeks nowadays.' Slim didn't even turn when he spelled this out. 'It's just that some of us haven't come out about it yet.'

'One geek in this house is all I can take,' my brother continued. 'Why open the doors to people with more interest in our lives than in their own?'

Slim let go of the controls with one hand and touched his temple. At the same time Misty halted in her tracks, right in front of the pipe, acting like she too wasn't going any further if she had to put up with any more crap from Pavlov.

'I hardly think we're in a position to be choosy here,' said Slim. 'If Cartier kicks us out we couldn't even cover a deposit on a new place, so be careful what you say about geeks. Unless Misty finds her winning streak fast, it might be you who'll be needing them more than they need you.'

I began to regret I had even mentioned the proposal. Told them if we fell out now we might as well just pack up and go. My brother shrank into his cushion, still grousing about the idea of being under surveillance.

'I don't hear Misty complaining,' I said, thinking we had done nothing but watch her back for the last half-hour. 'At least she's out there trying to sort our situation.'

Slim echoed my sentiments, and then went into a state of high alert when an avalanche-like sound spilled from the TV speakers. 'Holy shit!'

'What is it?' I turned my attention to the game on the screen, just as the feet and then the feisty form of another Misty Ventura popped out of the pipe.

'Oh, you picked the *wrong* man!' Had Slim's skills matched his excitement, his opponent would have been dead already. As it was, he fumbled with the joypad in such a way that his own Misty adopted a stance not unlike that of a chicken. 'Come on, then,' he said regardless. 'Who wants some?'

I glanced at Pavlov, who was already looking my way with a similar air of bemusement. Why? Because the opponent in question hadn't been customised so much as *miniaturised*. Everything about her was downsized and deflated. With her hair in bunches tied with outsized bows, she looked more like a little miss than a grown up Misty.

'This is like *Rugrats*,' my brother declared, 'only better.'

'What are you going to do?' I asked. 'Take her back to her parents?'

Slim narrowed his gaze, said, 'Don't be fooled by appearances,' and at the same time managed to persuade his Misty into some kind of fighting stance. At once, Misty Minor's eyebrows snapped into a V, then her mouth stretched into a sneer. Slim seemed taken aback, we all were, but my boyfriend had the controls.

'Mate, don't try to hit her.' Pavlov sounded a little alarmed as Slim's Misty hooked the air then jabbed an accidental right into the stone wall beside her. 'She's a child, for Chrissakes.'

'I'm trying to run away,' Slim pleaded, but by then it was far too late. In one fluid move, the kid spun full circle, came round with her leg outstretched and delivered a fearsome ankle chop. A move that left all three of us viewing the screen with our heads turned sideways.

'Are you dead?' I asked, watching the little scamp scuttle away from her victim. 'You look dead.'

Bravely, and with a little steering from Slim, Misty peeled herself from the subterranean floor. She looked a little unsteady, having struggled to her feet, then again Slim was still messing with the buttons. The action over, reality seemed to creep back around the screen.

'These webcams,' Pavlov sounded a little less defensive as he questioned Slim again, 'would you seriously let them into your life?'

Slim had Misty crawl into the pipe before he responded: 'All I'm saying is it's worth considering. People are naturally wary of new technology, but it hasn't outsmarted us yet.' A further moment of despondency for us all just then, as a headlong rush of water washed Misty to certain death. 'Storm drain.' Slim sighed, and hit **restart**. 'Always there's something.'

From out of the silence, Pavlov said, 'So what happens when you have to get undressed for bed, stuff like that?'

'Cartier's proposing a single cam in every room, which means making good use of your dead zone.'

'Your *what* zone?' I asked.

Slim looked one way then the other, and dropped the controls into his lap. 'The dead zone,' he repeated, and locked his arms out straight in front of him. 'Your basic cam has a limited field of vision, right? Just like any camera, even the human eye.'

'If you say so.'

Slim opened up the gap between his hands, as if he were about to make the TV levitate, then stopped to glance from one side to the other. 'So anything you want to do in private, you do in the dead zone, where the cam can't see you.' A further silence followed as my brother and I processed the concept, sizing up Slim and his little demonstration. 'Okay,' he relented finally, and reached for the keyboard at his feet. 'Let me show you in the flesh.'

Pecking at the keys now, Slim closed down his game, pointed his browser at a search engine and summoned up a menu of webcam sites.

'Wow!' I gasped as he scrolled down the screen for us. 'There are hundreds of them.'

'From arrival lounges to funeral homes, all humanity is here online.'

'Billy Goat cam?' Pavlov was scanning the list now. 'That doesn't sound very human to me. Is it American?'

'*Dentist* cam?' I squinted to check that I had read it right. 'That's what they put in your mouth nowadays?'

'Taxi cam?' Slim suggested instead, and read out the accompanying synopsis. 'A London cabbie invites you to see the sights. Click here, and enjoy the ride.'

'Commentary optional,' I finished for him. 'If only that were true in the real world.'

My brother's expression puckered in contempt. 'One question,' he said, and dropped in a pause as if we should know it already. 'Why?'

'Why not?' replied Slim. 'Because it's there, I guess. Even if nothing appears to be happening, there's something compelling about sticking around just in case the situation changes. Chances are you could spend eight hours watching the guy get grumpy in traffic. Then again, you could log off and what do you know? He loses the plot completely – gets out of the cab, draws a shotgun from under the seat, and goes postal in the Seven Eleven.'

I pointed at the screen. 'How about that one? Coral cam.'

Slim stopped scrolling through the list, highlighting the title and the synopsis for the cam site in question. Pavlov began reading aloud like it was some kind of riddle. '"Watch Coral do the housework. Follow her from room to room as she does her daily rounds."' He stopped and wrinkled his nose. 'This is entertainment?'

Slim hit enter, and said, 'Observe.'

Waiting for the website to load, I wondered whether now was the time to reveal how my conversation with Frank Cartier had finished. Quite simply, our landlord had let on that he could find other tenants who would kill to take up his offer. And if we didn't cover the extra cost of *not* going online we could always give him one month's notice. His words precisely. *One month!* That was four weeks' grace in which our luck might just have changed. And I had to turn him down flat: telling the man that if we couldn't meet his ridiculous rent demand on Monday we would ship out on the spot. I steeled myself to speak up, but the cam site arrived on the screen as I drew breath and suddenly there we were. Looking through the square window at a total stranger Hoovering.

'Is this a tape?'

'Live and direct, sweetheart,' said Slim.

The picture wasn't perfect, a few shudders around the edges, but it had an intimate quality unlike any film or TV show. I didn't feel like part of an audience; it was more intimate than that. In some ways it really did feel as if we had just stepped into someone else's house without an invitation. If this was Coral she was about the same age and build as me. She had a short blonde bob, although it was a similar colouring as mine at the roots, and was wearing the kind of clothes I might have bought for myself: pink pedal-pushers with a capped-sleeve cherry-red top. There was certainly a better standard of domestic cleanliness going on with her, but that was all. I watched her run the vacuum cleaner back and forth over the carpet, contemplating how I would feel in her shoes.

'This woman,' said Pavlov, after a moment, 'how is it she earns her living?'

'See the banner above the webcam?' Slim rolled the cursor

over an advert for some online auction house. He clicked on it, and another window popped up inviting us to put in a bid for a weekend break in Amsterdam. 'This is her sponsor, and she'll be paid by them for every page impression that comes in from her site.'

'So she cleans up on two counts,' said Pavlov.

'Depends on the traffic,' Slim said, 'but certainly if she's offering something a lot of people want to see, and the ads are targeted properly. Cash for clicks is what it is.'

'Cash for creeps more like.' The boys turned my way. 'Whatever I was doing,' I said, 'I'd feel weird being watched.'

'Think of the rent,' said Slim. 'It's not such an intrusion that way.'

'Do you have a problem with the camera?' my brother asked me next. 'Or a problem with the housework?'

'You've changed your tune,' I countered. He had the spliff now. I wondered if that was responsible.

'Money-wise, I can see it makes sense. Getting the rent paid for doing nothing.'

'In front of an audience,' I stressed. 'Pavlov, you won't even *eat* in public.'

'That's a chewing thing and you know it. With a camera it's different. I wouldn't have to put up with *seeing* people watch me masticate.'

'But you'd still know they were watching.'

'So what do you suggest we do?' he snapped at me. 'Rob a bank?'

'It's an idea,' I said, sensing my skin prickle. Why not? I thought, and held my brother's gaze. A one-off, like Rose had suggested. It was outrageous, way over the top, and a reward for anyone prepared to test the boundaries of their everyday lives. Pavlov looked set to query my emerging smile, but Slim cut between us and gestured at the screen. 'There she goes,' he said. 'This one's using her dead zone.'

I turned to the telly, saw the vacuum cleaner standing unattended now, a comfy chair in full recline and a breakfast bar in the background, but no sign of Coral.

'Where's she gone?' I asked.

'Who knows?' said Slim. 'But it looks like this girl knows how to work a webcam.'

'The more I think about it, we'd be crazy not to accept Cartier's offer.' Pavlov crushed the stub of the joint into the ashtray. 'If this is all it takes, I'm in.'

We both looked at Slim, expecting him to side one way or the other, not suddenly adopt a spellbound expression, his jaw dropping open, both irises shrinking to pinheads.

'What?' asked Pavlov, turning to see what had silenced him. 'Oh!'

'That's it.' A cursory glance was all it took for me to spring from the sofa. 'Count me out!'

'She's naked!' Pavlov switched his attention back to Slim. 'Did you just make her clothes come off?'

Slim lifted his hands from the keyboard, as if to protest his innocence. 'Maybe she just got hot,' he said.

I headed for the door, glancing at the online spectacle on the way, and told him that anyone else would have fetched a glass of water.

'Not all cam sites are so explicit.'

'I don't care. Clothes or no clothes, I'd sooner expose myself in other ways before exposing myself to the weirdos of the web.'

As Slim hurriedly toggled back to the index page, Pavlov said, 'Where are you going now?'

'To make some money,' I told him. 'Fast.'

'But is it legal?' he asked.

I left the room without reply, and braced myself for the pair of them to scramble after me.

17

Straight in. Straight out. Never look back. Never do it again. This
was my mantra on our way out to the country, motoring through
the rain. The three of us were in Slim's car. Some toilet-blue,
beaten-up Beetle with surf stickers in the rear window and wipers
at the front that sounded like nails across a blackboard. Hardly the
first choice of vehicle for your typical bank robber, but one more
reason why I argued we could get away with it. Slim and Pavlov
had both dismissed me outright at first. The pair of them laughing
when I said I was serious, then falling quiet when I swore I would
do it alone.

'Cisco, this is insane,' was my brother's first response, and one he
then repeated when I killed the engine and shut down the stereo.
'We're not gangsters. We don't do this kind of thing.'

'You're right.' I ejected the tape, slung it into the back. 'On the
way home we're listening to Madonna.'

Slim? He was the reason I was behind the wheel, the reason we
had been obliged to listen to Dr Dre for the last few miles of the
journey in a bid to psych him up. Slim being the one now crossing
the street on this drizzly Saturday morning in a small market town
in the Fens. Heading for a branch of the bank that had denied both
boys a loan.

I was parked in a narrow side road opposite, flanked by the kind
of shops that were never open – an antiquarian bookstore to my
right, a photographic studio on the nearside. The wedding pictures
in the window were so bleached out and seventies-looking that I
questioned whether any of the happy couples were still together.
Or alive, for that matter. Even the tomes on display in the bookshop
looked like fossils, while my brother sat so rigidly in the passenger

seat that he, too, might have been set in stone. I rubbed the fug from the windscreen, saw Slim glance back at us and gave him the thumbs-up. If Pavlov realised I was just as apprehensive, I figured he might freak out and reach for the keys. I regretted the show of bravado with the tape, though: the silence being harder to handle than a meaty-mouthed rapper from the hood.

'Look at him, he's swaggering.' Pavlov sat up in his seat. 'Like all of a sudden he's Snoop Dogg.'

By now Slim had reached the lobby doors. Through the raindrops snaking down the glass we saw him swing back on the handle, only to hold it there for an elderly, slow-shuffling couple, one of whom paused to thank him on the way out.

'Did I say Snoop Dogg?' My brother looked at me despairingly. 'I meant Deputy Dawg.'

'Will you give him a break?' I drew breath as the door closed behind Slim. 'A couple of minutes from now, all this will be over.'

'I'm an agony uncle,' he said, mostly to himself. 'What kind of message does it give to the young people if an agony uncle is busted on a bank job?'

'Maybe they'll think you were human after all,' I muttered, under my breath.

It was the sound of the siren that stopped us sniping at each other. Stopped us breathing, too. Sucking the air from the car, so it seemed, when a police van shot past out of nowhere. I admit I reached for the door handle, but relaxed when the vehicle hurtled past the bank. Unlike my brother, who was half-way on to the pavement when I hauled him back by the tails of his pastel shirt. 'Where the hell are you going?' I reached across to slam the door.

When I straightened back into my seat, I found Pavlov looking fiercely indignant. 'I need a wee, all right?'

Slim had gone in wearing a duffel coat and jeans, his dreads tucked away behind a woollen scarf and my bag slung over his shoulder. Mercifully, the balaclava remained at home. The one he had rooted out the evening before, and which had come to mark the first real test of our relationship.

'I'm doing this alone,' I had insisted. At the time, I was standing with him in the bedroom, tussling for possession. 'It's me who can't dismiss the idea, and if I come back with the money then we all get peace of mind in different ways.'

'Out of the question,' he had countered, the balaclava stretching way out of shape. 'Not without me.'

'I know what I'm doing,' I had said, and snapped it free from his hands. 'Think about it, Slim. Anyone walks into a bank wearing something as daft as this, they'd be wrestled to the ground in seconds.'

'So, what are you saying? That a pretty frock might *dazzle* them into doing everything you say? Cisco, you've got balls.'

'That's precisely what I haven't got.'

'Then why are you even thinking about taking on a bank?'

'Because I don't need balls to pull it off. I don't need ski masks. I don't need guns or any of that macho crap.' I had tapped my temple. 'All I need is a brain.'

'Who put you up to this?' We had both turned to my brother. He was watching us from the door, leaning against the frame with his hands in his pockets and a dry, puckered smile. 'Was it Sweet William? The man may talk the talk, Cisco, but he's a street florist. The closest he gets to robbery is the price he charges for sunflowers out of season.'

'Sweet William has nothing to do with any of it,' I had stressed, and hoped he wouldn't push me on this point. Had I confessed that the idea came from a conversation with his friend, a hospital-bound cat burglar, my position might have been a little compromised. Instead, I had said, 'Pride is behind this. Frank Cartier is capitalising on the fact that he caught me staying here, and it's time I took responsibility for that.'

'By hitting on a bank?'

'By acquiring sufficient funds without harming innocent people or leaving them directly out of pocket.'

All the glee had gone from Pavlov's expression when I said this, which left him looking at me in stunned silence. The pair of them listening at last, when I ran through the girl's guide to getting away with it. The calm, considered request for cash. No criminal history, no threatening notes or clown masks. Just a lot of charm and courtesy. Slim? He had heard me out. Looked first at my brother, then directly at me. 'So where's your firepower? You got to be packing something.'

'Packing?' Pavlov had snorted at the very idea. 'Mate, you come from Hertfordshire, not Harlem.'

'The street is the street. Doesn't matter what part of the world you're from.'

'You were brought up in a cul-de-sac. Somehow I don't think a 'hood like that lends itself to drive-by shootings. What did they do, three point turn before the hit or after?'

I had levelled a frosty glare at Pavlov, and confirmed there would be no guns, not because I was clueless as to how to get hold of one but because it wasn't necessary. 'We're dealing with rural folk here. I doubt I'll even have to resort to bad language to get what I want.'

'So what do you expect us to do while all this is going on? Stay at home? Make the place look pretty for your return?'

'That would be a first,' Pavlov had muttered.

'Slim, my mind's made up. At first light, I'm driving out of the city and I'm going to find me a bank to rob.'

'Then this really is a question of pride,' he had said. '*Male* pride.' Slim going on to declare that *he* would be the one to do it, even if he had to agree to play it my way. 'You're my girlfriend and I care for you. You're out of your mind, and I believe you'll go ahead with this no matter how hard I try to talk you out of it. But I wouldn't like myself much if you went off alone and didn't come back. That's why this conversation is closed.

Tomorrow morning it's me who'll be driving out of the city and finding that bank.'

Listening to Slim puff and rant, my first thought had been to remind him that I was free to do what I wanted, but the way he finished with a wink, a bloody *wink*, it made us both grin stupidly.

'Just then,' I had said, 'did you call me your girlfriend?'

'Might've done.' Slim had rubbed his elbows, and for once looked rather at a loss. 'Is that bad?'

'Not if you wanted to smooth-talk me into doing it your way. But I'm driving. You can't rob a bank *and* be the wheelman. It doesn't work that way. Someone has to have the engine running when you throw yourself into the back seat with all the loot.' Slim had looked a little taken aback, until I said, 'Unless you have a problem with me being in the driving seat.' First he had shrugged, then he saw the funny side and next his arms unfolded. I had stepped into the space between them and let him draw me closer.

'Get a grip, you guys.' This scornful voice had come from the doorway. 'You're talking it up like this is really going to happen.' We had turned to face Pavlov, the only one of us still smiling. 'It's a joke, right? You two, being funny with me.' Pavlov had held out for a moment, then appealed to his housemate with some urgency: 'It's not a game, Slim. We don't get three lives here. Shit like this gets us sent directly to jail. Ten years' sharing a cell with some steroid-crazed bitchmeister who can bench two-fifty and likes to be called Sue, you understand?' My brother's voice had pitched high just there, and then cracked completely. *'Prison scares me.'*

'So what are you telling us?' Slim had asked, quietly. 'Does this mean you're *out?*'

Pavlov had blanched and prickled at this. Raising a forefinger at us, he had wagged it like there should have been some words to go with the gesture, then given up and said simply, 'I'm not sitting in the back, okay? I get travel sick.'

115

Which was how my brother and I came to be up front in the Beetle opposite the bank, the pair of us stressed and bickering badly.

'For once in your life, Pav, can't you tie a knot in it?'

'I wish I could.'

'Look around you,' I said, 'there's nowhere you can take a leak. We're a long way from London, and you can't just pee in the street. The people here have standards.'

Pavlov pointed through the glass. 'I was thinking that tea-shop would have a loo.' Just having to listen to this pushed my adrenaline levels close to overdose. I gripped the wheel with both hands, watched the blood leave the skin over my knuckles. 'Look,' he said, 'they're just opening.'

'Maybe you could get some hot drinks to take out.' I trained my gaze on the bank door. Breaking off with the sarcasm to pray Slim was safe in there. 'And a Danish for your housemate would show you hadn't forgotten him at this time.'

From the fringes of my vision, I sensed my passenger turn to face me. 'Have you got any cash?'

'For God's sake, Pavlov, *that's why we're here*!'

My brother sank back into his side of the car, one hand on the dashboard, drumming with his fingers, both eyes boring into me.

'So,' he said eventually, 'is this love?'

'What?'

'You and "the boyfriend". Isn't that what makes two people temporarily take leave of their senses?'

'Not now, Pavlov.'

'Mostly it persuades the men to reappraise films starring Kate Winslet. Robbing banks is new to me but, hey, when you've just fallen head over heels I guess the world must seem like yours for the taking.'

'I said, *not now*! Anyway, how can you be so cynical and still call yourself an agony uncle?'

'Gallows humour,' he said. 'Comes with the job. So was that a denial?'

'It's an inappropriate question to ask at this precise moment, that's all.'

'So you don't love him?'

'Even if I did,' I said, 'Slim should be the one to hear it first.' Pavlov narrowed his eyes. Then he drummed his fingers a little faster, like I really needed to feel under observation at this time. 'Okay,' I said. 'Probably I do.'

'*Probably* you love him?'

Across the road, through the drifting rain, I saw the bank door fly open and a figure hurry out: Slim, with the shoulder-bag clutched to his chest and a look of grim determination that softened when he caught my eye. Instinctively I reached for the ignition key, fired up by his safe return and the way my feelings had suddenly pulled focus. So did I love him?

'Unquestionably,' I confirmed. The car started first time. I turned to face Pavlov. 'Now let him in and belt up. This conversation never happened.'

Music didn't accompany our drive back. Just the relentless call and response from the wipers. We stopped twice before the motorway, once so that Pavlov could urinate prodigiously into the hedgerow, the second time when Slim decreed that if he didn't swap places with my brother he would brain him.

'Can't we just put this behind us?' I pleaded, pulling away from the verge once more.

'Don't tell me,' said Slim, and shot a thumb over his shoulder, 'tell him.'

'When I said a Muppet could have done a better job,' came the voice from the back seat, 'I wasn't having a go.'

'Hardly a compliment, Pavlov, was it?' I adjusted my seat as I said this. Tried to make the journey home a bit more bearable. Like my brother, the road we were following seemed to go on endlessly. Nothing to distract us from the soggy fens and fearsome skies. I glanced at Slim on occasion. The man responsible for the fact that I was heading home with more on my mind than when I left.

'Guys,' said my brother next, 'there'll be trouble if I stay in the back. I'm feeling nauseous already.'

'Tough,' Slim growled. 'You're out of sight, you're out of mind.'

Five hundred yards of peace, and Pavlov had to come back by calling him a shit-out. The curse was barely audible under the wipers, but it was enough to bring Slim round in his seat and start yelling. 'I did *not* lose my bottle, all right? Why would I be frightened of two geriatric bank clerks?'

'You tell me.'

'Pavlov, when I walked through those doors I was pumped. The ladies behind the screen, they didn't know what was coming to them. No idea at all. They even smiled at me. So I smiled back, only in a more meaningful way, and decided it would be kinder if I addressed them both.'

'You don't have to go through this again,' I told him.

Slim settled back in his seat a little, still seething with Pavlov, but anxious to reason with us both. 'I just want you to accept that I was ready to ask for the money. Really. I had a script in my head, just as we rehearsed it, and I would've been word perfect too.'

'It's something we just didn't consider,' I cut in, still cursing myself for the oversight. 'We've been so tied up with the prospect of having some in our home, I guess none of us thought about the fact that the bloody things could be anywhere else.'

'Two closed-circuit cameras,' he went on, as if we needed reminding another time, 'both pointing right at me with their little lights blinking. What was I supposed to do? Smile for the tape?'

'Anyone else would've walked away with their integrity.'

'Don't start again,' warned Slim, but Pavlov was there already.

'Even I would've just left it, and I admit I make a lousy villain.'

'What matters is he tried,' I told him.

'Cisco, he opened a fucking *savings* account.'

Naturally I sided with Slim, out of solidarity and also sympathy.

But as I endeavoured to steer and stop them scrapping, I couldn't help wondering whether I would have been intimidated so easily. Rose had insisted nobody was going to link us to a robbery with clean sheets like ours, and that made sense to me. Even footage from a spy camera couldn't put names to faces. When they show that stuff on the crime programmes, *everyone* looks like they're up to no good. From the harsh contrasts to the unflattering angles, it even conspired to make innocents look like they had something to hide. If Slim had gone for the money, I thought, and left nothing but an image of himself, the law would have had to line up every slacker in the country if they'd wanted to track him down. It might have shut my brother up as well.

'Here come the cops!' he crowed suddenly. 'Get your head down, Slim.'

I steered wide of the bobby on the bicycle, watched him wobbling in our wake and told Pavlov he was pushing his luck.

'Just looking out for the fugitive.' He pressed his cheek to the window, scanning the vast skyscape. 'Can't see any choppers yet, but we'd better not be complacent.'

'I'm not listening to you any more.' Slim reached for the glove compartment. 'Where's my tape gone? The Dr Dre. He was in the player.' I told him it was in the back somewhere, that it had popped that way when we pressed eject.

Pavlov turned to look, first on the parcel shelf and then in the foot well, before rising up between our seats clutching something completely different. 'I have to tell you I just found something.'

It was a little green savings booklet. Fake leather finish. A sticker on the front with a cartoon goose and space for a name underneath it. I remembered getting one like that when I was a kid. We both had one, Pavlov and I, Junior Nest Eggs, or something. Which, as it turned out, was exactly what my brother had in his possession.

'That was in my coat,' Slim said angrily, and tried to swipe it from my brother. 'Give it back, you little thief!'

Pavlov held the book just out of his reach, claimed it must have fallen out when they swapped places. He sat back to inspect it further, licking a finger to leaf through the pages. 'Oh, man,' he said, stopping at the first. 'I can't believe you did this.'

'So I panicked – picked up the nearest application form.'

'Opening a kiddiewinks account is one thing . . .'

'Pavlov, just keep it to yourself.' Slim sounding sensitive all of a sudden.

'What?' I asked, switching my attention between the road and the rear-view mirror.

'There's twenty pounds in here.'

'No?' I fought back a smile.

My brother leaned forward to show me. Slim stared dead ahead.

'You go to rob a bank,' said Pavlov, 'and you *give* them money?'

'The last of our cash too,' I said, and sniggered with him.

'So the interest was good.' Slim gave in to a smile himself here. 'At least we'll make something from this day.'

'You know what?' I shifted into a higher gear, thinking no way now would I lose the roof over our heads for the sake of a lousy camera. 'I reckon you could be right.'

18

- THE TENANTS agree to live with a single web-cam installed in each room (excluding the bathroom/toilet).

- The content shall be used expressly by the Landlord as a showcase for his business interests in the property sector, and broadcast live from the Landlord's sponsored website.

- Webcams must be free from obstruction at all times.

- No obscene, offensive, unlawful or blasphemous behaviour. Showing off or staged acts are equally prohibited.

- The Landlord aims to present the house in the best possible light, and agrees to improve interior decoration and furnishing accordingly. Tenants will incur no extra charge for this service.

- Providing both parties comply with the terms of this Agreement, the Landlord shall agree to waive the Tenants' rent obligations until further notice.

'Look at what we're *creating* here! It's going to be beautiful. Even the sun is shining for us.'

Eight thirty, Monday morning. Blue skies overhead, a flower market in full swing, and our signatures still wet on the contract. The document was standard issue, with special amendments drawn up by the man behind the whole venture. Cartier himself had insisted on a little ceremony, gathering the three of us in front of the house like this. With the papers fanned out on the window-sill, he countersigned looking positively dewy-eyed. Even finishing with a flourish to match his manner. Our landlord was here to collect from us, and he hadn't stopped beaming since we agreed to his terms.

'These webcams,' I said, standing aside as yet another workman went into the house with cables looped over his shoulder, 'are they a problem to install?'

Frank Cartier grinned at the boys as if I was the only one to be concerned. He had been here ten minutes, tops, and already half a dozen of his people had passed through the doors. 'She's a star, isn't she? I *love* her to bits. "Are they a problem?"'

'Well?'

'Darling, not a problem you need worry about.' Cartier reached inside his camel as he patronised me. 'Home improvement has to be done properly if it's going to be done at all, and I am upgrading your house here.'

'Except the bathroom and the toilet,' Pavlov added hastily. 'That's what we agreed.'

Cartier said that was how the site would be, and casually produced a sheaf of cash from his pocket. It was the kind of wedge that justified the rubber band, and served to throw us all. 'You won't even know we've been in there,' he said, as two more labourers inched between us. They were hefting what looked to me like a cross between a computer and a sports locker. Slim reached out and touched it, making a sizzling sound as if the thing was red hot. 'That,' he said, 'is one hell of a server.'

'And a server is what?' I looked to them for an explanation.

'A server is our connection to the world wide web.' Cartier returned to the count, the money fanning from one hand into the other as if he was looking for something among it. 'Think of it as the brains behind the operation.'

'Can't it go in the yard?' asked Pavlov, and promptly caught his breath. 'What about radiation? Is this like a massive mobile phone?'

This time he responded with a bead on my brother that chilled me. His butcher's blue eyes, so steady under those hoods. 'Without a server,' said Cartier eventually, 'there would be no website. Without a website there would be no webcams. And without webcams you would have no yard, no *home*.'

The sound of someone hammering inside the house beat the silence into submission.

'The server is fine,' Slim assured him, glaring at Pavlov. 'We'll take good care of it.'

'Then I'll take good care of you,' said Cartier, and continued leafing through the rest of the money. As it turned out, my hunch was right. He had been looking for something. A calling card, trapped between the last two notes. He held it out between two fingers.

'What's this?' I asked, turning the card in my hand.

'Your new address,' he said. 'Virtually speaking.'

'*caminside.co.uk*?'

'Catchy, innit? Thought of it myself.' He broke off, and drew breath to deliver the obvious: '*Caminside*. Cam Inside. *Come inside!*'

'Inspired,' said Slim. He looked like he was talking to the cash curled up in Cartier's fist. 'You didn't go for the dot com, then?'

'The national ones are cheaper.'

'Very wise,' he agreed. 'Who wants to be a dot com anyway?'

'So when do we go upstream?' asked Pavlov. 'Or whatever it is you call it.'

All of a sudden Frank Cartier looked put upon, more so when the hammering stopped and the shrieking started. A kung-fu caterwaul coming through the open window followed by an indecipherable babble that sounded like swearing. He pinched the bridge of his nose, and then found that banded tuft of white hair at the back of his head. Eyes on the flagstones now. Squeezing on his pigtail until the shouting stopped. 'You'll pardon his French,' he said. 'Kenzo can get a little stressed under pressure, but he and his boys will be out by sundown.'

'This is going to take all *day*?' Pavlov looked panicked.

'We're dealing with tradesmen,' said Cartier. 'An hour's work can mean a week sometimes. What can I say?'

'But I can't stay away from the house that long!'

'He needs taps,' Slim explained, 'and I really should get back to my game.'

'Who's Kenzo?' I chipped in belatedly.

And that was when the money came my way. Cartier handed me the lot without a word of explanation. Then he returned his attention to the individual who had sparked the biggest objection. Adjusting the links on his bracelet as he waited for Pavlov to compute.

'Under the circumstances,' my brother said, 'I think we can survive out here.'

'Good. Now go and spoil yourselves.' Our landlord reached inside his coat once more. It wasn't a pistachio that came out this time, however, but a slim panatella. Rolling it under his nostrils, he said, 'Call it compensation. Call it a housewarming gift. Call it whatever you want. Just make sure you come back looking your best, because on the stroke of midnight we throw open the virtual doors and potential sponsors will be watching.' He fired up the cigar, then eyed us in turn. 'I want to see model tenants, all right? You've still got plenty of space to yourselves in there, so don't distress me in front of the webcams.'

'We won't,' said Slim. 'How could we?'

The money felt warm, but seemed to heat up further as he

reiterated the terms. I had no idea how much Cartier had just handed over, but it looked as if it could buy a lot of pampering, more than I would earn from a day temping. Or a month, for that matter. Which was why I hesitated before saying, 'We can't accept—'

'Without shaking on it.' This was my brother, stepping in front of me to pump our landlord's hand.

'But—'

'We really should leave you to get on with the job.' Now it was Slim who silenced me, and suddenly the money was in *his* possession, plucked from my grasp as he took my wrist and broke for the flower market with my brother blocking my protest from behind.

'It's going to be a great day,' he called to our landlord, and that's when I gave up the fight. 'Just you wait and see.'

'Oh, Mr Cartier?' Slim swung round so that he was walking backwards beside me, then cupped his mouth to be heard over the closing crowd. 'Could you leave the sofa? It's antique.'

Sweet William regarded the money on his counter, the sum both boys had insisted on presenting to him straight away. 'With that kind of green,' he said thoughtfully, 'you could buy a whole lot of flowers.'

Pavlov said it wasn't flowers he was interested in buying. It was the other stuff.

'You can't buy one without the other,' Willie cautioned. 'It doesn't work that way.'

'Sweet, this is a stack of money we have here.'

'And I have a *stack* of flowers,' he replied, winking at me. 'All this from a temp job?'

'Don't ask,' I said bitterly, still flanked by the pair of them. 'It's cash that comes with strings. We're expected to spend it on prettying ourselves up.'

'And you come to me for this?' He brought his hands in to touch his chest. 'Church aisles I can make pretty. No problem. People? They don't look so beautiful after smoking shit from me. So the world might look a better place to them, but only if they take my advice and stay away from mirrors.' He broke off, and considered us soberly from behind his counter. Slim and Pavlov were plainly itching to score, come what may, and I rolled my eyes when the florist and dealer focused on me. 'Have you three fallen out?' he asked, leaning on his forearms now.

'A minor disagreement,' said Slim, 'which is why we were hoping you could sort us out with something nice and mellow.'

'Magnolia is easy on the eye.'

'But not so easy on the *head*.' My brother sounded agitated now, retrieving the wedge and squaring it off against the counter. 'Do we have to find ourselves another source?'

Maybe the sun went behind a cloud in the moment that followed, but Sweet William's expression darkened considerably. He seemed to gain in stature too, pulling back like a wave on the verge of breaking.

'Could I have a word with Cisco?' The boys looked to one another, then made themselves scarce when he barked, *'Alone!'*

'Am I in trouble?' I asked, wondering whether I, too, should beat a retreat. 'I delivered the flowers to the hospital, just like you asked.'

'I know,' he said, still scowling over my shoulder. 'Rose called to thank me.'

'She did?' I sounded nervous. 'Was that all?'

'Nope.' And that was his last word on the cat burglar. Sweet's face softening back to dough as he pulled his hands from his puffa. 'Now, when can we take care of these?'

I'd forgotten all about my promise to do his nails, but covered quickly by saying I had been a little distracted of late. The bank botch I kept to myself, thinking if Rose had put him in the picture he would have probably come over the counter at us when we first pitched up. Instead, I glanced at my watch and said, 'We can do them now, if you like.'

His hands flashed back into his pockets. 'Can't we do them at your place?'

'No good. Not today.' I explained about our online agreement, showed him the calling card Cartier had given me. Sweet William turned it over and over as I stressed this deal had been down to our financial situation, that if we wanted to stay we had to do so under the watchful eye of the webcam.

'In my line of work,' he said finally, 'I get twitchy if I even *think* I'm under observation.'

'It's something we'll have to get used to.'

Sweet turned his attention across the market. This time I followed him round. The boys were sulking on the edge of the pavement opposite. They kept coming in and out of view behind the traffic of people drawn here by the upswing in the weather. 'How are you getting on?' he asked. 'Living together?'

'Good,' I said, perhaps a little too quickly, because when I came back he was waiting there for me to try again. 'Okay. The money issue has been a strain, but things can only get better now we don't have to worry about the rent.'

Sweet William looked over my other shoulder. 'Just don't let it come between you,' he said absently. 'Even goldfish can get on each other's tits.'

'They don't,' I said, half smiling, 'do they?'

'I would if I was in the bowl.' He tipped his head in the direction of our house. 'But Kenzo might disagree.'

I spun right round, prompted by that name. Cartier was still visible between the stalls, there in front of our gate, only now he was in close conversation with another man, a gaunt Oriental with feathery hair and arms that flitted about as quickly as he appeared to be speaking. The man had some bad tattoos, from what I could see, bad in the sense that he seemed to have a lot running from his wrists to the sleeves of his white T-shirt. From across the street they looked like scales. More so when Sweet said, 'Kenzo owns The Fish Eye.'

'What's that?' I asked, wondering why the man was so animated.

'A fish shop without the chips. I forget the proper name.'

'An aquatic centre?'

'That's what I said. At The Fish Eye you can find the rarest species known to man, and more. Weird-looking freaks like you wouldn't believe.'

'You've seen them?'

Outside our house, the two men had turned their attention to the bay window. Cartier was pointing at something with his cigar, while his associate stood there with his inked-up arms behind his back.

'Kenzo has webcams trained on every tank. Check out his website and see for yourself.'

'So that's why he's here,' I said.

'I believe you share the same landlord, like mostly everyone round abouts.'

'Including you?' I asked.

'Being strictly canvas, only one landlord calls the shots with me.' I turned back to the counter as he said this, only to be faced with the wildest bunch of flowers in the whole wide world – anemones, cornflowers and grasses of every kind, all spun together behind my back. It was a glorious sight, and I blushed when he said it was for me. Sweet William grinned shyly, gestured up to the pool blue skies. 'Someone's certainly watching over us this fine day, so why don't you do what the man said? Take his money and make the most of it.'

'I'm supposed to be at work at ten o'clock.'

'Tell them you're sick. Who's going to know any different?'

'Do you think I should?'

Suddenly his expression soured. At the same time I realised that the boys had dared to rejoin me. Hanging back sheepishly from Sweet and his bouquet as if fearful of being swatted.

'Will you just take these before I get offended?' he asked.

'What do I owe you?'

'Respect,' he said bluntly. I accepted the flowers, relieved to see his grin come out once more. 'Now make that call to the office, girl, then live it *large*! Have the best day out while you can, because from tomorrow you never know who might be checking up on you.'

19

'Are we live, do you think?' Slim said this as I closed the front door behind me. He flipped the switch and for a moment we all peered up and around, standing there unsteadily, blinking as our eyes adjusted, though it wasn't just the hall light that hit us.

'Never mind the webcams,' I said. 'Are you sure we're in the right *house*?'

We had arrived home at the stroke of midnight. The three of us rolling in like party pumpkins, back from our all-day ball. It was Slim Jim who was first over the threshold, and despite the dark I could have sworn he pushed the door open with his forehead. Pavlov shuffled in close behind, while I followed with the bouquet I had been clutching all day. A little wilted and in need of water, but radiant none the less. The flowers were in good shape too, unlike the boys who had already started on the sticky bud that came with it. I had only let them lighten this load from our florist and dealer on condition that they carried my shopping bags, which meant they were wiped out on two counts. Here in the hallway, however, Slim and Pavlov perked up notably, brought to their senses by the tang of fresh paint. Gone were the scuffmarks from the walls, as indeed was the carpet. Cartier had said he planned to make it look good downstairs, but this was *great*.

'Nice,' said Pavlov, as Slim whistled his appreciation. 'Stripped floorboards are so much easier to keep clean.'

'I feel like we've been done over by benevolent burglars,' I said, drifting along as if this was an art gallery we were in. 'It's *gorgeous*.'

'Cartier's done a fine job,' Slim added. 'The man has taste.'

'There,' said Pavlov, the first to sight the webcam. 'Above the kitchen door.'

It looked to me like a golden egg. One with a lens embedded in the fat end and a cable at the back that vanished into the plasterwork. The whole thing was clamped to the wall by a forked bracket. Staring up at it, I suddenly felt very self-conscious indeed. 'Is it on?' I asked, fixing my hair as a precaution.

'I guess.' Slim checked his watch to be sure the appointed hour had passed. 'From here on, we'll just have to get used to it.'

'Not before I take a leak,' mumbled Pavlov, and headed upstairs.

Slim turned to face me, his eyes pinked up but that spark still shining through. 'Shall we take a tour?' he asked, and invited me to link arms.

What we found marked the climax of a dream day. Make the most of yourselves, Cartier said, and we had really gone to town on his funding. I was glad Sweet William had talked me into it, even if he had been cooler about our landlord's venture. For my brother, the high point had been the lunchtime session in a sensory deprivation tank, while Slim got to sharpen his shoot-'em-up skills with the discovery of a new video-game bar – the Reload Basement, I think it was called: to be honest I only caught a glimpse of the sign before Slim had dragged me out of the sunshine to investigate.

A set of stone steps had delivered us into what appeared to be a converted crypt. The set for a sci-fi chiller, perhaps, when I took in the chrome bar at the back and gleaming ductwork overhead. Central to this subterranean space were four clusters of outward-facing monitors. Each cluster had been surrounded by inward-facing males, and left me wondering if there was such a thing as the digitally dispossessed. Slim had said they were playing a game called *Slay Nation*, though I quickly tuned out of his running commentary. Instead, my thoughts had returned to street level, specifically to the shoe store opposite, and within a minute I was there in body too. Slim elected to stay and take on his fellow daylight-dodgers while I went shopping, and that had been fine by me. I did wonder how healthy it was for grown-ups to express themselves in a fantasy like this, but letting him do his own thing meant he hadn't complained when we all met later and I continued to do mine.

As for Pavlov, he came out of the tank so chilled that he had been happy to go with the flow. In fact, he seemed quite happy for Slim and me to turn the rest of the day into a date – this from the man who had thrown up so much resistance to our relationship, only to force me to confront my deepening feelings for his housemate while we toughed it out in the getaway car. I even wondered whether it had been Pavlov's weird way of bringing us closer together, for having confessed to him that I was falling in love, I didn't feel I could rest until I told Slim himself. I wanted to share it with him now that we were home and alone together, but timing was everything. Because once those words came out they would never again have the same impact, and part of me hoped that Slim would be the first to say them.

Walking into the kitchen was like finding ourselves in the pages of a lifestyle magazine. In the wake of our landlord's makeover, we had access to steel tops and classy cupboards, a Belfast sink and a towering fridge with double doors. Open it up, and the halogen light and billowing vapour made you think we had heaven stored in there. 'This is too good to be true,' I said. 'What's the catch?'

Slim extracted one of those minuscule pots of yoghurt that are supposed to keep you regular and showed it to the webcam in the corner behind us. 'The catch is I can't nick stuff from Pavlov's shelf any more or scoff it at the table. At least, not without witnesses.'

The table, in fact, was about the only thing that hadn't been replaced, which was a relief in some ways. Even if it did look a little worn in the face of all this shiny newness, it served to make the place feel more like our own.

'Cartier hasn't missed a trick,' Slim said, when I shared my take on things. 'Sometimes show homes can be just too perfect. They may look lovely, but they don't feel lived in, and that can make them hard to sell. Virtually speaking, any viewers are going to be knocked out when they come through the front door, but if they pop upstairs they'll connect much better if the bedrooms are a bit of a tip. That's how it is for most people, after all, which can only help them feel at home.'

Slim's theory made sense, and I could see why it wouldn't apply to the front room, where we found his old sofa presiding over a palace.

'Look at this,' he said, and walked in turning circles. 'Look at *this*!' The lights were off in here, but a pale glow cut between the curtains from the street-lamp outside. Enough for me to note that we no longer had curtains but posh new drapes. Sensing other changes in the shadows, it felt as if we were taking a sneak peek at a present that wasn't supposed to be opened until morning.

'I could call this home,' I agreed, surveying the subtle abstracts that had replaced the kitsch prints on the wall.

Slim flopped on to the sofa. I watched his attention fall on the lacquered unit in front of him, with the television on top and his games console shelved neatly inside. It was enough to bring him right in front of it, dropped on to his knees. 'Cartier's even untangled the wires,' he said, and found the keyboard neatly slotted underneath. 'He certainly knows how to keep me sweet.'

I was on the sofa when Slim came back, pleased to have the weight off my feet. 'Why don't we turn in?' I asked, snuggling up to him in the half-light. 'I know there's nothing new to see up there, but I fancy getting familiar with our bed. Under cover of darkness, naturally.'

'Sure,' he said, only to start tapping at the keyboard. 'But there's something I want to see first.'

'What's on?' I asked, as he fired up the TV.

It was when the screen began to brighten that I woke up to the webcam high above it but I only realised what kind of show we would be watching when Slim replied: 'Us.'

20

A couple of keystrokes later, Slim and I prepared to view our new address. He was cross-legged in front of the sofa, the keyboard in the hammock-like crotch of his combat pants, pretending to be cross because I kept messing with his hair. 'Are you ready?' he asked.

'Let's see who's in,' I said.

With a ceremonious flexing of his finger, Slim hit the magic button. The browser window went white, and then the welcome page kicked in:

caminside.co.uk
Fine living spaces for fun-loving people

The show home is now open
(no appointment necessary)

Hall	Sponsor this webcam
Front room	Sponsor this webcam
Kitchen	Sponsor this webcam
Landing	Sponsor this webcam
Bedroom 1	Sponsor this webcam
Bedroom 2	Sponsor this webcam

chat   message   register

For a moment neither of us uttered a word. We just studied the menu, wondering how we would be served up.

'Fun-loving?' Slim shook his head. 'It makes us sound like a bunch of stay-at-homes.'

'I think that's the idea. No sponsors will be interested in stumping up for people to see an empty house.'

'Whenever someone makes a virtue of the fact they're having fun,' he went on, 'you just know they're dying inside.'

'So what happens now?' I asked. 'Assuming people don't share your scepticism.'

Slim said, 'Observe,' and clicked on the second webcam down. Immediately, a window popped up on the screen and there we were, Slim and I. The picture was a little broken up to begin with, but quickly found its feet in real time.

'Bloody hell!' I said, scrambling to sit up, then pulling a face when my image followed suit. 'How many people can see us now?'

We were framed from up on high, the street-lamp behind us transformed into a backlight.

'Well, there's the two of us,' said Slim, 'so we must be giving Channel Five a run for their money.'

'Channel Five do nudity,' I reminded him, 'and we don't.'

'Nor do we do sound,' Slim added, testing the volume with the remote, 'which is good news for us, and a royal result for lip readers.'

'There might be some out there,' I said, and realised I had just covered my mouth. 'You never know.'

Slim dropped the cursor to the chat icon, and an empty window opened out. 'Well, nobody's talking,' he said, 'but it's early days. The site's only been up a matter of minutes.'

'Maybe they're shy.'

'For the time being,' Slim assured me, closing down the chat room, 'there's nobody here but us.'

I asked him to click on the register icon next, still curious to know more. The page that kicked in pretty much begged us to enter our email address. According to the blurb, this meant we could receive 'more exciting details' about Cartier's property portfolio. But it seemed a bit sad somehow, being at the top of his list. 'I don't want to hear from my landlord any more than I have to,' I pointed out.

'Damn right.' Slim settled back beside me. 'It's an unwritten clause in any contract that the tenant should make every attempt to be out on rent day.'

'At least we don't have to worry about that.'

'There's not much we need to worry about at all.' Slim tapped away at the keyboard once more, and the screen revisited the webcam window with us in it. 'Right now, we could do anything we wanted and nobody would know.'

I watched him on the screen, turning roguishly to face me. 'I'll know,' I warned, but Slim went for it anyway. 'Cut it out. Not on camera – *stop it!*'

The sound of the loo flushing upstairs prompted us both to get a grip. I pulled away from him and smoothed out my dress, while Slim ignored his appearance in favour of the keyboard and deftly selected the landing cam.

'There's our man,' he announced, as the screen revealed Pavlov leaving the toilet. 'The sap of the show.'

My brother backed into the bathroom next. I could hear him upstairs, filling the basin, followed by the sound of furious scrubbing.

'He was in there a while,' I observed, and sensed Slim nodding beside me. When Pavlov scuttled out on to the landing again, he was clearly still unhappy. The thunder of feet on stairs preceded his appearance in the lounge, the Love Surgeon with a face to match his footfalls.

'Builders have been here.'

Slim looked at him questioningly, said we knew that. 'It was Cartier's people, Kenzo and the fitters. If it's going to mess with your memory, Pavlov, I don't think you should smoke any more.'

Even though the light was coming from the hall behind him, I could see the scowl on my brother's face.

'They've used the facilities,' he said, to expand.

'So?'

'Cisco, builders and toilets do not mix.'

'Someone forget to flush?' asked Slim.

'Going by the puddle I just had to mop up, I don't suppose they saw much point.'

'Oh, that's disgusting!' I grimaced.

'And so unnecessary. Why can't they sit down to do it like the rest of us?' Slim quit flicking through the webcams when my brother said this. A smile rippled across his face, but Pavlov hadn't finished. 'And you'll never guess where they put the server.'

'No way?' I said. 'In with the toilet?'

'I didn't even see it until I'd cleaned up the mess. I turned to sit down and there it was, sitting on a shelf above the door – humming.'

Slim said, 'You make it sound like a cottaging encounter.'

'It's not funny,' replied Pavlov. 'In the contract Cartier specifically stated that the toilet would be out of bounds, like the bathroom.'

'From webcams,' I said, to clarify. 'With no rent to pay, a server in there is a small sacrifice.'

'But I couldn't wee,' he protested, 'not properly. Not with that thing looming over me with its lights and wires and switches.'

'It's not watching,' said Slim. 'It's processing.'

'Yeah, and it's stopping me from doing the same thing.'

Slim changed tack, and invited Pavlov to step into shot. 'Let the people see you, mate. You're in the dead zone there.'

'I'd rather stay where I am, if that's all right with you. I'm more comfortable on the edge of things.'

'Like loo seats,' Slim suggested, sotto, and tapped back into the front room. 'Anyway, check this out. It's not so bad – nothing to see, really.' I curled my feet up and lolled my head against Slim's shoulder. 'I have to go to bed,' I said. 'Somehow I don't think we'll be missed.'

It was then that Pavlov begged to differ, pointing fearfully at something behind us. 'What the hell is *that*?'

I twisted round on the sofa with Slim, just as a blinding band of red light came out of the gloom back there. I ducked on instinct, sensed Pavlov crashing in beside me. I didn't have time to blink, breathe or shriek before Slim was up and squinting into the glare. My brother and I followed him, edging upwards together. Whatever it was, I could see now that the source was mounted above the window. A ticker panel, Slim suggested, like you see on the stock exchange or in a football stadium. I realised he was right just as all the points of light on it died away, leaving nothing but a dazed darkness, and then it blazed back into life: a string of words this time, flowing right to left.

WELCOME . . . HOME . . . DID . . . I . . . STARTLE . . . YOU?

'It's talking to you, Slim.' Pavlov shoved him on the shoulder. 'Sacrifice yourself.'

'Why me?'

'You connect with these things.'

'And you're the great counsellor,' he countered angrily, facing up to him now. 'The one with the so-called solutions.'

FRANK . . . HERE.

'It's Cartier,' I said, drawing them apart. 'Look.'

RUNNING . . . FINAL . . . SYSTEM . . . CHECK.

'Any minute now,' muttered Pavlov, 'this whole house will take off.'

YOU'RE . . . LOOKING . . . GOOD . . . LADS . . .

'I always do,' said Slim, throwing out any line that would make him feel in control.

I didn't feel so cocky. At first I was relieved to know who was watching us, but the next message to slide from the ticker had me spinning back into the sofa with a cushion clutched to my lap.

... BUT ... NOT ... AS ... GOOD ... AS ... CISCO ...

Slim dropped down beside me, and asked me not to put my foot through the screen just yet. 'He's only being honest.'

'He'd better not start on me,' warned Pavlov.

'This is what he's doing,' said Slim, back in command of the keyboard. He swung the cursor over the message icon. 'Look.'

MESSAGES
Say hi to the housemates here.
Then watch the screen behind the sofa.

```
┌─────────────────────────────────────┐
│                                     │
└─────────────────────────────────────┘
```

Just keep it clean!

'Why doesn't that make me feel any better?' I asked.

'Think of the rent,' said Slim.

'Everyone keeps saying that.' Pavlov lifted away from the sofa and turned his back to the webcam. He narrowed his eyes at the ticker, sizing up the situation, then dismissed it with a good long yawn. 'I have to go to bed,' he said, his wrists extending from his cuffs as he finished with a stretch. 'Sleep is the only way I'll get my head round this.'

Just as he began to bring his arms back in, my brother found himself bathed in a pinkish light.

SWEET ... DREAMS ... PAVLOV.

Pavlov made like a statue, as if the message was some kind of Medusa. 'How does Cartier know I'm ready for bed?'

Slim drew my attention to the screen, reminding me what the viewers could see.

'Unless you're about to perform a back flip,' he said, 'it is kind of obvious.'

Pavlov considered his hands, spread wide apart, and surrendered them to gravity. Still with his back to the webcam, he then lifted his middle finger. Just high enough to gesture at the ticker without being seen by anyone but us. 'Night, night, sucker,' he said, relishing this small victory, then turned for the door. 'Because this is where I leave the frame.'

Slim flexed his fingers over the keyboard before my brother had even reached the stairs, and I knew where we were heading next.

'Oh, come on,' I said, giving in to a private smile. 'Pavlov will go bananas if he knows we're spying on his bedroom.'

'No such thing as spying,' said Slim. 'In cyberspace this is a "shared experience".'

Footsteps overhead now, played out on the screen by the arrival of Pavlov in his room. The section captured by the webcam included his futon, but not for much longer, I realised on watching my brother drag his mattress out of shot.

'Pavlov told me he was going to do this,' said Slim.

'Is he allowed? The contract says we mustn't alter out habits and routines.'

'So Pavlov's having a room rethink. Don't we all from time to time? It's only natural, which is exactly what Cartier expects from us.'

I glanced at the ceiling, smiling to myself at the sound of goalposts being shifted. 'Smart move,' I said, and snuggled up to Slim. 'Beats robbing banks, at any rate.'

Slim put his arm round me, pulled me closer in. 'Anything's better than that, apart from writing agony columns, maybe.'

'That wasn't so bad. I'm just glad I could help.'

'Pavlov's still twitchy about it,' he said. 'Reckons his editor's going to suss it was written by a female.'

'Why? Because I spoke from the heart?'

His silence informed me that this was probably the case. Pavlov came back into shot just then, returning for the futon frame. Slim said: 'I feel bad that you have to live with this.'

141

'With what? Two bickering guys who secretly adore each other, and a landlord with a beaky nose?'

'Nobody outbeaks me,' said Slim archly. 'And I don't adore Pavlov.'

'Yes, you do. Don't be so shy with your emotions.'

'We tolerate each other. That's how I see it.'

'You're as bad as he is.' I tutted. 'Why can't you be more open and honest sometimes?'

'I can,' he said, 'if there's something in it for me.'

A play-slap to his chest from me, and we both returned our attention to the screen. By now, only the foot of the futon was visible, but then Pavlov returned to the picture, dragging his desk with him. A few minutes later, having plugged in his computer again, squared off his mouse mat, repotted his pens and arranged the rest of his agony accessories, the switch appeared to be complete.

'Awww, look,' I said. 'He's even feeding his Sea Maidens.'

Slim reached for the keyboard once more, and shut down the window. 'I think we've seen enough,' he said, still tapping away. 'Cartier too.' A warm glow on the wall behind the television prompted me to turn round.

WATCH ... THIS ... SPACE.

'Who wrote that?' I asked. 'Was that from him? Don't say he's still watching?'

'He might be,' said Slim, still pecking away with two fingers. He hit enter, the ticker refreshed, and the room turned red again. Just like me, in fact, when I read Slim's message. 'Right now,' he added, 'I don't mind if the whole of cyberspace is logged on with us.'

SLIM ... 4 ... CISCO

'Numbers now.' I came back down from this virtual carving to cup his chin my way. I was thrilled, but here too was my opening to play him for more. 'Back in infant school,' I said, 'that was a good sign.'

'It still is.'

He grinned and glanced back at the screen, but I held out for his full attention. 'What I said about being a bit more open,' I reminded him, 'why don't you give it a go? Think of words instead of numbers, and just see what happens.'

'Okay, I like you.' Slim paused to clear his throat. 'A great deal.'

'Like I like you?'

'I don't know,' he said, his eyes scanning mine. 'How much do you like me?'

My lips brushed the tip of his nose. I held his face between my hands, and then found the neck of his Aloha shirt. I brought him closer to me, pulling him by the palm trees. 'I'm not afraid to speak my mind.'

Slim considered what I had just said, and smiled. 'I was assuming you'd read mine for me.'

I moved back an inch, seeking some perspective, because I knew how *I* felt about Slim. My heart was busting to tell him too. It felt like I had a puppy in there, overexcited and hard to handle. But what if I let it out and he wasn't ready? Would he react badly if I sprang it on him, or was that what he was waiting for? I searched his eyes, but couldn't get beyond my own reflection. 'It's no good,' I said, partly joking. 'I haven't got a clue what's going on inside your head.'

'The same as in yours?' he ventured.

'You think so?'

'I do,' he confirmed. Then his mind appeared to catch up with his mouth and sent them both sprawling. 'But not in the wedding sense, if you see what I mean. I'm not saying I won't some day – of *course* I can see myself tying the knot eventually—'

I touched my finger to his lips, held it there until he stopped trying to speak, then set him free when the only thing that could follow was a kiss. 'Let's not spoil the moment,' I suggested, when he broke away to explain himself again. 'I wouldn't want you to tell me anything just because you think it might get you somewhere.'

'Oh, I'm already there.' His eyes glittered as he said this. Opening up in a way that invited me to laugh with him, though I was the one who led the way upstairs. The pair of us going on to shift our bed just as Pavlov had, with a little less precision but a lot more incentive.

21

It was Sweet William who made the first guest appearance. Several days after the house went online, the kitchen cam was treated to the formidable sight of a fourteen stone softie receiving a manicure from me. Not that anyone watching would have seen the big picture, I should say, for Sweet insisted that his hands stayed out of shot while I attended to his nails. Hence the slightly affected way he appeared to be sitting alone at the table. Staring up at the lens as if daring people to keep looking.

'Do I have bits in my teeth?' he whispered, from the side of his mouth.

'Not that I noticed. They can't hear you, Willie. Relax.'

'Nothing worse than being caught out with bits in the teeth,' he stressed, speaking up now but clearly uncomfortable about it.

'Except badly kept nails,' I suggested. 'Want me to do your toes too?'

He had to glance my way to see that I was joking. Even so, the cuticle creams and the pot of orange sticks clustered at the corner of the table served to return his attention to the webcam with an air of anxiety. It was my brother who was responsible for establishing the divide between what could and couldn't be seen. Pavlov had spent a good couple of hours marking out every dead zone in the house. As a result of his hard work, two lines of red tape splayed across the kitchen floor – originating from a point directly underneath the webcam. Even the table was marked off, which gave me a corner to work on Willie's nails where it wouldn't harm his reputation. My brother had segmented every room in this way, except the bathroom and the toilet, defining the boundaries where we lived and where we *really* lived. It certainly made being here much easier, but Willie was having trouble adjusting.

'What time will the limp dicks be back?'

'It was you who told them to leave,' I pointed out, sitting back on my stool. For the last ten minutes, I had been concentrating on just cutting down and cleaning up his nails. It was like unearthing antique porcelain, the way they gleamed as I removed the grime. Sweet William had nice hands, all things considered. Nothing delicate or slender, far from it, but there was something very touching about the fact he had entrusted the job to me. Going by the purple knots he had for knuckles, I figured he rarely let anyone appreciate them in this way, which made me wonder if he had shown them to Slim and Pavlov curled into fists. 'What did you say to make them vanish like that?' I asked.

'Nothing heavy,' he said. 'I never do.'

I had found Sweet William when I got back from work. The florist waiting at the gate in the late sunlight, despite the fact that Slim and Pavlov had been inside at the time. He hadn't said what he wanted, but then it was obvious from the way he avoided both the subject and my eyes, chattering instead about the forecast without once looking at the sky. He had only lifted his gaze from his bootlaces when I suggested that now might be a good time to find the emery board. It was with the boys that his manner hardened. All he had done was ask for a word with them in private, and seconds later they had hustled through the front door without saying goodbye. Pushing back a cuticle now, I said, 'You really mustn't worry what people think. My brother scrubs his own nails until they bleed at the edges, and Slim is worryingly in touch with his feminine side. I actually had to ask for my Alice band back this morning. Would you believe he's taken to wearing it?'

Willie turned his attention from the webcam and considered me for a moment. 'Bleeding Rose thinks you can do better than him,' he said.

The thing I had just said about Slim wasn't intended as a question or a criticism. It was just an observation to put Sweet at his ease, not leave me feeling tense. 'So what does Bleeding Rose know?' I asked cautiously, hoping this wasn't going to spark a lecture about crime and punishment.

'What *doesn't* she know?' He was grinning now that he had my full attention. 'She's a big *caminside* fan.'

'Rose has been watching?'

'Anything's better than staring at patients drifting past her window, but God knows where she got the laptop from. I drop by one day, she's given up on the book I bought her and booted up to be with you.'

Now it was my turn to look up at the lens. It hadn't taken me long to shake off the sense of being watched, to detach myself from the audience, but now that a face I knew was out there it changed things. I felt like an actress who steals a glimpse between the stage lights and suddenly wonders what the hell she's doing.

'Has Rose seen something?'

'Mostly your boyfriend's nadgers,' said Willie bluntly. 'Someone needs to tell him to tie up his dressing-gown before he settles on the sofa for the day.'

Sensing that he wasn't going to let this one drop, I felt obliged to defend Slim's name. The dressing-gown issue I would deal with by quietly binning the damn thing. 'He's been through a lot lately,' I said. 'Slim took me in when I had nowhere to go, and now it's my turn to stand by him while he gets his life back on track.'

'By playing computer games?'

'*The Money Shot* is more than a game. There's a million at stake.'

'Plus the chance to watch a make-believe fox wave her booty about all day.'

'Misty Ventura,' I informed him, then decided Slim needed no defending here. 'You know, the more I watch the guys in front of that game the less I like it.'

'Rose believes the man spends more time with her than with you.'

I was shaping off a nail when he said this, and came close to taking the skin with it. 'Misty isn't real,' I said, mostly to remind myself. 'I don't exactly have grounds to be jealous.'

Sweet William shrugged and returned his attention to the lens. There, his expression darkened considerably. For a minute or so I worked in silence, finishing his nails with strengthening oil, wishing Rose had kept her opinion to herself.

'I feel like a fish,' he said next, sounding agitated all of a sudden. I had nearly finished with the first hand, but now he wouldn't keep still. 'A fish in a bowl, with bad vibes instead of water.'

'Stop fidgeting,' I said. 'If you want nice nails you have to relax.'

'Doesn't it make you jumpy, all these eyeballs on you?'

I told him that, apart from the bed-bound, I didn't think many people were logging on to look. 'Slim keeps checking out the chat room,' I told him. 'He reckons we're up to maybe a hundred visitors a day. A hundred and fifty tops.'

'A hundred and *fifty*?' Suddenly Sweet stopped frowning at the webcam, and in one smooth move his brow went the other way. 'In my line of business that's an attractive market.'

'A hundred and fifty visitors a day is not that many, Willie, not for a venture with commercial backing. The boys reckon Cartier must have done some serious negotiating just to get them on board in the first place.'

'This place is sponsored already? Who by?'

I invited him to place his other hand in the dead zone, and said, 'I believe all the cams are covered but one.'

Instead of shifting his seat, Sweet William crossed his hands as if this was a table version of Twister he was playing here. A game for one person, from the point of view of anyone viewing the kitchen at the time. Still, he didn't seem to care about that right now. His sly grin told me he'd sussed which cam had proved the least financially attractive. 'The panty waist, right?'

'Pavlov will be covered soon.' I nibbled at his nail with the clippers, feeling some loyalty towards my brother.

'So who's put money into the kitchen?'

'Bleach manufacturer.'

'Makes sense,' he said, looking round. 'You could eat your dinner off every surface in here.'

'They wanted to clean up with the hall as well, but the pizza people got there first.'

'Isn't that the way of things?' he groused. 'Seems these days 'you can't turn your back on the door without a flyer dropping onto the mat.'

'It's a problem,' I agreed.

'How about the front room? Any takers there?'

'Air freshener,' I said, none too proudly. 'Same for the landing.'

'So that leaves your bedroom.'

I just knew he was going to end up there. Not that I minded the questions, but I was a little embarrassed to admit that it was covered by a condom manufacturer. More so when Sweet himself looked as if he wished he'd stopped with the landing. 'Sorry,' I said, 'you did ask. But there's nothing much to see – we've moved our bed round so viewers only see our feet. Now, who's going to get off on that?'

An awkward pause overtook us. I went back to his nails, feeling almost ashamed about the living arrangements we had here.

'He's a persuasive force, your landlord.' Sweet William was waiting for me when I glanced up. The expression on his face quite serious now.

'Is there something I should know?'

'The boys didn't tell you about him?' He seemed genuinely surprised, and quickly tried to hide it by going back to the webcam.

'Willie, will you spit it out?'

'The word on Frank Cartier, it's . . .'

'Go on,' I said, when he fell quiet again.

'Most probably bullshit. An urban legend. Forget I even mentioned it.' Which was where I guessed the florist hoped to leave it, had he not then felt one end of an emery board press knife-like into his neck.

'Try me,' I murmured in his ear.

22

I needed chocolate like Willie needed air. His nails looked good when he left, and I felt a whole lot better when I found the newsagent had a stock of Crème Eggs. They might've looked like a nest of webcams, there in the display basket, but that didn't stop me from buying several.

Maybe the boys had been watching the house, waiting until it was safe to return, because they were back before me. Slim was with Misty in the front room, and I could tell my brother was watching them. Indeed, the conversation they were having persuaded me to hang back in the hall.

'I hear she does it if you hold down both buttons for ten seconds and then make her do a monkey grab.' This was Pavlov, talking over the game's background beats and the sound of Misty panting.

Next came a distracted sigh from Slim. 'Now is not the time to get complicated,' he replied, 'not with another Misty watching. What's my opponent going to think if my Misty suddenly pulls a stunt like that? It's hardly an act of aggression, is it?'

'You never know, it might flush her out.'

Slim tutted irritably, as if he'd been pressured about this for some time. 'Let me settle this thing,' he told my brother, 'and then we'll see who's the daddy.'

'She certainly looks capable of doing it. Maybe they both are. Can you imagine if they could do it to each other? All covered in mud and sweat? *Hoo, baby!* I always wished they could've made Lara do something like that.'

'Do what?' I asked, and watched their attention spin sideways as I came through the door. 'I thought Lara could do most things.'

151

'Cisco!' My brother tensed, then shrank into the corner of the sofa. 'We didn't hear you come in.'

'Obviously.' I ran my finger round the foil at the top of my Crème Egg, tearing a long strip from it. 'Come on, boys. Why hold back from little me?'

Slim froze the game, and tried to cover with a smile. Then he clocked my expression, and his smile seemed to stick there too. He cleared his throat, said, 'Pavlov was suggesting ways we could improve Misty's performance.'

'In the strategic sense,' my brother clarified. 'Nothing to worry about.'

I bit into the crown of my egg and lapped out a little of the yolk. 'Like what I hear about Frank Cartier. Is that "nothing to worry about" either?'

It was a question that seemed to bring darkness in from the edges of the room, as if a spotlight had been cast upon the sofa, then Slim asked what I had heard. 'You know damn well,' I said bitterly. 'Apparently everyone knows round here but me. The word on our landlord and his associate? The one who was right here in our house recently? Who most probably has a set of keys too!'

Pavlov stopped me there. 'Kenzo is retained by Cartier to keep his properties in order.'

'And his tenants,' I added. 'Sweet William told me all about it.'

'Sweet William should have known better,' my brother said, 'spinning crazy stories like that.'

'Which crazy story did you hear exactly?' Slim was standing now. He plunged his hands deep inside his pockets, looking a little uncomfortable.

'How many stories *are* there?' I was incredulous. 'The one I heard took twenty minutes to extract, and that was crazy enough! If Willie is to be believed, guys, Kenzo has done time for torturing a tenant. With fish hooks.'

'I see,' said Slim, and looked to his toes. 'That's the really crazy one.'

'Willie said it was the poor soul next door, the one who won't leave the house any more because of what was done to him.'

'Allegedly,' said Pavlov firmly. 'You know, it's probably something Cartier dreamed up himself – a way to make sure that all the people on his books pay the rent on time. Honestly, do you think we'd want to be here if that story was true?'

'So why don't we do the neighbourly thing, go and see how he is?' Pavlov opened his mouth but the coward in him stole his powers of reasoning.

'Let's not forget we're here for free now.' This was Slim speaking for him now. 'All we have to do to pay the rent is hang out in the live zones a bit. It's going to be difficult to fall short on payment, I think.'

I levelled my gaze at Slim, as best I could considering his lofty height, and told him that I still should have been informed. 'What Willie told me about Kenzo was *horrible*. And now I've signed a contract with the man who pays his wages. Jesus, you two. Had I known how Cartier handled people, I wouldn't have set foot inside this place, let alone moved into it.'

Slim crossed the red tape on the carpet as I said all this, coming into the dead zone to comfort me. 'I'm sorry you had to hear that story at all, Cisco, but look at you. This is why we kept it to ourselves.' He paused to plant a kiss on the crown of my head. 'Nothing will happen to us,' he promised. 'We're safe as houses here.'

I looked up into his face. Slim was smiling for real now, and I did feel secure in his company. I still had some issues to clear up, but I needed his full attention for that. It was only a glance he gave the screen, nothing more, but enough for me to check out what had distracted him. Sure enough, there was Misty, standing breathlessly in front of a lagoon with a plunging waterfall in the background and rocks strewn on either side. I turned back to him, and just knew he was itching to get behind his joypad. 'Unfinished business,' he ventured sheepishly.

'Is it this thing you're supposed to make her do?'

'Not that,' he assured me, and broke for the sofa as if my question had been a form of permission. 'There's another Misty behind that boulder. She's been on my trail for a while, but I turned round unexpectedly and I think I have her cornered. With this game you can call a truce for five minutes max. It's like a live pause, but if you don't get back to it within the time allowed you're toast.'

I sat beside the boys, conscious of the cam but keen to see the outcome. Slim resumed the game, turned Misty one way then the other. 'Where is she?' I asked, scanning the screen for an opponent. 'I can't see anything but bits of fallen-down cliff-face.'

'See that spike glinting behind the boulder?' said Pavlov. 'There, by the edge of the waterfall.'

'Uh-huh.'

'That's her nail gun.'

'Oh, crikey! What have you got?'

Slim jabbed at the joypad. Misty raised her bare fists. I couldn't tell whether he was doing this for me or as a blatant provocation. Whatever his intention, the Misty with the big bad advantage stepped into the open. She was better proportioned than Slim's effort, apart from the weaponry she had levelled at him, which was so big it might have been wrenched from the top of a tank.

'Shit,' said Slim, and twiddled his fingers uncertainly.

'Don't run away,' my brother advised. 'She'll turn you into a pin-cushion.'

'Run *at* her,' I suggested. 'Do the unexpected.' Both boys looked at me. I shrugged, nibbled at my half-eaten egg. 'Put it this way, your boobs are your biggest defence. Anything that hits those ridiculous stacks will bounce away harmlessly.'

'Make a decision,' Pavlov urged his flatmate, looking back at the on-screen action, 'because she's just started running at *you*.'

Sure enough, big bad Misty was splashing along the shore of the lagoon, taking aim as she closed in on kill-me-quick Misty. It was a pathetic way to die, and would have been gruesome, too, had

Slim not started pumping the buttons on his joypad. It didn't make her do very much on the running front, but jumping-wise it was impressive. All forward motion and little lift. A rocket-like charge, in some ways, that came right up under her assailant's chin and sent her crashing back into the shallows. The incidental music soared in response but this Misty stayed down, spread out in a star shape – a crimson halo thickening in the water.

'*Yes!*' Slim leaped to his feet. Rooting himself to the carpet with his spine arched back and his fists lifted high. '*Way to go!*'

'First blood,' Pavlov proclaimed, grinning as his housemate made a little victory lap of the sofa.

'*Who*'s in charge?' Slim crowed, bringing both thumbs in to his chest.

'Oh, you're the man,' I confirmed, swivelling the half-egg in my hand, looking for a way in. 'I feel so much better now I know you're here to look after us.'

'Didn't I tell you we're going to make a million?' Slim missed my point. I wasn't even looking at the screen as he said this, though we all returned to the game when a frenzied snorting built up around Misty. 'Oh, shit,' he said. 'I forgot about the—'

'Pigs.' Pavlov reached for the joypad on Slim's behalf and punched restart. The screen went black like a blink, and when it opened up again Misty was back at the start of the level. 'She was about to die horribly just then. It's fun to watch the first time, but we don't have time for that now.'

'All right,' I said, when Slim didn't complain. 'What does all that mean?' I set about my egg once more, and rather wished I hadn't taken such a big bite as Slim went into details.

'The pigs are killers,' he said. 'They can detect the scent of spilled blood so as soon as you make a kill they come running. It means you have to get out fast or they rip you to shreds. I was so excited about taking out my first Misty that I forgot all about them, but I'm young. I'll learn.'

'That's hideous,' I said, screwing up my face.

'No.' My brother swapped a glance with Slim. 'That's gaming.'

'But all this violence and aggression,' I maintained. 'Look at the effect it just had on you both. Slim killed his opponent with his bare hands—'

'Forehead,' he cut in, and nutted the air in front of him. 'A Glasgow Kiss is what did it. Always guaranteed to finish the job.'

'Which is what worries me,' I said. 'You're not a nutter, but it's easy to see why people believe this kind of thing can turn you into one. I know it's only a game, guys, but you have to admit there's a fine line between fantasy and reality here.'

I think we all took in the red tape at this point, the fine line currently defining our own existence. When I looked back, Slim had assumed control of the keyboard again. Summoning up the browser and directing us back to our virtual home: the webcam window with the three of us in it.

'This is our reality,' he said. 'Effectively we're being paid to do nothing. Now that's what I call work.'

My brother looked across at me and grinned. 'Don't worry,' he said. 'If the landlord gets nasty, Slim here can kiss him in that way of his.'

My thoughts cut back to Cartier, specifically this thing about his business practices, and I wondered whether I might have crossed a boundary of my own. I had seen what a wind-up artist Sweet William could be with the boys and it wasn't so hard to imagine him testing me too. 'I just don't want there to be any secrets between us,' I said. 'It's bad enough we have to keep stuff out of the webcams, but at least let's be open and honest with each other.'

'Actually,' said Slim, brightening as he glanced at my brother, 'there's something else you should know.'

'No, there isn't.' Pavlov seemed agitated. 'It's not a share thing.'

'What?' I popped the remains of the egg into my mouth, sucked my fingers clean, and said, 'I could use a laugh. Go on.'

'You heard your sister.' Slim grinned wickedly at my brother. 'Give your new friend a little wave.'

'No way. It'll only start up again.'

'What friend?' I asked, and wiped a dribble of chocolate from the corner of my mouth. 'Pav, you just agreed there'd be no more secrets.'

I heard him sigh from his side of the sofa, but it was on the screen where the action happened: a shot of my brother waving for the webcam without a hint of warmth or sincerity.

'Now check this out,' said Slim, gesturing for me to turn round, which I did just as the ticker above the window came to life once more. The display may have been less than dazzling in natural light, but the content was arresting enough.

HELLO . . . TO . . . YOU . . . TOO . . . BUNKMUFFIN . . . XXX

I looked back at the boys. 'Someone's talking to Pavlov? Do we know who she is?'

'Who says it's a *she*?'

Now my attention focused on Slim, and when I turned back to the ticker my disbelief lost out to laughter.

WHAT . . . COLOUR . . . SKIMPIES . . . ARE . . . YOU . . . WEARING . . . THIS . . . EVENING?

'These little messages started arriving this morning,' Slim went on. 'First it was just pleasantries, compliments about his shirts and stuff.'

'How was I to know it was a bloke?' Pavlov came close to snarling at the lens just then. 'Bastard didn't let on he was a guy until way after lunch-time.'

'By which point your brother had struck up quite a friendship.' I asked how he knew. Slim blew me a kiss, said he had caught him knocking out stuff like that.

'It was a distraction,' Pavlov countered. 'My editor's gone quiet since I passed off Cisco's column as my own. Waiting for his

157

response has left me feeling vulnerable. It's only natural I should pick up when someone says I've got "come to bed" eyes.'

'Do we know who he is?' I asked.

Slim said this was cyberspace. It could be anyone.

'Maybe even a woman masquerading as a man,' my brother suggested, so thinly I don't think even he believed that was likely.

'You'll just have to ignore the ticker,' I told him. 'Whoever it is will soon get bored and find another website.'

We contemplated the window on the screen, the ticker behind us looking ominously dormant. Waiting, it seemed, for an attentive audience.

WOULD ... YOU ... LIKE ... TO ... KNOW ... WHAT ... I'M ... DOING ... RIGHT ... NOW?

'*Nooo!*' we yelled as one, but made all kinds of different stop signs.

'I knew it,' said Slim, and finished with a universal gesture. 'We're dealing with a one handed browser.'

'I'm out of here.' Pavlov marched into the dead zone. From there he informed us that he was going to check his email, on his own computer in his own room, and if his personal stalker wanted to click along to watch the wall then so be it. 'The bastard can speak to the nape of my neck, because that's all he's going to see of me.'

HE'S ... SO ... CUTE ... WHEN ... HE'S ... ANGRY.

Slim watched Pavlov flounce from the room, and took a moment to pull himself together again. 'Do you want to eat something?' he asked me. 'Or was that Crème Egg supposed to be your supper?'

'It wasn't even a snack,' I said. 'It was therapy.'

'Then I should cook.' Slim rubbed his hands together. 'We'll go oriental. It's a speciality of mine.'

'Really?' I said. 'Does it involve fish? I'm off seafood until further notice.'

Slim told me that one taste of his chicken and noodles in black bean sauce would have me hooked. All I had to do was nothing and he would have it ready in a flash. 'Put your feet up,' he said, on his way through to the kitchen. 'Watch yourself for a while.'

'Why would I want to watch me?'

'Because you're the best thing on the box.'

'What about the creepy guy?' I called after him, aware that if anything came out of the ticker now it would clearly be meant for me.

I was about to call after him again, but Slim popped his head back round the door, his dreads swinging low, that brow ring twinkling. 'Do you mind if we don't ask him to join us?' he said. 'I've only got enough noodles for three.'

23

My feet belonged to someone else. At least that's how they looked through the webcam lens. I barely recognised the soles. With my legs crossed at the ankles, and my heels resting on the footstool in front of the screen, I studied the picture in front of me and wondered whether cosmetic surgery extended that far south. I needed a toe tuck ten times over. A pedisuction, if such a procedure existed. Anything to make them more shapely. My nails were in good condition, a shining example for Sweet William, but the varnish had been a mistake: a glittery silver that demanded all the attention it could get, and yet couldn't quite disguise what was wrong underneath. Big hair worked on the same principle, I realised, and I had always been so *careful* in that respect.

For a minute or so I kidded myself that it was the wide-angle lens playing tricks with the perspective, but eventually I quit trying to arch my feet and curl my toes so they looked smaller. Instead, I just sat there feeling like I should be on the Springer show or something. Which, in a way, I was already. The circus act on the sofa, waiting for my perfect mismatch – the man with the fungal feet.

'We'll be right back,' I said to myself, and shifted the keyboard on to my lap. I had seen enough of myself, so I returned the browser to our menu page and wondered where to go next. *Caminside*, it said across the top, though I still felt like I was on the outside with my nose pressed to the window. That's why I clicked on the chat room icon – thought I'd eavesdrop on any visitors looking around and see how it was for them. Slim had been keeping a weather eye on it, monitoring the trickle of traffic we had attracted so far. I had wondered why a property player would actively encourage people to fraternise with each other on a tour through the house. Pavlov reckoned it was a spin on one of the oldest tricks in the rent book: having the prospective tenants view a place together so that they felt pushed into making the first offer. The chat window opened up just then, revealing just a few screen names hanging out together. Even so, it was few too many for me. I took one look at the scrolling conversation they were having, and immediately scrambled to plant both feet firmly back inside my shoes.

HeelSpike:	No way could that girl suck her own toes, Sockboy28 is living in a dream world if he thinks she'll go down that far.
Sockboy 28:	Sometimes the chunkier ones can be quite supple. It's gotta be worth hanging out here, just in case she tries.
ToeKarla:	HeelSpike is right. It takes months of practice. All she does is sit there looking like she wished a bowl of ice cream would land in her lap, there's no way she could make it.
FunGal:	People, we're not thinking here! Do we really want to see a chick with *corns* go to work on herself? That's a fetish too far for me.

'I haven't got corns,' I protested. Louder, when I switched it into a question. Then I went into a complete wig-out and yelled, 'Slim, they're talking about *me* in here!'

'Who is?' he asked, sounding a little distracted, his question underscored by the hiss and spit of hot oil in a wok. 'Can it wait? I'm a little tied up right now.'

ToeKarla:	Maybe with a pedicure she could be kinda cute.

Sockboy 28:   Oh, dude, imagine! The cotton balls between the
                toes!

FunGal: Mmmm!

'Believe me, Slim. Nothing can be more important than this.'

'Gimme a moment.' He sounded much more harassed this time, the oil a little more urgent, fierce and unruly. 'I'll be right through.' Even as I heard him say this I was scrambling to get out of the chat room. I hit a key. Any key. Kept hitting the keys, in fact, until the offending window closed. Witnessing this presence in our house was like finding we had a family of rats behind the skirting-boards – a low-level threat that made me want to jump on a chair and scream. I would have exited the website completely, but in my haste I managed to tile the screen with feeds from the landing, the hall and the kitchen. There was nothing going on with the first two, but the culinary cam drew my attention. It showed Slim brandishing a spatula in one hand and the wok lid in the other, inching slowly backwards like he had a tiger in there with him.

'Do you want a hand with the cooking?' I called out.

'No need,' he trilled. 'Be with you in a tick.'

The luminous glow inside the wok lid increased my concern. That and the fact that the crackle I was hearing sounded like ten feet of tin foil being crunched up in a ball. I was about to get up and see what was happening, when the window on the screen showed Slim make a sudden advance across the frame, out of the webcam's reach. Then came an abrupt clatter followed by silence. A second later, Slim appeared at the door. Instead of the lid he was holding a tea-towel. He dabbed his brow with one corner, then slung it over his shoulder. 'Where's the emergency?'

'I was about to ask you the same thing.' I switched back to the chat room; this was the fire that needed stamping out. Except now the foot fetish circle had been joined by several more screen names, and the discussion was moving on to other matters.

DeliaDoesDallas:	The dumb ass should've got the chicken pieces in quicker. No wonder it went up like that.
Gateaux-Fabulous:	But it's essential to have the oil searing hot. He just didn't stir enough.
ToeKarla:	Anyone see if it spat on his socks?

Slim looked at me uneasily, and said, 'Everything's under control.'

I knew he was talking about the kitchen, but I had other concerns on my mind. 'Doesn't it disturb you?' I asked, trying hard not to lose it again. 'I'm beginning to think the only property people come to view is *us.*'

Slim twisted a button on his beach shirt, then enquired tentatively what it mattered. 'Even if they are talking about you, me and Pavlov,' he said, 'they can't touch us.' He motioned at the tape on each side of the sofa. 'As soon as we cross the line, we stop being the entertainment.'

I was about to ask how he thought this might limit the things we could do together, when Pavlov appeared at the door, grinning like it would hurt him to stop. 'Cisco, I could kiss you.'

'Easy,' warned Slim. 'This isn't Alabama.'

'Your column,' my brother said. 'It'll be in the next issue of *Sparkle!*. Word for word as well!'

'That is good news,' I said, beaming back at him. 'I told you our luck would change.'

'My editor adored it. He emailed to ask why I hadn't written with such candour before.'

'Honesty is everything,' I said, with a side glance at Slim. I wondered whether he had deliberately positioned himself in front of the screen, covering up the chat room and the kitchen exposé. Still, I didn't ask because this was Pavlov's moment, and I got up to give my brother a hug. Leaving the live zone felt strangely liberating, and I decided that in future I should spend more time on this side of the tape. Even if I wasn't doing anything special in front of the webcam, it was clearly more than enough for some of the viewers.

'Can I smell burning?' Pavlov addressed this to the chef, not me. He tipped his head to one side, crinkling his nose. I looked back at Slim, adopted a more knowing expression.

'Okay,' he relented, and ditched the tea-towel. 'Who fancies a takeaway?'

24

It was Pavlov who volunteered to collect the pizza. Slim had pointed out that it was just as easy to order in a delivery. We didn't even have to bother with the phone, he added. Now that a third of the house was sponsored by Poppa Italiano we could just click on the banner ad, and most likely a Turkish boy on a moped would be here within minutes. Pavlov insisted he should go, if only so he could witness it being cooked with his own eyes. Make sure nobody hawked into the topping, stuff like that.

'Thanks,' I said, as he was leaving. 'That's really helped me work up an appetite.'

Slim waited for the front door to slam shut, then flashed me his bedroom eyes. 'I know other ways.'

'So do I,' I said flatly, 'but you don't simply switch me on like you do your games.'

For a second he just stood there in front of the sofa, regarding me quizzically. 'Have I done something wrong?'

I was about to invite him to sit down so we could talk, then considered what people might read into it. Which was how we came to conduct this heart-to-heart in the far corner of the front room. Out of eyeshot of the rest of the world.

'It's not you,' I told Slim, when I faced him in the dead zone, 'it's everyone else.'

'The viewers?'

'I hear what you say about them, but I can't switch off from the fact that they're out there now. It changes things, makes what intimacy we have seem a little forced.'

'Oh, I don't know,' said Slim, and I just knew it was the fool in him that was going to answer next. 'If you ask me it's kind of kinky.'

I turned to the window behind him. 'I know you're having second thoughts about this cam thing too,' I said. 'I *wish* you'd just admit it.' Dusk was closing fast, as was the flower market. The traders out there hauling away their carts, trolleys and crates. They formed a rag-tag procession, trailing petals and cigarette smoke in their wake, but every one acknowledged the florist at the far end. I could see him standing sentry in front of his stall. The one with the fresh blooms and the fairy lights. 'Sweet William warned me there could be more to this than met the eye,' I said. I felt Slim's hands on my shoulders as I spoke. A tentative touch that only settled into something more certain when I reached up to give them a squeeze. He said, 'This morning, a message came through on the ticker to belt up my dressing-gown better.'

'I've been meaning to talk to you about that.'

'At first I was really embarrassed,' he went on, 'but then I wondered what I had to hide.'

'Are you asking for reassurance?'

'When a guy's packing double figures down there, Cisco, *he*'s the one who has to do the reassuring.'

'Double figures?'

'That's what I said.'

'Slim, if that were true I'd need counselling before I even let you *near* me.'

'I swear that's how I measure up,' he insisted. 'In centimetres.'

I smiled to myself, still watching the florists float home. 'I thought inches were the industry standard with you boys.'

'They are,' Slim confirmed, 'but ever since I converted to metric I've felt so much better about myself.'

'That's still no excuse to let it peep out in front of the webcam,' I said. 'Anyone could be watching.'

'Sure they could,' he agreed, 'but I've no idea who they are, and that's what makes it bearable. They're just screen names. Made-up monikers. Why should I care what TickleChix thinks of my tackle?'

'Tickle-*what*?' I asked, twisting round now.

'I don't remember the precise name,' he said quickly. 'My point is these people aren't part of my life like you are.'

'Don't get smooth with me.' I poked his chest with my finger. 'Anyone with that kind of screen name gets in touch, I deserve to know.'

That grin of his eased across his face. 'Actually, she was keen to know more about you.'

I wasn't sure whether he was hoping this would flatter me, but all it served to do was bring me full circle. 'I'm in a relationship with you, and nobody else,' I said, and suddenly felt lighter than air. 'I want it to work, really I do, but if we can't keep some of the more intimate aspects to ourselves, the secrets, as you once spun it for me, then I have to ask what we're doing together.'

Slim seemed alarmed at my change in tone, his elongated face looking even longer. It wasn't a threat, what I had said, just a venting of frustration, because this house was making it hard for me to tell him how I felt. Still, at least I had been honest. I only hoped he would follow my lead.

'Tonight,' he said, 'after we've eaten, let's spend some time alone together. Create a few secrets, so to speak.'

'I don't feel like going out,' I said. 'I'm working tomorrow. Another day dealing with people who actually enjoy being in front of a camera.'

Slim smiled, marked by the sound of the key in the front door, then asked who had said anything about going out. 'So people might follow us on the bedroom cam, see the empty frame and know exactly what we're up to, but they can't touch us, Cisco. It doesn't matter what kind of misfits are drawn to the website, the screen is where they stop. As far as we're concerned, they might as well not exist.'

I could see where Slim was coming from, but then Pavlov hurried into the room. He stopped suddenly, breathing like a sparrow in shock.

'What's wrong?' I asked.

My brother was clutching the pizza box in his hands. Judging by his entrance, I sensed we weren't going to like what was inside. As it turned out, the contents of the box were fine. What troubled him were the contents of a car outside. Pavlov cleared his throat, but even then his voice was just a whisper. 'There's an old boy parked up in a Morris Traveller.'

'Is he lost?' asked Slim.

'You could say that,' said Pavlov. 'He's wearing a red dress.'

The pizza was cold when I got round to dividing it up. None of us seemed very hungry, however, and not just because we left it so long the surface had glazed. Slim Jim, Pavlov and I, we just didn't have the heart to tuck in. Despite external encouragement.

BUNKMUFFIN . . . YOU . . . SHOULD . . . EAT.

My brother scanned the ticker, then took his plate to the far side of the room. 'Is there a word to describe a gathering of stalkers?' he asked. 'A stakeout, maybe?'

BUILD . . . UP . . . THAT . . . BODY . . . BABY.

'A shadow,' I suggested. 'A shadow of stalkers.'

I was cross-legged on the carpet, facing my brother from the other side of the room. I had my plate in front of me, just over the line of red tape. The way I felt then, a glimpse of my picked-at pizza was all I was prepared to give our audience. Only Slim remained visible to the webcam, fretting at the hastily-drawn drapes.

'Can you make out what he's doing behind the wheel?' asked Pavlov. 'Maybe *he*'s behind the ticker.'

Slim stole another look. 'I don't see a laptop in there with him,' he said, 'but I can't be sure where his hands are, either.' He glanced back to ensure we had understood him right. 'Don't make me hazard a guess, guys.'

'Why don't you just go and speak to him?' I suggested. 'It's not like we're asking you to rob a bank.'

'What if he's dangerous?'

'Does he look it?' This was my brother, pausing next to review the question. 'The man might think he's dressed to kill, maybe.'

'So why don't *you* deal with him?' said Slim. 'What I'd like to know is how this fruitloop found out where we lived.' He said this with a hint of suspicion. Something neither of us liked – especially me, the one person he was supposed to trust on every level. Indeed, my expression dropped several degrees when he stopped peering into the street and asked us again directly. Who spilled the beans?

'Maybe you could tell us,' I said.

At first, Pavlov had wanted to call the police and get the pensioner in the car arrested. For what? Slim had asked. Possession of an offensive frock? Despite being shaken by the sight of him out there, I had to concede that Pops had good taste. A sheer strappy number, I had discovered a few minutes earlier, when they let me take a look through the window, but not as my brother had described it. For a start it was a *négligé* – from Victoria's Secret, I guessed, possibly Ann Summers, and certainly not very appropriate for an old soldier with hair like an emperor's wreath. More to the point, as I had told the boys, the colour was *vermilion*, not red. It was then they suggested that I deal with the pizza and leave the surveillance to them. Them and the rest of the virtual world, I had muttered to myself, on cutting Slim his slice.

COULD . . . BUNKMUFFIN . . . WIPE . . . HIS . . . MOUTH . . . IN . . . SHOT . . . PLEASE?

'You wish,' said Pavlov. 'Whoever it is clearly had issues with his mother at mealtimes.'

Slim came over to join me now, outwardly the most upset by the invasion. Gone were the wisecracks and the way-it-goes attitude. I gave him some space as he sat down beside me. Straight away he sank his teeth into a triangle of pizza, though he hadn't finished with Pavlov. 'You're the one who started the fan club,' he said, chomping at the strings of cheese that stretched out on him. 'I watched you flirt with the ticker all morning. It was a desperate thing to witness.'

'I didn't know he was a guy!'

'So you're at pains to tell us.'

The telephone put a halt to this. Ringing out once, twice, a third time too.

'Someone pick up,' I said, meaning Pavlov, who was closest to the handset. But instead of reaching across he let it go until the answer-machine kicked in. A crackle came through the speaker, then a crunch, not a static crunch but the one I had been hearing in my head lately whenever I thought of Frank Cartier. I wondered what condition his molars must be in, crushing hard nuts like that, day in, day out.

'I know you're there,' our landlord could be heard to say finally. 'I know because I can *see* you.' I glanced at Slim. Cautiously he brought his feet back over the red tape. A pained sigh came down the line. 'Are you deliberately hiding from the webcams? Slim? Were those your toes? Pavlov? Cisco? What's wrong with sitting on the sofa? Being bashful in the bedroom I can understand, but this is disappointing. I should remind you that we have a business arrangement here—'

'*Answer* him,' I said urgently. 'Pavlov, you're nearest.'

My brother merely showed me his palm. Squinted as if it would help him hear better.

'Model tenants, is what we agreed. Model tenants in a happy house, not a hideaway. If there's a problem I can always ask Kenzo to look into it.'

'What does that mean?' I asked. 'Bloody hell, speak to him! Tell him we've got stalkers.'

Slim, like Pavlov, remained locked on to the speaker. The pair of them straining to listen, with no intention of intercepting the call, even when Cartier's tone began to lighten. Our landlord buttering us up with compliments and click reports: two hundred and fifty hits a day. Just enough to satisfy the sponsors, he said, which included the one he had recently secured for Pavlov's room. But there were still costs to cover, which was why he needed us to honour our part of the bargain and *relax*. That was how he finished before hanging up. A second later the boys tuned back into the room.

'What's his number?' My brother reached for the handset.

'Call last number redial,' Slim suggested. 'That'll get him.'

I stared at them both in turn, shaking my head in disbelief. 'What the hell was wrong with picking up?'

Pavlov had the receiver to his ear by now, and glanced at Slim as if it was down to him to explain the obvious. So I looked at Slim expectantly.

'Men talk to machines,' he said, with a shrug. 'We open up to them a little more freely than we do with people. When it comes to leaving messages, a lot of guys end up saying things they would otherwise keep back.'

'He was calling to check up on us,' I said, 'not *break* up with us.' My brother pressed two fingertips over the mouthpiece. 'Business or pleasure, it's the surest way to get a man to speak his mind.'

'Frank Cartier doesn't strike me as a man who's easily intimidated.' I took another slice of pizza to the sofa, mugging a face for the webcam just so our landlord could see that I was doing so under duress. 'What's he got to hide from us, anyway?'

'All that stuff about expecting more from his tenants,' said Slim, 'that's a standard line from any landlord who wants to assert authority. But we let him roll with his words and it turns out we're not doing so badly after all.'

'Oh, yeah,' I said bitterly. 'We're doing great.'

'Guys.' This was Pavlov, still hanging on the phone. 'Will you keep it down?'

'So now you're going to ring back and tell him about the stalkers. At the very least you could've saved the cost of the call.'

'A small price to pay,' said Slim. 'Knowledge is power, after all.'

'Mr Cartier?' Pavlov ducked into the handset, then turned away, seemingly embarrassed to be in my presence. 'If you can hear this, would you pick up the phone, please?'

26

I forced myself to tackle my pizza, chewing through it bit by bit while my brother reported the problem with the ticker pest. I kept telling myself I should eat something now before my appetite deserted me completely, but by the time Cartier's answer-machine had run out of space I was fit to burst. Not with pizza, but with anger at Pavlov's rambling confessional. My brother having tripped over his own tongue to admit that *he* was the one who had broadcast our address to the virtual world. We watched him return the receiver to its cradle. In the long silence that followed, I wondered when he was going to meet our gaze again.

'You wrote our address on a postcard?' Slim said next, condensing what we had just heard. 'And you held it up to the *webcam*?'

Pavlov motioned at the ticker. 'I had her down as a party girl, like I said. Not some guy aiming to mess with my head. Some of the things I was reading up there were too good to be true, promising all kinds if I revealed my whereabouts. I guess I got caught up in my own fantasy, okay? As a free agent, it's only natural to play along with something like that.'

'As an agony uncle,' I said, reminding him of his position, 'how many times have you advised people never to give out their details online until they're sure they can handle the consequences?'

'That's agony, Cis, and this is the real world. What was I supposed to do? Tell a *grown-up*?'

'It was a dumb move,' said Slim. 'All that time spent making excuses into Cartier's answer-machine and you know what? You didn't even mention that your virtual indiscretion means we now have a very real stalker outside.'

'Did I forget to say that?' Pavlov looked genuinely surprised. 'Damn. Shall I phone back?'

'Stay right where you are!' Slim darted across to retrieve the phone, and backed away as if my brother was a baby snatcher. 'Don't even think about taking it away from me.'

'At least he owned up in the end,' I conceded. 'If we want things to work out we have to stick together. Until we find our feet career-wise, living here rent free is a golden opportunity.' I realised I sounded like Slim, and in some ways I was speaking for him, but the conflict this arrangement had caused between us left me feeling uneasy. 'We'll just have to be more vigilant, learn to live with people watching, and use our dead zones wisely so we know where the boundaries are. Even with the webcams,' I finished, 'there'll always be space for ourselves.' I faced Slim when I said this, hoping he would realise that the space beside me on the sofa was where I wanted him to be. Not back there by the drapes, which was where he went again. Putting me on edge with his constant checking.

'So long as it doesn't encourage any more freaks,' he said reluctantly.

'And keeps the fish-hook man from our door,' I added. 'Even his tattoos scare me.'

'What they say about Kenzo is a myth,' stressed Pavlov, with a note of finality. 'Try to exercise a little self-control over your anxiety.'

'Like you did with your *mouth* just then?' snapped Slim, turning on my brother again. 'Next time the beeps kick in, hand the phone to your sister, turn round then quietly leave the room.'

Pavlov looked set to defend himself, but an interruption from the street had him on his feet for a different reason. 'Is that what I think it is?' he asked, as the engine turned over a second time before firing into life. That the vehicle could be heard pulling away served to drag some of the atmosphere with it. Slim lifted a corner of the drape, and confirmed 'the dude in the dress' had gone.

'Thank God for that,' I said, with a sigh. 'I didn't think I'd sleep, knowing he was out there.'

'Me neither,' my brother agreed. 'I almost feel like celebrating.'

Slim remained less than relaxed, however, and focused on Pavlov. 'Part of me wants to wind down with a spliff,' he said, 'but somehow I feel obliged to keep in view of the cams tonight so Cartier doesn't think we're doing something illegal.'

Pavlov seemed uncomfortable, rocking from one foot to the other. For a moment I thought he would make his excuses and join the server in the toilet. Instead he pointed prayer hands at his housemate and repeated his apology.

'Give him a break,' I said, in his defence. Pavlov had been foolish to broadcast our address, but we needed to move on from that now. I said this, but Slim didn't respond. Even Pavlov looked like an actor who had forgotten his lines, and that's when the ticker kicked in again. Blinking into life like some kind of malicious autocue.

BUNKMUFFIN ... IS ... ADORABLE ... WHEN ... THERE'S ... TENSION ... IN ... THE ... HOUSE.

Pavlov glared at the intruding comment. 'I feel like I'm responsible for a pet nobody loves.'

'That reminds me,' I said, seizing on what I saw as a chance to lighten the mood. 'How are you getting on with the Sea Maidens? Have you purified the water like it said in the instructions?'

'What with?' My brother stopped right there. His question turning in on itself. Sucked into the space left by the fact that he had clearly forgotten all about the stuff that had come with the box.

'How about the growth powder?' I asked, but the answer was already on his face. 'There were two tubs, Pavlov, but you can't use one without the other.'

My brother forced a smile, collected the keyboard from the carpet and joined me on the sofa. 'I guess this thing has its uses,' he said, conjuring up the webcam for his room. The window opened on his desk, but I didn't even look for the aquarium. Not when a banner advert framed the shot demanding my attention.

Despair-Direct
Because things can never be this bleak
click here for counselling and comfort.
All major credit cards accepted.

'This is my *sponsor*?' Pavlov clicked on the link, then squeaked indignantly at the chat room that opened up for him.

CounsellorTim: :o)

'Why is he smiling?' Pavlov's fingers ran scattershot across the keys.

I expected Slim to seize the moment at his housemate's expense, but he was beyond that. I sensed him behind me, his hands on the back of the sofa, braced for my brother's response.

Pavlov: What's your problem, pal?

CounsellorTim: I'm here to help with yours. If you'd like to tap in your card number, I can offer head relief for £50 or £75 for the full couch.

The Love Surgeon addressed the screen directly next, inviting the man to go Freud himself before he sought him out and shut him down in a way he would never forget. It was a startling outburst, but therapeutic. In fact, Pavlov seemed positively subdued when he switched back to the front-room cam then removed himself from the image on the screen. 'I'm going to my room,' he said, in a whisper. 'Promise you won't watch.'

'What are you planning on doing?'

'Nothing,' he told Slim. 'I just need some time alone.'

Which was exactly what Slim and I had planned as well, but not like this. My boyfriend took the seat vacated by my brother, there at the far end of the sofa.

'So,' I said, hoping he'd come closer, 'where were we?'

He smiled thinly, then dragged one hand down his face as if hoping to erase something from it. The way he went on to stare at the webcam made me wonder whether I was the last thing on his mind. In mine he was at the head of the queue. 'This is going to come between us,' I said, gesturing at the lens, 'isn't it?' I felt my throat knotting, then goosebumps all over.

'All this attention,' was all he could say, 'it can't last.'

Hearing this, I couldn't help but think Slim was talking about us here, not the cams and the creeps they attracted. I could almost see it on the screen: the couple on the sofa, taking stock of their situation.

'Why don't we take this to bed?' I suggested, standing. 'I could use an early night with you, away from prying eyes.'

'You go ahead.' Slim didn't blink as I crossed in front of him. 'I'll be right up.'

I hesitated, felt my heart sink some, then decided that perhaps we could follow Pavlov's lead. Use a minute alone before making out together.

'Don't be long.' I dipped back to kiss him on the lips, the sound like a ringpull lifting, and hoped he wasn't going to blame himself for all this. Slim might have talked us into accepting the webcams into our lives, but it was my signature on the contract – Pavlov's too. Nobody had forced me to put pen to paper, or move in with a guy I barely knew for that matter. On both counts it had seemed like the right thing to do. Still did, when the old Slim returned for a moment and asked me to warm the bed. 'Okay,' I smiled, 'I'll be waiting.'

Some time just before dawn, I was disturbed by a faint, high-pitched shriek. A woman, I felt sure. I lifted my cheek from the pillow, and sleepily sought some kind of focus. The bedroom light was still on. So, too, were my bra and panties. I hadn't expected to be wearing them at this time. As Slim wasn't here with me, my brain slow-processed that I must have fallen asleep waiting for him. Another sound, a building series of gasps from the same girl, and this time I was bolt upright in bed, my mind's eye working hard to contain the scene downstairs. I knew where he was now. I also knew exactly what he was doing without me, and for some reason I felt curiously cheated.

Slim was missing because Slim was with *her*, Misty Ventura, and at a time when I needed him most. I had an overwhelming desire to bawl him out for staying up late, and a nagging inclination to forget about it and go back to sleep. *The Money Shot* was only a game, after all. Misty wasn't real. This submissive Amazonian and her assault-grade weapons – could I seriously regard her as competition? Had it not been for the red tape on the carpet at the foot of the bed, I would probably have gone down there and dragged him back to bed. As it was, that dividing line between two zones woke me up to a couple of things. First, I wasn't dressed to be seen by the webcam stationed in the corner of the bedroom, but more importantly, there was another way to see what was going on.

If Slim's shrunken dressing-gown was a little revealing on him, it left me feeling like a total strumpet. I actually had to breathe in to knot the sash, which also served to squash my boobs and lift the hemline high up my thighs. I checked myself in the mirror, considered finding a sweater, then persuaded myself to forget it and broadcast live like this. The panting I could hear downstairs was just too much to handle. As I booted up Slim's own laptop, in full view of the bedroom cam, I imagined that some dedicated viewers had to be punching the air right now. Except I knew that this was all they were getting: the angry cow in her undies, stomping through cyberspace until she found the window that revealed a whole lot more.

'Now I see you,' I said to myself, staring at the front room on the screen. For there was Slim, just as I had suspected, positioned so close to the edge of the sofa that you could have taken the bloody thing away and he would have stayed in the same position – elbows locked like his knees, joypad held like a hymnbook, his face a palette of emotion, with Misty heading for the horizon, as reflected in his eyes. I had never seen him this alive before, so dedicated to one thing. It certainly wasn't the same man I had invited to join me upstairs, the one who had blown me out for something that was evidently much more important to him. I watched my brother's housemate grin and grimace for a while, his dreadlocks swaying like the way I remembered she moved, and then found my fingers seeking out the message window.

I typed without looking at the keys. I didn't need that kind of guidance. Not with the words appearing as I wrote them, gliding across the ticker behind Slim. A message I doubted he would see, but which served as a release for me. For somehow it completed the picture before I slipped back to my side of the bed.

YOU ... DON'T ... KNOW ... WHAT ... YOU'RE ... MISSING.

27

I was wide awake when Slim crept into the bedroom. Not that he knew it. I kept my eyes closed when his knees tucked in behind mine. His arm looped round my waist next, but I couldn't bring myself to stir or register his presence. Within minutes his breathing had softened against the nape of my neck, little wafts of toothpaste and tobacco, and I knew for sure that he was asleep. Dropping off, just like that! The player at rest. I wondered what kind of perfume a girl like Misty might wear because it would have rubbed off all over Slim, had their interaction been real. Something slutty, I imagined. A cheap, overpowering brand. It just about summed her up in my mind, but it didn't make me feel any better. I glanced at the clock-radio. It would be another hour before the weatherman helped me choose my outfit for the day. The prospect of seething in silence until then was enough to persuade me to make a forecast of my own. I slipped out of bed, showered until the water ran cold then dressed to suit my mood.

Being watched without knowing who was out there made it hard to switch off. I was making myself some tea and toast, in full view of the kitchen cam, aware that people were picking up on every move I made. I imagined some were talking about me in the chat room right now, but this time I didn't care. *Why is she dressed in black today?* they might be asking. *What's wrong with using a plate to catch her crumbs? How much longer is she going to leave her fucking roots?* All that crap they could have for nothing, it was just so trivial. So skin deep. What mattered to me was the stuff inside, the things no cam could see.

I drifted through to the front room, left the drapes shut despite the breaking dawn, and thought about the last person who had been in here. Slim's imprint was still on the sofa, the joypad abandoned beside it. Last night had been an eye-opener, but on reflection it was also an inevitable part of our relationship. Our whole thing together had been so immediate and intense, a chemical attraction almost, and now the smoke was clearing. It meant I could begin to see what he was really made of, even though we had already bonded in places.

With men, it was usually hobbies, stuff they didn't exactly sing about on a first date. I once had a fling with a guy who flew kites in competition. Another who had aimed to collect the football programmes for every single match that Manchester City ever played. I could live with these pursuits: they were non-sexual, non-threatening and invariably non-interesting. Technically speaking, Misty Ventura was non-existent, so I should have been able to handle Slim's interest, but something inside me wouldn't let it lie. In some ways, I felt as if he had turned to her in our time of crisis. I sipped my tea, still dwelling on the night's events, only to jump and have it wash over the rim when the ticker read my mind.

THERE'S ... MORE ... TO ... THIS ... GAME ... THAN ... MEETS ...
THE ... EYE.

'Not *again.*'

The sentence rushed across the screen, red lights blinking on black. That it was followed swiftly by another stopped me checking for a car outside.

TRUST ... ME ... HONEY ... I'VE ... SEEN ... IT ... ALL.

I'd been addressed like this once before, could even recall her bittersweet voice when the next line joined the chase.

WHAT ... ELSE ... CAN ... A ... GIRL ... DO ...

LAID ... UP ... ON ... HER ... BACK ... ALL ... DAY?

'Rose,' I said, relieved. 'It's you.'

PAY ... ME ... A ... VISIT ... SOME ... TIME.

'I will.' I turned to mouth the words at the webcam. When Sweet William first mentioned that Rose was watching, I had felt very weird about it. Now I had a clearer picture of what attracted our audience, I welcomed her virtual presence. In some ways, I wished she could have been here in person because I certainly felt like opening up to someone. I waited for the ticker to light up again, but it didn't happen. Even so I carried on staring at it while I finished my tea, wondering whether goldfish had hang-ups too.

I had an age to fill before work. I just didn't know how to use it constructively. Half of me wanted to head back upstairs and give Slim hell. The other half knew that kind of wake-up call wouldn't go down well, so I took myself to the sofa instead and settled into the place where I had watched him on the webcam. I toyed with the joypad for a second or so, wondering how Slim would react if he knew how I felt about his make-believe mistress. Then I realised that when it came to affairs of any kind a man would instinctively deny everything. Far better, I thought, as I powered up the games console, to seek out the truth from the other woman.

The Money Shot menu informed me that Player One hadn't quite completed a third of the game. The level he was on, I discovered at the touch of a button, had been attempted eighty-seven times.

'Now that's disappointing,' I said, recalling the frenzied fingerpad action I had witnessed the previous night. 'Misty must be deeply frustrated.' I decided to start where Slim had left off. I logged on to the online arena, selected **continue game**, and braced myself accordingly. The menu opened out like a double door, and suddenly

187

there she was, all bullet bra and buttocks, ready to obey her master's command. The bitch.

Misty was facing a towering curtain of rock, standing so close I wondered if someone had sent her there for being naughty. I was just considering how to turn her round when somewhere off-screen a pig started squealing. The leader of the pack, I realised, as the scene went pink and a thousand and one murderous-looking trotters turned Misty into something a little more scarlet.

'Oh, yuk.' I winced at the carnage, and immediately hit restart. This time I knew the killer pigs were coming. I could also see why Slim had endured such a tough time, having reached this apparent dead end. I didn't rate my chances of doing any better – mainly because I had no idea how to make Misty stay upright, let alone take emergency action. There was a rock ledge a couple of feet above her, which looked like the only way out, but all I could do as the pigs rushed in was press every button wildly. In response, Misty appeared to go into some kind of major seizure, and I figured she was dead again when the first pig pounced. Another random jab, and this time we both got a grip. Misty exploding into a gravity-defying back flip that saw her alight on the ledge just as a sea of snout and spittle crashed in underneath her.

'Go, *girl*!' I said, and not just to myself this time.

Another ledge jutted out to Misty's right, and another above that one on the opposing rockface. I studied the controls, tried to recall the sequence I had just achieved, and was thrilled when my guess proved right. It was beautiful, and my confidence grew as Misty made it from one outcrop to the next. A variation with the buttons and I added pirouettes and tumble tucks to the ascent. This wasn't climbing, this was *dancing*, and it was truly a joy to watch. The squealing below just fading away until the summit beckoned and I overreached myself. Pushing poor Misty to such an extreme that she was left clinging to the ledge by her fingernails. Which was good in a sense, but not so great when I had only mastered how to make her move from the knees down. I squeezed the button at the back of the controls, hoping to see her pull herself to safety. But instead she let go with her right hand. The pair of us gasped, though only one of us sounded like the sort of thing you hear through a bedroom wall. Anyway, I listened to the loose stones fall away like beads from a broken necklace, and figured that in her position I would probably be screaming my ass off.

'Come on,' I urged her. 'We can do this.'

I realised where I had gone wrong, so I thought, and tried again with another button pressed as well. It was an involved move I would come to remember by heart, but never divulge to the boys, for this one left Misty in the same perilous position, wearing nothing but her boots.

'My God,' I marvelled at her naked tushy, and the dark cleft in-between, 'I *did* it.'

'Did what?' A voice at the doorway. My brother, looking like a man who hadn't so much stirred from sleep but booted up fully functioning. 'What did you do?' he asked again. 'Apart from use all the hot water.'

'Nothing.' I dropped the joypad and smiled innocently at Pavlov. It didn't last, it couldn't, what with the background sound of a plucky female adventurer plummeting to her doom. A crunch. A squeal. A guilty shrug from me.

'Is this *The Money Shot*?' He came out of the dead zone just as Misty became history once again. By the time he saw what was going on, all evidence of her naked body had been ripped into a million pixels. My brother grimaced at what was left. 'Slim will go mad if he catches you messing with her.'

'Not as mad as me, had I confronted him here last night.'

He took a seat beside me, his eyes locked on the webcam. 'I know what happened,' he said. 'I was watching from my workstation.'

I faced my brother and waited until he had eased up with the lens. 'So you couldn't sleep either?'

'Not since we went online,' he said. 'Every time I shut my eyes I start to hear the server. I can't help thinking it's humming through the walls just for me.'

I understood, nodding now. Thinking at least he would agree that Slim had been out of order.

'So what did you think?' I asked.

'About last night's performance?'

'Uh-huh.'

'Mostly that you really shouldn't sit at your laptop in Slim's dressing-gown. It's indecent.'

'You were watching *me*?'

'I was one step away from coming in and throwing a blanket over you, that's for sure.'

'What about Slim? Did you even bother checking up on him?'

'It's not Slim I'm worried about,' he said bluntly. 'It was your reaction to what he was doing that concerned me.'

Ruefully I faced the menu screen, the high scores listed on it. 'Can you blame me? I know he's stressed about being watched, we all are, but he chose to work it out with Misty instead of me.'

Pavlov studied the scores, but didn't say anything. He was probably balking at the number of attempts Slim had taken with this level. 'Cis, playing like this isn't going to make you feel better.'

'You'd be surprised.'

'No, *you* need to talk,' he insisted. 'Find a good time when you're both calm and let him know how you feel. Also, give him a chance to speak about the relationship from his point of view. Find that middle ground, Cisco. It's the only way ahead.'

'Thank you, Uncle Pavlov, but sometimes compromise is not what you want to hear. I know Slim hasn't played away in the real sense, but I feel sidelined all the same. When am I going to read a column from you that advises a girl to get *even*?'

Hesitantly, Pavlov said, 'When you write the next one for me.'

The way he slipped this in made me laugh. 'Are you saying I need to find my own solution to the problem here?'

My brother extended a finger at the statistics on the screen. 'If

Slim could just master this game, there wouldn't be a problem. At the very least he'd get it out of his system. At best, we'd be a million dollars richer.'

'The way he plays it,' I said, 'I'm not sure the money matters any more.'

'Well, if Slim can't master Misty, I doubt that anyone can. I hate to say it, but he's the best gamer there is. The only man for the job.'

I dwelled on his comment, then reached for the controls. 'Watch the screen,' I said.

'*The Money Shot* is one of the most touch-sensitive games on the market,' said Pavlov, sneering a bit too, just as the menu mixed to the opening scene: Misty at the foot of the cliff with her kit back on, just a moment away from being mauled by marauding porkers.

'Fasten your safety-belt,' I said, as the game began. 'We understand each other.'

'You reckon . . . *whooaaah*!'

My brother's jaw descended with every ledge that Misty reached. Midway up, pointing dumbstruck at the screen, he finally made it through a sentence. 'I never knew she could bust those kinds of moves.'

Another three-sixty side-somersault, followed up with a reverse pike flip. 'Call it female intuition,' I said.

'But what she's doing goes beyond all physical limitations.'

'If you're a guy, maybe. It's really just basic gymnastics.'

'Goes beyond my *fantasies*, too.'

I didn't like to say what I could make her do at the top. Instead, on reaching the summit successfully this time, I had Misty collect the handy pistol that happened to be lying at her feet, then turned her to face the panoramic vista. The camera spun round accordingly, chasing her rear end as if that was all there was to see. The glorious rendering of rainforest canopy and mountain ranges being secondary to the sculpted orbs that formed her backside – even though you could see most of it through the gap between her legs. In some ways, I thought, this was more voyeuristic than anything a webcam could offer.

'So what now?' I waited for my brother to refocus. 'Should I carry on without Slim?'

Pavlov looked at me, and I could see he was about to ask whether I was still talking about the game. When I didn't answer, he said, 'Slim's come a long way. It would be a shame, I think, if you were to leave him behind at this stage.'

My thumbs hovered over the control buttons. Misty at the cliff edge, her porn-star ponytail stirring in the breeze. The slightest touch from me, and it would all be over. Misty herself remained unfazed. I guess she was used to facing her maker. Biting the dust wasn't exactly a big deal for her, after all. I glanced at my brother, thought about Slim in her shoes. 'It's really not as hard as he thinks,' I said. 'Being committed is fine, but it takes consideration too.'

Pavlov scratched under his chin. 'A team talk is all he needs.'

'There you go again,' I said. 'You're so fucking reasonable. *Sparkle!* were mad to think you weren't still perfect for that job.'

'I mean a talk from me.'

I pulled back a little, digested what he had said. 'Do you think he'll listen?'

'Sure,' said Pavlov, 'providing I don't give him the agony spiel. No guy's going to listen to that. It's got to be something that cuts deep without making him feel like a plonker. A different language, almost.'

'Yeah? What language is that?'

'Bullshit, basically.'

'Oh, come on.'

'I said you wouldn't understand.' Pavlov returned his attention to the game, and now it was my turn to question whether he had been talking about *The Money Shot* all along. More so when he said, 'Slim has to learn to take stock of where he is, not simply push on regardless. Just like you have here.'

Although it was barely breakfast time for Pavlov and me, the sun was on the wane with Misty. Out across the bosom of this digital earth, flocks of flamingo could be seen gliding over the treetops. Even their shadows had been considered, as had the mist that fringed the distant mountain shapes. I pictured the game's designer sitting at his screen with a white robe and a trailing beard, a geek God before his online creation. One with Eves all over the shop, and not an Adam in sight.

Pavlov was right. There was just so much to take in.

I was focused on Misty, but still thinking about Slim, wondering how he might see things after Pavlov had spoken to him. I glanced up at the cam, wishing I could get the view from the outside. Then again, what did the web-watchers know? They could probably make a decision about which shade of lipstick I should wear for work, or bitch about my eating habits, but the bigger issues went beyond them. Misty, meanwhile, continued to survey the course of her achievement so far. It seemed unfair to let Slim drift downstairs and find I had beaten him at his own game. With this in mind, it was with mixed emotions that I volunteered her to step into the abyss.

'Ouch.' My brother grimaced at the tapering shriek that followed, and so did I when the picture shuddered to the sound of her impact. Somewhere far below, a herd of sadistic swine could be heard receiving second helpings. Pavlov stood up, and smoothed down his shirt – buttercup yellow today. 'Cruel but kind,' he said. 'You did the right thing, Cisco. Now let me do my bit. I'll talk to him, let him know that you need a little more TLC. It'll be better coming from me. Don't worry.'

'When you care about the issues,' I said, 'you give good advice.' I tossed aside the joypad, then followed my brother from the sofa pleased that I had achieved something significant so early in the day.

'Does that mean you'll help me with this week's questions?' he asked.

'Because you don't care about them?'

'No,' he said, 'because I don't know how to show that I care like you do. At least, not since my job went on the line.'

'For crying out loud, Pavlov, you're not too old to give advice in a teen magazine.'

'I'm over the hill,' he stressed, 'and after the reception your column got it seems I'm also too male.' My brother turned his attention to the dormant ticker. 'If you write it up before office hours I can be fairly sure my editor won't be watching.'

'How?'

'I have a hunch,' he said, and narrowed his gaze.

Now it was my turn to glance at the ticker, though I still couldn't see what it had told him. 'You'd better show me to the problems,' I said. 'Looking at things from a boy's point of view is getting to be enlightening.'

28

'How do you make CDs stick to your nipples?'

'Too weird.'

'Is clitoral piercing safe?'

'Too wild.'

'I yearn to sleep with my cousin!'

'Too rural. *Sparkle!* is very metropolitan in its outlook.'

This was in Pavlov's bedroom. Every problem I picked out, it seemed my brother had a reason why I couldn't answer it. We were sitting in front of his workstation at the time, our backs turned to the webcam. Pavlov only sifted through the email submissions. He didn't like to touch the letters – not since the youth with the itching anxiety. The one who had asked him to identify the mite Sellotaped to the corner of the page. Along with a strand of pubic hair.

'Okay, how about this: I'm obsessed with Britney.'

'That's not a problem,' said Pavlov. 'It never troubles me.'

'I had a thing about Kylie once, but I think I just admired her and got a bit confused about my feelings.'

'Even so, you mustn't tell Slim. He'll never sleep again.'

I glanced at the time in the corner of the screen, wondered whether he would even *surface* before I went to work. Then my brother pointed out that the Britney crush question came from a boy, as had many others.

'Really?' I said. 'Like what?'

'The piercing one, for a start,' said Pavlov. 'He was worried about what it might do to his manhood if his girlfriend went ahead and got it done.'

'Is clitoral piercing safe *for him*?' I had only scanned the first line of the question. Had I read it in full, I would've hit the delete button. 'How self-absorbed is that?'

Pavlov shrugged. 'The problems from boys always boil down to their dicks.'

I scrutinised the screen once more. 'I assumed only girls wrote in to a magazine like *Sparkle!*.'

'You'd be surprised. Loads of problems come in from readers' boyfriends or their brothers. They see the mag lying around the house, scan the agony page when nobody's looking, and fire off their problems.'

'What's wrong with their magazines?' I asked. 'Why can't they seek advice there?'

'What magazines?' he asked. 'If you're under sixteen and you have a problem with your computer hard drive, your drum machine, or your model train, then fine. There are titles with expert panels who can help. But if you're after the male equivalent of the girl's teen titles, one that addresses *personal* issues, forget it. Boys just can't be seen to buy that kind of gear, so the industry doesn't go there.'

'I see.' I was scrolling down the emails now, looking for a female name. 'But you don't actually feature boys' problems on your page. These lads must be desperate if they write in knowing they're not even going to see an answer.' Pavlov's silence seemed to confirm things. I wondered how it had been for him as a teenager, but didn't like to go any deeper in case that's what had shaped the man. 'How about this one?' I said, and stopped scrolling. 'This is one I always wondered about: Why do guys *always* want girls to swallow?'

Pavlov read the email for himself. 'Keeps the sheets clean, I guess.'

'Somehow I think that's a reason held by nobody but you.'

'Nutritionally, it's not so bad.'

'As too many men have tried to convince me.' I remained unimpressed.

'You get protein,' he went on, 'enzymes, zinc and vitamin C. Plus it's only five calories per serving.'

I gave him a moment to retract his statement – at the very least his use of the word 'serving'. But my brother was looking at me like he'd just sold a miracle slimming aid with one hand on the Bible.

'Next you'll be telling me it makes a great face pack.'

'It does.' He seemed almost affronted by my cynicism. 'Some guys swear it works like an aftershave, too. A dab behind each ear and—'

'*Stop!*' I showed him my palm. 'I might never date again.'

'Aftershave isn't for everyone,' he conceded. 'Anyway, it's still not something I can address in the agony column. I'm a teen love surgeon, not an adult sex therapist.'

'But we've been through loads of questions here. It doesn't matter who they're from, sex is the main concern.'

'The magazine's advertisers worry about it too,' he said. 'That's why I can't deal with problems like that. It's the fluffy stuff they want from me.'

'Don't girls write in about romance?'

'Of course,' he said, 'but it's always the same thing: How do I ask him out? Why does he blow hot and cold? What can I do to be sure he'll stay faithful? And you try answering that one without mentioning sex.'

'So what do you do for variety?' I asked. 'Make them up?' When Pavlov didn't say anything, I began to question his integrity. 'The problem about roots being a turn-on for a man, it came from *you*?'

'That one was genuine,' he ventured, but stopped short of naming Slim as the one who couldn't get it figured for himself.

I drew his attention back to the long list of emails in front of us. 'These girls are crying out for important sex advice and you're *ignoring* them? God help the boys, but don't let everyone down.'

'What can I do? I have an obligation to deliver fresh dilemmas every month that won't offend the people who pay the cheques.'

'You have an obligation to your audience,' I said, selecting the oral question. 'If anything you'll be empowering them by addressing

197

these issues. Next time one of your readers is cuddling up to her boyfriend and feels his hands push down on her head, she'll feel better about resisting the pressure.'

'Cisco, if I deliver an explicit question like that my editor might sack me on the spot.'

'He might,' I agreed, 'but he'll sack you for sure if he finds out that it's me behind your advice.'

'But you can't deliver an agony column where all the problems are genuine,' he argued. 'It would be so, so ... *unprofessional.*'

'Okay,' I said, 'I'll compromise. Oral sex stays, and I'll make up a couple of relationship questions for you.'

'Such as?'

'My boyfriend's behaving like he's seeing someone else.'

'Now that is a good question.' He smiled. 'Somehow I feel confident you can give a good answer too. What's the other one?'

I reached across the desk for the aquarium, lifting off the handkerchief that covered it. 'He hates my present.'

I held it in front of the monitor. Lit from behind, the algae-ridden water brightened into something more like pickling vinegar.

'It doesn't look good, I accept that.'

Cheek to cheek with my brother, I was reminded of how we were as as kids in front of jam jars brimming with pond life. The big difference being this wasn't pond life we were looking at here. This was primordial. A soup so fetid I could barely see through to the other side. And yet, despite the lifeless state of the water, I had the ominous sense that something in there was watching us.

'The water purifier might've helped,' I reflected. 'The poor things.'

Bubbles appeared from the depths, wobbling to the surface like a fart in the bath.

'The growth powder went down well,' said Pavlov, optimistically.

'I bet. What did you give them? A pinch every other day?'

'To begin with,' he replied. 'Then I got scared and tipped the lot in so they wouldn't go hungry if I left them alone for a while.'

'You got *scared*? Of what?'

'Infection.'

This time I responded with a little less sympathy. 'What we're looking at here, it's not water from the Ebola river. The box said it was suitable for six-year-olds. There's no reason to be frightened.'

'Let me see *you* take the lid off.'

I jiggled the aquarium, just enough to make the water slosh and turn, and the pair of us snapped back smartly when two loch-like specimens yawned in and out of view. Still passing for fish poo, but with bigger eyes and wraith-like faces. 'They don't look like this on the packaging,' I said.

'Cisco, they don't look like anything on *earth*.'

It had only been a fleeting glimpse, but I was rattled just knowing that something was in there – most probably watching us.

'How about Kenzo?' I suggested. 'He owns an aquatic centre. Maybe you could take them there for advice.'

'Have you seen the place?' Pavlov's tone led me to believe it was probably something I wouldn't have forgotten in a hurry. He took the mouse, opened up his web browser and tapped in a web address. 'His homepage is about as close as I'll go.'

And I could see why. A site that opened up in black was never a good sign. The copperplate lettering that spelled out The Fish Eye reminded me of old curiosity shops that nobody ever dared visit. Then a grid appeared on the page. A webcam gallery, I realised, as the empty frames began to fill.

'Feeds from his tanks,' my brother said. 'It's mostly so Kenzo can keep watch on things when he's away torturing tenants with fish hooks and gaffs.'

'Funny guy,' I said, deadpan, though any hint of humour was lost to the more immediate spectacle on the screen. Imagine the opening credits to *The Brady Bunch*, but with the ugliest fish in each frame. That was what I found myself gawping at: bloated, whiskery things in a state of suspension, so it seemed. The kind of catch most anglers would tip back into the water and then head for the pub with the story under their hats.

'Kenzo is a collector of rare breeds.'

'I'm so glad they're not commonplace. Doesn't he have plain goldfish in stock?'

Pavlov scrolled down the page, revealing a window at the bottom that spanned the screen. It was host to another webcam, and the feed revealed a tank with a small shark circling inside it. 'Not something your average cat would attempt to scoop out with its paw,' my brother observed, 'although I'd like to see one try.'

'Is that allowed?' I asked, watching this sleek destroyer trace a helix through the water. 'Who would want a shark for a pet?'

'I don't believe that one's for sale,' he said. 'It's what Willie told me anyway.'

'Still,' I said, with a fleeting glimpse at Pavlov's own Jurassic pot, 'Kenzo might be able to do something with the Sea Maidens.'

Turning his attention to me now, he said, 'Do we care enough about them?'

I drummed my fingers on the desk, wondering what Darwin would've made of our conundrum, whether he had deliberately left out species like this from his seminal tome in case they put readers off. Compromised the sales potential, stuff like that.

'So what would you like to do?' I asked. 'I don't mind if you want to get rid of them. I only bought them to cheer you up, but I can see they might have an opposite effect.'

Reluctantly, my brother took the aquarium into his possession. 'The toilet?'

'Cruel but kind,' I replied. 'In the absence of a cliff edge.'

Moving into the dead zone now, my brother said, 'This column I have to deliver, the boy's view, I don't suppose there's any chance you could answer *every* question before you go to work?'

I faced the monitor, and sighed like a builder constructing a quote.

'What do you reckon?' He stopped there, working on an estimate of his own. 'How about we make an early start every day this week?'

I repeated his suggestion, playing him for a beat before shooing him away.

'Go flush the fishes,' I said. 'I'll have it wrapped by the time you get back.'

And I did. This agony thing was easy. The blowjob dilemma virtually answered itself: next time a guy gets you to go down on him, I advised the girl, don't spit or swallow, *share*. Come back with a loaded kiss, and give him a taste of his own medicine. The issue about the unwanted present wasn't a problem at all, more a springboard for me to launch into an attack on men who refused to appreciate a gift unless they could drink it, watch it or hang it from a tool belt. It was the last one I had to think about.

The relationship question that came from the heart.

She hadn't been dating her boyfriend for long, this one said. In fact, she had pretty much moved in on the first date. It had taken a moment of madness to make her realise how much he meant to her, but the fact that she was in love with this guy now threatened to come between them. Why? I knew the answer to that one, living as I did with a virtual peephole in every room. Because the more you see of that special someone, the less you understand them. Anyway, this girl was locked in tight, and if it turned out that her boyfriend wasn't in there one hundred per cent it would pull her apart. That's why she was angry with herself, that's why she was scared, and that's why she was seeking advice from an expert.

Of course, she didn't say all this in the question, especially not the bit about the botched bank job. With a thirty-word limit imposed on all problems, it basically ended up sounding like a relationship that risked burning out because it had started off too quickly. Which was why I couldn't face answering it.

'Don't worry about that one.' I surfaced from my thoughts to find that my brother had returned from his mission to lose the

Sea Maidens. 'If I can't answer it,' he said, and returned the rinsed aquarium to the back of his desk, 'I know someone who can.'

He'd have to wake him with a bucket of cold water first, I thought, glancing at my watch. It was time I left for work, which came as something of a relief. 'I have to go,' I said. 'Tell Slim I said goodbye.'

'We'll have that chat,' my brother assured me. 'He'll listen.'

I moved over the red line to peck my brother on the cheek. Even if he did wipe it away as I headed downstairs, at least he knew that someone cared. Which couldn't be said for everyone, I realised as I left the house a few minutes later. For as I pulled the door shut behind me, I swore I heard another one creak open upstairs and figured it must be Slim. Had he been awake all this time? Tuned into Pavlov's bedroom courtesy of his laptop and Despair-Direct? Maybe he had even read the screen over my shoulder, waiting until it was safe to come out. I turned to face the flower market, picking up the pace once I'd snapped the gate shut behind me.

29

Sometimes you can step outside and feel as if the whole world is looking at you strangely. Bad hair days are often to blame. Hangovers too. Or those times when you creep out of some guy's flat without waking him because you can't remember his name. The walk of shame, that's what it was, and even though I wasn't wearing a cocktail dress to work I still picked up on the classic signs: the stolen glances from strangers, the small talk in my wake. Usually it was down to paranoia, but as my house was wired up with webcams I had good reason to think I was being watched.

It started with Sweet. The florist on the far side, breaking off from a customer to squint across at me. I carried on walking, swinging my bag from one shoulder to the other. I was in a huff about Slim, mostly. Resigned to the fact that it would cast a cloud across the length of my day. So when the funny looks continued I swivelled round and took it out on the wrong person. '*What?*' I snapped. 'Is there a problem?'

For a second Willie seemed taken aback, only to put a crease in his waist and show me the seat of his ample sweatpants. 'Your dress!' he bawled, and the crowd seemed to part so his voice could reach me. '*You got your dress tucked up in your knickers.*'

I was still blushing as I came out of the flower market. There were fewer people around at this end of Columbia Road, but I was just as sensitive to my surroundings, picking up on things like the slate grey Morris Traveller. The one parked facing into the sunshine up ahead. I couldn't be sure it was the one from the night before. Back then it had been too dark to determine the colour, and now it was too bright to see who was sitting inside. That is, if anyone was inside at all. The glare against the windshield was so intense it hurt to look. I picked up the pace, still trying to steal a glimpse, but my eyes began to smart. A teardrop coming down that could've been followed by more had I dwelled on recent events. That was how vulnerable I felt as I distanced myself from the house, heading for the bus stop on the high street because I couldn't hack a journey by tube. Too many faces in my personal space, with nowhere to turn for air.

A small queue had formed at the stop. Nobody seemed to notice when I joined it, apart from the pinstripe in front of me who seemed to shrink away – but, then, I was looking a little emotional, struggling not to sniff too much or throw myself into his shoulder and beg to be hugged. Strange, I thought, that people don't want to know when you really need some attention. Men were the most reluctant. The ones least likely to step across the dividing line that showed they had a heart. And the stupid thing was they had a boundless capacity for passion and feeling and love, but you had to be in the same zone before they truly opened up.

In a bid to get a grip, I reminded myself that Slim and I had been together for a matter of weeks. By rights I should have been able to climb out of the relationship, towel myself down emotionally, and take stock of things from the side. Instead I felt like I was already in the deep end, depending on him to keep me afloat. Why? Because Slim wore my scrunchies and my Alice bands, and I had never met a guy so relaxed about that. He could deal with my brother, too, and my crazy ideas to find money fast, and no other man I knew would rob a bank on my behalf. But ultimately it was because we had been through hard times. That was what united us. What was tearing us apart was technology: the cameras that covered our rent and the online game with a hidden million. The things designed to enhance the way we lived our lives.

It was a white-van man who brought me out of myself, some idiot leaning on his horn as he whizzed by the bus stop, leering at me as if I should be grateful. At least Slim wasn't *that* inconsiderate, I thought, and for a moment I found myself at the front of the queue instead of the back. All this attention made me feel like I was breathing the wrong mix of air. I couldn't even taste the exhaust fumes being laid out left and right, which was worrying because I could see slashed veils of the stuff hanging over the tarmac. Wondering if I looked as detached as I felt, I turned to find my reflection some place, and promptly found myself fuelling the gasp that followed with whatever I could bring into my lungs. For it wasn't my reflection that came into focus but the tanks behind the glass and the sign with the copperplate lettering.

'The Fish Eye,' I said, under my breath, gazing at the waterborne leviathans I had witnessed via webcam earlier that morning. The place itself looked like an old electrical store. The difference being it wasn't old tellies stacked up on racks in the window. The beasts on display appeared bigger than they had on the screen, even more bloated and blotchy, each one just hanging there in different shades of silted water, some with weeds and some with nothing but rocks. I had no idea what kind of specimens I was looking at, but they all looked like bottom feeders to me.

I left my place in the queue for a closer look, intrigued at finding this place for real. More so when I noted the miniature cameras mounted on the rim of each tank. The way they had been positioned made me think of kingfishers braced to strike into the water. Resting my hands on my knees now, I peered in low between two racks. There were tanks tiled along every wall, but it was the long one at the back that drew my attention. Especially when I saw something sleek and grey turning in it.

'Cor,' I said to myself, 'it's Jaws Junior.' I cupped my hands to the glass for a better look, just as the owner himself crossed in front of the shark. Kenzo was frowning into the phone, an old-style receiver with a cable that yawed out from the counter in the far corner. The man consulting with his paymaster most probably. Discussing what to do if we tried to leap out of our own bowl. With so many tanks in the window, what little light that made it through quivered eerily on the walls. I could see why Pavlov didn't fancy paying a visit to

205

this place. Kenzo seemed quite at home in there, however. Feeding his stock with his free hand, dropping in flakes like seasoning. The fish responded well to him, which made me wonder whether I had been wrong about my assumptions. Maybe it wasn't Cartier he was talking to, maybe it was his mum, or perhaps he was making a charity donation. I was only looking in after all, and appearances could be deceptive, as I knew from experience. I got so wrapped up in the idea that I might have been passing judgement a bit too quickly of late that it took me a moment to realise Kenzo had noticed me. The man with the bad tattoos cutting out of his phone conversation just as I registered his face. He must have wondered what was with me when I spun away from the shop. Carried round by a sharp intake of pollution, then a longer exhalation as the bus arrived to sweep me into the day.

At work people were on the lookout too. But, then, I was temping in a profession where people earned a living like that. Not that anyone made it obvious between the hours of ten and twelve. Dark glasses all morning were compulsory in the modelling industry, unless you worked behind the reception desk as I did. It was the bookers and the agents who fascinated me – the way they always came in scanning both sides of the lobby without turning their heads. The models themselves picked up on it, I could tell, because they made every effort not to notice. I found it both distracting and compelling, the way we watched each other without being seen ourselves. It was only when I caught these people clocking me that my insight fell away. Maybe I'd been brooding about Slim too much, because I was obviously giving off some commanding vibes – with all the double-takes I was receiving and the looks that lasted just a beat too long, I began to think of myself as a human photo-fit. A composite of familiar features unrecognisable as a real person.

Days before, I had felt capable of pulling off a bank robbery without anybody knowing. Now I couldn't even fix my hair without someone making a mental note of it. The one time I reached for the grips, this woman glanced across from the sofa. Despite the retro shades, I knew she was taking me in because her head tipped to one side. I placed her in her late fifties, although I had never seen skin so flawless, or cheekbones so pronounced. She wore a plain silk headscarf that made her look older but more graceful with it. I didn't notice that she was smiling until she took off her sunglasses and crossed towards the desk, looking at me like she'd discovered something, and for a beat I thought I had made it. Paris or New York, I thought. Was that where she planned to take me? Then she opened her mouth and nothing of the sort came out. 'I have a meeting upstairs in five, and I'd like you to make some calls for me.'

She reached across for my notepad and pen, scratched out a long set of digits. 'This is the number for my flight tonight. I want you to confirm the reservation is for club class, and insist on a seat at least three rows clear of any children. The number underneath will get you my husband's office. Call and tell him the wolfhound needs walking this evening. That's if he doesn't have other dogs to entertain while I'm away.' I think she must have mistaken my sagging expression for something like empathy, because she came down from her high-flying instructions and leaned in like she was my best mate all of a sudden. 'I'm sure you can handle him. If he gives you any bullshit, tell him I'm on an open return.'

'Of course,' I said sweetly, wondering if she would like me to drop round later and cook his meals. Maybe even blow the guy so he didn't feel the need to stray. I scanned the number she had just given me. The same number was printed at the top of my payslips, I realised. It belonged to my philandering middleman at the temping agency. I looked up, primed to ruin his wife's day, only to remind myself why I couldn't afford to lose this job. The rent was no longer an issue, but if the general public had to take liberties with me it was easier to handle out here than in my own home. My smile was beginning to make my mouth ache at the corners, so I folded away the paper and said, 'I'll take care of it right away.'

'I'm sure you will,' she said, and slotted her shades back on. It was the knowing look she offered over the rim that left me wondering if she was already aware of the connection I had here. 'You look like a girl I can trust.'

30

Bleeding Rose was absent from her room when I turned up at the hospital. The traction frame had gone too, but I knew she hadn't been discharged because her Jackie Collins was on the pillow. She couldn't be far away, I thought, and set off along the corridor to find her.

I had decided to drop in on my way home from work. I was tired, but it wasn't sleep I needed – I was tired of being read for all the wrong reasons: first the florist, then the fright outside the fish shop, and finally the full hour of phone calls it had taken to settle the affairs of a woman I gathered was a major talent scout. That's what I heard on the grapevine, at any rate, and it just about summed up my life. The girl behind the girl, that's who I was. First with Misty, and now with the models. I felt like a good book busting to get out of a lousy jacket. I wanted to be opened up and *understood*. That was why I didn't head home straight away. Choosing instead to visit someone I could rely on to look at me and read between the lines.

The corridor took me past a little garden just outside the ward. It was a suntrap of a square with grass and shrubs and wheelchairs angled randomly with each other. A nurse was out there with the patients, but only one had a florist and dealer for company. I hung back behind the glass door, unsure what I might be interrupting. Bleeding Rose had her crook leg in a cast still, and a magnificent bouquet of parrot tulips on her lap. The floral equivalent of flames, wrapped up tight with a twist. The nurse moved among the wheelchairs just then. Medication time, I realised, watching the cat burglar slip a hand between the blooms when nobody was looking.

Sweet William was sitting on his hands beside her chair, his knees tucked up like a little boy. A very big little boy. So big, in fact, that I wondered if he would ever get up again. He'd done something with his hair, I noticed too, put in a side parting that was struggling to return to the wild. But what really grabbed me was the way he kept looking up at her when he thought she wasn't watching him. He reminded me of a St Bernard – trustworthy to the end, but so damn melancholy it hurt to have him around.

Part of me wanted to push through the door and shake some sense into the man, urge him to relax and *tell* her what was going on inside his head. Nice nails or not, if he didn't open up he risked losing her. I even closed my hand around the exit bar, but I didn't take it any further. How could I? Invading their space like that, and with my own agenda? So I doubled back down the corridor instead, leaving Sweet William to sort out his life while I tracked down a phone booth to settle my own.

It was Pavlov who picked up. I was relieved it wasn't Slim, but at the same time just a little disappointed. 'Have you spoken to him yet?'

'Give me a chance, Cisco.'

I came further into the phone booth, hunkering under the Perspex hood as if I had a thing about emergency sprinkler systems. 'But you promised,' I persisted. 'Is Slim with you now?'

'He's just been crushed to death by a rockfall, if that's what you mean. So, yeah, he's with me until he hits restart.'

'Then go for it,' I implored him, 'you and Slim. It's really important to me.' A clacking sound came down the line: my brother opening his mouth before he knew what he was going to say. So I got in again, just in case he was going to change his mind. 'I'm depending on you, Pavlov.'

'And I'll do it,' he insisted, sounding defensive now. 'It's bad enough I get grief from the ticker all day, please don't make it worse for me.'

'Are you still being pestered?'

'Put it this way, if I'm in the front room and I drop something in the live zone then that's where it has to stay.'

'So leave it there,' I said. 'Do something more rewarding. A team talk, perhaps.'

'There's a time and a place,' he replied, a little frostily. 'And a way.'

I considered what I had just said and apologised for being so snappy. 'It's just been on my mind since I left for work. Everywhere I go I think I'm being watched, and I just want to come home to a house where I can relax. At least I know when I'm under surveillance there.'

'I'm surprised you got out at all.'

'Eh?'

'This morning,' said Pavlov, 'an hour after you left, I was on my way out to buy some milk when I found a mound of pizza flyers on the doormat. The letterbox itself was so rammed I wondered whether the world outside had been submerged under a sea of cheaply printed menus.'

'Must be a price war,' I suggested.

'More like a siege,' he said. 'I tried to open the door and it jammed from underneath. I had to open a new bin bag to clear them away. Can you believe that? Slim thinks it's the rivals to Poppa Italiano, trying to curry favour so Cartier switches sponsors.'

'Curry pizza? That's a good idea. It would be like two take-outs for the price of one.'

For a moment Pavlov didn't say anything. I pictured my brother, wondering why I had just been so flippant, and then reviewing his rant for an answer.

'All right,' he relented. 'I'll talk to him, but the flyer situation is another issue that needs addressing.'

'I know,' I said, smiling into the receiver. 'We'll put one of those signs up forbidding free sheets and salesmen and stuff.'

'Signs on doors are no good,' he said. 'If the kids in the street see that, we'll end up with turds through the letterbox and all sorts. The only way to make a change is by talking to these people directly.'

'You do that,' I said. There was no need to add that I had Slim in mind. I just gave him time to work it out before saying, 'I'm relying on you, Pavlov.'

God knows when Sweet William had lumbered by, but he was gone when I returned to the garden. There was only one way out of the hospital from here, and it would've taken him past the phone booth. I dwelled on this, and found myself checking my bag before I walked out into the sunshine – making sure he hadn't dropped something into it while my back was turned. A sign that someone was looking out for me.

'*Cisco*, look at you! In the flesh again at last.'

Bleeding Rose didn't say this so much as bawl it like she was sitting in the bleachers. The headphones she was wearing explained this startling response when all I'd done was amble up and say hi. For the umpteenth time that day, people turned to check me out. I ducked down beside her wheelchair, took the place on the grass flattened out by Sweet. Rose was all bound up in a plum silk dressing-gown with a silver sash and a dash of ash down one side of her lapel. She squeezed a smile at me, the cigarette between her lips lifting into the horizontal, then popped off her phones. The cat burglar seemingly oblivious to all the attention she had attracted.

'What are you listening to?' I asked. 'Would I like it?'

The lead trailed towards the tulips on her lap. It was then I realised she didn't have a Walkman underneath but a notebook computer. It was closed up like a clamshell, and I figured that whatever music was coming out of it had probably been nicked via the net. Then Rose put a name to the tune, and that was enough to restore my full attention.

'The theme to *ER*,' she said, 'plus the incidental music from the first series.'

I waited for the real answer, then realised she had just given it to me.

'You're listening to that?' I paused to take in our surroundings. 'In *hospital*?'

'It blunts the boredom,' she said, and pinched the dog end from her mouth. 'Makes me think this is an exciting place to be. On that show there's always a drama unfolding. Here, the only thing unfolding is the sheets.'

'Right,' I said, and wondered what it would take for me to get into her mindset. 'So I guess this means you're keen to get out?'

'Keen?' Rose reached for her wheels, braced to rev the chair. 'I'm going *crazy* in here, honey, waiting to get discharged.' She tapped her cast. I noticed she'd been using a pencil on it to cross off the days. 'Once the shell comes off,' she went on, 'I'm back on the rooftops. Doing what I do.'

'Don't do it,' I said, with some conviction. 'Crime doesn't always pay.'

'Willie won't like it, but I can't ignore my calling.'

I turned to her flowers, and said how nice it was to have someone who cared for her. Wasn't that enough?

She shrugged. 'Maybe.'

'*Rose!*' I was almost scandalised. 'You know damn well how he feels about you. He's really making an effort with himself just so you'll notice. Look at his nails. It took a lot of courage for him to get them sorted.'

'I know. I watched you shine them for him.' All it took was a wink, and once again Bleeding Rose brought home to me how public a slice of my life had become. I knew bits and bobs had been caught on cam, of course I did, but I never considered that I might be held accountable for it. For a short while I just sat there as Sweet William had, legs crossed, pulling up grass, unable to look at her directly. 'What else have you seen?' I asked.

'I saw virtually everything this morning,' she replied, 'until you left for work.'

'Then I should tell you what a day I've had—'

'No need. I can tell it's been a dog.'

213

'You can?'

'Sweet might be a little shy with his effort to win me over,' she said, 'but he's there for me when I'm at my most vulnerable, unlike a lot of guys.'

Guys like Slim? That's who Bleeding Rose was comparing him with and that's what she confirmed when I asked her outright. 'Willie said you had your doubts about him.'

'For someone who spends all day in female company, honey, he has a lot to learn about the opposite sex.'

I thought about my attempt to play *The Money Shot*, but didn't feel Rose needed to know that I had managed to make Misty's clothes come off.

'You know, that game isn't so hard,' I said instead. 'I took Misty Ventura about as high as she could go.'

'And then you let her drop.'

Which was what my heart did next – for a beat, at least, as I asked myself how the hell she could have known that just by watching me at play on the sofa. The webcam was mounted above the screen, after all. I searched her expression for clues then realised it was what she had done with me when I was sitting on the sofa. Picked up on the way I had responded to my fortune with Misty and drawn her conclusions from that. It had been the same with Slim the night before. The TV might have been in the dead zone beneath the cam, but I had been able to see what was going on because it was written all over his face.

'Now you've got me thinking,' I said. 'Jesus, I suppose with a little imagination the viewer can get a *whole* extra perspective on things.'

She didn't respond – not with words, at any rate, but wheels. The patient reversing on to the path, leading the way to her private room, she said, where we could log on to my public house in private.

'Too many people out here,' she said, and glanced at her fellow patients. Most of them were dozing in their own wheelchairs, however, slowly deflating or, quite probably, dead. At least, that's how they looked to me, all folded up in their chairs with their heads hovering over their laps. I really didn't consider it a problem, I told her, but Rose was insistent. Said she always surfed behind closed doors because of what she enjoyed looking up.

'Pornography?' I asked, as we reached her room. Rose seemed quietly amused by my assumption. 'That's for the boys.' She lifted her laptop on to the bed and opened it up like a chest of treasure. 'The webcam sites that turn me on have very different works of art in them.'

Bleeding Rose used a skeleton key to ease out the cable from the bedside phone. The connector didn't look as if it was meant to come out at all, so I shut the door on the corridor while she slotted it into the back of her laptop. I even closed the curtains, certain that I was about to witness something illegal. By the time I came back with a plastic chair we were all wired up to the web, her browser locked on to the front façade of some stately-looking home. One from her folder of favourites, no doubt, going by the way she had selected it so swiftly.

'Now, this gets me hot.' Rose's face seemed to shine when she said this, but it wasn't all down to screen glare. 'It's great that people are so keen to throw open their doors online. It makes my job just that little bit easier.' There was a menu at the foot of the screen, and each button took Rose to a different part of the house. It was in the drawing room that I realised why she was here: the cat burglar was casing the joint from cyberspace.

'Does this mean you've been watching our place with a view to *robbing* us?'

She cackled at this in a high-tar, unfiltered way. 'Honey, I never rob from my own.'

I wasn't sure what this said about our social standing, or the state of our place, but then she pulled out of the big house and I realised I would soon be able to judge that with my own eyes. 'My brother's in right now,' I said, 'talking to Slim, I hope.'

'Let's see, shall we? I've been busting to have a word with him myself.' Rose stabbed the return key. 'Your boyfriend needs to sort himself out,' she said, 'and I don't just mean with a haircut.'

The welcome screen began to build, completed now with links

to all our sponsors. I found myself blushing – not just because it was so weird to have someone talk about my life as if it was a soap plot, but because we weren't exactly looking at a website backed by Microsoft and Nike.

caminside.co.uk

Fine living spaces for fun-loving people

The show home is now open

(no appointment necessary)

Hall	Poppa Italiano Pizzeria
Front room	The Air Police (lemon)
Kitchen	Sink Terrier Bleach Products
Landing	The Air Police (lavender)
Bedroom 1	Ridge Runner Inc.
Bedroom 2	Despair-Direct

chat   message   register

'These sponsors,' she said. 'Do you use any of them?'

I was about to say that Slim and I didn't rate the condoms, but the thought sank into my stomach before I could spit it out. So I told her the pizza sometimes, but never the freshener or the helpline because both would make my eyes water. Rose sympathised, adding that Sweet William packed that brand of bleach whenever she called him out on a clean-up operation.

'He'd make a good house share,' I remarked.

Rose moved her cursor down the menu. Then she glanced across at me, and I thought she was going to ask if I was sitting comfortably. Instead, she said, 'Let's see how yours are shaping up.'

It was strange, seeing our front room without being in the house. That the site was devoid of sound made it all the more unusual. Even on the visual front there wasn't much to appreciate. An empty sofa with a gaming magazine splayed over the arm, and a mug on the carpet next to the keyboard. In the background the late sun was fanning through the bay window, just as it was in the hospital. Here it was defined by the heat on my back, at home by the glittering shoal of dust. I didn't think The Air Police would be happy about that, and wondered whether I might return to find the door smashed open and the place smelling synthetically fragrant. I turned to Rose, wondering what she made of it all. 'Sorry about the mess,' I said.

'Don't apologise.' She seemed almost amused. 'It's what makes it real.'

Even if this was supposed to be a slice of everyday life, I still wished Slim would tidy up a bit more, or at least confine his slacker habits to the dead zone. That would be an improvement. Then I wondered whether he had done just that, and pictured two shores of rubbish on either side of the lemon-scented room. As Rose switched into the hall, I realised I was doing exactly what we had just discussed outside. Making assumptions based on what I *couldn't* see. Right now, I was looking at an empty hall wondering where Slim was hiding out and whether my brother was living up to his promise.

'Try the kitchen,' I said. 'We do a lot of talking in the kitchen.'

'Let's hope it's an improvement on the cooking,' she said, and clicked from one cam into the next. 'Slim should never be allowed in there alone.'

'It was only a stir-fry,' I said, in his defence, but my attention turned to the feed that came through just then: for the boys could be seen facing each other across the table, but only Pavlov was properly visible. Slim was little more than a nose and chin, the extremities of his profile, with the occasional flash of brow ring. I couldn't tell whether or not he was deliberately confining himself to the dead zone. Privately I hoped it was the force of Pavlov's argument that had him in retreat.

'At least they're talking,' I said. 'Do you think he's getting through?'

Rose didn't need to answer, because Pavlov folded his arms just then and slumped back in his seat. Slim had obviously come back at him with something, because a hand dropped down on his side of the screen and began to heft the air. He was articulating something heavy, it seemed to me, while my brother pinched the ridge of his nose and nodded solemnly. Watching this silent scene play out, I immediately assumed the worst and imagined Slim was saying he couldn't deal with this minor crisis of mine. That I was too pushy, too paranoid and could learn a trick or two from Misty. What he was saying was all in my head, but it didn't stop me going cold. A sudden, shocking shift in body temperature like being in the shower when someone messes with the taps elsewhere in the house.

'This is worse than knowing nothing,' I said finally. 'All I'm doing is putting words into their mouths that I don't want to hear.'

I looked at Rose, caught her considering the keys and not the screen, her mouth bunched to one side, like she wasn't sure where to go next. Then she turned my way, and compassion came into her expression, that pitying smile you get from someone when you're about to hear bad news. 'What I said to you this morning,' she said, 'about there being more to the game than meets the eye?'

I blinked at her, and returned to that moment in the front room, to my earlier misgivings about her insight into my playing ability. 'You weren't talking about *The Money Shot*, were you?'

Bleeding Rose flattened her lips. 'Honey, I was talking about a lot of things.'

Instinctively I faced the screen again, still questioning what she meant by this, but sure somehow that I was looking in the right direction. Slim's disembodied hand continued to chastise my brother, but it was impossible to suss what was going on. Short of being in the house, there was no way *caminside* could offer that kind of access, which was when I found myself looking at the scene like a thief – wondering if there was another way in. I turned to Rose again, aware that I was closing in on her outlook. 'There's a bigger picture here, isn't there?'

She answered me first by reaching for the keyboard, and I knew now where this was going. 'I think it's best you watch.'

So I did. I watched and wondered. It was all I could do, in fact, as Rose summoned up another website, a site that looked just like the last but with a very different view of the same scene. Watching now from directly *over* the kitchen table. Wondering how many more cams Cartier had secretly squirrelled away.

'This isn't happening,' I said, almost tripping over the words. 'This isn't *caminside. What is this?*

'Your landlord's second site.' Bleeding Rose sighed before she spoke, as if her conscience was glad to be shot of it. She directed her mouse to the navigation bar. It was split into a grid, the squares numbered one to thirty, and the selection she made lit up like neon. At the same time the picture cut to the view from the clock on the shelf behind Pavlov. I knew because two blurred hands obscured the boys slightly, which just made the action beyond look even more off-limits.

'I can't believe what I'm seeing here!'

'Welcome to *camplicity.com*,' she said, and brought her hands away from the laptop like a bomb that had just been primed.

'Cam *what* dot com?'

'As in complicity,' she said, reluctantly stressing each syllable, sounding less like a mentor now but a friend who knew she had to hurt me before she could help. 'To be involved with others in an evil or illegal activity, such as the installation of secret web cameras inside a household duped into believing there's just one in selected rooms.'

I heard her right but I didn't take much in. How could I when Rose had put a full stop on her revelation with a single keystroke. One that completed the picture by bringing *sound* into the mix. Out of nowhere, I could hear my housemates in heated discussion. But not as Pavlov had promised. From this fresh perspective, I could see that the subject matter wasn't my feelings for Slim but a half-eaten Crème Egg in his possession, previously hidden

221

from shot but which he was now showing straight to camera. My boyfriend, the accidental presenter.

'Observe,' he said, through the laptop speaker, a voice that was all treble and no bass. He lifted the egg to his lips, the crown already consumed. 'It's all about where your tongue goes first. Does it go for the sweet fondant centre, which is the obvious draw, or the upper wall?'

'Slim, you're avoiding my question. I never asked about the egg.'

'Not an obvious choice, the wall, because you have to work at it before it melts. But when it does succumb,' Slim turned the egg as if it were a precious stone, 'the reward justifies all that extra effort.'

'Will you put it down for one second?' We were looking over his shoulder at the time but I just knew my brother was sprung tight inside. 'I'm talking about my sister here.'

'I know.'

'*Slim!* She's really upset about last night.'

'So I was working late,' he said dismissively. 'Big deal.'

'Call it work if you want,' said Pavlov, 'but please don't play your relationship like that. You're both on the same side, and she talks about you like this could go the distance.'

'You've spoken to Cisco? About us?'

'Outside the bank that time. Waiting for you to complete your comedy routine.'

'What did she say?'

'That she was in love with you.'

Slim seemed to think things through here. Whatever was behind the confectionery riff he had been running with, it appeared to fall away with a nod for my brother. 'I hear you,' he said, and I heard him too. Wishing I could walk through that kitchen door right now and slip my arms around him. 'I want to make it up to her, really I do.'

'Good,' my brother said, relieved. 'Glad to hear it.'

'But first tell me how *you* go to work on an egg.' And there he was again. The Slim I didn't recognise, back with the idiot grin, but for a reason I still couldn't fathom. Even so, I could have strangled him. 'Come on, man, you're the one who raised the issue.'

'All I said was you spent too much time nibbling at the crown.' This was Pavlov again, talking about the chocolate. 'It wasn't meant to be an allegory for anything.'

'But you had a point,' Slim insisted. 'An important point with sexual, psychological and philosophical implications.'

'Slim, you're talking crap. Utter pants.'

I began to wring my hands, flattened by what I was hearing, furious that I was even party to it. Then Slim levelled the egg at my brother, and every feeling fell away but for a sense of foreboding.

'I stand by my word,' he insisted, and I could see in his eyes that I wasn't going to like it one bit. 'The way you go down on a Crème Egg reflects the way you go down on a girl.'

That was it. I clasped my hands across my forehead and groaned, long and hard.

'I didn't know how to tell you.' Rose sounded anxious, and returned to the keyboard. 'It was something you had to see for yourself.'

'Leave it on.' I realised she was about to close the window, and asked if I could assume control. 'Let me get some perspective on this.'

I came in for a closer look, but this wasn't Slim I was seeing here. This wasn't the man who wore my hairbands and swaggered into banks on my behalf. This was an *amoeba* of a man who was making a meal of *my* egg. The last one too. I had stashed it in the fridge, kept it chilled as an emergency measure. In a time of crisis, all I had to do was break the seal and binge myself better. Even Pavlov's Sea Maidens hadn't turned quite so monstrous. It was then that Slim stuffed what remained of the egg into his mouth, and I found myself with Rose again, looking any place but the laptop.

'That's not remotely sexy.' My brother with the commentary as I stared at the tiles under the bed. 'And you'll spoil your dinner.'

'If Slim mentions dessert,' I muttered, peering up again, 'I swear I'll reach right through that screen and smack him off his chair.'

'It's just two boys shooting the breeze,' said Rose. 'That's what you have to tell yourself, honey. This wouldn't be happening if you were at the table with them.'

'This shouldn't be happening at *all*!' I said, angrily. 'Jesus Christ, Rose, I feel so violated.' All manner of thoughts spooled through my mind, each one resurrecting an encounter with our landlord. Cartier crunching nuts at the bedroom door, creeping up on me in the kitchen. The man with his ideal living arrangements. 'A slice of life was what he proposed.' I felt compelled to come back to the screen as I said this. 'That was the agreement we had with him, Rose. A slice, not the whole fucking cake.'

Which was exactly what Slim looked as if he had packed inside his mouth. His eyes pinched into triangles, laughing inside as he consumed my Crème Egg. It was a struggle to watch. The same for Pavlov, it seemed, who left the table then and crossed behind Slim for the door. And yet despite myself, I couldn't turn away completely – not when Bleeding Rose asked if I was braced for a tour of the house. The full extent of our landlord's deceit.

'I only discovered this second site by chance.' Rose clicked back a couple of pages, returning to *caminside.co.uk,* the virtual show home created by Frank Cartier that I now regarded as little more than a front. We were looking at the welcome page once more, but in a different light. I didn't care who sponsored us now. My eyes were locked on to Rose's cursor as it sank towards the three options at the foot of the screen: passing over the chance to chat or send a message to the ticker, but hovering ominously over the option to register. 'I was interested in seeing what other properties Mr Cartier had to offer,' she explained. 'Normally a rental isn't the tastiest target, but a good thief never ignores an open window, does she?'

'So what did you find?'

Rose highlighted the field requesting an email address. 'I received the list as promised, plus an invitation to sign up for the second site. Premium-rate membership, of course, but people are happy to pay for this kind of kick.'

I wished we had filled in the form, then figured our rat of a landlord would have recognised our email address or programmed his mail out thing to block us or something. I didn't know how and I didn't care. I'd had it with technology. I was through with geeks.

'Show me Slim again,' I asked her. 'Let me see what I'm missing.'

This time Rose returned from another angle, slipping back into *camplicity.com* courtesy of a camera in the kitchen cupboard. This one let us peek out between the slatted front, looking down sharply at my brother. His return serenaded by the whistle and squeal of water pipes. Meantime Slim was picking his teeth, a stranger at the table. He was resting his elbows just behind the red tape. Keeping himself out of sight, or so he thought. 'Damn, that tasted good,' he told Pavlov.

'I don't want to know, mate.' My brother was losing his hair on top, I noticed just then, a thin whorl in his crop that he probably hadn't picked up on, though I couldn't speak for his editor. 'I just want to be assured that Cisco's going to find a new man when she comes back.'

Slim wiped the corner of his mouth with the heel of his hand, nodding now as if it wasn't just the egg he had digested. 'I like your sister,' he said. 'I like her a lot—'

'Which means he's in love with you.' This was Rose with her interpretation. 'But I accept that's hard to believe right now.'

'It always was,' I replied, my eyes bright with tears, 'because he never actually said it.'

'Cisco, it's how men are. They express themselves differently. You know that.'

'Oh, I do now.' I reached for the laptop, operating now on emergency power, and closed it down. 'The camera never lies.'

32

I arrived home well after the watershed – ten, eleven, maybe later. To be honest I'd kept track of the drinks that evening, not the clock behind the bar. I found Slim and Pavlov in the front room, the pair of them flopped on the sofa, watching a wildlife documentary.

'Cisco, we were worried about you.' My brother straightened up as he said this, swallowed the last bit of the banana he was eating. Slim looked at me anxiously. Even the ticker flashed a greeting, but I didn't give a damn who was behind it this time. I just stood there at the door to the front room, light-headed from alcohol but with my attention fixed on them both. Apes were hooting on the TV, gearing up for some kind of drama, such was the upswing in their excitement.

'Where have you been?' It was Slim with the question and the edgy smile.

'People-watching,' I said abruptly, so he wouldn't ask more. I gestured at the screen. 'Have I missed much?'

'Just the usual.' Pavlov reached for the controls and brought down the volume. 'It's all about animal behaviour in the wild. Footage of primates scratching their arse ends and squabbling over who gets to squat in the best bit of the tree. Stuff like that.'

'I think it's a repeat,' said Slim helpfully.

On the telly, an ape, maybe a baboon, picked a tick from his pelt. He examined it as if he'd never seen one before, then hoovered it into his mouth. After that he found another, did exactly the same thing.

'It looks familiar.' I faced back to the boys, feeling a little unsteady on my feet, and found them both watching me.

Pavlov said, 'I think you two could use some time alone,' but didn't slip seamlessly from the sofa because I laughed out loud. Not so much because of the irony in what he was saying but because I had known he was going to say it. I clapped my hand across my mouth, aware of the alarm I was causing. 'Ignore me,' I told my brother, as he finally made it to his feet. 'You wouldn't find it funny.'

Pavlov consulted the webcam, then crossed the line on the carpet. Like it mattered what zone he was in any more. 'Have you been with Sweet William?' he asked. I shook my head, but it didn't seem to make any difference. 'Never accept seeds from that man, you hear me? Even if he makes out they're just for planting.'

'I'm fine,' I said, and glanced over his shoulder. 'Just a little keyed up.' Slim was sitting on the edge of the sofa now, watching the primates but evidently waiting for an audience with me.

'We've spoken,' whispered Pavlov, as he passed into the hall.

'Is that so?' I said, without looking back.

The moment I learned about Cartier's cam con, my first instinct had been to pluck the boys from the spotlight and bollock them. I had left the hospital with every intention of heading home and inviting them outside for a quiet word, but all that changed when I pushed through the exit doors. It was like an air lock, coming out into the twilight and the sudden plunge in temperature. Back into a world that had moved on without me. The city seemed so empty, all the people gone home to enjoy private moments with their loved ones. That was what had struck me most forcefully when I sat down on the steps and covered my face so that nobody would see the tears. Even if it had been just the guys monitoring the traffic cameras, looking for a way to kill time until the next rush-hour came round.

I was in love with a stranger, that was how it seemed to me then. I had left the house that morning thinking maybe there was more to Slim than met the eye, but never *this* much. Rose had shown me a whole new side of him, and from a viewpoint that outraged me. Even thinking about Frank Cartier made me want to scream. What he had done was unforgivable, but it was his second site that had laid my boyfriend bare. The two seemed inextricably linked, which was why I had turned west instead of east. I felt shabby heading away from home, as low as the spies under the sofa, but before I could act I had to see it all: the full extent of our landlord's scam, played out in my absence.

The cybercafe was just down the road from the gaming basement, the digital dive where Slim had once taken me. I marched by the latter without looking down the steps, my fingers itching for some keyboard action of a different kind. Despite the empty streets, the cybercafe was wired in every way: ranks of browsers stationed in rows, from suits to students, backpackers and bohemians, all of them seemed lost in their virtual worlds, oblivious of the tense, troubled-looking girl and the corpse she had to step across to reach the bar – okay, so the only stiff was the gin and tonic I summoned, but I swear you could fall down dead in one of these places and nobody would notice. Unless, of course, it was reported to them in a chat room or posted on a message board. I slipped on to the bar stool, faced out across the cafe and wondered which guy I could pick off just to punish Slim. Two rows down, a suede head with sea-green eyes might have made my day *and* my night if he had known what I was thinking. But ultimately it was just a distraction. A means of keeping my mind occupied until a workstation came free. And when it did, there was only one man I wanted to observe.

I found Slim with Pavlov, standing at the window in the front room in a state of some anxiety: the pair of them taking turns to peek through the drapes. I did wonder how many people, like me, were watching from the wings. For I had slipped in through *camplicity*, courtesy of Rose's password, to find yet more covert operations – each cam fused into the framework of the building, hidden behind the bricks and mirrors, the paintings and plasterwork. It really was like peeping through a spy-hole with some of them. The fisheye lenses, partially obscured views and raggedy frames conspiring to make the whole set up seem all the more illicit, possibly illegal and potentially explicit. This was my house under full surveillance here, and it felt like a game show rigged against us. I located the sound bar, but kept the volume low. In my state of mind, I really didn't need people looking over *my* shoulder.

'It's a different négligé,' was the first thing I heard, Slim sounding all top end again through the speaker. '*Cream*, I think your sister would call it.'

'But is it him?' asked Pavlov. 'I can't cope if it's another stalker with a taste for women's clothes.'

Slim came away from the window. Solemnly, he said, 'It's definitely the same guy as last night.'

'Then we should call the police.'

'Pavlov, we have to take this into our own hands. I am *not* going to dial the emergency services because there's a cross-dressing pensioner parked outside my house. We'd run the risk of being done for time-wasting, and if they came inside I'd most likely be done for possession.'

'For what?' My brother grinned. 'Inappropriate hair for a white guy?'

'Says the man with the illegal shirt on his back.' The spark returned to Slim's eyes, a mischievous glint that had once been like a magnet to me. This time, however, it went the other way. 'What colour do you call that?' he asked. 'Nectarine?'

Pavlov considered his shirt, shot his cuffs and said, 'Dreads on a honky is punishable by a longer stretch inside.'

'Not if they were to take your whole wardrobe into consideration.' Slim gestured high, drawing his attention to the dormant ticker. 'The freak who's been harassing you could probably claim just provocation. That might mean damages, old son.'

'Then I would have to cut a deal,' said Pavlov, from his corner of the front room. 'Inform them of your crimes against my sister.'

'That wasn't a crime,' Slim crowed, quick as a blink. 'She *consented*!'

I sat back for a second, struggling to believe he would talk about me in this way. Even Pavlov seemed appalled, but didn't come close to my own sense of outrage. Not least because straight sex was all that had featured in our relationship to date. If Slim seriously thought he might move into any other kind of zone with me, he could whistle for it. I had always figured guys quit this kind of crap when they lost their virginity. Making up stories about their sexual conquests was what schoolboys did so they wouldn't stand out from all the other liars. I just hoped my brother had grown out of believing everything he heard. The way he began nodding to himself, it seemed that Slim had certainly given him something to think about.

'Wilful girlfriend neglect,' Pavlov said softly. 'That was the charge I was going to bring.'

I could feel the tension building, the screen between us like an open window. Then Slim let it all out with a sigh, and looked the long drop down to his feet. 'You've made your point,' he assured Pavlov. 'A new man is what Cisco will find when she comes home.'

I glanced across at the suede head, a dish just a few workstations away, and wondered how Slim would react if I didn't come home at all. What he had come out with was unforgivable. Then again, it was no more unforgivable than the fact that I had come here to watch him say it. I switched to the cam we were all supposed to know about. It was available on this site too, and somehow I felt more comfortable watching from there, despite the addition of sound. On the screen, my brother began fussing with the drapes again, folding one over the other, then patting them down as if that would make it safer inside. 'When she gets home,' I heard him say, 'you're on your own.'

'Aren't you going to stick around?'

'Slim, you don't need moral support to say sorry.'

'Supposing she gets heavy?' he said. 'At least if you're in the room she won't press me about things like commitment.'

'You haven't been seeing each other for long,' Pavlov reminded him, both boys standing behind the sofa at this point. 'Don't be the guy who thinks a couple of weeks together means you're "in too deep".'

'Pavlov, I want things to work out as much as she does. But any discussion about the long term isn't something you rush into, is it?'

'Why not?'

'It's a big step,' said Slim, 'talking intimately like that.'

'A commitment, you mean?'

'Exactly.'

My brother let Slim have a second to think about the subtext there, then gave up and checked his wristwatch. 'Cisco could be back at any time,' he said. 'The moment she walks through that door you'd better be ready for her.'

Slim said, 'You're right,' and began patting down the pockets of his combat pants. Somewhere below his knees (I had to guess because his excuse for a sofa was in the way), he appeared to find what he was looking for. Even so, he didn't bring it into view. Instead, Slim glanced at the one webcam they knew about, looking right at me, it seemed, then dipped out of sight. 'I always think if you're prepared for the worst it can only get better.'

'It's a lover's tiff,' said Pavlov, addressing his own shoes, it seemed. 'Cisco isn't going to murder you.'

In response a wrist shot up from behind the sofa, grabbed my brother's elbow, and promptly dragged him out of view. Had I been watching via *caminside*, unaware of this second probing site, I might have switched off and done something less boring instead. As it was, I had an arsenal of cams I could call upon to find out what they were doing. A reverse switch to the bay window, and there was Slim, backed up against the sofa with a badly buckled joint. He had already fired it up, and was examining it between drags.

'Watch the carpet,' he said, on passing it to Pavlov. 'If Cartier finds burn-holes he'll know what we've been doing.'

I reached for the mouse, thinking this was all wrong as I went right under the sofa to settle on the rear view from there. I couldn't see much, just a brick of light that defined the space between the two boys' backsides. In fact only the ashtray between them was completely visible. Then again, it wasn't the shot that bothered me but the comments scrolling up the chat window. The one that had popped up under the picture when I crawled under there.

VaxMe:	Look at the dust balls in this place.
Trodden 28:	Filthy. There's nothing worse than domestic tumbleweed.
Lust4Lint:	Hey, fellas! You don't like the dirt? Go higher.
VaxMe:	Higher? Have you seen the cobwebs in the lamp cam?

What I read was lower than the foot fetish people, as if the audience attracted to this site only really found their voice at ground level. I was just gearing up to introduce myself via the keyboard and claim responsibility for the blonde strands with the darker roots that they went on to pick apart, but my brother got in before me.

'This place could use a spring clean,' I heard him say.

'It's fine. Good for another month.'

A hand came down just then and ruffled the carpet. 'Feel it, Slim, there's biscuit crumbs and all sorts.'

'Is this need to clean a hormonal thing with you? It's like your sister, coming over all sensitive about nothing. Except she's a girl and that's allowed.'

I saw Pavlov's fingers find some fluff and flick it at his flatmate.

'It's a question of human decency,' he said. 'God knows what's under the sofa.'

I reached for my drink, saluted the screen, then found I had already drained it dry.

33

The bartender was quick to serve me. He had been unloading the glass-washer when I left my station and closed in on him. I guess the Reaper-like shadow that fell over the poor guy had persuaded him it could wait. I was in hell, knowing what I did, and my instinct was to erase it from memory by getting thoroughly pissed. I watched the pocket of air float up the optic as he served me, and considered suggesting that he just spun the valve wide open and prepared me a pitcher or two.

'Are you seeing anyone?' I asked. The bartender came round with the glass, but kept his distance. I wasn't sure which of us was more surprised by the question. It had just spilled out. An impulsive need to speak with someone. It helped that he was good-looking, in a slightly startled, boyish kind of way. 'Don't worry,' I said. 'I'm not about to jump on your bones. It's your mind I'm interested in, for the time being.'

He relaxed a little, gave the bar top a careful wipe with his cloth then set down the drink. 'I'm in a relationship,' he confirmed, smiling shyly.

'Good,' I said, feeling foolish. 'So am I.'

'Great.' His smile eased into something more playful. He leaned on his elbows. 'We have so much in common.'

I looked along the length of the bar, biting back on the temptation to ask if he fancied a fling anyway. 'I just wanted to ask if your other half knows everything there is to know about you.'

When I turned back I found him considering my question, not me. I felt a hint of disappointment. I'd been quite enjoying the attention for a change.

'Can I just say that you're the third person to confide in me this week?'

'You're kidding.'

'This is a cybercafe.' He shrugged. 'Romances formed in here tend to rely on reinvention. People come to flirt anonymously in chat rooms or conduct email affairs with strangers, but there's always a danger that some will fall for their own fantasies.'

'How so?'

'Online, reinvention cuts both ways. But that's easy to forget when you're carried away by your fingertips.' He lifted his chin, looked over my shoulder. 'Eventually they find out their playboy prince is nothing more than a beer-guzzling trucker and break down at the bar.'

'Typical,' I muttered. 'Bloody men.'

'Oh, the women are just as likely to mask their true identity,' he assured me. 'They don't set out to deceive like guys. It's more about covering up what they consider to be flaws and imperfections in their looks or character. Yesterday I had a guy sitting right where you are. For months he'd been exchanging emails with Miss Detroit 1997. Finally she comes clean about this little secret of hers and it shocks him so deeply he can't even blink.'

'Like what? She's married?'

'She didn't win the pageant.'

'That's not so unforgivable, especially if they'd formed a bond.'

'Turns out she's a beer-guzzling trucker.'

'Oh,' I said, and consulted my drink. 'But she was female, right?'

'The trucker aspect was enough for him to deal with.'

'I can see that would be a problem,' I agreed, after a beat, 'but he must've laughed it off?'

'Eventually I called him a cab,' he said flatly. 'He was in no fit state to drive his rig that night.'

'The *guy* was a trucker too?'

'Not when he logged on to reinvent himself. Before his sweetheart broke the news he had been whatever she wanted to hear.'

I regarded the bartender over the rim of my glass. The story was too good to be true, but so was he. Helping the man get home had been so *nice* of him – the sort of kind-hearted gesture that Slim wouldn't have hesitated to make either. Slim did a lot of things without thinking.

'I'm Cisco,' I said finally. 'Don't ask.'

'Maximillian.' He nodded graciously. 'Likewise.'

I lifted myself on to the barstool, caught his eye, and that smile came into play once again.

'Well, Maximillian,' I settled in close, 'that tells me how it is for everyone else, but how is it with you?'

'Please,' he insisted, 'call me Max. My partner calls me Milly sometimes, but it's guaranteed to make me cranky.'

'So, does she know you inside and out?'

The barman said no, then slipped in that she was a he.

With my cheeks heating, I attempted to apologise for making assumptions, but ended up just slumped in front of him. 'Well,' I said finally, 'that pretty much sums up how well I can read a man. For a moment back then I thought you were flirting with me.'

'I was,' he said, 'but I wouldn't want my partner to know. It never looks good, even if I'm so faithful I could weep.'

I considered this, thinking that ultimately the same applied to me. Then I looked at him squarely and said, 'You obviously know your partner pretty well.'

He shook his head. 'It's the same as I tell all the lost souls who wash up here, you can't know somebody one hundred per cent. You just can't. Even if they have nothing to hide, there'll always be things you didn't know about them and wouldn't want to either. It's like looking into a black hole. Everyone wants to discover what's in there, but you have to risk it all to find out.'

I jabbed a thumb over my shoulder at the workstations. 'I think I just took a peek.'

'Ah,' he said, like this made a difference, 'and now it's threatening to tear you apart, right?'

I told him that's where I was – facing into my own personal heart of darkness. The ultimate girls view of what guys were like behind closed doors.

'So you have two options,' he said. 'Log off now, and hope your relationship can survive the suspicion you're bound to bring to it, or go in with your eyes wide open. Find out everything you can about this man of yours, then ask if you still love him. Because if you do, and you make it through to the other side, nothing else will *ever* come between you.'

What he had said just blew me away. And yet now here he was, the bartender called Maximillian, casually reaching for his cloth to wipe the surface once again.

'Thanks,' I said, a little in awe of him, and lifted my drink clear. It reminded me I hadn't paid. 'What do I owe you?'

'What do you owe me?' At first I thought he was totting it up in his head, but then he went back to work with a grin. '*Details*, girl. Fast, unlimited net access is a fine perk of the job, but nothing beats the gossip I get to hear.'

Now it was my turn to outshine him with a smile, and it felt so good because I didn't think I had it in me at the time. Nor the resolve that told him to watch out for his new straight best friend. Get the glasses sparkling and a fresh lemon sliced, I said. For I had a voyage of discovery to make at my workstation, and I'd be coming back for refreshments.

Max whistled through his teeth, but I figured he had more of an idea what to expect than I did – especially when he looked me in the eye, and said, 'Are you sure you can handle it?'

'Whatever happens,' I assured him, 'you can guarantee that when I go home I'll be raising the roof.'

34

Baboons – screeching and squabbling, canoodling and copulating. That turned out to be the soundtrack to my late-night stand-off with Slim. Pavlov had kept to his promise and left us alone together. He was upstairs now, draining cisterns and filling sinks, while we looked for a way to get things flowing too.

'These apes,' said Slim, with a nod to the screen, 'there's a theory that some mate for life, but you wouldn't think so, judging by the way the males behave sometimes.'

I faced the documentary, unwilling to join him on the sofa, and saw one of the males hanging from a branch by its toes. I could tell it was male because its testicles were hanging down and it appeared utterly spellbound by the sight of them: reaching up to bat them this way and that, making a big noise so everyone else could see what he had found. I may have been first with the dry smile, but it was Slim who broke the silence. 'I told you it was a repeat.'

'Slim, I—'

'I'm sorry about what happened last night,' he said. 'I let you down, and I apologise. Pavlov told me how much my session with Misty upset you. All I can say is this cam thing just got the better of us all.'

'You can say that again.'

'We should talk to Cartier, consider getting him to take us offline after six maybe. Normal show homes don't stay open twenty-four hours, why should we?'

'I think he has his reasons.' I sighed, wishing he would shut up and let me speak. Not leave the sofa to check on the space outside our house again. Watching Slim slip his nose through the drapes, I could sense he was avoiding the inevitable. Pavlov had primed him for a heart-to-heart about where we were going, and here he was with his back turned to me. 'Slim,' I said firmly this time. 'There's something you should know.'

'It's okay,' he replied, raising his hand to stop me there. 'Our friend in the dress, I can see him for myself.'

'That's not what I wanted to talk to you about—'

'Was he asleep at the wheel when you walked past just now?' Slim glanced back at me, a hint of panic in his eyes. 'There are many things you can be forgiven for when you get old,' he went on, 'endless nostalgia, reeking of gravy, nodding off every ten minutes, but wearing a *négligé*? It wouldn't surprise me if he turned up in one made of human skin.'

'That *négligé*,' I cut back, 'is butterscotch, not cream.'

Slowly, as if I had just put the tip of a blade to his back, Slim returned his attention to me. Coming round as if maybe he hadn't heard me right. Like I was the one who was stalking him now.

'Did I say it was cream?'

I felt myself wobbling, inside and out, and wondered how many people were getting off on this – not just from the view we all knew about but the second site too. I looked across at Slim, bracing myself to come straight out with it, give him the wide angle on the whole story, everything I knew, but something held me back. An instinct untouched by alcohol or emotion that urged me to sort the personal issues before the public concern. So instead of sweeping my hand around the room, pinpointing spy microphones and covert cams, telling Slim I knew exactly what he had said about the old boy's outfit and more, I just said, 'I know you too well,' and retreated to the kitchen.

I needed space, a glass of water, and room to breathe. The water was on tap, but privacy was impossible and not just because Slim followed me in. I could sense him behind me, keeping his distance, probably asking what it would take to win me over. Once again I toyed with telling him. Just turning from the sink and blowing him away as I ripped out webcams left, right and centre. The place was a mess as it was. Unwashed plates in the sink. Breadcrumbs on the surface. Shreds of foil on the table. The legacy of my last Crème Egg and a sure sign that it was Slim's turn to tidy up.

'Is it Misty?' I heard him clear his throat. 'If it is, I'll stop right now. You mean more to me than finding the prize money.'

'It's not that.' I found a glass and filled it, let the water spill over the rim. 'Not any more.'

'It isn't?' He breathed out so sharply I pictured him deflating. 'You won't believe how many levels we got through today. Misty climbed this huge rockface with all kinds of rewards at the top. First we found a pistol and then a map. A *map*, Cisco!' Slim was talking now like *they* were the team. 'My guess is the game's creator didn't leave too many of those lying around, and my Misty must be among the first to find one. It was a real morale booster. What's more I've got her sprinting – I mean, really motoring along, and in the right direction too. X marks the spot with the bank vault, and with every *Money Shot* mile I'm getting closer and closer and closer. So stick with me, Cisco, we're on to a winner . . . Cis? What's the matter? Hey, you're crying. This is a *good* thing I'm talking about. Come here. Shush. Now, what's with all the tears?'

The Slim who took me in his arms just then wasn't the one I had observed from the cybercafe. That one had finished the joint with my brother then kicked back on the sofa. The pair of them loafing in front of the webcam we had agreed to let into our lives – blissfully ignorant of the fact that they might as well have been going out live from Leicester Square, surrounded by spotlights and a silent crowd.

What had troubled me most was the trivia, the way guys together discussed truly meaningless issues instead of the stuff that mattered. Listening to Slim argue that repetitive-strain injury was under-represented in movies had been like getting an extreme close-up on his mind and finding nothing there but fluff.

All the keyboard action you get nowadays, was how he began,

241

and nobody ever had a problem with the pain? *The Matrix* was a little implausible on that front, he went on. How Keanu saved the future for us all without even a twinge in the wrist, it just didn't compute. When my brother pointed out that Reeves did more fighting than typing in that flick, Slim came right back with *You've Got Mail*. Tom 'n' Meg get it on in a chat room, and we're supposed to believe they don't have *any* cybersex? Excuse me, he said, but where was the netiquette there? You hook up with someone in a chat room, it's impolite *not* to ask if they're naked. Even if that kind of communication had proved too frantic for the censors, he went on, a support bandage on one of them would've conveyed the same meaning. Pavlov had suggested that might be a scene for The Director's Cut, but I hadn't caught Slim's view on that. Opting instead for an emotional break at the bar and some expert analysis from Max. The first of many, in fact. Not least after I returned to my workstation to find the boys had moved on to *The Money Shot*. The pair of them sold on Misty's progress, heading deeper into the realm of male fantasy.

'If this game was made into a movie,' Slim had stirred to say, joypad in hand once again, 'who would play Misty?'

'Britney.'

'You always say her,' he complained. 'It's no fun when you don't give it any thought.'

'She's a talented artist.'

'Who would happen to look a treat in cycle shorts.'

'So who would you choose?'

Slim had chewed on this for a moment, negotiated the pneumatic one across a frayed rope bridge and said: 'Anyone who would let me co-star, basically. That would be a dream. Can you imagine, teaming up with Misty? Crossing into her world.'

'What? For real?'

'Into the game, yeah. Getting so close to the prize money you could smell it.'

'I don't think you'd get far,' my brother had said. 'You'd be too busy trying to find the cheat that gets her kit off.'

Slim hadn't answered for a moment. That he had just inadvertently let his heroine drop into a stretch of quicksand demanded all his concentration. 'I think the problem would be if she tried to take *your* kit off,' he said eventually, watching Misty slowly sink.

'It wouldn't be an issue,' my brother had insisted. 'Providing Miss Ventura agreed to drop her smalls then I would be happy to dangle in the face of danger and get on with the task of getting rich quickly.'

'Right.' Slim hadn't sounded too convinced. 'And when was the last time you tried sprinting with no pants on?'

'Um? When I was about three, probably. Then I realised underwear made life much easier. Something I can't stress too highly.'

A change of cam had told me that Misty was up to her neck in quicksand at this point. Meantime, Slim was wringing the joypad this way and that as if steering it might help her out.

'Just think about it,' he said absently. 'We're not exactly aerodynamically designed down there. It hurts even *jogging* without support.'

'Ah, but in this game you can customise your body, right?'

'Agreed.'

'Then I would make mine long enough to double up as a belt.' My brother seemed quite proud of his gaming strategy. 'That way if I had to start running I could just secure it round my waist.'

'Good call. A useful weapons holster, too.'

'Exactly. Why bother with knapsacks?'

For a moment the pair of them had fallen silent just there – watching the quicksand close in over Misty's crown. Then Slim had exhaled heavily, and said, 'A dick that length, I could've thrown her a line. Hauled her to safety with it.'

'Now that's something you wouldn't see in a movie.' Pavlov had reached for the keyboard at this point, shaking his head as he squared it up on his lap. 'I think we've seen enough of Misty for now. What's Cisco going to think if she finds you playing with her again?'

'Hold on!' Slim had sounded agitated. 'You just logged me out of the session!'

'Keyboard overrides joypad. It's the natural order. Though the remote will rule forever.'

'Give me a break, Pavlov. One more attempt. I've come so far today.'

'Enough is enough,' was how he finished, pecking at the keys. 'Besides, we have housework to do.'

What I had gone on to witness from the cybercafe demanded yet another return to the bar. I hadn't bailed out there or broken down, but I did get through a lot of gin, sympathy and napkins, courtesy of my new gay best friend. Eventually Max had persuaded me to face up to going home, if only to hear what Slim had to say. By that time, I believed I knew my so-called boyfriend better than he knew himself. And though I had been left feeling shelled like one of Cartier's bloody pistachios, I figured that at least I could never be let down by a man again. With the insight I had gained into the male psyche, I would always start off disappointed. In fact, that's exactly how it was when I logged off from my workstation. I had been obliged to squeeze past the suede head on my way out. The way his attention stayed with his screen, however, I could've been dressed in nothing but a pair of kitten heels. Then I had seen what he was watching, bloody *camplicity*, but what really hit home was that it so mesmerised him. Even when I tapped him on the shoulder and said, 'There's one hell of a row coming up.'

'Yeah?' He had twisted round, eventually, and then caught his breath when he saw who was looming over him, invading his personal space.

'Keep watching the screens,' was how I had left him. 'I'll be home in twenty minutes.'

I had gone on to let myself into the house with the key and a sigh. A sigh dragged on by the door swinging over the pile of pizza flyers on the mat. Judging by the racket in the front room, I realised that the boys hadn't finished with this housework thing of theirs. I made a point of crashing the door shut, and hadn't been surprised that the vacuum cleaner shut down dead. Why? Because we didn't own a vacuum cleaner that powerful. Ours was an old wheezer that did little more than cough repeatedly whenever we set it to work. The model I had heard was a dream, as was its owner, and neither were in the house, for this was a webcam broadcast the boys had been enjoying – and I knew because I had witnessed them logging on to it! Coral was her name, and cleaning up was her game. With the help of a credit card, you could watch her getting into every nook and cranny – behind her lounger, under her coffee table, everywhere. Pavlov and Slim had gone no further than the free preview, but I was in no doubt that this was down to our crappy credit rating with the bank.

The silence had been replaced by the sound of grunting primates as I made my way along the hall. I had turned into the front room, thinking that it sounded like a jungle in there, but finding only Slim and Pavlov. The pair of them flopped on the sofa, making out they had been watching a nature documentary all along. It was late, I had realised then. Way past the watershed.

'Cisco!' This was my brother, and that was how I finally came home to them, feeling like I hadn't missed a damn thing. *We were worried about you . . .*

35

The Slim who went on to hug me in the kitchen was the only one I wanted: he took me in his arms as if he expected the whole house to collapse around us. The roof, the joists, the bricks, the works. All I could do was cling to him, sobbing against his chest, as close as I could ever be to his hidden heart.

'Talk to me,' he kept whispering. 'Let me in.'

I wanted to open up. I was committed to telling Slim everything. But being here with him, feeling the heat of his body against mine, it simply overwhelmed me. For I was with the man I loved, despite everything the day had thrown at me. I still resented Slim for what I had seen, but all that was from a distance. This was here. This was now. The two of us together, but not yet alone. He pulled back a step. I lifted my face and found him waiting there, braced for me to open up.

'I can't do that.' I wiped my eyes, cleared my throat. 'Not here.'

Slim brought his hands to my wet cheeks. 'Let's go to bed, then. We can talk there.'

'*Where?*' I sensed his hands fall away.

'The bedroom?' he said. 'Or have I just said the wrong thing?'

After all that time in front of the second site, it was only now that I came to consider my own place in it. Slim was all I had been interested in, but now here I was interacting with him and everything was threatening to go horizontal – in public. I didn't know what to say. I fired off a 'yes', recoiled with a 'no', then winced and admitted I was spinning out here.

'All the more reason to lie down,' he advised, and I steeled myself to tell him that it wasn't just the drink that had got me into this state. I levelled up as best I could, only for Slim to seize the moment with a kiss to my temple, my cheek, my lips. He came away smiling fondly, swept back a bang that had come loose from my grips. 'Get some sleep, Cisco,' he said next. 'Whatever's on your mind, we can talk about it in the morning.'

'But—'

'Don't say another word.' Slim touched a finger to my lips. 'I'll take the sofa, give you some space. I have to wash up anyway.' He turned to the plates in the sink. 'It's about time I took some responsibility for the mess.' I wiped my cheeks with the heel of my hand, and told him he didn't have to do that.

'What?' he asked, and faced me with that spark in his eyes burning brighter than ever before. 'Are you saying I don't have to wash up?'

Sex. Now *that* was in the air. I could almost feel the charge as I closed the bedroom door, but it wasn't coming from me. I could sense eyeballs all around the room – as if the viewers in the kitchen had flocked up the virtual staircase to be here before me and shut off the lights to set the scene. Even the moonlight through the blinds kept giving way to a wash of neon pink. This was down to the screensaver on Slim's laptop, I realised. He had left it up and running in the corner of the room, an image of a Cheap Motel sign blinking on a loop. I was just beginning to wonder if things could be any more sleazy when the low-rent strains of a jazz trumpet started up through the wall from Pavlov's room. My brother was working late again, I thought, blinkered like my boyfriend to the stage show we were in.

I had to tell them. No more delays. Keeping quiet about *camplicity.com* made me no better than those who were paying for the privilege of spying on us. I had messed up in the kitchen because my feelings for Slim had overwhelmed me. Now I was in the bedroom, having drifted up in a daze, but the thought of blowing *anything* here was out of the question. I turned to the bed, drawn that way as I considered what the viewers might have regarded as a regular event. I ought to have been outraged, but I was way beyond that. At least they wouldn't see any more, I resolved, and promptly wondered what was keeping Slim downstairs.

One last look. That was all I intended before I fetched my brother and my boyfriend and insisted that we speak out on the street. I knelt in front of the laptop and tapped out the website address. I just wanted to check that Misty was out of the frame, that I would have Slim's full attention and, indeed, the front room turned out to be satisfyingly empty. The only aspect of the shot that rattled me was the fact that he had shut off the lights already. Even so, the picture was perfect. A little bleached to the bone, but that's how it was with cameras that could keep the night at bay.

Infra-bloody-red. Had Cartier stopped at nothing? The way it was going, it would be no surprise to find he had wired the place for X-rays too. That was when I should have made some noise, but the music coming through the wall from Pavlov's bedroom had a head start on me. The beats now driving that trumpet refrain were frantic. I could still hear Slim clinking crockery in the kitchen, but this sounded more like someone tumbling down a flight of stairs with a tray of cups and spoons. I watched the cursor on the screen float towards the webcam menu, barely registering that I was responsible for directing it there. I even stole into my brother's bedroom thinking of Rose, and immediately found myself wishing Max was here to put his spin on things.

'Oh, my God.' I heard my own voice and my senses snapped to attention. '*This* is what he does in there?'

Pavlov's music might have been a little intense through the wall, but now that it was coming out of the laptop speakers I wondered why his ears weren't bleeding. The horn was squalling over a storm of percussion. Some jazz standard dragged through jungle hell, that was how it seemed to me, but it clearly hit all the right notes for Pavlov. I had assumed my brother was working to music, not working *out* to it. This wasn't even air guitar I was watching him play, but something altogether more compromising. Air drums, at a push, I could imagine, but air drum *and* bass?

Watching Pavlov flail around his dead zone was like witnessing an electrocution. Then the tune fell away and that brought him down, only for the introduction of a belting female vocal to energise him again. This time with his eyes knotted shut, his head tipped back and an imaginary microphone cupped in both hands. My brother, the club-anthem diva. It wasn't pretty but, then, it was a personal moment. Not intended for public broadcast.

'One down,' I muttered, levelling the cursor over the kitchen icon, sure that Slim was washing up because that's what I could hear him doing downstairs. Even so, I hit the cam key with a hint of dread. 'One to go.'

He was at the sink, to my relief, the red tape enclosing the dead zone a couple of feet behind him, not that it made any odds to me from this vantage-point. A pinhole cam in the tiles told me he was making a thorough job of it, as did the soap-sud fetishists in the chat room that went with this picture. Despite their concentrated commentary, I felt touched by this portrait of my boyfriend in a good light. Pavlov's own moment might not have matched it, but I decided that all the compromising stuff I had seen of them just wasn't valid. I couldn't use it as a criticism in any way. How could I, when I had basically trespassed into their lives to witness it? I mulled this over watching Slim wipe down the surfaces then twist the cloth dry. A change of heart on my part that was subsequently blown out of the dishwater when the man opened his flies and washed his penis in it.

36

'I have to come clean about something.' This was the first thing Slim announced, when he walked into the bedroom. Even if he was about to say that he would walk over burning coals to be with me, he stopped short when his senses caught up with his gob, for there was no fake flashing neon in here any more, just a thinning bar of light from the hall that vanished when he clicked the door shut. The darkness seemed absolute for a moment, but then the moonshine became apparent, slanting through the blinds to sketch zebra stripes across the bed. Which was how Slim found me as his eyes adjusted, lying underneath a sheet with the top end clutched around my throat. 'You turned off my laptop,' he observed. 'What would I do without you?'

'I'm sure you'd survive,' I said.

He began unbuttoning his Hawaiian. 'Are you cold?'

Cold? Watching Slim carry out that kind of ablution in the sink had turned my heart to ice. My affections had threatened to deep freeze when he used the tea-towel on himself too. I had been so appalled by this domestic atrocity that I hadn't even noticed him leave the kitchen, just carried on staring at the screen until the sound of footsteps on the stairs sent me scrambling to cover my tracks. Had Slim come in to find me prying on him like that, I'm not sure who would have been more compromised. It had left me with no alternative but to slam down the laptop, hurry under the covers and curse my handling of the situation. I had come home to rescue the boys, from the house and from themselves, and now I couldn't find a way out for any of us. Being under total surveillance made it impossible to get ahead of the game. Slim was already climbing out of his combats, and my instinct was to stop him but I couldn't.

By the time I had taken the audience into consideration he was snuggling up to me. The distinctive lemon fresh scent coming off him didn't help matters either.

Slim settled his hand on my hip, then lifted his head away from the pillow. 'Cisco, you *must* be cold.' He peered under the sheet, glanced back up as if something had just frightened him. 'Or are you trying to tell me this is just a temporary stop?'

I was still in my clothes, and cornered now. This thing could go no further, but rather than play for the audience, I made the most of my surroundings. Snapping the sheet right over our heads, I leaned in and found his ear. 'We're being watched,' I whispered.

'I know,' he mouthed back, as if he understood the reason for my subterfuge. I sensed him make some space between us, creating a cavern with one hand so that I could see to the end of the bed. 'Our feet are in the live zone,' he said, and I realised he was still in the dark. 'Just keep your socks on and we're covered even if the sheet rises up.'

'You're wearing socks in bed?'

I knew it wasn't the main concern here. It was also a bit rich coming from someone who had tucked herself up in the dress she'd been wearing all day. Still, if Slim had been hoping to strike lucky with me he'd let himself down yet again.

'It's the toe-suckers in the chat room,' he said, unsure why I was so anxious for him to keep his voice down. 'Can you believe I've had email from some of them? Treatment tips for my fungal thing. Nail-care advice too. Like a guy needs to worry about that.'

'This isn't a joke,' I said, under my breath. 'I have to tell you something.'

Slim propped himself on his elbow. I thought he was there to listen, but instead he whispered, 'Things won't seem so bad when the sun comes up,' and for a beat I just gave in. I couldn't see much with the sheet pulled over us, but Slim's presence cocooned me somehow, protected me from prying eyes. 'You know,' he went on, barely audible now, 'it doesn't matter what you're wearing when you stir in the morning, it'll always be the prettiest thing. Sometimes I wake up just to see it happen. Your lashes part, you look at me, all this colour and light comes into the room.'

I folded my arms around his neck, drew him as close as I could, and just came right out with it. 'Do you love me?' I asked, and I didn't care if anyone could hear. I still had stuff to tell him, but first I had to be sure of this. 'Because I'm in love with you, Slim, but you're still just such a mystery.'

His dreads formed a curtain around the kiss that came down next, sealing us in even more. It was a deep, searching kiss, and I responded willingly until he broke off. His lips forming three words I couldn't quite hear because he sank away from my embrace just then. I raised my head from the pillow, heard him murmuring mantra-like under the sheets, and wondered where he was going. Then I felt his hands slip under my skirt, reaching up for my knickers, until I pulled back in a panic.

'What's the matter?' he asked, kneeling over nothing now. He shrugged off the sheet from his back. 'Did I do something wrong?'

'Can we talk about this outside?' I was right up against the headboard, couldn't go any further back.

Slim looked perplexed, a little self-conscious, too. He brought his knee up to his chest, not so happy to be naked now. 'Are you okay?'

'No,' I snapped, startling him. 'I feel like a Crème Egg.'

'Ah.' He mugged a face, but loosened up some. 'I'm afraid I might've had your last one.'

'*That's not what I meant!*' I swung out on to the floorboards, and almost took him with me. Anger carried me round the bed, humiliation catching up quickly. It wasn't just that I knew the pet theory behind his practice, what really hurt was that he believed he could make good by going down on me. Still, at least I was dressed. It didn't do to be struggling into clothes at a time like this.

'If this is about chocolate,' he said, 'I'll go out and get some more right now. Even if I have to walk into town.'

'It's too late for chocolate.' I jerked open the door. Light swept over the bed, forcing Slim to shield his eyes and instinctively his genitals. 'It's too late for a lot of things.' For a man who dipped his dick in the washing up water, who boasted to my brother about things we had never done, he seemed so vulnerable now. Exposed to such raw scrutiny, while naked from the ankles up. 'Congratulations,' I said, thinking of all the people watching. 'Pavlov and me had our most embarrassing moment on a lake in Italy. You just earned yours right here in your own home!'

'Cisco, we're in the dead zone . . . Where are you going?'

'Out,' was all I said before slamming the door shut behind me. *Offline.*

37

Misty Ventura would have dealt with things differently: faced with a guy handling her like a chocolate egg, she would have responded with a cool high kick or just wasted him on the spot. I doubt she would have fled down the stairs like me, choosing instead to back flip through the window or lift her way into the loft – most probably with Pavlov slung over her shoulder too. But then Misty was a long-limbed action figure who didn't exist outside the screen. Unlike her, I had a life beyond what she had. I had feelings to contend with, just as I had faults, but I also had friends – and this was where we differed. Misty Ventura dealt with her wounds by searching for med packs, while I stumbled towards the fairy-light strings that squared off the stall at the end of our street, the only one trading at this time, and with more blooms than you could imagine. You didn't get a florist-and-dealer in *The Money Shot*, a mountain of a man who let his business slide for the night just so he could sort me out, who gave me the spare room back at his place and told me I could stay for as long as I liked. Misty missed out on the little things like this, magical moments that kept the real world turning. Everyone needed a friend like Sweet.

I don't remember falling asleep, but it must have taken me down deep because when I stirred next morning I had to question everything around me. I opened my eyes, let an unfamiliar space come into focus, and found a butterfly resting on my nose. Balanced right there on the tip, its peacock wings seemed to blink like my lashes. I gasped and it fluttered away. Lifting my head from the pillow, I realised the room was littered with them: clinging to the bedposts and the open curtains, and flitting through the sprawling sunlight as if this was a meadow not the uppermost floor of a mansion block. Through the open window I could hear an opera diva practising her scales, belting it out from a flat on the opposite side of the quadrangle. I could also smell molasses, and wondered what on earth Willie had cooking in here.

'Look at you,' was the first thing he said, even though he had his back to me. I tightened the sash on the silk kimono I was wearing. Something I had found in Sweet's wardrobe among a lot of sleeveless puffas. 'You want eggs?' he asked. 'I can do sunny side up, or nothing at all.'

'I'm fine,' I said, 'thanks.'

I had found him in the kitchen area. The man was shirtless, and wore an apron striped like toothpaste. He was kneading dough in a big china bowl, his meaty shoulders pumping in turn as he told me eggs sunny side was the greatest comfort food ever. I said I'd grab something on my way to work, not because I wanted to avoid sitting down and talking through my troubles but because the weirdness I had just woken up to extended beyond the spare bedroom.

'What's with the butterflies?' I asked instead, turning now to take in his whole space – bamboo furniture, throw rugs and bongs, fluttering wings just everywhere. 'Are you some kind of collector?'

Two balcony windows commanded a view over the rooftops, with a gilt-edged gouache in between, a still-life study of a tipped-over vase. For a moment I thought Sweet was being funny when I heard him say, 'Painted Ladies.'

'Pardon me?'

'It's what they are,' he grumbled, padding around me now with both paws dusted in flour. 'Hazard of the job. You take a consignment of buddleia, forget to close a window overnight, shit like this is what happens.' He opened the broom cupboard, stood aside to show me his harvest of arching purple blooms, and let a few more butterflies spiral out in the process. 'I'd haul it all down to the stall, but not with these buggers flapping about behind me. I'd feel like such a bell end. A bit-part player in a Disney flick.'

'It would be a lovely sight,' I suggested. 'Really pretty.'

'Cisco,' he growled, like I had forgotten this was Sweet, 'until darkness falls on this day, the buddleia stays right here.'

I let the issue drop, unwilling to rile someone who had shown me such kindness, and came back to his mixing bowl. 'Is that a normal kind of cake?' I asked, wondering whether perhaps it would end up as the sort that got chopped up into squares and flogged at festivals.

'Naturally.' He weighed a hunk of dough in his palm. 'What else is there?'

'It smells good. There's nothing like a man who can bake.'

'Really?' He faced me once again. 'You think so?'

I had to smile. Willie was so transparent with his affections that I could almost see the herb rack behind him.

'It's good you're baking for someone special,' I said. 'A cake made with love always tastes so much better, I think.' I didn't need to mention Rose by name because all of a sudden he couldn't meet my eye. 'If you like I can deliver it to the hospital,' I said instead. 'I'm a regular visitor nowadays.'

'No need.' He wiped his hands on his apron and pulled out a carton of cigarettes from his pouch pocket. 'Rose bust out yesterday evening.'

'Bust out?'

'All right, she was discharged. Had the plaster off and insisted she could walk. It wasn't until she got through the doors that she took my advice and got into the taxi.'

'Rose seems like a very independent lady,' I said, 'but I'm sure you saw her home safely.'

'I always do,' he assured me, 'though I suppose I should check up on her later, see if I can help out in some way.'

'Like satisfying her appetite for cake.'

At first Sweet seemed affronted, and I was a little embarrassed at the dig myself, but despite the problems with my own love life I was determined to get him talking freely about his. He tapped out a cigarette and slotted it behind his ear. I

257

was relieved to see him grinning as he did so, saving it for later.

'She's worried about you, Cisco. We both are.'

'Rose put you in the picture, then?'

'It was the picture on her screen spoke for her,' he said. 'I pitched up to take her home, found her glued to your landlord's website.'

'Which one did you see?'

'Does it matter? A fish tank is a fish tank, whichever way you look at it.'

'It's different when you're on the inside with the other fish.' I sighed, my feelings rising up again – conscious of the two fish still in there. After a moment to reflect I realised I had been staring, but Sweet didn't seem to take it personally. If anything, he had used the opportunity to roll his sleeves a little higher. As if the work ahead might get messy.

'Wanna know what I saw?' he asked.

'Go ahead.' I took a seat at his table. 'It can't make me feel much worse.'

'Cisco, I saw three housemates living their lives.'

'Then you weren't watching the right cams,' I said. 'I'm off men big-time after yesterday.'

'It was nothing unusual, the scenes I caught.'

I told him about Slim and the thing with the sink. Willie didn't even catch his breath, just shrugged and said, 'At least he keeps it clean.'

'I'm talking about his penis, not the plughole.'

'Lotta men wouldn't bother with either.'

'You're not shocked?'

'Your boyfriend had no idea he was under surveillance. We all do stuff differently when we think we're alone.'

'Do we?' I said tartly.

'We do,' said Sweet, and waited until I had his full attention. 'Every single one of us.'

I tried to hold his gaze, but he was already in there. All this time spent focused on the boys, I had barely considered what people might have seen of me. The things I did in my own time and space.

'Look at me,' I said, 'I'm blushing.'

'Look at *me*,' he said, and showed me the back of his hands. He wiggled his fingers, and ten pearly nails sparkled wildly in the sunshine. 'Knowing what you do about how they got to look so fine – now, that's embarrassing.'

'Willie, I fixed up your nails. It's no big deal.' I was about to suggest that more people had probably seen me in the buff than noticed the buff he had on display there. God knows what I might have been doing at the time, I said, but it beat being outed as a man who went in for a little pampering.

'Can you keep a secret?' he asked, a shift in gear from the florist in the pinny, and one that stopped me in my tracks when he told me the most personal thing I had ever heard from anyone. It was an admission that made absolute sense, and went some way to explaining his reluctance to take things further with Rose. 'Tell me that's not embarrassing,' he finished, like it was a competition all of a sudden.

'But there are pills for that,' I said. 'Injections, too. All kinds of different treatments. Impotence is a growth industry, if you see what I mean.'

'Sometimes drugs just don't do it for me.' Sweet William thumped his chest. 'It's gotta come from in there, or not at all.'

'Nonsense.'

'It's a guy thing.' A butterfly alighted on his ear as he said this, but he didn't seem to mind. 'I figured it might help if you knew private stuff about me as well, but I didn't expect you to understand it.'

'And you think Rose wouldn't want you because of that?' I sat back in my seat. 'You're right. Only a man could make that kind of assumption. Jesus, Willie, share it with her. Take it somewhere.'

'I can take it everywhere but up,' he said flatly. 'Where it matters.'

'First Slim and now you.' My voice lifted a little. 'Like my brother said, it always boils down to your dicks.'

Sweet William reached for a book of matches on the counter. 'Pavlov takes a leak sitting down,' he said, and his eyes shot up to catch my response. 'Even lays out paper on the seat. In his own home.'

'He never does?' I sat back as he nodded solemnly. 'Really?'

'The way your brother settles there, Cisco, it's a dick problem all right.'

'Oh,' I said, conceding the point, only to pick it right up again. 'Ohmy*God*, there are webcams over the *toilet*?'

'And in the bathroom, but it was all a bit steamed up when Rose showed me.'

'Oh, shit. *Of course!*'

'I didn't see nothing.' Willie pulled out the chair opposite, gently brushed two butterflies from the seat before sitting down. 'But I did persuade Rose it was something you had to see. We talked about it yesterday, in fact. Burned my nose sitting outside in the hospital garden.'

'I saw you,' I said.

'Yes, you did,' he replied disarmingly, and removed the lid from a small silver cask. I watched him strip five sheets from a book of cigarette papers, and wondered if he was expecting visitors. Maybe that was what made me pick up the pace, because I reeled off the fact that Frank Cartier had given me his word those two rooms would be out of bounds. 'Can you believe he looked me in the eye when he said that?'

'Sure,' said Sweet between licks. 'Keeping you in the dark was what made you such a valuable property to him. Your landlord knew the punters would only pay top whack to watch if you were unaware. Everyone hoping for a chance to see that money shot.'

'They're *gaming* fans?' I said. 'Don't tell me Misty is the big attraction?'

Sweet William looked mystified. He took the cigarette from

behind his ear, sliced it open with his fingernail, and tipped the tobacco into the paper trough he had made. At the same time, he told me that wasn't what he meant by the money shot. 'In every good movie,' he explained, 'there's a moment that guarantees bums on seats, right? A key image or a scene the audience come to see. The bit that everyone talks about.'

'Like the platform scene in *Brief Encounter*?'

'That's a chick clip. Involve me here, babe.'

'All right. Like what?'

'Ever see *Independence Day*?'

'Hardly a notorious chick flick, Willie. That film was about aliens zapping the White House. It was a geezer-pleaser.'

'But you paid to see it?'

'I might've rented it on video,' I said awkwardly.

'And you remember the bit where the White House got toasted?'

'Sure. It was the bit we'd all heard about.'

'That's your money shot.' Sweet William extracted a sizeable chunk of hash from the box. 'How about *Titanic*?' he asked next.

'Actually I never got round to seeing it, but I could probably describe the moment when the ship went down. So many people relived it for me.'

'There you have it again.' He pushed back his chair, and reached round to collect the lighter from the kitchen surface. I didn't realise he had gone there to create some leg room too, until he winked at me and scissored his big fat thighs. 'Sharon Stone in *Basic Instinct*,' he said. 'Now that was some money shot, wasn't it?'

'Point taken,' I said, and flashed back to my own situation. Wondering how many times I had tried to get comfy on the sofa in a skirt. 'Why don't people just rent a porn video for that kind of thing?'

'There's a different kind of money shot in that genre,' he said, and seemed to retreat from the conversation as he loaded the joint. I didn't think it was wise to push for details, but I only had to question what kind of moment he could be talking about and there I was, heating up like the hash under his flame.

'At least with a dirty movie the action's guaranteed,' I said, wishing we could move on.

'Sure it is,' he said, 'but there's more dough in the *possibility* of seeing it all. The punters tune in, find they can't stop watching in case the good stuff kicks off.' He rested the joint in the palm of one hand, used the other to twist it together like a little bouquet. I had never seen a joint rolled in this way before. 'People stick around because there's no script and no censors, and Cartier cleans up as a result. Charges by the minute, according to Rose.'

'Without our permission,' I pointed out. 'Or our knowledge.'

'That's his unique selling point.' Sweet William stoked up the spliff, took a single hit, then spoke with a catch in his voice. 'Take that fish-tank show been on the box lately. You can put all the extroverts you want into one house, manipulate the mix to maximise the chances of tension and sex, but the bottom line is they know they're being watched. Every move they make, everything they say, it's a performance. With you, Cisco, your boyfriend and the uptight, they see you crossing out of that zone into the other. They see you with your guard dropped, where the show's really going on. That's where it's at.'

'It's a liberty is what it is,' I muttered, conceding that the spliff was solely for him. I rested my elbows on the table, and pressed my palms to my temples. 'I feel so cheated, Sweet. So *angry*.'

'Privacy is a precious thing,' he said, with a note of lament. 'Seems people have lost sight of that lately.'

'What am I going to do?'

'Go back for the other fish,' he said, his eyes pinking up as the joint burned down. 'Just don't judge them by the stuff you weren't meant to see. Especially not your boyfriend.'

I considered what Slim had once said to me, repeated it for Sweet. 'Where would a relationship be without its secrets, eh?'

'Exactly.'

'So I should just *forget* about what I saw? Wipe the tape, so to speak?'

'Hell no,' he croaked. 'This show must go on.'

'Willie, you should stop smoking so much. You're not thinking straight.'

'Food for the soul,' he said, turning the spliff in his hand. 'And fuel for your plot.'

'What plot?'

'The one I'm cooking for you now,' he said gruffly, as if I was distracting him from the bigger picture. 'I'm thinking reconciliation,' he continued. 'I'm thinking *ratings*.'

'Ratings?'

Sweet William consulted his spliff, thickened the air for the butterflies before expanding. 'Your audience share.'

'What share?' I asked. 'The creeps logging on to *camplicity* belong to Cartier. He's the one making all the money here, not me.'

'So give them something else to watch.' The fat man sitting archly at the far end of the table now, looking down his chins at me like this was *Alfred Hitchcock Presents*. 'Give them something only you can offer, Cisco. A unique show. Something they can't afford to miss.'

38

Another two days ticked by before I took the call from Slim. In that time I stayed with Sweet, I went to work at the modelling agency, and I did a lot of thinking. The thinking I did behind the reception desk. Standing there with a warm, welcoming smile I could probably maintain in my sleep. Not once did I let it drop. Even when the bossy old bitch came back from her travels. The one who had issues with her husband, as indeed I did with them both. I smiled for the photographers and the talent scouts, too. I even stayed sunny in the face of all the double takes that kept coming my way. The hint of recognition that crept into the faces of so many people here for faces other than mine. Except now I knew where they had seen me before. Wise as I was to *camplicity*, it meant I had a window on *their* private lives. I knew what total strangers got up to behind closed doors, in front of their screens. And that put a smile behind my smile. Stopped me crumbling on the inside.

It was Willie who insisted that I bide my time before making contact with the house again. He had assured the boys I was safe and well, and that neither of them would come to any harm providing they took his word for it. I wanted to go back to them, of course, but Sweet insisted that I got myself together first. He said it was vital that I broke the news calmly so they didn't get hysterical and screw things up. In what way? I had asked. Sweet said guys didn't tend to think straight when told they had been stitched up, urged me to use my intuition. Which was why I kept it simple when I finally stopped ignoring my mobile and took the call from Slim. I let my smile fall away on hearing him breathe out and then asked him to meet me away from the house. On neutral territory. The place I suggested had nothing to do with Frank Cartier, but everything to do with us.

Getting a drink in the Reload Basement was easy. All I had to do was catch the bartender's eye, give him a second to register that a female really was there voluntarily, and he came over like I owned the place. I hopped on to the barstool, ordered a vodka and tonic, then watched him work out how to put one together as if all he ever served was Diet Coke and bad coffee.

I had arrived a little earlier than arranged, keen to get as comfortable as possible in this alien, almost hostile environment. I slipped the straw between my lips, then swivelled round to take a long sip and a longer look. It seemed like nothing had changed since my last fleeting visit. I heard the same battle sounds, saw the same low lights, silver pipes and ductwork overhead, with the same four clusters of inward-facing males surrounding four clusters of monitors. This time, though, I didn't feel so intimidated. People came here to lose themselves, after all. The world around was of no concern to them, that was how it seemed to me.

Some guy descended into the basement just then, dipped his head to avoid clipping the pipes, and made his way to the other end of the bar. He had a relaxed but clean-cut look, a black tapered suit with a blue cotton shirt undone two stops. I only stole a brief glimpse, but he looked like he was going places. I did wonder what business he had here and flirted with the idea that maybe he was the owner. I couldn't resist glancing across from my drink one more time, just to confirm that he hadn't wandered in accidentally, and gasped when I found him looking straight at me.

'Slim?'

He approached cautiously. 'Good to see you,' he said.

It took a moment for me to match the voice I knew to the man before me, and another to concede that when it came to being in another world I was as guilty as the game heads.

'You cut your hair.'

He dragged a palm from his crown to the nape of his neck. I watched his short tousled locks springing out underneath and still couldn't believe he had done it. The ropes were gone. Those dreads that framed his face and defined his way of life had been cut back and shaped up into something altogether more striking. Something on the way to a shag was the only way I could define his new look. Even the brow ring was no longer a feature, which meant his face assumed a natural symmetry. Near perfect, to my eye.

'D'you like it?'

'It brings out your nose,' I said, 'in a nice way.'

Slim accepted the compliment gracefully, and then came over all upbeat. 'Sweet William told me you've been staying at his place,' he said, still barely recognisable to me. 'He wouldn't tell me where it is, but I've always wondered what it looked like, where he lives.'

'Willie's place?' I thought about this for a moment. 'Nice. Clean and airy. Very feminine in a lot of ways. I even found a nice kimono in his wardrobe.'

'Seriously?'

'Please don't tell him I just said that.'

'Do I look like a fool?'

'Slim, you're many things,' I said, 'but you're nobody's fool.'

He gestured at the bar, blushing just a bit, and reached inside his jacket pocket. 'Can I get you anything?' he asked, and came out with a clutch of coppers. I shook my head. I was doing just fine under the circumstances. With the barman still waiting for his order, Slim sheepishly counted out enough for a Coke – Diet, if he had any in the chiller.

'At least you look the money,' I said. 'You're not due in court or anything?'

Slim Jim laughed, and invited me to appreciate the cut. 'Your brother helped me out,' he said, as I ran a thumb inside his lapel. 'I told him I was due for an upgrade. He said only geeks got upgrades. Said what I needed was a decent haircut and a set of threads.'

'That's good advice.'

'Either way, I was through with the old model. It wasn't performing properly.'

He was close now, his elbow on the bar top, fingertips brushing mine. Close enough for me to feel uncomfortable meeting his eyes, knowing what I had seen. I was going to have to tell him about *camplicity*, come what may. It was just a question of building up to the moment of truth.

'So how's Pavlov?'

'Good.'

'Yeah?'

'Fine.'

'And the stalkers,' I said, faltering now in my attempt to find a way in, 'have they been behaving themselves?'

'As well as can be expected,' Slim told me, in all seriousness. 'The ticker's gone into a sulk because we've been blanking it, while our friend in the *négligé* has taken to pulling up every evening and dozing at the wheel. His routine is really shaping up now, which is good, I think, for someone in the autumn of their years. It's when the everyday habits start to slip that you know the mind's going the same way.'

I laughed despite myself, enjoying Slim's company all over again. His new look really was something special – understated, but overwhelming in a lot of ways. 'And what about Misty?' I asked, some play in my voice this time.

'She's good.'

'Yeah? Getting anywhere with her?'

'All the way,' he said, smiling with me now.

'What? *All* the way?'

'All right, a beach is where we are. We've been all around the world in a hundred levels and more. Misty and I have negotiated mountain passes and desert dunes, dry riverbeds and winding goat tracks, and now we've hit the beach. The map indicates all the money is in the vicinity, and I know for sure we're the first to get that far because there are no other Misty footprints in the sand.'

He broke off there, probably reminding himself that I didn't live it as he did, only to come back with conviction: 'I'm closing in on the cash, Cisco. I really am. I just don't know where to take her now. The ocean is out of the question. It's the edge of the world in virtual terms. You don't fall off if you go any further, but you risk crashing the game.'

'Maybe you could have her catch up on her tan,' I suggested playfully. 'Some people have assumed I do my clearest thinking on my back.'

'That would mean dropping my guard,' he said, riding out my dig. 'My kill count is good right now. A Misty every morning this week.'

'Now, that *is* an achievement.'

'I thought so too,' he agreed. 'Just a shame nobody was around to witness it.'

'Don't be so sure,' I muttered into my drink.

'She sends her love.'

'Who? Misty?'

'Really. She misses you. We all do. It's not the same without you watching over us.'

A pause fell over us. Slim was the first to draw breath by asking me home, but I had just one thing on my mind and now was the time to share it. Without once taking my eyes from him, I brought the houselights up on Frank Cartier's second site.

Slim reacted to this revelation by shutting down completely. I told him about the hidden webcams, highlighting what I had seen, why I had walked out, and how he would have to trust me now if he wanted to see Cartier punished. He didn't say a word throughout. Just leaned into the bar then leaned into his hand when I finished. Looking inwards, it seemed, like that was the only space he could be sure he still had.

A minute later, my brother responded in a very different way. I called him at home on my mobile, ordered him to step outside, then repeated everything I had just said. When I finished, I was forced to tip the handset away from my ear. Even Slim stirred when the bone-chilling shriek come out of it. I had anticipated that Pavlov would be much more vocal than his housemate, which was why I had opted to tell him from a safe distance.

'So, what now?' Slim asked, sounding broken in the same breath.

I shut down the phone, swigged my drink, and told him what he'd come to hear. 'Let's go home.'

'We can't,' he said. 'How can we?'

'Call it a trial period,' I said, and gestured for him to lead the way, 'but there'll have to be some changes.'

'Like what?' Slim asked, walking straight past the gaming screens as if they didn't exist.

'Don't worry,' I said, smiling to myself, thinking of the plan Sweet William had seeded for me. 'You've made a good start already.'

39

We found Pavlov waiting outside the house. He looked like a lock-out, standing there on the step, shifting from one foot to the other. A latch-key kid in need of a loo.

'Marvellous,' he groused, as Slim and I came out of the flower market. 'Didn't I say no good would come of all this?'

'Relax,' I said, and extracted my own set from the pocket of my shoulder bag. 'There are all kinds of rewards waiting for us inside.'

'What are you doing?' he asked, blocking my path. 'We can't go in there again. The place is *crawling* with cams.'

'Not quite,' I said. 'There's a blind spot on the landing. Just at the top of the stairs. It's the only true dead zone in the house. We're okay to talk quietly in that bit too, because there are no microphones nearby.'

'How do you know?'

'I've had a few days to familiarise myself with the second site.' I pushed the key into the lock then turned to address them both. 'Now we're going in, and we're going to act natural. Is that clear? Slim, I want you to fetch your laptop from the bedroom, boot it up in the blind spot. Pavlov, you look like you're going to have an accident if you don't relieve yourself soon. Do what you have to do, but don't let on that you know you're being watched.'

'Oh, like that'll work.' He appealed to Slim for support, but Slim had barely spoken since leaving the Reload Basement. The man was in shock, it seemed. 'It'll be like using a public facility!'

'Pavlov, we could just stand here and wait for your bladder to burst, but somehow I think even you would rather perform for an audience than suffer that indignity.' I opened the door an inch, felt some resistance from yet more pizza flyers, and invited my brother to lead the way. 'Now, get in, but don't give the game away.'

'Is that all this is to you?' he hissed. 'A game?'

'Whatever it is,' I said, and gave the door a shove, 'the next move is ours.'

The first time we walked into the house after it had been wired up, the changes had taken our breath away. From the new carpets to the catalogue kitchen, it had seemed like an ideal home. This time, it just felt fake. A studio set with cardboard walls and more life going on behind the scenes than in it. Still, the boys didn't let me down. The pair of them acting as I had asked, even if they were a little wooden. It was what I had to show them that worried me – the guided tour of the second site, before I revealed the plan I had hatched with Sweet William. I did consider taking them through it from the cybercafe, but what I had to propose was an inside job, so I figured we should start as I meant to go on.

'Look at this place,' Slim whispered, on clicking inside *camplicity* for the first time. The three of us were stationed at the top of the stairs, huddled inside the blind spot. 'You can even see under the sofa.'

'You'll also find one trained on the kitchen sink,' I said pointedly, but just then Pavlov took charge of the laptop. All of us falling quiet as he clicked upstairs to the toilet.

'This is outrageous,' he whispered, racing full circle round every angle on offer in there, not stopping to catch up on the gossip going on in the chat room attached to each cam. *'Unspeakable.'*

'Do the bedrooms get this kind of coverage?' Slim caught my eye across the keyboard, and took that as a yes.

'And after all that crap he gave us about having them look "lived in",' growled Pavlov. 'The next time Frank Cartier lets himself into this house, he'll be leaving in a body-bag. See how he likes to relax in that.'

'Can you quit being such a hard-on?' This was Slim, firing up now that he had seen the site for himself. His voice strained to break out of a whisper. 'Now is not the time for bullshit bravado. That kind of macho crap isn't going to get us anywhere.'

'Thank you, Slim,' I said, thinking he had shaped himself up in more ways than one. 'I'm glad we're on the same wavelength at last.'

Slim nodded graciously. He waited for Pavlov to settle down, then suggested torching the place instead. 'Why not?' he reasoned when I frowned. 'Nobody gets hurt.'

I glanced at my brother, who was sprinting through the cams now like a virtual avenger. When Slim asked him to find the front door cam, 'because doormats burn the best', I almost believed I could smell the testosterone coming off them both.

'Guys.' I raised my voice just a notch too high for my liking but it was the only way to keep a lid on things. 'Violence is not the answer. I have a plan, and it'll bring us everything we're owed and more, but I'm not going to start until you've calmed down. Why don't you close your eyes and count to ten?' The pair glared at me, but I was deadly serious. 'Go on.' I waited for them to comply, smiling only when they grudgingly submitted. 'Now, we have to stay cool here. Think rationally. Use our heads. Which means listening to me, and doing exactly what I say. Is that clear? Good. Okay ... One. Two. Thr—'

It was on this third stroke that a familiar sound issued from the laptop speaker. A sound of something slipping covertly into the house that prompted both boys to snap their eyes wide open. The webcam window, still trained on the front door, confirmed what they had heard.

'*Got you!*' Pavlov sprang over the screen in his bid to get downstairs, clipping one corner with his heel. 'I'll teach you to take liberties with our lives.'

'Wait!' I snapped up the laptop before it got trampled on, and scrambled to follow him. Which was difficult enough in an ankle-length skirt, but almost suicidal with Slim all over my back. 'Count to *ten*!'

You work as a pizza-delivery boy, it's not exactly a career move. The only perks you get are the moped with the big box on the back, the scratched-up helmet and the red zipper jacket, at best a tip or two. So you do your job: you deliver pizza, and when you're not delivering pizza you deliver pizza flyers. You don't expect a tip for that, of course, but neither do you expect to be confronted by a crazy in an agony shirt who attempts to shove a fistful down your throat. Not that you'd know what an agony shirt looked like, being a pizza-delivery boy, although I figured it had made an impression on this one.

'*Irritating, isn't it?*' my brother was yelling, as I struggled to pull him away. The poor guy was pinned to the wall of the porch, his eyes shot through with terror as another flyer got crammed into his mouth. 'It's a letterbox, not a litter bin, so don't darken my door with your rubbish again, understand?'

'Pavlov—'

'Because next time, I swear to God, I'll shove them up your *arse*!'

'Pavlov, people are watching.' This second stab at turning his attention came not from Slim or me, but from the other side of the gate. I was the first to glance round, see the man pop a nut into his mouth and grin at his companion. A crescent of spectators had formed behind the two men, drawn from the floral thoroughfare.

'*Cartier?*' Slim was beyond shock now, his hands falling away from my brother's shoulders just as I let go of him too. The look on our faces was probably what persuaded the people to move on. All three of us wheeled round, and immediately the gaps between the flower stalls became a big draw for them, which left just our landlord and the gaunt Oriental leaning up against the gate beside him. The one who wore the fish tattoos like long sleeves under a capped T-shirt. He had a toolbox at his feet, I noticed, and that just alarmed me even more.

'Be nice to our sponsors,' said Cartier. He extended a ringed finger at my brother. 'Pizza is your bread and butter.'

'Do as he says, Pavlov.' I shot him a fierce look so he wouldn't question me, hoping he might see that I was thinking on my feet. Reluctantly, my brother stood down. The pizza boy crumpled to the floor, his baseball cap knocked sideways, spitting out mulched-up flyer.

'Hope we're not intruding?' said Cartier, sounding unusually friendly. 'Kenzo needs to run a systems check on the server.'

'Are you *intruding*?' Pavlov was incredulous, and I knew he had a whole different spin on the question.

'Let me tell you something about the system running in there.' Slim looked set to square up to the pair of them, but the pizza boy moved faster – seizing the opportunity to spring from behind us and scramble over the railings in front of the bay window. By the time Slim had recovered from this distraction, I had already stepped in with my receptionist's smile.

'Mr Cartier,' I said, 'your system seems to be running like a dream, but what do we know? We're just the talent. If Kenzo would like to come in and dust it down, then, please,' I said, and swept my arm towards the open door, 'be our guest.'

I batted my baby-doll glance at the boys, but laced it with a look that told them to shut up and agree with me. We had nothing to hide, after all. I knew that, having rescued the laptop from a stomping by Pavlov before rushing to rescue the pizza boy from the very same thing.

Frank Cartier nodded approvingly at my invitation. 'Is what I like to hear,' he said, loosening up with me, maybe, but keeping a bead on Slim. 'Nice haircut,' he said to him next, having given the nod to his associate. 'Sharp suit, too. It's good you're putting in the effort to make this venture work.'

I could sense Slim bristling again, which was why he felt my heel on his toes as I stepped aside for Kenzo and his toolbox. Pavlov yielded too, but that was because he was a pussy. As Slim would later remind him.

'So,' I said, praying the boys would fall in behind me, 'have you been seeing much of us, Mr Cartier?'

'With my property portfolio?' he said, like I should know. 'I barely get to see my *own* home. Every day I'm here in town because that's what my business demands. There's repairs to be carried out, tenants to keep happy, problems to be sorted.' Cartier focused on Pavlov, standing behind me still, and chewed on a thought for a moment. 'Maybe you should take a look at my life. I could use some professional advice to help me sleep at night.'

'I can make some suggestions,' my brother grumbled, but Cartier wasn't listening. Looking in on us from the outside, there behind the gate.

'I was right when I said this would be a great day,' he declared next, considering us each in turn. 'Didn't I say this arrangement was going to make us all happy? Just look at it.' He was addressing the house now, leaning away from his outstretched hands. 'The bricks behind the clicks. That's what it is. People are *queuing* up to rent from me, that's why I'm so busy, and judging by Slim's threads you must all be seeing some extra readies as a result.'

I was convinced the boys would explode at this, but if they blew it now we'd never get even, so I got in first. Played this game as innocently as I could. Sweet William would have been proud of me as I told Cartier what he wanted to hear. I even caught a glimpse of the man himself, keeping an eye on us from the far end of the flower market. 'So how's your own place shaping up?' I asked our landlord. 'Still got the builders in?'

I had been hoping to get Cartier talking about himself instead of us, just until Kenzo came out and they left us alone. What I didn't expect was for the smile on his face to contract into a grimace. The corners of his eyes tightened, narrowing his gaze. 'You know what?' he said. 'Sometimes I wish I was in your shoes.'

'Do you?' This was Slim, sounding surprised and perplexed.

'Being a tenant,' he said, to clarify, and reached for the pistachios in his pocket. 'If there's a problem with your property, you make a call and the owner will pay to get it fixed. Simple as that. Me? I got nobody to call and a place that could fall into the ocean unless it's shored up and strengthened. So, yeah,' he said, returning to the question, 'I got the builders in. Nine to five they're crawling all over the property. Taking my cash. Stealing my privacy too.'

'Can't be much fun,' I said. 'Living like that.'

'It's hell,' he agreed, and seemed to turn instinctively towards the neighbouring house. 'Some days I feel I'm caught between the devil and the deep blue sea.'

I didn't dare turn to see if he had sighted someone through one of the unwashed windows. Didn't even want to ask if he had meant to load his comment like that. Cartier reached for his snowy hair stub again, surveying the neglected façade like it actually hurt him. 'Another thing about being a tenant,' he said. 'You have rights.'

'*Rights?*' This was Pavlov striking out again, astounded by what he had heard.

'That's what the man said.' This time it was Slim who silenced my brother. A leap of faith, backed up by a wink for me. 'Where would us tenants be without our rights, Mr Cartier?'

'You'd be on the street,' he said absently, stepping back to get a better perspective on the state of the place next door. 'As a tenant, you have the right to lock yourself in. You could let the place decay from the inside out, if you wanted. Refuse your landlord access to carry out repairs. Create all kinds of problems, though God knows what would possess you to do such a thing.'

'A breakdown in relations?'

Cartier dropped a look at Pavlov that told him not to go there. 'If my tenants are unhappy,' he said, 'they only have to come to me.'

'That's good to know,' I said quickly, and was relieved to see Kenzo float out of the door. A fish out of water, if ever there was one. He nodded at Cartier, in approval of sorts, which was

277

my cue to shepherd the boys over the threshold. 'If we ever have any trouble here, Mr Cartier, you can count on us. We'll bring it directly to your door.'

'Is what I like to hear,' he said again, this time sounding genuinely pleased, and opened the gate for Kenzo.

40

Straight in. Straight out. We'd been up for it once before, but this time we were going all the way. What could stop us now? It wasn't even a robbery. We were attempting to *give* this time, not take away. That's how I spun it on the drive down to the coast. The three of us heading for Cartier's place on the cliffs. Motoring through wet weather again, in the same toilet blue Beetle with the same stuck wipers. It seemed like a fitting vehicle for the fix we were in, and one more reason why I argued that we had to do this. Sure, we could have abandoned our house, strapped our stuff to a roof-rack and gone the other way, but the sense of injustice would always be there in our rear view. At first, Slim and Pavlov had both dismissed my proposal. The pair of them laughing when I had said I was serious, then considering the precedent when I swore I would take a day off work and do it alone.

'Cisco, this is beyond insanity,' was how my brother had responded, and he repeated it once again when I killed the engine at our destination.

'Pavlov,' I twisted round in the driving seat, 'shut up, all right?'

Slim? He was the reason I was in the driving seat. The reason I had banned all gangster rap on the journey in case it messed with his mindset. My new improved boyfriend being the one who had insisted on going inside instead of me. We watched him now, crossing the coast road then striding through the gates, this drizzly, windswept morning: exchanging nods with the labourers like he knew them all personally, even daring to high-five one hod-carrier as he headed up the drive towards the looming pile with the towers and the scaffolding surrounding it. Frank Cartier hadn't been boasting when he said he lived in a big mansion. It was *huge.* One of those granite affairs with high windows and steep, sloping roofs, way too big for a single occupant. He hadn't been wrong about the erosion problem either. The grounds stopped just yards from the rear of the mansion, with nothing beyond but the sky and the sea line. I was parked on the farm track opposite, flanked by palsied trees, wishing the sunshine would break through the clouds a bit more. Every now and then I would see light lick across the water, and figured it probably wasn't so bleak under better conditions. Just then, however, the weather was the least of my concerns. I rubbed the fug from the glass, saw Slim glance back at us, and gave him a covert thumbs-up. This time there was no hiding the fact that we were all just as shit scared as each other. The only difference was that Slim was out there while we were in the car, watching from behind yet another kind of screen.

'He's got it all wrong,' said Pavlov, perking up again. 'Pizza boys don't walk like that or talk to strangers. It's too cocky for the service industry.'

'Do you see any builders taking notes?' I asked, thinking that would shut him up. 'It's not a show event. Someone on site is hungry. Slim is here to deliver. That's all they'll think when they see him.'

My brother and I watched him follow a path around the house. A bank of overgrown rhododendrons obscured our view, but I knew Slim was seeking out a side entrance. He came into view just briefly, his crash helmet bobbing up and down, the bright red zipper jacket marking him out as a man with a mission to deliver. All it had taken was a profuse apology from Pavlov, a ready-rolled joint with pure grass in it, and the boy from Poppa Italiano had loaned us his outfit for the day. He had even thrown in the kingsize cardboard box for good measure, giving Slim something to hide his gear in.

Sadly, it also gave my brother one more thing to fret about. 'He's not even holding it flat. *Look!* Did you see him then? It's like he doesn't give a damn what condition the pizza is in. If that turned up on my doorstep, I'd ask for his manager's number.'

'Brother, nobody's going to check because nobody's ordered anything.' I gestured at the hard hats dotted around the grounds, the lawns turned to mulch under their boots. There were labourers everywhere, coming and going from the house, climbing up and down the cage erected round it. 'What do they care if a pizza delivery pitches up? There's only one man who would ask questions, and he isn't here.' I reminded my brother that Cartier was all business and no pleasure, that our landlord had confessed as much. 'Trust me,' I said. 'He's gone for the day.'

Pavlov knew I was right, and reluctantly conceded as much when I pointed out that his car was missing from the drive.

Meanwhile Slim had disappeared from view, slipped inside the house as planned.

Pavlov consulted his watch. 'Ten minutes,' he instructed me. 'We can't hold on any longer than that.'

'We're here until Slim comes out.' I gestured at a line of manky Portaloos at the side of the drive: nobody would notice if he wanted to use the facilities, I told him, and signed off one potential complication as he made himself comfortable like me. 'Face it,' I said. 'We're in this together.'

I had said the very same thing when pitching the plan in the first place, just after closing the door on Cartier and Kenzo – when the boys had rounded on me to explain why I had sucked up to the bastard. In response, I had invited them into the yard, as I always meant to do, and told them about the scam. What I proposed was a sting that would put our landlord in the spotlight instead and even make us a few pennies in the process. Yeah, right, they had scoffed. Create a cam site with Cartier in it? Nice idea. Just a shame none of us knew where to start. Slim had confessed that he didn't have that kind of coding know-how. He said we only knew one person with the skill and experience, and Kenzo was on Cartier's payroll. So I had laid it out for them right there. Said, what did they want to do – clear out or clean up? Because if it was just a question of finding someone who could lend a hand with the housework ahead of us, weren't they familiar with the ultimate in domestic help?

'Coral is a nice girl.' Pavlov sank back in the passenger seat, nodding to himself. He had been silent for some minutes now, just watching the clouds bundle over the sea, and I wondered if she was all he had been thinking about. 'A dream to work with.'

'I bet.'

'She must receive hundreds of emails every day, requests for this, that and the other, but she got back to mine within the hour.

'She seemed very familiar with you,' I remarked. 'Like perhaps you already had some kind of correspondence going with her?'

Pavlov mumbled a denial, but I didn't believe him and neither did I care. Unlike him, my concern was with the figure I pictured tiptoeing through the big house up ahead.

'Maybe she fancies you,' I said, without thinking, and hoped to God that Slim was all right in there.

'D'you think so?'

I turned to face my brother. Found him straightened up and waiting for confirmation.

'Pavlov, what do I know? I think we should be grateful that she agreed to come on board as our technical adviser.'

'I think Coral and I have some chemistry,' he said proudly.

'You've never met,' I pointed out. 'All the technical advice she's provided has been via email.'

'A virtual romance would suit me, though. All that intimacy without touching.'

'Plus you're offering her a twenty per cent cut on anything we make from a camsite featuring Cartier. I'd say the girl's using her head, not her heart.'

Pavlov went quiet. I glanced across, and apologised straight away. I didn't have to explain myself, he knew why I was on edge, and the pair of us retreated into a shared silence. In my mind's eye, I was with Slim in the corridors. Seeking out Cartier's computer terminal, then opening the pizza box that contained all the technology to connect him to the watching world. When Pavlov surfaced with a question, I wondered if he had been reflecting on how well we worked together.

'Are you two good again?'

'We're okay.'

'What does that mean? Girls write to my agony column when things are okay but could be better. In my experience, you say things are okay that means not good.'

'Things are okay,' I insisted. 'They could be better if I knew how Slim felt about me, but that's my lookout. Anyway, I figured you'd be relieved if things weren't going well between us.'

'Cisco, I want you to be happy.' A brief smile from my brother told me he meant it. 'Just happy.'

The truth was, I still felt raw inside. Slim had been exposed by the webcams, the way he behaved without me served up for all to see, and I couldn't forget about it. All right, so Sweet William had convinced me that our landlord was the only one guilty of a crime here and, yes, I accepted that Slim was an innocent victim, as indeed we all were, but only time would tell if we had both learned something from the ordeal. Slim might have scrubbed up on the outside, but I had to be sure that the change came from within. Pavlov unfolded a paper handkerchief from his pocket, and used it to clear the windscreen again. Still thinking about Slim, I rolled down the side window an inch and said, 'I think we could use some air.'

'You don't need air,' my brother replied, and the look we shared made me realise he had been tuned into my thoughts all along. 'Nor do you need time to think or space to breathe,' he said. 'You just need to use your eyes.'

And I did just that. I returned my gaze to the house and fixed it there, concentrating on nothing else until the front door opened and our very own pizza boy slipped out. Even the sunshine emerged to mark the moment, bringing light into the Beetle as I fired up the engine – ready for his return.

'Let's take this home,' I said to Pavlov. 'Slim and I will work it out, if we ever have a moment to ourselves.'

Say you're a subscriber. That *camplicity.com* was a regular feature in your surfing schedule. What happened is you visited the first site, keen to see a little bit of life in rented accommodation. Maybe you were thinking of moving into the area yourself, so you sign up for all the properties this landlord has to offer and receive an invite to see a whole lot more. The dead zones, dished up for a fee. So you pay your money, because you're curious to see what these guys do when they move out of frame. It's a buzz, the first couple of visits, it really is. A novelty. A laugh. Gradually your confidence grows, and you try out the ticker. It's just like waving for the camera, really, except you're saying hello to yourself.

Ultimately you're here for the housemates. All the time you're watching the three of them pick their toenails, hoping for a fall-out. Even some flesh if you keep up an online vigil. Pretty soon you're into the chat rooms too. You make friends under the sofa, over the beds, behind the kitchen sink. The site becomes a talking point in your life. Maybe you mail the link to friends, once, twice, multiple times, and relive those magic moments around the water-cooler at work. Without even knowing it, you're building up the fan base. You feel as if you know these people intimately. You've seen them eating and sleeping, fighting and fucking, laughing, loafing and most of all *living*. Whatever they've done, you were there when they did it, and somehow that makes them family. So when one of them emails you out of nowhere, the girl in the group with the roots and the invitation to see behind the scenes, you leap at the opportunity. It might cost a little extra, but why not? It'll add a whole new level to the experience. And she asked so nicely.

'All right. Here we go. Ten, nine, eight ...' It was Slim who said we should have a countdown, Pavlov who suggested bubbly for breakfast, even if he did put his shirt before the celebration. My brother draping a tea-towel over the bottle before he popped the cork.

'Seven, six, five . . .'

I didn't mind how the other two chose to mark the moment, so long as I was the one who got to hit return and launch this site for all to see.

'Four, three, two . . .'

'*One!*' we chimed, as discreetly as we could. Stifling our giggles when the bubbly fizzed over Pavlov's sleeve, then reminding ourselves where we were as the webcam window opened up. The three of us were back in the blind spot, crowding around the laptop, braced to view the result of our hard work. Twenty-four hours after Slim had stolen into Cartier's cliffside mansion, a new webcam site revealed itself to the waiting world.

'Ladies and gentlemen,' breathed Slim, 'we have contact.'

'We did it.' I tipped my glass to him and to my brother, who proposed the toast.

'Welcome to *getcartier.co.uk*.'

Get Cartier. That was the plan, and this was our turning-point, our chance to collect from the landlord. It was a new day, in every sense. As my brother had once said, there's always room for a third way. So what do you get for your money? A two-shot set-up, basically: one in the library, overlooking Cartier's desktop computer, the other in the adjoining room, pointing directly at a full-length mirror. The interior had revealed a collision of styles, one that borrowed from so many sources in a desperate search for its own identity. The only uniting element was that everything in it had been reproduced from the original: mock-Tudor glass in *faux-*Victorian windows, reproduction Georgian coving and even dodgy Elizabethan portraits of the Cartier clan. It was there for all to view, now that we had the place under surveillance, and conspired to heighten the fact that the house just didn't fit together properly.

The state of the place made Slim's task much easier. He had hidden the webcams beautifully, customising two stuffed hunting trophies so that both possessed the gift of sight once more. The eagle on the bookshelf in the library sported a new eye, while the grizzly bear in the next room had an obstruction in its throat that wasn't there when it died. There had been no need to drill a hole through the wall to connect the cable to Cartier's computer. According to Slim, his playboy pad really was past its prime. He said the walls sported so many cracks and fissures he could have squeezed through them himself. As a result of all this installation work, we were opening up the opportunity to see a man alone with his machine and also with his own reflection.

Coral had been the one to suggest framing Cartier in front of his monitor. She reckoned the *camplicity* disciples would go crazy for it. Having hacked into the server from her end and extracted the member database, our virtual consultant claimed that a view of our landlord overlooking his creation would be like watching some kind of malevolent god. According to Slim, two doors accessed the library. The main door was closed to the central hallway, but the side door next to Cartier's desk had been wedged open with a slipper. There wasn't much in this room, just a mirror on one side and a big old bear on the other, but with enough space between them, he said, for a man to seriously humiliate himself.

There was no need for chat rooms here, a message ticker or any other means of interacting. What we offered was *insight*, pure and simple. It took a leap of faith on my part, but nearly every member of the second site signed up to watch. Each paying ten pounds for the privilege or a fiver if they recruited a friend. Coral had good business sense: she knew how to attract a full house. Even if it was just geeks who were queuing to get in. I bowed to her wisdom in every way. And yet despite having made first contact with Coral, my brother didn't click with the final product quite so quickly.

'Is this it?' Pavlov was staring at the window. A static screen shot with the message that read: *'Live broadcast most evenings!'*

'The site complies with the specifications laid out by your girlfriend, yes.'

'Coral is not my girlfriend,' he told Slim, 'but she does have a schedule for her web casts, and a picture archive if you log on and she doesn't happen to be online at the time.'

Slim Jim lifted his eyes to the ceiling – like he hadn't been through this enough times for my brother. 'The Cartier cam kicks in when Frank chooses to power up his computer. These things don't run on thin air.'

'Spare us the technicalities.' Pavlov surrendered. '*Just give me content.*'

I glanced at Slim, saw him bite back all the put-downs that would have poured from the old model. Even if my brother had just come across like a new media asshole, there was only one man we wanted to bring down.

'As soon as our landlord goes online,' I explained, speaking for Slim now, 'everyone will know about it. The fact that it can happen at any time is all part of the draw.'

'Automatic email alert,' Slim added proudly. 'Wrote the programme myself.'

This time it was my brother who resisted the temptation to weigh in, switching instead from Cartier's place back to *camplicity.com.* A quick click through our house showed that nobody was home. At least, that was how it seemed to anyone watching right now. For our sting on Frank had a sting for us too.

'I can't live like this for ever,' said Pavlov. 'It isn't natural.'

He was speaking for us all – whispering, to be exact. Gathered as we were at the top of the stairs again, squashed into the only place where we were invisible to the watching world. For a beat the three of us took stock of our surroundings, silent but for the fading fizz in our glasses.

'You're right,' said Slim eventually. 'It isn't natural. But natural is what we have to live and breathe if we're going to make this work.'

Pavlov turned to me, testing for second thoughts on this project of ours.

'He's right,' I said. 'If Cartier susses that we know about his second site, if we even *look* like we're wise to the fact that this whole house is live online, he's bound to smell a rat.'

'More like a mouse.' Slim was waiting for us with his brow hitched high, but there wasn't much room for laughter in the limited space available. 'Guys,' he said, when his gag fell flat, 'it's a small price to pay for what we stand to make.'

Slim wasn't just talking about money here. Pavlov and I knew how much we had to earn back first, and that would take some time. We couldn't dictate when *getcartier* would come online and expose our landlord to the web, but every time we stood to feel a little better about what he had done to us.

'Okay,' my brother said, and drained his glass. 'Let's go to work.'

'Be careful out there.' Slim watched him climb into view of the cams, and came back round, like me, to the laptop. Not to follow Pavlov; but to check that our consultant had witnessed the launch. All I had to do was collapse the view from Cartier's second site, and there she was, underneath it, in a window we had kept open since recruiting Coral to our cause. The feed from her own site told me she was watching *camplicity*, because her face lit up as my brother emerged from the blind spot.

'Someone's found a number-one fan.' I glanced over my shoulder, leaned away so Pavlov could see her on the laptop screen. Then I looked across at Slim, and wondered if we could say the same for each other. I might have taken the opportunity to find out, but my smile was required at the modelling agency and Slim was expected to assume control of a pistol-packing click-chick while he lay back on the sofa. For the sake of appearances, it was business as usual. Which meant I wasn't surprised when Pavlov asked if I could hang back for five minutes.

'My editor thinks I'm on a roll,' he explained, coming back into the blind spot to speak a little more freely. 'He's even invited me in for a review first thing next week, so it's vital I keep up the good work.' He adopted a quietly pained expression. 'Please, Cisco. Your boy's view for *Sparkle!* is unbeatable.'

I sighed and twisted a glimpse at my watch. 'I'll write it up now on the laptop,' I told him. 'Lock yourself in the toilet, and I'll knock when it's finished.'

'The toilet?' Pavlov looked worried all of a sudden. 'Why?'

'Because you're always in there,' I said. 'It's the most natural place for you to be. What if your editor was in on *camplicity*, and he caught you pacing behind me while I wrote your column?'

'Maybe he has already.' My brother said this with some bitterness, as if it was something he had considered for a while.

'Either way,' I said, 'if you want to keep your job we just can't take those chances.'

'But the cams!' he pleaded. 'Facing the server was testing enough, but now I know what's really in there I have to screw shut my eyes whenever I take a leak – think of a special place where no one can see me.'

'What did you say?' This was Slim, suddenly concerned. I felt myself prickling too.

'I imagine I'm in a soundproof room,' Pavlov went on, regardless, 'no server humming or pipes sloshing underneath me. I'm convinced there's a block forming down there, Cisco. Now, that would be a nightmare.'

'So you're closing your eyes in there?'

'Got my fingers in my ears too.'

'You're kidding?'

'It's all I can do.'

'Not if you want me to be your agony uncle,' I said sternly. 'This has to look convincing, Pavlov. We must look at home in *every* room of this house. Otherwise the curtain's going to come crashing down.'

A good actress should feel at home on the stage: out there under the spotlight is where she comes *alive*, her body and soul thrown into the performance. At least, that's what they all bang on about when the magazines are invited into their lovely homes. I've always been a bit cynical about 'the craft'. You learn your lines, you hit your marks, what's so life-affirming about that? Then I stepped out myself, got into a little improvisation routine along with a couple of other amateurs, and the sense of accomplishment put a smile on my face that came from the heart.

For once, I wore it to work. I showed it to Sweet William on the way in, and even shared it with the proprietor of The Fish Eye while I waited for the bus. Kenzo was tending his tanks on the other side of the shop glass. He caught me beaming at him from the queue and seemed somewhat bewildered. My bus pulled up at the same time, but I managed to steal a glimpse of the shark in its tank. I didn't like to think what fuelled its relentless stealth, but even that couldn't wipe the smile from my face. Nothing could. Not even the sight of my favourite talent scout, and the demeaning demands she had lined up for me that day.

'Call my husband,' was the first thing she said. 'Tell Mr No-Show that the wolfhound is with me. I got back to find the poor thing hadn't been walked in *days*. God knows where he's been, but when you speak, stress that I have people to see this morning, and be sure that he feels bad because I've left you to look after it.'

'Sure,' I said fragrantly, and didn't flinch one jot when a big silly dog lifted its paws on to my desk and drooled all over my doodle pad.

The boys played it well too. I know because I spent my lunch-break at the cybercafe. Did the same thing all week, in fact, quietly taking my place among all the other people who had come to check up on them. Word was, most of the viewers were pleased that Slim persevered with *The Money Shot*. He might have wound up in a rut on a beach, but watching him struggle with Misty was a reward in itself. My brother joined him regularly on the sofa to watch. He would have provided a steady and ever-cynical commentary as well, had he not kept breaking off to quarrel with the ticker. Still, it looked authentic. Especially when they took time out to smoke a spliff in the so-called dead zones and banter like a bunch of berks. Slim and Pavlov played guys together to a *T*! They were naturals at it. One time, Pavlov drifted back from the little boys' room, accepted a joint from Slim and even made a big thing about keeping behind the red tape.

'Can I ask you something?' he asked, and pinched the spliff between his lips.

'Sure,' said Slim. 'What's on your mind?'

Pavlov gathered the front of his shirt, lifted it above his belt buckle and looked at him searchingly. 'Does my dick look big in this?'

Slim checked out the grin cracking open on his face, but didn't once look at his slacks, just came back with an observation of his own. 'My dick is so big, it has people on the payroll.'

'Yeah?' My brother seemed impressed.

'An entire entourage, mate. Straight up.'

'You think that's big? My dick's *people* have people. You want to talk to my dick's PA, you get in touch with the assistant first.'

'Mine has an agent,' Slim countered, this time with a note of finality. 'That's how big my dick is.'

'Mine is bigger still.' Pavlov jabbed his thumb nonchalantly at the window. 'Check out the tour bus.'

It was a class act, and I frequently shared the highlights with the bartender. My drinks served up to perfection in return. Coming as they did with ice and reassurance.

'You're doing okay,' Max kept saying, which would've been good had I not still been dwelling on my brother's agony interpretation. It wasn't until the last day of that week, however, that I asked him to break from serving and elaborate. The place had grown so busy over recent days, it was all he'd been able to say. 'Cisco,' he declared, feigning shock that I'd even had to question it, 'it's *great*! If you were doing good then you'd be trying too hard. Keeping it real is where it's at, which makes *camplicity* almost as compelling as *getcartier*.'

'You're a subscriber?'

My new gay best friend said he didn't need to be, and invited me to look round the ranks of surfers in here. 'The people watching your housemates right now are basically killing time. Waiting for the main event.'

'That's brilliant,' I said. 'Frank is a hit!'

'Last night, I'm shaking up a daiquiri, it's like the whole place goes beep.'

'Beep?'

'They got mail.'

'Ah,' I said, up to speed with him now. 'We receive the same alert at home, but knowing our landlord has just booted up his computer is not exactly an invitation for us to log on.'

'Very wise,' he agreed. 'From what I've seen, all he does in his spare time is monitor *camplicity*.'

I was finishing my drink when he said this, and came away with a whistle. 'Imagine if Cartier caught us watching him.'

'Don't go there,' said Max. 'I believe there'd be hell to pay.'

When I returned from lunch that Friday, my favourite scout was already waiting for me at the reception desk. She looked as if she had been there for some time. The woman refusing to be helped by my cover, the temp behind the temp. The way her face set hard when I shrugged off my coat and beamed at her, I believed she had a new low lined up for me: a request, perhaps, to wear a wire when I next picked up my wages from her old man's temping agency. Having dealt with everything from her hire-car people to her hairdresser, I was ready for anything. Except, that is, the offer of a new job.

'You're good with people,' she said, 'and I'm on the lookout for a booker.'

'Pardon me?' At first I thought she had said *hooker*. Asking me to sleep with her husband would have been the ultimate low, but I kept my composure which was a good call, because she removed her presidential shades and went on to detail the kind of demands that would come with the position. The cosmopolitan travel and the clothing allowance should have been enough for me to ask when she wanted me to start. The way she outlined my career prospects if I worked as hard as I had for her here, it sounded too good to be true.

'So what do you say?' she asked, and her glasses went back on again. My head screamed at my mouth to say yes, to sign on the dotted line before she had even drawn up a contract. Here it was, my chance to go places at last! I drew breath, trying hard to contain my excitement, but my heart got in there before I could stop it. 'Can I give you an answer on Monday? I'd like to talk it through with someone first.'

Looking at Slim, when I found him waiting nervously outside the agency after work, I believed he'd smashed something precious belonging to me. That was my first thought when he handed me the brassy bunch of tulips and euphorbia. 'Misty and I needed some space,' he said, playing with me now. 'I thought it might be nice to get out of the house for a while. Meet my girlfriend after work, see how she's doing.'

Slim was wearing a shirt that might have belonged to an agony uncle before colour was invented. The creases in his trousers looked sharp enough to draw blood, and I could see my reflection in his shoes. Complete with his cut-down hair, he looked like a man on the move. I thought about telling him my good news, but we had a lot more to talk about on the slow stroll home.

'Did you two have a row?' I asked, though I didn't just have Misty in mind.

Slim smiled, and handed me the bouquet. 'We'll sort it out,' was what he said. 'It's all about team work.'

I cradled his offering, and was surprised to find the wrap coming apart in my hands. I actually had to put a twist in it to keep it together. 'Don't tell me you bought these from another florist?' I said. 'What will Sweet think about that?'

'Willie had his boy running the stall. He told me the boss was helping to rehabilitate a friend.' Slim stopped there and looked at me as if our dealer was assisting a drug casualty or something. I was busting to tell him about Rose, not least the unspoken issue in Sweet William's life that stopped him from being a man about his feelings for her. Had my own private affairs not just been seized upon by the public, I might have shared his secret with Slim. As it was, I just said, 'Willie looks after his own.'

'Sometimes I wish I could be more like him.' Slim said this so quickly and so quietly that I wondered whether he was talking to himself, like his thoughts had just slipped out unchecked.

'There's no need.' I said. 'You're doing okay.'

'Is that good?' Slim reached up to touch his brow ring, and grinned when he found nothing there. 'Usually with an upgrade you get a manual or a help desk. Some way to check you're doing the right thing.' He tapped his temple, then shook himself down inside his shirt. 'I'm all trial and error.'

'So long as we aim to learn from our mistakes,' I said, smiling when Slim insisted on carrying my shoulder bag. 'That's what matters most.'

We reached the bus stop, and continued walking, ignored the tube station too. I didn't realise we had passed it until the next one loomed, and even then we drifted on. Easing our way through the rush hour like everyone else in this city, forgetting passing faces just as they left ours behind. The anonymity meant everything to us, and we seized the chance to talk, opening up about where we'd come from and all the places we could head to from here – not just in our work but out of it too. Behind us the late sun blazed between the clouds. It served to lengthen our shadows as we gravitated east, lengthening our shadows, almost pointing out where we had to go first.

43

Things came undone in Columbia Road. We crossed into the flower market, holding hands for the first time in a while, and immediately I sensed that something wasn't right. Dusk was falling fast, stealing the colour from the petals underfoot. Most of the traders were packed up for the day, and already the cars had crept back in. Filling the spaces left by the stalls, just as they always did.

'Seen a ghost?' asked Slim, as my hand tightened in his. We were standing on the white line, midway across the road.

'Our stalker.' I gestured at the gap outside our house. '*Where is he?*' We both looked to see if he had parked elsewhere, but the sound of a motor turning into the street stopped us in our tracks. We spun round to face the far end, and there it was, prowling towards us with the sky sliding up the windshield: the old man's Morris Traveller.

'He's home now,' was how Slim greeted the slow closing motor. Several pigeons sprang from its path, but they needn't have got so flustered. If the figure behind the wheel planned to mow us down, we could have smoked a last cigarette before he reached us. For the car was simply coasting, and came to a halt just a yard from our feet. Was he dead in there? I wondered. It happened to men of his age, certainly more frequently than a belated desire to climb into frocks and hound people. A sudden crunch from the gearbox made me catch my breath, but that turned to a sigh when the vehicle reversed into its usual spot, just in front of our gate.

'I was worried there for a moment,' I said, as we hurried for the front door. 'I thought he'd gone for good.'

Inside the house, Slim and I discovered we weren't alone in picking up on things that were missing from the frame. Despite all that chat about where we'd been and where we might go together, there was something about where we were *at* that remained unspoken. It was a fixture in any other relationship that had been absent from ours since the cams crawled out of the woodwork. We might have pledged to put on a show for our landlord, to be everyday in every way, but one thing just wasn't in my repertoire. An act I refused to perform now that I knew there would be an audience, and which had kept Slim and me apart at night – sexiles in the same bed.

I might have been tempted a couple of times but whenever we came close I sensed other people getting closer still and then zooming in from every angle: jostling for the best seats in the house. It was frustrating, not least for the hardcore element of our audience, as we were to discover from the man who believed he was running the show.

'Look at you both,' declared Frank Cartier, welcoming us into our own kitchen like he hadn't seen us in years. He turned to Pavlov, who was sitting at the table fretting at the corners of a napkin. 'Don't they make the perfect couple?'

My brother complied as if the man had him hostage, agreed that we were made for each other without pausing to consider the question.

'It's always good to see you too, Mr Cartier.' Slim cleared his throat. I hoped it would stop him sounding so unsettled. 'Nothing wrong with the server, is there?'

'Far as I know the server is firing on all cylinders.' He was a big man, our landlord, not as big as Sweet William but he seemed to fill as much space just by standing with his back to the sink – his shoulders squared by his camel coat and those hard, hooded eyes that always found you first. 'Technology is a wonderful thing,' he said to us now. 'Once you get a system up and running, the only thing that can screw it up is human error.'

The way he said this, making out we were letting him down somehow. It was an issue that became even more apparent once he persuaded Pavlov to give us a moment alone. Cartier didn't even have to ask him to leave: he just ran a glass of water, left the tap dripping into the sink, and watched my brother take himself upstairs. 'Thirsty work this property game,' he said, between gulps. 'Been checking up on tenants all week. Making sure everybody's cosy.' He paused to finish his drink, then levelled with us both. 'Everything's all right between you both, isn't it?'

'Fine,' I said quickly. 'Never better.'

Cartier gestured at the one cam in the room that we were supposed to know about. 'It's not getting on your tits, then?'

'Absolutely not,' I said, wondering if he had meant to be so literal.

'You're sure about that? If I was living with little segments of my house online I might get a bit . . . self-conscious, you know. A bit cranky sometimes. A little *uptight.*'

'Not us,' I said, and shook my head.

'Because I wouldn't want this to come between you.'

'It's touching that you're so concerned,' Slim assured him, 'but we're more relaxed about the webcams now than we've ever been. Honestly, I barely notice the red tape around the house any more. I really think we're on top of the situation.'

When he said this I thought I might laugh, for it was perfectly clear to me why Cartier was here, circling the subject like a marriage-guidance counsellor. The man trying too hard to make out that he gave a damn about our welfare.

'Happy tenants is what I like to see,' he said. 'It's all I ever want.'

I was tempted to drop the act and tell him we didn't cater for an adult audience. Even if it did boost membership to his secret second site, the only screwing that would go on under this roof was what he was doing to us. I considered a showdown, right there and then, but at that moment Pavlov returned with a complaint of his own.

'That's it,' he said, sounding panicked. 'It's blocked.'

'Then stop putting so much paper down there.' Our landlord addressed Pavlov but looked at Slim and me. I slipped my arm around Slim, gave Cartier what he wanted to see.

'It's not that kind of blockage,' Pavlov continued. 'This seems to be more of a . . . a tidal thing.'

Cartier turned round slowly, wincing as he faced my brother. 'A tidal thing?'

'The water goes up and then it goes down. If I flush on a high it'll flood.'

'And you bring this to me now? Last thing on a Friday?'

'You *are* the landlord.' Pavlov stood his ground, matching the man's steady gaze. The sanitary condition of the house was a point of principle for him.

'All right, relax,' said Cartier eventually. 'I'll have Kenzo look into it, but don't expect him before Monday. You'll just have to improvise until then.'

'Improvise?'

'I don't know. Use a milk bottle. Go next door.'

'Next *door*?' My brother had something to say about that, but whatever it was came out as a squeak instead.

'We'll be fine if we flush on a low,' I said, to compromise. 'Nobody likes to be disturbed at the weekend.'

Frank Cartier chewed an imaginary nut, nodding in agreement, then stuck a low-slung finger at Slim. 'Look after this girl, you hear me? Treat her right on her time off. She's a star. She deserves the very best, body and soul.'

'I know that,' said Slim, and drew me close. 'I'd be a fool to let her out of my sight.'

'Then my job is done here.' Cartier flexed his shoulders under his camel, told us he had to go if he was going to get home before dark.

'One more thing,' said Pavlov, stepping out of his way.

Cartier didn't turn around, just stopped in the hall with his back to my brother and his head bowed low. 'Whatever it is,' he said gruffly, 'I believe it might spoil my weekend.'

'But Mr C—'

'*Monday*, Pavlov. Hold on to something, for once in your life.'

'I should've told him about the stalkers,' said Pavlov later that evening, and not for the first time either. It was as if he hoped that repeating himself might change the outcome of Cartier's visit. 'No landlord would walk out on his tenants if he knew they were at risk. Had I told him, he would've dealt with it. Maybe killed two birds with one stone and sorted the loo as well.'

'A blocked toilet might be his problem.' Slim handed the spliff to my brother. He'd only just fired it up, but then Pavlov had been stuck in high gear since our landlord left. 'A geriatric gender-bender is most probably ours.'

'I still think it's outrageous.' My brother broke off to take his first hit, which thankfully served to downshift him into something approaching silence. We were squeezed into the blind spot again. The carpet at the top of the stairs was starting to look a little grubby we spent so much time there. Mostly it was dropped ash, but then it wasn't our carpet, however, and our respect for the house had taken quite a nosedive lately.

The boys were kneeling on either side of me, the three of us studying the laptop in front of us. We were logged on to *camplicity*, and I was pleased to see that the webcams reported nobody at home. Okay, so a determined browser with an eye for detail might have noticed the twist of smoke floating towards the ceiling, but not the spliff that we shared out of shot. Slim just kept cranking them out, more so since the trap had been set in Cartier's house. I could have refused but here in the house it helped to take the edge off our situation. Blurred the boundaries, so to speak. Just as long as we didn't hear the fire truck while we smoked, and kept our voices down, it was safe to say that within this square we were invisible to the outside world. I extracted the joint from my brother, who had kind of died there with it between his fingers.

'What do you think he does with himself?' I wondered aloud. 'Cartier says he's all business and no pleasure, but people are shelling out to watch him in front of his computer.'

'Why should we care?' asked Slim. 'Having spent time on the wrong side of a webcam, I'm not busting to swap sides and watch someone else.'

'Come on,' I said. 'It would be great to get some dirt on him.'

'We're making money from the man,' Slim reminded me, 'maybe not a fortune but at least I can sleep at night again. Why would I want to give myself nightmares by joining the audience? Leave it to them, Cisco. They're paying us for the privilege, after all.'

'But he practically asked us to make love online!' I said, upon which my brother jolted back to his senses. 'You know, perhaps it's time we got out of here while we still can.'

I said this without thinking, but clearly it sounded the right note for us all. Even if the chime we actually heard marked the arrival of an email. A green light, of sorts, from *getcartier*, triggered by the fact that the man himself had just logged on from his own computer. It was our cue to get into character, to got out and go live. By now the boys were conditioned to act on the prompt. Slim took off to the front room and resumed his relationship with Misty Ventura, while Pavlov retreated to his bedroom and got on with his ironing. Me? I improvised. I didn't have a routine. I fitted in around them, but just then I didn't want to fit anywhere else but here. Alone in the blind spot with a half-smoked spliff and a laptop link to our landlord's library, I was exactly where I wanted to be. The boys might have claimed not to care, but I couldn't ignore my curiosity. So what did I see through the eagle's eye? A skewed view of Frank in front of his monitor, positioned so that I could see what he was watching. It was nothing fancy, but more than enough for me. I watched our landlord settle into his chair, and decided that he'd only just got home because he shook off his camel like it was an afterthought.

'Hello, Mr Cartier.' I steeled myself for anything as he began to work the keyboard, wavering only when the welcome screen for our second site popped up on his monitor. Still, I thought, at least I could keep an eye on him this time. 'Wipe your feet on the way in,' I said, and eased back the laptop lid to make things more comfortable for me.

For the first time, I realised I was looking at him without him looking at me. It took away some of the intensity from his gaze. Made Frank seem a little less imposing. But then his expression assumed a harder edge. He stabbed at the keyboard, muttering what looked like curses.

'What's the matter?' I could see from his monitor that he was with us in the virtual sense, moving through the cams downstairs, into the kitchen already. 'What are you looking for?'

Another click, and Frank entered the front room. Slim could be seen on his screen now, cross-legged on the sofa with his joypad and a look of strained concentration. I thought our landlord might settle there too, spend a little time on him, maybe reverse the shot to see how Misty was getting on, but he clicked out again, and swung up the stairs. I watched him leap through the landing cams, and I swear it felt as if a ghost had just passed through me. Next up was Pavlov's bedroom. He found my brother steam-pressing creases into his socks, and made a quick retreat. It was when Frank entered the second bedroom on the menu that my core temperature dropped by a degree. The way he slowed down here to appreciate the many different pictures on offer. The dropped G-string. A tissue I had used to blot my lips, followed by the depression in my pillow on the bed. I watched him lean in close to his screen, and pulled away, disgusted.

The creep was here for me.

This wasn't just business, I realised, as he consulted the chat room inside my knickers drawer. Nor was it just pleasure. The man was getting cash *and* kicks from the clicks he had set up here. Just to be sure, I crushed the joint and visited the boys in turn. I spoke to

Pavlov first, just a quiet word in his ear, then headed downstairs to nuzzle up to Slim and share the same whispered request. Slim did exactly as I had asked him. When he left me alone on the sofa, and joined Pavlov in the blind spot, I could only guess that Cartier was shadowing me. I would know for sure once we'd run this test shot. I felt like bait, sitting there on the sofa while the other two watched our landlord from the laptop. I was tempted to pick up the joypad, but I didn't think Slim would appreciate me messing with his game at this stage. Misty herself was panting on a shoreline somewhere, just as Slim had said. A digital sun hovered over her horizon, laying out light across the water. I wished I could have joined her some how. Get out of this world and into another. Instead, I received a summons from my brother, delivered by Pavlov who appeared at the door with the colour pressed from his lips.

'You're right,' whispered Slim, when we joined him round the laptop. 'Cartier got close up to you, then went under the sofa, into the chat room to share what he had seen.'

'You should've read the comments.' This was my brother. 'On second thoughts, just accept that the man is a voyeur of the lowest order.'

On the screen, I watched Cartier working his own keyboard. He was picking through the cams in our landing, circling like a virtual vulture, probably wondering how we had managed to disappear. At one point I caught sight of the crown of my head. I ducked away, cursing quietly, but this had nothing to do with my roots situation.

'That's it! We have to shut this thing down.'

'Cisco's right.' My brother squashed in tightly beside me. 'I've never felt so claustrophobic in my life. As soon as he logs off, we're leaving.'

At the same time, Cartier appeared to give up the search for us and clicked into the toilet. The shot he had of the pan was just distasteful, but what really sickened me was that people had been watching us from that vantage-point.

'High tide,' Slim noted. 'Check it out.'

Sure enough, the water looked dangerously close to the rim. I half expected Pavlov to break down on the spot. As it was, we all did – not because the toilet threatened to flood, but because Cartier took a plunge into it, pointing his browser to a cam we hadn't visited ourselves. A cam we didn't know *existed*, located way beyond the U-bend, that went beyond belief. On a website where nothing was sacred, in a world where every stone hid an entertainment opportunity, the man had installed a sewer cam.

'Mother of God.' I pressed my hands to my cheeks and stared dumbly at the revelation on Cartier's screen. It looked like an image beamed up from a sub on the ocean floor, something so far down and desolate it was all done by remote. I could only think the cam was a probe of some sort, for a jaundiced light pushed through the gloom, too weak to pick out anything more than particles suspended in the water. Frank swivelled round in his chair to the cabinet beside his desk and extracted a bottle of Scotch. I didn't blame him for needing a drink. It was a shame that he went back for a glass, in some ways, because he missed the moment on his monitor when the sewer light halved in reach and flashed a silvery green. 'Did you see that?' I masked my mouth with my hand, mindful of the noise and the fact that I felt a bit sick. 'There's something *moving* down there.'

'Whatever it was,' said Pavlov, 'I'm about to freak out.'

'Is it a turd?' Slim peered a little closer as another shredded shape slid through the light. 'It's a good footer by my reckoning.'

'A foot,' I said. 'That's monstrous.'

'It's worse than that,' my brother said with a note of dread now. 'It's moving against the current.'

The three of us closed in on the laptop as if it was sucking the air from the house, drawing us through our screen to Cartier's own monitor. Because that was where the gloom was eclipsed by a curious, stalk-like eye. An extreme close up that moved Slim and me to face Pavlov, who turned to the heavens and wailed so quietly he could've been a lost kitten.

'*The Sea Maidens!*'

Was it fooling with Frank? Playing peep-po with the man as he poured himself a drink? That was how it looked when the beast backed away from the lens to bring its friends in on the act. For the second or so that it lasted, a shoal of bloated mutants crammed the frame – scattering when Cartier came back to the keyboard. I remembered to blink just then, my dope-shot mind still struggling to make sense of what I had seen. The silence didn't make it any easier, which was why I filled it with the first thing that came into my head. 'It said in the instructions they were playful.'

'It said a lot of things in the instructions.' Slim glowered at my brother. 'But I don't think it touched on what happens if you stoke them up with growth food and flush them down the *bog*!'

'Let's get out of here,' said Pavlov, sounding beyond all reason. 'If the sanitation goes, so do I.'

'Wait!' Slim lifted a cautionary finger and levelled it at the laptop. Cartier had just switched off his monitor, and was collecting his camel from the back of the chair. 'This fucker has to pay.'

Our landlord did what I was desperate to do: he knocked back a stiff one and he walked away. The three of us left there in the eagle's eye, watching him slip out of the library.

'Go grizzly,' my brother urged Slim, calling the shots for real this time. 'He's heading into the next room. Give me the bear. *Give me the goddamn bear!*'

Slim stabbed at the keys, and the feed on the screen cut to the second cam. It might have been a cave we were watching from here, such was the view from the grizzly's gullet. Through the space between its jaws, we could see the beast in full, reflected in the mirror on the far side of the room. It had been mounted on its hind legs, raised on its haunches with both paws lifted high, which was potentially quite scary had it not served as a coat-stand.

'Here he is again,' Slim said as Frank walked into shot, coming right up to the webcam, so it seemed. I could tell he was hanging his coat, but all I could see of him beyond the bear's canines was a serrated sliver: a ruddy cheek, a cauliflower ear, then a glimpse of something else as he turned to face the mirror.

'That's more ugly than the Maidens,' said Slim. 'I just hope he does something seriously embarrassing now.'

'How many people are watching, do you reckon?'

Slim turned to Pavlov, said even if it was just the three of us that would be enough.

'So long as he doesn't do naked,' my brother warned. 'Anything but that.'

Frank Cartier didn't appear to be preparing to slip into something unsightly, but what I had seen him slip *out* of his coat pocket demanded closer attention. Standing now with his back to us, he rolled his shoulders then shadow-boxed with his reflection like the winner he probably thought he was. That little pig tail of his snapping up and down as he danced from foot to foot.

'If I could make this bear move,' said Slim, 'I'd step forward and kick his butt.'

'Don't be too hasty,' I said, my eyes locked on the screen. 'Check out the cash he's got in each fist.'

Slim leaned in, like my brother, and I waited for them to spot what I had seen already. But it wasn't a roll of pennies Frank had there, an old boxing trick that even I knew packed a mean punch. This was strictly paper weight, at least a couple of grand in each paw, which told me everything I needed to know about his form.

'Look at that,' said Pavlov, his voice riding up the scales. '*Look!*'

'Friday.' Slim gave a little whistle. 'Rent day.'

'For what?' I asked. 'The property he owns offline or online?'

'Either way,' my brother observed, 'I hope he washes his hands.'

'That kind of dirt doesn't come off easily,' I said. 'Not if it's come from *camplicity.com.*'

Frank gave a jab and a hook as I said this, and bounced round now as if ready for the bear.

'Jesus Christ, *get out of the mouth*!'

'Don't move.' Slim grabbed my brother's wrist, stopped him bailing out. 'Don't even breathe.'

We had been rumbled. Cartier was wise to the cam. He had to be, didn't he? The man standing there with two bunches of notes, squared up to the grizzly with a look on his face like he was about to deliver a punchline. He reached out next, as I had feared he would, but his fingers didn't find us. They went low instead. Somewhere in the region of the bear's guts, I thought. The way our picture began to rock back and forth, it was certainly deeply invasive.

'What is this?' Slim whispered, but he didn't need to ask again. Not when Frank Cartier stepped aside and began to root around in the pocket of his camel coat. I knew because we could see the bigger picture in the facing mirror: the grizzly with its pelt peeled apart, opened up by a zipper to reveal the stuffing inside, all of it banded into bricks, exactly like the two he had just deposited in there.

'What it is,' I said, as our landlord returned to pack another wedge inside the cavity, 'is one hell of a money shot.'

From the shoreline next day, with the late sun laying out light across the water, I turned to Slim and said, 'These things always look so much better for real, don't you think?'

'I'm not so sure.' He kicked a little sand with his boot. 'I could seriously use a sofa.' We had dressed to suit the part. Slim wore a black turtleneck with his combats, a rope looped over his shoulder and his balaclava rolled back to the tips of his ears. For the bank robbery a mask would have gone too far, while a pizza-boy's outfit was just perfect last time around. On this occasion, I didn't have a problem if his ensemble made him feel better about the job ahead of us. My boyfriend looked like a semi-skimmed version of the Milk Tray man, but nobody would see him this time – so we hoped. 'Keep it together,' I said, to encourage him. 'If we pull this off, you can lounge in luxury for ever more.'

My mobile rang just then, as it had every thirty minutes since we pitched up on the beach below Cartier's mansion. We had made it down here just after midday. Abandoned the Beetle way down the coastal road, then spent the afternoon waiting for the all clear. It had been a tense, frustrating experience, watching the sun sail out of the sky, the sea breeze sharpening underneath.

'Talk to me, Pavlov,' I said, into the phone. 'What's happening at home?'

'No change,' he said. 'The pig is in his pen.'

I sighed, masked the mouthpiece and translated the message for Slim. 'Frank is in the house still,' I said. 'Did you tell my brother to talk in code?'

'I might've done,' he said sheepishly. 'It's what they do, isn't it?'

I said he'd been watching way too many movies, then went back

309

to Pavlov and told him we couldn't wait any longer. 'We have to act before nightfall. We can't risk missing out, and I don't want to get wet if a storm breaks. I only washed my hair this morning.'

A pause down the line, then, 'So you want me to feed the pig?'

'Eh?'

'Like we discussed. I'm ready to fill the trough. Give me the word, it's as good as done.'

'Pavlov,' I said, after a pause, 'just run the tape, all right?'

'Roger. That's a big ten four.'

'Oh, for God's sake, what's wrong with a simple "yes"?'

'*Smokey and the Bandit,*' he said. 'It's what they say to sign off.'

'Forget what they do in films,' I replied. 'We're not watching this on a screen. The conventions don't count out here.'

'Okay. I read you.'

'Bro, shut up and play the bloody tape. Slim and I are ready to start the climb.'

'Good luck, you guys,' he said, like I was the one wasting time.

I shut down the phone, then zipped up the puffa I was wearing. It was a sleeveless affair, with a collar like a yoke. A gift from a florist I had stayed with recently. Sweet William kept a stock of them to cover for every extreme. I hadn't packed for my week with him, and this was one of many kind gestures I had been too scared to refuse. And right now it provided just the comfort I needed.

Slim was standing with his back to the water, sizing up the cliff fall behind us. What had been a sheer chalk wall was reduced to a scarred basin here with hunks of rock damming the rubble behind it. Wild grass and gorse spotted the slope itself, and meshing had been laid down to prevent further erosion. Towards the top, a stratum of steel piles jutted from the rock. Underpinning work was what it was, but it made the mansion just behind the summit look like a fortress. Even the ivy spilling over the edge could have doubled as a balustrade. Slim slipped the rope from his shoulder. I didn't like to say it was all just a matter of perspective. The slope didn't look that hard to conquer. We could probably just hike up most of it, I thought, but decided to keep that one to myself. Slim was clearly busting to assume control of the situation, and I didn't want to spoil his moment. If anything, I hoped that by letting him go first he would get it out of his system before we found ourselves in real danger.

'Are you sure you don't want to wait here for me?' he asked. 'It's going to be tough.'

'Don't worry about that.' I looked out to sea, saw the first fingers of cloud clawing in from the wings. 'Let's just get inside the house before it rains.'

Straight in. Straight out. Only this time with a sting that would guarantee some serious relief. There had been no need for me to spin it to the boys: after everything Frank Cartier had put us through, the time had come to go beyond just getting even. Wiring him up to a webcam might have levelled the score, but it was never going to net us the kind of prize money we had witnessed him squirrel away. The night before, we had checked out of the bear and agreed that a rebate was in order. It had taken some foresight and planning, of course, a little intuition on my part as to what made Cartier tick. I even had Coral instruct us on how to shut down *getcartier* to the viewing public. That way, there would be no more shots of the grizzly spilling its golden guts for all to see and, crucially, no evidence of our impending visit to lay claim to it. From here on, it was strictly closed-circuit. The feed from the mansion went no further than our laptop at home, and Pavlov was under strict instructions to report in regularly on our landlord's position.

Following Slim over the boulders at the base of the slope now, I wondered how far the boys would have got without me in this bid to hit Frank where it hurt. The front-door bell probably. It was that kind of mindset I was dealing with here.

We had squabbled over the plan, of course, but eventually both

Slim and my brother conceded that we should approach from the cliff side, seek out the weakest part of the property and gain entry that way. Even if we had to break glass I was confident that our landlord wouldn't hear it: the distraction we had cooked up was just too good for him to miss, as was the window of opportunity it would open up for us. Right now, as we picked our way up the scarp, I knew he would be in the library watching *camplicity*. The cams inside the eagle and the bear confirmed that he had been logged on like that since first light. If he left the frame it was only to fetch food, drink or the paper. According to a recent update from Pavlov, the man had yet to get out of his silk dressing-gown. It was as if Frank Cartier lived his life in front of his computer in the hope of catching the best of ours.

What Cartier didn't know was that Slim, Pavlov and I had been up through the night, preparing for the dawn of this day. Because if we didn't get to his mansion first I feared someone else would. We could only guess how many people had been watching when Frank stashed his cash inside the grizzly, but it was an open invitation to every crook in cyberspace. That was why we got it together while the world outside was asleep, going so far as to film a little footage for Pavlov's new friend Coral to feed into the server. Something to guarantee that Cartier's bum stayed on his seat while we went to work. It had been Coral's idea to record a scene that would dupe him into thinking I was at home, enjoying a moment all to myself. I had only agreed to go ahead and tape it on condition that the bedroom door was locked and the curtains closed. I wasn't alone with the digital camera, of course. Anyone could have been in the room with me, thanks to our landlord's secret set-up. Anyone except the man himself, because I didn't start filming until the house lights went out inside *getcartier*, and that was all that mattered to me.

'What you filmed in the bedroom.' Slim was just ahead of me when he said this, leading the way up the slope. 'Will I get to see it some time?'

'It's private,' I said. 'For Frank's eyes only.'

We dropped down to all fours as the incline grew steeper, scrabbling for purchase on the chalk. Even so, Slim didn't need the rope. It was just a question of considering our footing: concentrating on the climb with the same focus we had put into the groundwork. The real challenge was in our hands – not just because we were exhausted from lack of sleep and strung out for all kinds of reasons, but because of what we were actually *doing* here. The pair of us seemed way beyond our boundaries now, attempting a third excursion into the world of crime. A world in which I had no place, but was compelled to visit if we wanted a return to normality.

Up ahead I could hear Slim breathing heavily, grunting as he negotiated a loose pocket of stones. 'Couldn't you just talk me through the highlights?' That was what came down from him next. 'Specifically the big moment.'

'The tape is supposed to distract Cartier, not you!' I tried to catch up with him, but the chalk face was a little unforgiving. 'Thirty minutes' grace is what it gives us. Thirty minutes' knowing that he's shut inside his library. So keep quiet and climb.'

Maybe it was my fault, I was stressed about this whole ordeal, but yelling like that marked the moment Slim lost his footing. I saw the sole of one boot seek an outcrop of rock, and barely had time to shield my face as a shower of chippings exploded over me.

'*Shit!*' I yelled, and so did he. It was only when the dust cleared with the stiffening breeze that I dared to look up again. Relief came over me next, when I saw that Slim was still there, grinning from his foothold on a tuft of grass. He seemed quite casual about it, in fact. 'Will you stop with these movie moments?' I said. 'I really thought you'd hurt yourself there.'

'Not even a twist,' Slim insisted, upon which the grass gave way beneath him.

46

I find men tend to go one of two ways over an injury: either they make out nothing's wrong or they strike up a great big fuss. It's one or the other. No middle ground. No *honesty.* Had it been my brother who had wrenched his ankle out there, I imagine he would have dialled 999 straight away. I could just imagine the rescue chopper dropping level with us, the pilot assessing the situation from the air, before his crewmate whips out the megaphone and bawls us out for time-wasting. That would have drawn Frank Cartier from his computer. Fortunately, under the circumstances, Slim was the type to bite down on his lip and assure me he was fine. His pride might have taken a tumble, but the rest of him had only slid a couple of yards down the slope. Watching him claw his way level with me, however, I could tell he had hurt himself. The way he winced every time he pushed up with his left, it was clear that I had to take control.

'Give me the rope,' I said, reaching out to pull him level, but Slim made out that he hadn't heard me. 'Come on, you're in pain. Let me make things easier for you.'

'Do you want to tie yourself to me?' he asked.

'No. I want you to tie yourself to *me.*'

'You're going first?'

'Trust me,' I said. 'You do trust me, don't you?'

The light was pulling away from us, and I could feel bad weather behind it. Dusk approached darkness too quickly, while the wind was beginning to bluster off the water – pushing my hair across my face. One thing I hadn't thought to bring was a scrunchie. Slim had no call to pinch mine any more, so I improvised with the bracelet he had given me. Once I'd bound my hair into a ponytail, I bound Slim to me with his rope.

'I hate to refer to the films again,' he said, holding his arms apart as I struggled with the knot, 'but aren't we supposed to be tethered to something other than each other?'

'Oh!' I faced back to him. 'Is that how they do it?'

Slim confirmed that in *Cliffhanger* Sly Stallone never made a climb without being tethered to his buddy or a babe. Didn't matter which, they were always tethered to the rockface by extension.

'You're right,' I agreed, then considered the rope around his waist. *'How?'*

Slim shrugged. 'It's a mountaineering thing, I guess. More importantly, it looks good for the camera. Shows a spiritual kind of bonding.'

I tugged at the knot to tighten it, and watched the whole thing snake apart. We looked at each other, then eased into the same grin. I retrieved the rope, but felt no need to forewarn him when I slung it from the slope. We had to get back to basics here. We had to be *ourselves*. 'Follow me,' I said, and struck out for the top once more. 'Let's dare to defy convention.'

Where Slim had gone for great big hobnails, my boots proved more fitting for this climb. The soft leather, flexible soles and good ankle support served me well as I negotiated a path towards the underpinning. I was quite chuffed by my whole choice of outfit, in fact. Jeans would have chafed on a climb like this, and anything more than a high-cropped vest would have been equally restricting. Okay, I was a little chilly once I'd shrugged off Willie's puffa, but at least I was free to find a space between the steel piles and ease my way through. After that I could breathe easy, as the bars formed a platform to stand on. It gave me a chance to shift my shoulder-bag on to my back. With the puffa rolled up in there, I found it was more comfortable. Weighted just fine. It was only as I adjusted the straps that I wondered what was taking Slim so long. I peered between my feet to see if he needed a hand, and found he hadn't moved one bit.

'What's the matter now?' All I could see was a rapt and awestruck face. For a beat I thought I had a rip in the seat of my shorts. I called out his name, even had to snap my fingers to bring him back to me. 'Is there something you want to share?'

'God no!' Slim clawed his way closer. He brought his face up to the steel piles, grasping at them like a prisoner on lock down. 'Unless you've brought a change of bra—'

'Slim,' I stopped him there. 'You're in shock.'

'Shock?' he said. 'I'm stunned.'

I didn't give him a chance to elaborate, even though he seemed busting to speak up. 'You've had a lucky escape,' I agreed, 'but now is not the time to dig for sympathy. Try to stay focused and get yourself up here.'

The beach was just a band below us now. The bay shaped like a scallop. Same colour, too, now the clouds had begun to clasp and bruise. By the time Slim had hoisted himself up to my level, I was itching to finish the climb. We didn't have far to go – I could actually touch the ivy spilling over the summit. The problem was it had grown in such abundance that we were faced with an overhang. I was just sizing up the best way over when my phone began bleating again. I unclipped it from my belt, said, 'Talk to me, brother.'

'Fifteen minutes left on the tape,' he said, pressingly. 'Are you in?'

'The mansion?'

'The pen sounded so much better, but we'll call it the mansion if we must.'

I glanced at Slim, caught him checking me out in a weird way. 'Will you stop it,' I hissed, breaking from the call for a beat.

'The tape is working a treat,' my brother continued. 'Cartier's watching it so closely I can't even be sure he's still breathing. Soon as he saw what you were up to in the bedroom, he poured himself another Scotch and made himself very comfortable indeed.'

'Can *you* see what I'm doing on his monitor?'

'I've conditioned myself not to focus on that section of the screen.

I don't even want to know what you did to leave him so transfixed. Soon as this is over, I'm destroying the tape.'

I glanced at Slim. It was a relief to see him sizing up the last of the incline now and not me.

'We'll be into the grounds soon enough,' I told Pavlov. 'Call me if Frank gets restless.'

'Even if he blinks, I'll let you know.'

'We're relying on you,' I said. 'No toilet breaks, you hear?'

'Understood.' Pavlov said this just a little too quickly. I sensed my spirit sink before he spoke again. 'Don't do anything drastic in the next sixty seconds, okay? I'll be right back.'

I closed down the phone, wondering how he'd manage with that milk bottle, then turned my attention to the summit again.

'What now?' Slim sounded a little defeated.

I turned to face him in profile, and saw only one way up. 'Get on your knees,' I said. 'From your shoulders, I reckon I should be able to do it.'

'With your boots on?' Slim seemed to perk up all over again.

'Once I'm up there, you take my hand and I'll lift you. We haven't got time for power plays right now.'

'Yes, ma'am!' He went down on one knee and lowered his head, braced for a little more weight than I was entirely happy about. With my heart racing, I stepped on to his shoulders, and walked my hands up the last of the rockface.

'Nice and easy now,' I said. 'Up you come.'

I reached for the foliage, grateful that he gripped my ankles when his own legs locked in place. All of a sudden the wind seemed a little keener, the salt tang sharper. I heard gulls overhead somewhere, distraction all around. But I did it. I clawed one hand over the next, clutched at a tough-looking tendril of ivy, and lifted myself from his shoulders. I seemed to swing outwards before I went up, submitting to the overhang with nothing underneath me.

Slim was calling my name, but it didn't register. I was on my own from here. I reached out blindly, did the same again, and the gable end of the mansion appeared from behind the foliage. The place looked proud in the face of all this ruin, defiant to the last. Just like me. I giggled at the thought, feeling absurd and disembodied. That haul-yourself-from-a-swimming-pool sensation when you're so exhausted you could happily sink back and drown. With my abdomen supporting me on the edge of the cliff, I made one last push upwards, my elbows at right angles, fingernails buried in the soil. I gave it everything I could, spreading my load on the palms of my hands, only to find myself grasping wildly at the wind as one side gave way completely. The house seemed to tip into the air, ivy snapping at the same time. I heard the breath rush out of my lungs and Slim below yelling, '*Cisco!*'

Then everything swung still. Stones stopped drumming beneath me. Slim was silent too, leaving nothing but the white noise of the waves in the background. I opened my eyes, and found my hand wrapped around a length of ivy. A length sporting withered yellow leaves that were gradually being flattened as they passed through my fist. 'Slim?' I breathed. 'This is bad. I'm going to fall.'

'You're not going to fall,' he said, automatically. '*Come on*, Misty. Be strong. Be focused. You can do it. I know you can.'

My hand seemed to squeeze a little tighter when he said this, going beyond what I believed I had left in me. Just then I called on muscles I didn't know I possessed, willing myself to make it to the top now that everything else had fallen into place.

'What did you just call me?'

'Cisco, there's a big old root I can see just above you. Reach that and you're there. It'll take an elephant.'

I ignored the implication, spelled it out again. '*What* did you just call me, mister?'

A short pause, then a reluctant voice said, 'Misty. It was a slip of the tongue.'

'Then say it again, but louder this time.' I looked up again, found a lowering sky then the root he had described to me. '*Say it, Slim!*'

'Misty?' he said as if to confirm.

'Again!'

'You want me to call you Misty?' It was exactly what I wanted to hear, the jolt I needed to see this through. I launched my free hand towards the big root. Fired up to get to the next level now, I found myself thinking all kinds of ridiculous things in the terror of the moment. Like maybe this was the move that would make my clothes fall off. 'Come on, girl!' I heard Slim shout. 'That's it. Go for it. You're nearly there. You've got it. *Go, Misty!*'

The grass at the top was damp with dew. Lying there with my backpack underneath me, I could feel it tickling my calves and the nape of my neck. I watched the storm clouds meshing in the gloom and figured my hair was going to get wet whatever. That's when my surroundings made sense again, triggered by something so trivial, and I realised I was in full view of the mansion's rear windows. At any time I feared a light would snap on and this would all be over. I sat up, and was about to shriek Slim's name when the man himself picked his way over the cliff face. The earth I had pulled away had pretty much left a set of steps for him, with bushes for bloody banisters. He climbed into my embrace, feeling warm against the wind and good to hold. Then I pulled back, shared his fond smile, and socked him round the chops. 'You just saved my life,' I told him. 'Don't *ever* do it like that again!'

Somewhere inside I was showing on a screen. Not an exterior shot that captured Slim and me creeping around the mansion perimeter, there wasn't that kind of security here, but a close-up in my bedroom. The one I had made earlier, recorded as live for the titillation of our landlord. As far as Frank was concerned, I was sitting on the edge of my bed just then, peeling off my stockings. He sees me arch my foot, flex my toes, and *ping* – it comes away like a slingshot. Next I cross my arms and take off my top. In my underwear now, I stand in front of the mirror, and try out different attitudes. Haughty at first, then flirty and coquettish. That bust-up with the boyfriend must be behind it. The girl seeking out her sexiest pose to remind herself of what he might have lost. At least, that's how I hoped our landlord would read the unfolding scene. Especially as I was scaling his scaffolding in a very different way at the time.

'How's your ankle?' I turned to Slim, a couple of bars below. I might have slapped him so hard his cheek burned red, but I still found myself looking out for him and worried that he was lagging. Rain had begun to spot now, gusting in from behind us.

'I'll survive,' he said eventually, 'so long as I don't muddle my names again.'

I had gone for a curving wall that flanked the main wing. My guess was it housed a spiral staircase. All we had to do was squeeze through one of the windows up there and we would have access to every level. Slim was quick to agree, not least because the decks and guardrails surrounding the wall made the ascent almost hazard-free. The first two windows turned out to be barred, however, and the one above that blocked by chipboard, which left the loft window in the upper gable.

'Look at this,' I said, when Slim clambered up behind me. 'It's broken already.'

'From the outside in.'

He was right: shards lay scattered on a tea chest in there. We glanced at each other warily. At no point had this seemed like a good idea, but now, more than ever, it was starting to feel like a very bad idea indeed. Of course, we weren't alone in knowing where Frank hid the money: anyone who had logged on to *getcartier* when he banked his cash in the bear would've shared the same insight as us. What worried me now was the audience share that might have been persuaded to act on it.

'Are we too late?' I asked, thinking the glass left in the frame looked horribly jagged.

'Nah.' Slim grabbed one of the couplers on the scaffolding, and gave it a little rattle. 'Cowboy builders probably bust it accidentally. No respect for people's property.'

I smiled thinly. 'At least they have something in common with the owner.'

I went through feet first, kicking out the last of the glass, anxious to get this done. Once inside, I reached back for my bag and found the Maglite I had packed.

'Can I just say,' said Slim, as he followed me through, 'I do believe you're everything a guy could ever wish for.'

'How flattering.' I twisted the light on now so it shone right into his eyes. 'Does that make me your girlfriend, or Player Two?'

'Both.' He grinned, shielding his gaze until I switched the beam on to more immediate matters. Slim shared my apprehension, I knew him too well now, but I was glad he could cover it up. For one thing, it stopped me losing my nerve now that we were in the mansion. Outside, I had been frightened of falling. Here, the sense of danger was in the unknown, which made it all the more immediate. It was dark, it was draughty, and the timbers were creaking like a galleon ship.

My torch beam cut through the dark, spotlighting maritime

trunks, tea chests and stacking plastic chairs. There was junk from every era, stacked up high with a passage running through the heart of it. A wider sweep of the beam picked out pewter jugs and Persian rugs, a commode and even a Commodore computer. I only knew what it was called because Slim pointed it out. He even nipped across for a better look, forcing me to remind him that we weren't at a bring-and-buy.

'But it's from the *eighties*!' he stressed, as thunder grumbled overhead. 'That's not just antique, it's an ancient artefact. Something like that is a collector's item.'

'And so is the money downstairs,' I hissed across the rafters. 'First come, first served. Remember?' It was another distraction I could have done without. One more way for Slim to avoid the reality of our situation. 'Let's move!' I said. 'You can't just press pause in here!' Slim stroked the computer with a fondness reserved for a pet facing the final injection, then fell into line again. I shone the beam at my wristwatch. We had ten minutes at most.

'You're not holding that right.' Slim was so close behind me now I could feel his chin brushing my shoulder. 'Unlike a normal torch, a Maglite is designed to be gripped overarm, you know? Elevated so everyone can see you've got taste. It's a design classic you have there. It's important you do it justice by handling it right.' I turned to face him, held it as suggested, and then clonked him on the forehead. 'How's that?' I asked. 'Or shall I try again?'

Slim didn't answer. He didn't even have a chance to nurse his brow because another voice called my name, I was sure of it. Way down in the building somewhere, there it was again – '*Cisco*' – louder this time and unmistakably male. I whipped the beam one-eighty, found a stuffed owl with a pair of boxing gloves hung round it, then levelled the light into the passage.

'It has to be Cartier,' breathed Slim. 'Oh, shit.'

Now I knew that I had a weapon in my hand, I hefted the Maglite as Slim had instructed. The light found a corner in the passage, a dog-leg of sorts. 'Come on,' I whispered, and began to follow the beam.

'What? You're going to *look*?'

'Slim, we don't have time for this.'

'But didn't they teach you anything on your media course?'

'I'm not going to die, Slim. I completed the scary-movie module.'

'Investigating like that on your own marks you out as a victim.'

'Why?' I said, thinking the only way to snap him to his senses was by defeating his argument. 'Because I'm female?'

'Partly,' he said weakly.

I thought about what had gone unsaid. 'Because I smoke pot and have sex?'

Slim bowed his head, clearly uneasy with his argument.

'Bad girls never make it to the final frame, right? Is that what you're saying? That the ones who fool around are dead meat?' A glance from Slim confirmed the point. 'In that case,' I said, 'I have nothing to worry about.' That earned me his full attention. I held the torchlight under his chin, anxious to complete this wake-up call. 'We haven't slept together for some time,' I reminded him, 'and I don't need any more dope to cope with all this craziness. If anything, it's made things seem *crazier*. You could say I've seen the error of my ways, Slim, which makes my odds for survival better than most. Okay? Good. Now stick close behind me.'

A girl who knew more about the big screen than he did? It was enough to bring him back to me. As someone who had slept through a degree in the subject, I never thought it would be so relevant to anything I did in the real world. It also helped that, by then, I had put a face to the voice that kept calling up to me. *It was Slim himself.* A feature of the recording still playing in the library downstairs. The moment cued up in my mind, which only fuelled my loathing of the bastard who was watching it right now. Having seen me in front of the mirror, trying out different clothes and poses, I estimated that Frank currently had a view of me stretched naked on the bed. Revealing myself for his benefit – but ultimately our own. Indeed, things were really hotting up in that bedroom when Slim had started yelling my name. My boyfriend calling up from the foot of the stairs back at home, which is what we had been hearing.

I knew exactly where we were on the tape when I heard myself acknowledge Slim. '*What?*' I had yelled back, sounding somewhat irritated by the disturbance, only to be reminded that we had to be out of the house in minutes. A party of some sort, but it was none too clear what Slim was saying through a locked bedroom door and I don't suppose the viewer cared much anyway. If we had played it right, Cartier's only concern was how much more he would see as I searched for an outfit *I really* liked. I had even set this final tease to music, cranking up the stereo to get me in the mood.

'Kylie?' Slim was up to speed himself now, the music lifting through the mansion into the loft. He nodded approvingly. 'An artist sorely overlooked for soundtracks.' Whatever he wanted to say about it, the music had been a masterstroke. For it meant we had a means of locating the library. Somewhere in this cavernous mansion, I placed Frank Cartier so close to his computer screen that he could see his own breath on it. I also realised that we didn't have much time before the tape ran out, so I let the Maglite lead the way – shining it around the corner in the passage then drawing to a dead halt.

'What is it?' Slim with his hands on my shoulders.

'The loft hatch,' I said. 'It's open.'

I killed the beam, headed for the square of light ahead, then pulled up again as another sound came through it. At first I thought it was timbers groaning, but the groan became a moan followed by a faint appeal. I dropped to my knees, crawled the last few yards, and then inched forward to take a look.

'Oh, Jesus.' Immediately I wished I hadn't lobbed the rope. 'We have to get down there.'

Slim joined me at the edge. Way below, in a grand hall, lay a semi-conscious figure. She was sprawled on her back, with one arm bent in a way that shouldn't have been possible. My choice of music didn't seem so fitting now. Kylie's voice sailing up the spiral stairs, urging us all to spin around or some such.

'Her name is Bleeding Rose,' I said.

'You *know* this woman?'

Slowly her eyes blinked open, stirred by the sound of her name. 'Honey.' She winced as if it hurt her to speak. 'Didn't I tell you to quit after the first job?' The cat burglar had her hair tied up on top, and was clad in a black-leather one-piece. She wore a lot of jewellery with it, including a belt of silver hoops that held the tools of her trade. A weak smile, then her lashes closed again.

'Rose is a big fan,' was all I said to Slim, wondering what next without a ladder. The one lying across her legs was redundant from our point of view. It appeared to have come off the rails up here, and I worried that we weren't far behind.

'I can get down there.' Slim was like a spring, coming out of the dark behind me. He hopped across the open hatch and lowered his legs into the light.

'Wait up,' I said. 'The drop is too much for me.'

'I know that.' His voice strained as he took his own weight, and began to sink out of the loft. Then, stretched to his full extent, he looked up and urged me to climb down him. 'Find that money, Cisco, I'll take care of your friend.'

'What?' At first I didn't think I'd heard him right.

'I'll only hold you back,' he hissed. 'Now are we in this together, or not?'

Aware that precious seconds were slipping just like Slim, I said, 'God help me if this is another moment from one of your movies!'

'It is actually.' He sounded agitated, which was understandable as he was hanging by his fingertips. 'I play myself in this one. Only neither of us is will see it through to the last reel unless you finish the job.'

I didn't argue. We had no time. I folded my arms round his shoulders, and began to shin down his torso. Rose was watching from below, but the sparkle had gone from her eyes. She looked pale down there, defeated. 'You get what's owed to us, Cisco.'

'Slim—'

'You're the star,' he grunted. 'You always were.'

Everything was going fine until I reached Slim's waist. Clinging to his combats, I found myself slipping south without making much effort to do so. The last thing we needed now, I thought, was for *his* clothes to come off. Then I felt my toes touch the floorboards. I prepared to drop, but Slim got in before me – losing his grip on the loft hatch so we both went down together. We made some noise, at least I did, but Kylie covered for us. Hitting her stride as we collapsed in a heap beside the cat burglar. As I waited for Slim to lift himself off me, I opened my eyes and saw Rose lying there with just a trace of a smile. 'Hi,' was all I could think to say. 'Have you met my boyfriend?'

'We do everything as a couple,' Slim added. 'We're very close.'

48

Lieutenant Uhuru. That was what Slim was busting to say when I flipped open my mobile to call up my brother. I could see it in the way his eyes lit up, as if it was a struggle to stay silent. And yet I think even he realised there was no place for that now. This was real. Very real. Rose had one life left, and if I didn't claim these final minutes our own game would be up too. That was why I wanted to check in with Pavlov, get the view from the bridge. I punched in the number, waited for a response, but he didn't pick up.

'What's wrong?' asked Slim when my own expression darkened. 'Don't say this is a bladder thing?'

I snapped shut the handset, told him I couldn't get a signal here. Which wasn't strictly true but it didn't matter. I wasn't going to give up now.

'Break a leg, Cisco.' This was Rose, barely with us but still rooting for me. 'You can do it, I know you can.'

Slim was kneeling beside her now, binding her bad arm with his belt. A makeshift sling padded out with the balaclava. 'You heard the lady,' he said, and winked at me. 'Scram!'

I smiled grimly, impressed nonetheless by his bedside manner. Downstairs, Kylie moved over for Madonna, who slowed the pace right down with 'What It Feels Like For A Girl'. In terms of a soundtrack, a ballad seemed even more out of place for the all-action moment I was in. I just had to keep reminding myself that it wasn't playing for me but the man in front of his monitor. From Frank's point of view, I hoped it would heighten the sense of intimacy in the scene still beaming from my bedroom.

Tape-wise, I was just slipping into my panties and bra. I'd had absolutely no reason to get out of them in the first place but, then, how many men watched a scene like this for the plotline? I didn't think Frank would break for coffee now, especially when he saw me reach into the wardrobe for a seriously skimpy dress. Once I'd worked my way into it and fixed up my hair, I would swish out of the bedroom and the show would be over. According to our plan, Slim and I were due to be swishing out of Cartier's mansion before that happened, which flagged up the fact that time wasn't so much running away from us but sprinting into the distance. Even thinking we might fail persuaded me to leave Slim with Rose and turn for the spiral stairs. For in a sense Frank was having his way with me, and unless I moved fast he would get it all for free.

The first window I passed was boarded up, and I guessed it was the one we had tested from the outside. The gale was kicking like a mule now, judging by the way it buffeted the chipboard. As I made the first flight, I began to realise that it wasn't just the joists that were frail in here. The whole damn building was complaining. Maybe the scaffolding was just rattling in the wind, but it was enough to quicken my footfalls.

'This isn't me,' I muttered to myself, and it really wasn't. I should have been at home, soaking in a bath with a glass of wine and a good girly read. Creeping down the steps while Madge set out her stall, I promised myself that was exactly how I would reward myself if I ever got out of here. Just then the money seemed worthless. I wanted bubbles, Beaujolais and *Bridget Jones*. And yet despite the fear and loathing behind this escapade, privately I had to admit it was an unbeatable buzz – one that had me thinking about who I was and where I was going, not just in my career but the cosmos. I was alive. *Exhilarated*. Even if I did yearn to uncork a bottle, spin the hot tap and escape into something fluffy.

The stairs unwound into a hallway. I was looking at oak panelled walls, heavy doors, and a grand lobby at the far end. Without the industrial roof supports, it would've been impressive: less like a mineshaft and more like the playboy mansion our landlord lived for. It was an ambitious undertaking he had here, for the balance was all wrong. The high ceiling didn't appear to sit straight with the floor, and the shadows were just too skewed. I crept across the tiles, heading for the last door on the right. It was open a fraction, and light spilled out with the music. The preceding door was closed, but the source of the sound was coming from there and I knew that had to be library. I smiled to myself as I tiptoed by. The pig was in his pen.

I was pleased to spot the bear through the open door, its paws held high as if it was a nice surprise to see me. To my alarm, the connecting door to the library had been left wide open. The lights were off in there. I couldn't see Cartier but I could place his computer: the marine-like glow coming off his monitor almost pulsed in time with the sound coming out of his speakers. Even in here the grizzly's eyes were twinkling. I wondered whether my brother was back behind the laptop, watching me from behind those bleached incisors. I slipped towards it, and immediately picked up on movement behind me. As I turned, I actually reflected on whether my folks were watching over me, and promptly scared myself in the mirror. That's when I ordered myself to get a grip. There was nobody else here, and I had come as close to Cartier as I dared. So close that I could hear myself on *complicity* now, singing along with Madonna. Even my landlord joined in too – Frank getting off on the closing minute of this bedroom scene while the star got on with the business of robbing him.

I found the zipper in the bear's pelt and began to ease it south. My heart was hammering so hard I was worried it could actually be heard. And then, out of nowhere, I found myself thinking of the antiquarian bookshop opposite the bank we had attempted to rob. It was the first thing to strike me when that musty smell spilled out with the money. You don't get a sense like that watching webcams. You missed out on a lot of things, I thought, and slipped the bag from my shoulders. Another long chorus and I was finished. I had to shake down the bag a couple of times so I could squeeze in every last note, but it was worth the effort. The bear didn't look good gutted, but it gave me some idea of how Frank would feel when he found it. I snapped tight the drawstring and rose to my feet. Madonna was on her way out but I would get there first. This was it. We had stolen into Cartier's innermost cave, and now I would leave through the front door! I crossed back to the corridor with victory bubbling in my blood, but the fizz went flat without warning when my mobile started to bleat.

'Hullo?'

I took the call. I can't believe I did, but that's how it was. A panic response to shut it up.

'The tape's coming to a close.' Pavlov was whispering like he might be heard. 'You'd better hurry.'

'Thanks,' I said, my eyes on the library now. The sound of a chair scraping back.

'Uh oh.' My brother stopped there. Watching his screen, no doubt. 'The pig is leaving his pen. Repeat, *Frank Cartier is leaving the library!*'

'Yes, I can see that.' The man emerged at the door just then. I swear he seemed twice his size, the way he filled that frame. 'Thanks, Pavlov.'

'Are you out of the house yet? Give me your position.'

'My position?' I masked the phone to confer. Came right back and summed it up in one word. 'Fucked.'

49

Frank Cartier came out of the library like he had just been hauled from his bed. He tied off the sash on his dressing gown, blinking into focus. I took a step away as his stare began to harden, and reminded myself to breathe.

'It's not how it seems,' I said.

'It never is.' He reached behind the door, came back with a poker. Slim would have said that was the bad guy's prerogative, always with the first dibs on the weapons. But Slim was looking out for Rose and I had never felt so alone. Cartier weighed the instrument in his hand, and I could almost see his mind processing how I could be in two places at once. 'Fuck me,' he said eventually, as our plot fell into place. 'It's a pleasure having you here.'

'Take the money.' I shook the bag off my back and tossed it between us. Frank grinned and shook his head. It wasn't what he wanted to see come off me, I realised with a chill. Moments earlier I had been on that screen in the library, giving him what he wanted – my tits, my ass, my *everything* – but all from a distance, cut off from Cartier. Now here I was making a special appearance, cut off from the world outside. Thunder crashed over the mansion just then, though we felt it mostly underfoot.

'You shouldn't have come.' Frank rested the poker over his shoulder, and glanced at the ceiling. 'It's not safe here.'

I shrank from our landlord as he stepped towards me, praying that all those stories about tortured tenants were just that – stories. 'You're not going to hurt me, are you?' I gestured at the poker, saw shadows shifting in the library behind him and breathed out hard.

'Not unless you'd like me to,' he said, and once again I found myself faced with a man who wanted to play games. Only this was the worst kind of man, and the game he had in mind just summed him up. 'Me and you, Cisco. What do you say?' He wagged his albino brows, his eyes burning right through me. 'Sleep with me and I'll even split the money.'

Frank said this, made me an offer I couldn't believe, and that was when the bomb went off.

'*Stop right there!*' I yelled, so abruptly I surprised myself. 'Have you no respect for people? No moral boundaries?' For some reason I found myself squared up to him now, looking up into his hairy nostrils, not giving a shit about the poker on his shoulder. 'You really think you know me, don't you?'

'Inside out,' he said, as if it was something to be proud about.

This time it was my turn to shake my head. 'Just knowing you've been watching every move I make, Frank, that says *so* much more about you.'

He tipped his head, working on what I had said. 'So, does that mean we have a deal?'

I laughed, spitting it into his face, almost. 'Okay,' I said, but not to him. 'Let's do it.'

Frank frowned, unsure if he had heard me right, then his expression snapped into surprise when a hand grabbed the poker from behind.

'Pesky kids,' hissed Slim, wrestling with him for the instrument now. 'I bet that's what you're thinking, Mr Cartier. I would if I was in your—'

Shoes. That was what he was going to say. Until Frank found one of his fingers, and used it as an anchor to twist round. Slim's expression rotated by the same degree. More so when our landlord began to bend the digit backwards. 'Please don't,' he whimpered, sinking to his knees. 'Not my trigger finger.'

'Where's your gun?' Cartier pulled up there.

'He doesn't have one,' I said, but Frank had his back to me. As far as he was concerned I was out of the frame. 'Just a joypad.'

'For gaming,' Slim pleaded, but it fell on deaf ears. What followed was a splintering crack, but I was responsible for that: tweezering my fingers inside the bear's jaw then tugging at the webcam until it came free. I don't suppose it minded losing a few teeth at this stage in its life.

'Go ahead,' I said, and directed the cam at the scene of the crime, the cable feeding from its throat as I closed in. 'Just so you know that anything you do now could be used in evidence against you. It's all going off in Columbia Road, Frank, and the laptop *never* lies.'

Cartier dropped Slim's hand as if a current had just run through it. Slim responded as though he had received a similar shock, flapping his hand as he returned to my side. 'It's just a sprain,' he said, like I cared at this point. 'I'll survive.'

Frank was standing directly in front of us now. He showed me his palms, and I *knew* I had him. Brandishing the cam between both hands, I almost felt like I could blow him away with it. 'Don't come in too tight.' He pointed at the lens. 'You might miss something'

'*Cisco!*' Slim yelled, but his warning came too late. Mid-step, the cable reached its full extent and popped from its socket in the back of the cam.

'What next?' I appealed to Slim, but the bear made the next move, and we both leapt out of its way. Toppled by my last tug on that cable, the big guy keeled towards Cartier. He backed away but the bear was faster, coming in with the grizzly version of a Glasgow Kiss. Our landlord roared, struggled to keep his balance, but the bear's weight took him all the way. Pinning him to the floor, right beside the money.

'You know what to do.' Slim grabbed the bag, slung it at me, then limped into the corridor. 'Run!'

'Not that way,' I cried. I figured he'd go for the front door, not back towards the stairs, but it only made sense when I chased after him. I found Slim crouched beside Rose. She was slumped outside the library where he had left her. Slim hefted the cat burglar over his shoulder, wincing until his ankle accepted the load.

'Go, Cisco!' He gestured at the main entrance, urging me to lead the way. I didn't even glance through the door we had just come through, but I sensed that Cartier was almost on his feet. With the bag clutched to my chest, I weaved between the roof supports, picked up the pace through the lobby and hit the door handle at speed. I snapped it down but nothing gave.

'It's *locked*!'

'This way.' Slim doubled back through the lobby, saw Cartier crash into the corridor, and swung full circle looking very freaked indeed. Even Rose picked up on the panic, urging Slim to watch his back as the man closed in on them from behind. Slim looked one way, then the other, saw an open door and said, 'The kitchen. You can always find a way out through the kitchen.'

I don't know what I was expecting. Staff, maybe, an island worktop with rows of steel utensils hanging overhead, chaos breaking out as the three of us whizzed through the doors. Instead, what did we find? It wasn't a damn kitchen at all, but a utility room – no window, no exit, nothing. Just a line of wellies, some clothes lines and an aluminium chute. The hatch had been left open. It was wide enough to slip inside. We didn't have much choice.

'Are you kidding?' Slim struggled to catch his breath. 'Haven't you seen *Star Wars*?'

'You go first,' I said, wrestling Rose from his shoulder. 'Someone's got to break her fall.'

'But it's a *trash masher*,' he insisted. 'Bad shit happens at the bottom of those things.'

'It's for laundry.' Rose came away from him as I said this, and insisted she could stand. But it didn't make any difference to our exit strategy. 'For Chrissakes,' I screamed, 'he's *coming*!'

'I might be crushed—'

'Where are you going?' We spun round on hearing him. Frank was in the lobby with the poker, Cluedo gone chaotic.

'Now!' I yelled at Slim, though he was half-way into the chute already. 'Do as Misty would!'

He went down head first, yelling all the way. A battle cry that lasted a lot longer than I had anticipated, however, and even turned into a shriek. The gloopy splash that followed was a real surprise. It didn't sound like socks and sheets down there, but I lost the chance to call after him for Frank was with us now, his nose all pulped and bleeding. He brandished the poker in one hand, reached out with the other. 'Give me the bag. The *money*, Cisco.'

'Go to hell, honey!'

Cartier switched his attention to Rose. I must admit I would have just handed him the cash – anything to get out of this place.

'Who's your friend?'

'Your *worst* nightmare,' she spat, her eyes pinching in like her mouth – East End all over. Even Frank looked a little unsettled. More so when a hammering started up outside the front door. The storm was still battering the mansion, the wind howling relentlessly, but this hadn't come from the heavens. At first I figured it was Slim, and it knocked me back how relieved I felt. Then a voice that wasn't his yelled, *'Pizza!'* and the three of us looked at each other.

'For you?'

'I didn't order anything,' I assured Frank, confounded. 'Did you?'

'Not me.' He seemed woozy on his feet. Disconnected, somehow. I watched him touch his nose with the back of a hand, surprise in those eyes when it came away sticky. He turned to Rose. 'How about you, lady?'

Another hefty rap on the door drew his attention from her, which was probably for the best because he didn't need upsetting any more. Whoever it was didn't sound too happy either, waiting around in this downpour. Cartier looked torn. 'Have you eaten?' he asked.

I had no appetite whatsoever, but this was the only break we had left. So I said, 'I could always go a slice on a Saturday night.'

Another pounding pushed Frank into a decision. 'Don't move,' he warned, and showed us both the poker tip. 'Lucky I got the cash to cover it.'

He marched into the lobby, digging for his keys. A silhouette suddenly, when lightning flared through the vaulted windows. Before the dazzle had left my eyes, Frank was hauling open the door.

'Someone order the special?'

I could just make out the pizza boy, looming large on the step. Rain was bouncing off his helmet and the cardboard tray between his mitts. He had a moped on the gravel behind him, ticking over on its stand. It was so small it might have been a toy. Frank checked out the man and his machine, said, 'You must have the wrong address.'

The pizza boy consulted a soggy receipt. 'Awww, you're right. I should be next door.'

Cartier tucked the poker under his arm and took hold of the tray. The pair of them squared up over the corners. I glanced at Rose. She linked her good arm with mine.

'Next door is three miles down the coast. Let me take it off your hands.'

'Not sure I can do that, boss.'

'I have hungry guests here.' Cartier snatched it free. 'What's in the special, anyway?' Below the pizza boy's helmet, two huge jowls began to tighten. 'Well, why don't we take a peek?' he suggested.

Frank popped the lid, but had barely registered the topping before the boy took his fists under the tray, smashing it into his face. A train came through the door just then, not a takeaway delivery. That's how it looked as tomato paste detonated in all directions and Cartier slammed back several steps. His assailant followed him in with another mammoth shove, then turned to us and saluted with one finger. Not a boy. Not a man. But a florist-and-dealer, our very own guardian angel.

'It's my own recipe.' Sweet William grabbed Cartier by his lapels, steadying him before he delivered the final blow: a sucker punch that saw our dazed and drooling landlord connect with the roof support behind him. I felt the impact all around me this time, and not just through my feet, as if the mansion itself was struggling to absorb the blow. Willie took off his helmet, watched Cartier sliding slowly down the skewed and buckled support. 'Consider it a Sweet special,' he said, and shook himself down. 'Easy on cheese, *extra* heavy on herb.'

50

Bleeding Rose had someone to look out for her. Watching her stumble across the lobby, heading for Sweet's embrace, I gathered she had managed to call him from under the loft hatch. Summoning the man on her mobile before the impact of her injuries had dragged her under. The cat burglar made such a hullabaloo over his appearance, in fact, that I was worried it would rouse our landlord. He might have crumpled into unconsciousness, but Rose kept shrieking and hooting as she planted kisses across Willie's face. Still, I thought, they made a good couple. Worked well together. Me? I had Slim Jim, the man who appeared just then at the front door. Emerging from the darkness and the hammering rain with all kinds of refuse hanging off him – bacon rind and banana skins, dental floss, porridge slops, and other stuff I didn't want to think about.

'Man, what's that smell?' Sweet William seemed alarmed by Slim's presence, and stepped in front of Rose to shield her. 'Where you been?'

Slim brushed away an epaulette of potato peelings, and blinked at us through a mask of grime. 'Laundry duties,' he said. Glaring at me. Talking to Willie still.

'You did a good job,' I assured him, and was glad to see him match my smile. It was a shift in expression that came to overtake my own as I came out into the storm and hugged him. Yes, he was a mess but he was mine, and the filth washed away as we clung to each other.

'You're forgetting something, honey.'

I looked back at the mansion to see that Sweet William had truly swept Rose off her feet now. He carried her, Kong-like, over the threshold, pretty much supporting her in the crook of one arm. Rose was holding my shoulder-bag, but it was only when I collected it from her that I remembered why it was so heavy. I said she should take half the money, only to be told I was having a laugh.

'It's all yours.' She rested her head against Willie's shoulder. The buffeting wind not touching her now. 'I got my fair share right here.'

I beamed at Sweet, beamed at Bleeding Rose, and swung the bag on to my back. Then I turned to Slim, and found him beaming like I needed the back up.

'Way to go, Willie, you saucy dog!' He stepped across the gravel, socked the big man on the shoulder, and knocked a cheeky wink at Rose. 'This guy *always* delivers, believe me.'

Sweet William didn't blink in the wake of this blow, though he did respond to the compliment. Just not in the way Slim was expecting. 'See that?' he said, gesturing at the moped still idling in the downpour. 'I'm gonna let you ride it home.'

'What? I *can't*, Willie, it's a moped.'

'Yes, you can,' he growled, and the thunder seemed to back him up. 'I promised I'd return it. Gave my word to the Turks at Italiano's.'

'Why can't you ride it back?'

'Because Rose needs to get back to hospital, and there's not enough room for the three of us, a big bag of money *and* your fool mouth.'

'Oh,' said Slim, subdued by this sudden assault.

'Just don't waste your time with the front brake,' Sweet added. 'There isn't one.'

'But I might die.' Now there was panic in my boyfriend's voice. 'If I don't come off it, the shame will surely claim me.'

'So keep your lid on.' Sweet William threw him the helmet. Slim caught it like a slug to the stomach, but held on nonetheless. 'Now, be a good boy and close the front door before your landlord's lobby gets all messed up and wet.'

'Did I speak out of turn?' he complained.

'Just shut it,' Willie asked him one more time, like it wasn't even the door he was talking about now. 'Then hit the road.'

Reluctantly, Slim did as he was told. I watched him trudge back through the slanting rain, buckling up the chinstrap on his new helmet. The garbage on his back kept lifting away as he approached the house, the force of the wind throwing scraps into the lobby and spewing it all out again. Such an unholy maelstrom was beginning to form in this pocket that Slim had to fight to pull the door shut.

'What about Frank?' I called out, but my question was lost to the Wagnerian crack that followed. It wasn't just the sound of the door slamming, even if the wind had given Slim a helping hand. Nor was it the fact that the low-slung skies lit up like an x-ray at precisely the same moment. Lightning may have struck nearby, because the earth seemed charged up all of a sudden, and yet the thunder that followed didn't decay. It gathered ground instead, joining forces with an ominous creak from the back of the mansion. Glass could be heard tinkling next, then wood splintering. A mounting din that fanned out through the building and left with something like an avalanche. Slim didn't move from the step when this went off. I screamed for him to come back to us but he clung to the door handle while the whole damn mansion collapsed like a badly made soufflé: bricks and mortar going down, coming up as dust for the gale to sweep inland. I shielded my face, sensed an aftershock under my feet, followed by a strange calm. The storm was still ranging across the cliffs, but all I really picked up on was the sound of rain on gravel, thinking at the same time how it could've been quiet applause.

That's when I braved looking back, saw the cliff with a bite taken out of it.

Nobody moved as we took stock of this sudden shift in boundaries, especially not Slim who found himself right up there at the edge. What had just happened seemed both unreal and inevitable, but I didn't question things further. That would have meant stepping forward to peer over the edge, and I only had to use my imagination to know what I would find.

'What a trip!' This was Sweet, the first to speak, and the only one to whistle his appreciation. 'Now that's something you can tell your grandchildren.'

'The moment we'll all remember,' I agreed.

Slim Jim stirred next. He let go of the handle, just dropped it into the abyss and came back brushing his hands. 'What a waste, more like. A Commodore computer getting all smashed like that. It breaks my heart.'

Willie muttered something sorry about geeks. A last word on the subject, it seemed, as he turned to leave with Rose in his arms like she was the damsel, not me. Still, I had a role of my own now, and hoped Slim would be the one who defined it.

Clearing a lick of wet hair from my face, I said, 'We made a good team, didn't we?'

'I had a *great* team leader,' he replied, coming closer now. Instinctively I knew this was our moment. There was nobody here but us, after all. He drew breath preparing for a speech of sorts, only to falter when the wind tipped over the moped and stalled it.

'You'd better kick start it quick,' I told him, enjoying the exchange even if it had been cut short. 'Before it cools down, y'know?'

The bike was one of those step through affairs, but Slim held my gaze heroically as he eased on to the saddle. Then he looked down at the machine between his legs, and even I would have found it hard to look anyone in the eye again. So I showed him two crossed fingers and gave him the space to master it without losing his dignity.

Sweet William was approaching the main gate when I caught up with him. He didn't seem troubled to be carrying Rose all this way, and I was tempted to ask if he could manage me as well. At the same time a buzz like an angry bee began to build from behind, then a beam of light veered across Willie's back. I looked round to see a single headlight coming at us, and joined the other two on the verge.

'Is he insured?' Rose raised the question just as Slim clipped left into the lane, taking some of the hedgerow with him. I turned back to answer, and found her looking at the ruins we were leaving behind. A man had met his fate back there, I realised for the first time, and yet all my thoughts remained homeward bound.

'Insured for what?' I asked her, unsure who she had in mind here. 'Building, contents or life?'

We trudged on, heading for the Beetle parked way down the lane. Through the rain, I watched the tail light gradually shrink from view. I kept my eyes fixed on it so intently, in fact, that it never quite faded to black.

51

The storm stayed with me all the way back to the house. It went on over my head when I stopped off at the hospital, and was lashing the street by the time I took the space behind the Morris Traveller. There it was, parked as usual in front of the gate to our house: something else that wouldn't leave me alone. The glass was misted from the inside, but I could see the old boy sitting there, watching our front window through the rain. After all the grief I'd been through, I was tempted to jerk open his door and bring him up to speed – just in case he was wondering where we had been all this time. I actually approached the driver's door, only to catch sight of something through the quarter-light and hurry for the pavement. The man was dressed like a lady, which was nothing unusual. It was what I had caught sight of him stroking that persuaded me to leave things alone. I couldn't quite make out what his hands were doing down there on his lap, but I didn't think it would be healthy for me to investigate further. Besides, I had a bone to pick with someone even closer to home.

'*Pavlov!*' I didn't bother with my boots when I came through the front door, just marched right in leaving wet prints behind me. 'You can't hide from me now.' I had tried to reach him on the drive back from the coast, but all I got was the answer-machine. Having messed up in his role as our lookout, I figured my brother was just too ashamed to explain himself. I'd left a couple of requests on the tape for him to call back – nothing terse or angry in my tone, not with Sweet William's face filling my rear-view mirror. Our florist-and-dealer could have sat back a little, but chose instead to lean between us, his forearms forming headrests for Rose and me. His opinion of my housemates like a radio I couldn't switch off. If

Willie had realised that I was pissed off with my brother, I knew he'd snatch the phone and steal my thunder. That was why I kept my cool when Pavlov failed to pick up. Played it like the calm before the proverbial, then unleashed my full fury as I marched into our front room.

'For an agony uncle, you have a *big* problem.'

'Cisco,' he said quickly. 'Stay calm, please!'

He looked a little jumpy when I found him on the sofa, especially when I opened up the bag and showed him all the money. And yet, he stayed there on the edge with the keyboard balanced on his knees and a tense, almost pained expression. I glanced at the screen. He was still logged on to *getcartier*, even though the site had gone down. There was nothing to see any more, just a webcam window with a connection error in it. Seeing my brother like this made me feel almost sorry for him. I imagined he had been staring blankly at the TV for some hours, hating himself for being absent from his post when we needed him most. A sense of self-loathing that probably hadn't been helped by his trial by milk bottle.

'You're going to have to learn to regain control of your life.' I sighed. 'We've come a long way this evening, but the rest is down to you. Just *relax*, Pavlov. Loosen up about yourself and wake up to all the good things you can offer people. Your advice, for a start.' I realised that the rain drumming against the window didn't help matters, all that water spilling from gutters to drains, but in some ways this was his chance to break free. 'Forget about waiting for the toilet to be fixed,' I told him, coming in to block his view of the screen now – anything to draw him from the torment he appeared to be in. 'And after what I've been through tonight, I strongly suggest you don't answer the door when Kenzo comes knocking next week.' I stopped there, because Pavlov began typing rapidly. I watched his fingers fly across the keyboard, and almost simultaneously a warning crept across the ticker behind him.

HE'S ... BEHIND ... YOU ...

A tattooed forearm locked round my throat, stealing my instinct to scream. Tuna breath on my cheek next, a fish knife under my nose, and a voice from the hall that conspired to keep me from breathing.

'Easy, Kenzo. We're guests in this house.'

Cartier. Frank fucking Cartier. My eyes slid sideways, as did my brother's, and there was our landlord looking more battered than ever before. His face was a mess, and it wasn't just down to the pizza Sweet had served him. He had a livid gash across his forehead now, scratches all over and brick dust in his once white hair. But the man was standing, just about, and that's when the fear struck home. Kenzo released me from his grip just then and shoved me on to the sofa. He did it with a knee in my back, and I cursed him as I fell beside Pavlov. It beat crying, which could've sprung so easily from either of us – not least when Kenzo went back to the tackle box he had brought with him. 'Tools of the trade,' quipped Cartier, like this was going to be a party.

'How did you get out?' I sounded even more rattled when I travelled further with the thought. 'How did you get *here*?'

'Maybe he knows the cheats,' muttered Pavlov.

Frank seemed amused by this too, but didn't disagree. My thoughts flashed back to the slog home from the coast. The Beetle had seemed a little low on its springs, even after I made the hospital drop. Waiting for me to draw my own conclusion, our landlord pulled a pistachio from the pocket of his ragged dressing-gown. All this way in the boot, I thought, riding unseen with the car jack and crush injuries, and he still had to snack. I glanced at Pavlov, considered what he had said about the cheats, then glared at Cartier. 'He certainly doesn't play by the rules,' I concluded. 'Online or offline.'

Frank shelled the nut with his thumb and forefinger, bobbed his head as if I had just paid him a compliment. 'It's why I never lose,' he said, though he didn't sound much like a victor here. The way he slurred the delivery while his lids lowered beyond a blink. I could only think he was running out of charge.

'But look at the price you paid,' I observed, and watched those butcher's eyes snap open.

'Kenzo,' he said, 'check the bag isn't missing any money.'

The Fish Eye proprietor stopped using the blade to pick under his fingernails and dropped down as instructed. They were bad nails, too, I noticed, watching him go through the cash packets: soft and lacking lustre, a sign of too much time in water.

'I'm giving you notice,' Cartier said next. 'With immediate effect.'

'We can go?' Pavlov sounded surprised. 'What is this? *Eviction night*?'

'I need a place to live. It's not right, a landlord with no roof over his head.'

'You brought it on yourself,' I said. 'Every brick.'

Cartier closed his eyes. His head bowed a little and I thought he had passed out on his feet. But then he spoke again, sounding utterly switched on despite his outward appearance. 'Of course,' he said, 'I'll have to conduct an inventory. Inspect the place for damages.'

'*Damages?*'

Pavlov heard him right, because that's when our landlord came back to us again. Woke up and confirmed that was exactly what he intended to do, as the owner of this property. 'Wear and tear is understandable. It always is. But negligence and breakages? The tenants have to pay, any way they can.' As he said this, Kenzo finished counting the money and returned to the tackle box. I watched in silent terror as he opened up the tiered trays and lifted out a pinch bag packed with fish hooks. Frank Cartier smiled genially. 'Time to settle up, folks.'

'You can't,' said Pavlov, weakly. 'This isn't in the contract.'

'Right,' he said. 'So sue me.'

'You still can't touch us!' I invited him to look around. 'The entire place is wired. You set us up yourself and it's all going out on *camplicity*. Every move you make!'

'So it is,' he said, quite calmly, and I realised he had considered the cams already. 'I imagine my subscribers must be glued to their screens right now.' Frank paused as I glanced at Pavlov, and must have known that my brother had lost all fight. He was just slumped there watching Kenzo size up hooks, as if this was another TV documentary. Cartier winked at me, and said, '*This* is why people are watching, Cisco. They're happy to sit through hours of navel-gazing for the chance to witness something truly unique, and now that's about to happen. Sex and squabbling have a certain appeal, but this is the ultimate shot. Believe me, they'll be compelled to keep watching to the bitter end.'

'Crap,' I said, wishing my brother would back me up. 'Maybe I have more faith in human nature, but nobody's going to sit back and watch us come to harm.'

'We're talking about a website for voyeurs,' he reminded me. 'This isn't *Crimewatch*. There are no grass lines for people to call. Should anyone feel the need to speak up,' he finished, addressing the room now like some cracked clairvoyant, 'I can always call upon their registration details for addresses.'

'I'll make a big noise,' I assured him. 'Just watch me.'

'No tenant of mine has ever complained about their treatment.' Cartier reached round to tighten up his pigtail, oblivious to the state he was in, and came back with blood all over his hands. 'How could they?' he asked.

52

Those stories I had heard about the next-door neighbour, they no longer seemed like urban legends. Our landlord might have adopted that punchline-pending smile again, but Kenzo continued his preparation with deadly intent. By now he had half a dozen hooks out, a mixed gauge selection that gleamed like surgical instruments. The display might have been bluster, of course, except that he had pinned each hook to the webbing between one thumb and forefinger. Kenzo seemed oblivious to the pain, and maybe it just didn't hurt, but every addition made me wince and look away. This wasn't happening, I kept telling myself. We were in the wrong place, at the wrong time, and in the wrong zone too. I wanted the storm to vanish and the night to lift, because this just wouldn't play out in the same way with bright sunshine flooding the room and coffee in the pot. I missed Slim, wished Sweet William hadn't made him ride the moped home. At least the three of us would have had an advantage in numbers.

'Shall we start the inspection in here?' Frank drew breath to continue, but it came out in an angry cough instead. He snapped his hand to his mouth, but I caught sight of scarlet flecking his palm.

'Please,' said Pavlov, stirring at last, 'it doesn't have to come to this.'

Cartier wiped his hand over his dressing-gown. 'If you'd prefer just to pay for the damages now, that's fine by me. It won't be painless, but it'll be over quicker.'

He didn't look good when he said this, grimacing as he swallowed whatever had just worked free from his lungs.

'Well, we still have a blocked toilet.' Pavlov gestured at the keyboard. With Frank's consent he brought up an overhead shot of the bowl. Even Kenzo halted in his handiwork to watch. 'It's been threatening to flood all day.'

I didn't need to look for confirmation, though I struggled to believe he had just reminded Frank about our plumbing problem. Then my brother rested his hand on my knee, and patted it reassuringly. It was the agony uncle in him, I realised. The one who had left him temporarily, spinning a solution to the problem at last.

'The toilet will cost you large,' warned Cartier. 'You want to make me an offer, or wait until Kenzo has completed the assessment?'

'Maybe he can fix it?' suggested Pavlov, and I started to see what he had in mind here. 'At least let me pee before I pay the price.'

Frank gave my brother the gimlet eye, staring at him intently despite wavering on his feet. After what had come down on his head, he clearly wasn't right upstairs. 'Fair enough,' he said finally, emerging from some inner consultation. Kenzo seemed disappointed, but closed down his tackle box and prepared to move out. The hooks in his hand stayed in place, even when he lifted the box. I didn't want to know when they would come into play.

Pavlov said, 'I think the problem is beyond the U-bend.'

Cartier made sure we saw him take possession of the blade from Kenzo. I sensed my brother deflate a little, and figured that his plan had been to rush our landlord once we had him on his own. Cartier's cohort never said a word on the way out. Even so, The Fish Eye proprietor left an unbearable silence behind. There might have been a storm going on outside, but it was nothing compared to what we had here. I glanced at Pavlov. He was lost to the shot of the toilet pan, torturing himself, so it seemed, from the way his face had tightened. Frank appeared to revel in his discomfort. I looked back and he rolled his eyes, making out that my brother's bladder would be the death of him. It was only when Kenzo's head floated into frame on the TV screen that Pavlov sighed and said, *'At last!'*

'Are you really that desperate?' asked Cartier. 'Jesus, you have issues.'

'He's been this way since I moved in.' I was watching Kenzo crouch over the bowl when I said this. He took the lid off the cistern next and peered in. 'You can't really blame us for being tense,' I added. 'We live in a house with hidden surprises.'

Cartier looked hurt, and not just physically. 'Cisco, this is rented accommodation. Hidden surprises are part of the package. At least you don't get damp with me. You don't get roaches, mice or fleas.'

'I'd sooner live with *the lot*,' I snapped back, 'than with another webcam.'

'That's if you live at all.' Even Pavlov picked up on the menace in his voice. In fact, my brother jumped even higher than me at the hammering that came through the ceiling next. The image on the screen put the sound into context: Kenzo was on his knees behind the toilet, attacking the soil pipe with a monkey wrench. I prayed that this approach would drive out the obstruction we knew to be in there, for I really didn't want this to be a problem any more – not if it was going to cost us. To my horror, however, the water level came *up*, rising to the rim, even spilling over a little, before draining down with a glug. 'That,' said Frank, and sank his hands into the pockets of his dressing-gown, 'is what I like to see. Now perhaps Pavlov would like to relieve himself. Then we can get down to business.'

'Straight away?' He sounded panicked. His plan gone pear-shaped now that Cartier had the knife. 'Shouldn't he make sure it flushes first?'

Frank pulled a pistachio husk from his pocket. He examined it like that ape we had seen on the telly and promptly hurled it into the hall. It was a sudden shocking shift in mood. One he took even further by bawling up the stairs at Kenzo, demanding that his associate guarantee a faultless flush because he couldn't stand my brother's complaining. Then he came back in and asked if we had any nuts.

'I'm sorry?' I thought I had heard him right. I just hadn't been expecting him to ask so nicely. Losing it in one breath like that, requesting nibbles the next.

'Makes me irritable,' he said, 'not having any.'

'I don't think we have any nuts in the house,' I confessed, braced for another outburst.

'Yes, we do.' Pavlov turned to point at the window. 'Parked up in a Morris Traveller out there is the biggest nut you ever did see. Some doddery guy – turns up in a different dress every evening.'

Cartier frowned, the jammy stripe glistening across his brow. 'Is this true? You have a *stalker*?'

'See?' said Pavlov, before I could respond, and his hand went down on my knee again. 'I told you Mr Cartier wouldn't be happy.'

'He's no bother,' I said innocently. 'It's like he's part of the furniture.'

'Not in my house.' Frank lurched towards the window. He jerked back the drapes and came away with a face boiling up like the storm outside. 'Excuse me a moment, will you?'

The man was out of his mind – not the one in the car, I didn't know what to say about him, but the one who marched out to confront him. Meanwhile, on the screen Kenzo was lowering himself on to the loo seat with his trousers crumpled around his ankles. Either he had more in common with my brother than I thought, or he was the sort of man who took *big* liberties away from his own home. Clearly he didn't care about the cam, but at least I could see he was otherwise occupied when I slipped out after my brother.

Frank had left the front door wide open. Just steamed out in his dressing-gown, despite the downpour. We stopped at the porch, and watched him march up to the car outside our gate. A delta of lightning surged across the sky, just as Frank rapped on the quarter-light with his pinky ring. 'Can I have a word, sweetheart?' He cupped his hand against the glass, and peered inside. 'Anyone takes an interest in my property, *they come to me first!*'

I wondered if the old boy was having a seizure in there. It certainly wasn't the kind of conflict that would bring the residents to his aid. Normally, when this kind of yelling kicked off in the street, people moved *away* from the windows. Then Pavlov tugged at my sleeve, and I decided that he would just have to look out for himself. If he didn't have Frank in his face then Kenzo would soon be here to fish him out, and we weren't going to hang back for that.

I followed my brother's lead, and ducked out under the bay window. If the pizza boy could escape over the railings so could we. Frank was thumping on the car roof now – kicking the door so hard it left dents, even with bare feet.

'Perverts like you should be locked away!' he raged, but his tirade ended there because the car door swept open, knocking him back a pace. And that's when we saw him, resplendent in a mid length sequined number with matching strappy sandals and full make-up. The old boy emerging from his zone for the first time, with a handbag over his shoulder and an industrial size power tool levelled at our landlord.

'*OhmyGod!*' My brother clung to my arm, while Frank just froze there on the pavement. 'That's *a nail gun!*'

I was going to scream, but Kenzo beat me to it: a frenzied caterwaul coming from inside the house, just as it had when we first encountered him. At the same time, another noise competed for my attention, a poor excuse for an engine, but building all the time.

'Kenzo?' Frank Cartier said this without once taking his eyes off the man who had him at nail point. '*Come quick as you can!*'

'Don't do this!' I implored him. 'Drop your tool!'

'Cisco! Come back!'

I was on my feet and up at the railings before Pavlov could stop me, pleading for compassion before I had thought it through, only for the nail tip to swing my way. The old man behind it looked scared and confused by all this attention. For a seventy-something he was in good shape, but all of a sudden he didn't seem so comfortable at being out in public with a dress.

'Take it easy, Gramps!' I tried to hide my near-hysteria as Pavlov came up beside me. With our hands held high we urged calm, but the mounting chaos made it hard to be heard. Kenzo was still making an almightly racket inside the house, and that persistent buzz was growing louder by the second – drilling a hole through the darkness, it seemed. With the rain still pelting down, it was no surprise to see Cartier seize the chance to run: turning on the pavement to break away then stopping short when he saw what was bearing down on him. A bike. That's what it was. Some pizza boy with his moped at full throttle. *Slim had made it home!* Frank threw his forearm in front of his face, but the headlight already had him.

'Brake!' my brother yelled.

It was beautiful, the way he steered the moped. Slim with the handlebars locked to one side, leaning the other way until the bike began to glide, and those little tyres screeching as he came to a halt right in front of our landlord. Now Frank found himself fenced off at both ends, and he knew it. The nail gunner stepped forward, his frock getting ruined in this rain, closing in like Quentin Crisp meets Quentin Tarantino.

'Stay away from me, you hear?' Cartier whipped back to face Slim, kept spinning in such a panic that his dressing-gown came undone, but he didn't seem to care about that. He was too busy fumbling with the gate to the neighbour's house, whimpering as he hurled himself at the door. 'Let me in! Now. *Please!*'

A light was on upstairs but, then, it never went off. Our landlord didn't look like he was going to give up here, not when a nail thwacked over his head and sank deep into the rotten door.

'*No!*' He wheeled round, saw his own worst nightmare at the gate, advancing towards him now. Frantically he fumbled in his pockets, and something told me he wasn't looking for a pistachio. Then a jangle and his keys came out. Cartier raced through the set as he turned to find the lock, sobbing as another nail narrowly missed his hand, then falling quiet as the door opened an inch from the inside.

I couldn't see who was behind it, but the way Frank's face stretched it clearly shocked him to the core. The keys dropped from his hand. He glanced round and I saw horror move into those eyes. Forced to choose between the lesser of two evils, I believed he would face the nail gun. Cartier certainly squared up to the old man as he came through the gate, even knotting his sash to reclaim his honour in this end game. But then he took a step backwards, a retreat that saw the door open further to accommodate him. It was only on the threshold that Frank wavered, catching my eye just for a moment, before sinking into darkness with his head bowed. God knows who was behind the door, but it kicked shut with such violence that I did wonder whether our landlord had made the right decision. Not least because the figure who had just forced his hand stood down with his weapon.

'Which one of you is familiar with Misty Ventura?' he asked, before spinning round so quickly that his hemline took a moment to follow.

'Him!' Pavlov pointed at Slim. 'My housemate is a *huge* fan.'

I didn't see Slim take the key out of the ignition just then, but his moped suddenly died beneath him. It was then I realised that I could no longer hear Kenzo. I couldn't hear anything, in fact. No rain. No wind. No thunder. Nothing. It was as if a bell-jar had come down on this moment, sealing us in with a madman.

'Do we know each other?' asked Slim cautiously.

The man nodded and came up close to him. 'You killed me,' he croaked. 'By the waterfall.'

'I didn't.' Slim's voice faltered. 'That was *you*?'

'What's your name?' the old man barked, his guard redoubled. 'When you're not being Misty.'

Slim told him, and pleaded that whatever he had done in her name was a mistake, a big one, that he'd never been comfortable with a joypad: the buttons were too close together, he said, beginning to gibber, and although he may have been responsible for that fateful head butt, it was a terrible accident that would never be repeated. Ever.

'Please,' I cried out, and just spoke my mind because it was all I had to defend us, 'I'm in love with him.'

'And I'm in love with her!' Slim added, pleading for compassion even when the nail gun came up under his chin. 'At least let me tell her,' he cried. *I never told her before!*

That Slim had just confirmed what I longed to hear should have been a moment to treasure. Instead, I feared it might be his last. That frock, too, had seen better days, was what I mainly remember thinking. Braced as I was for an execution, my senses picked up on anything but the inevitable. The weather we were having. My offer of a new job. The fact that I was *way* out of my zone here, barely able to believe that this wraith in women's clothing, who had stalked us for so long, would then wilt into my boyfriend's arms.

'Young man, I love you just as much,' he said, choking up now. All I took in was the clatter of his nail gun on the flagstone. Even Pavlov just stood there with his jaw hanging slack. 'That cursed game,' he sobbed, 'it was driving me crazy.'

'It was?'

'*Insane.* Day and night I stayed at my screen, but could I find the vault?'

Slim glanced across at me, looking a little self-conscious before he patted his ex-opponent on the back. 'Okay, geezer. Let it out. I've been there – not quite as far as you but close.'

The old man pulled away, and insisted that being killed by Slim was the best thing that could have happened to him. 'It took me a while to make sense of it all,' he said, still weeping. 'The truth is, I had a lot of anger when I first tracked you down. You murdered me, after all. But over time it helped just to be here outside your house. It meant less time playing *The Money Shot*, and more time getting back in touch with myself.' He looked up at Slim, those kohl-dark tracks tracing all the way to his jawline now. 'I played that game so much I was beginning to lose touch with the real world.'

'It's a very obsessive experience,' Slim agreed.

'No shit.' This was Pavlov, but it failed to hit home because that

awful howling started up from our place again. I looked across at
our front door, just as Kenzo crashed into the rain: the man with
the bad tattoos looking like he'd just been stung by a swarm of bees.
He certainly seemed to believe he was under attack from something,
the way he swatted at his half-hitched trousers. For a man who said
nothing, he careened into the darkness making a lot of noise. Any
other time, I might have worried about the neighbours.

'Let me take care of him.' Slim's special friend stooped to collect
his nail gun. 'You finished my game, now I'll finish yours.'

When he came back up to his full height it was clear that
something had unhinged behind the eyes again. Certainly none
of us dared to stop him trailing Kenzo through the space between
the cars. It was all too much for a lifetime, let alone one night, and
I felt sure the boys agreed. With all this madness spiralling around
us, there was only one place I wanted to be. And that was a place
called home.

53

Waking up with the weatherman can set your mood for the day. You have your highs and lows, your changeable periods. It can be hard to take in when you're dozing in bed, incapable of silencing the clock-radio. Sometimes the forecast is so different from what's been happening outside that you wonder if you're still dreaming.

'Cisco! Don't do it! *Stop!*'

I never did like Mondays. That early start always comes as a jolt. Usually I blame the alarm call, but after the weekend we'd just come through it was my conscience that messed with my mood. As a result, I was up before the weatherman, braced to seize the day: slipping barefoot into the yard at daybreak, in a candy pink slip and no face on.

'No!'

A branch lies on the cobbles out here, fall-out from the recent storm. It looks like a buckled-up broomstick, with a spray of leaves for bristles. God knows where it's come from, because I can't match it to any of the trees in the adjoining gardens. Normally I'd find petals out here from all over the world. California sweethearts, Dutch tulips, peonies from Patagonia and once even Arctic lupins. Not that east London is known for its converging trade winds, of course. It only takes a rogue gust through the gutters out front and all kinds of floral confetti can float over. Little things like this tend to keep you in one place. Stuff you don't find elsewhere, that you'd miss if you moved. For me, it has to be the flower market. I love being able to step out of my front door, come rain or shine, and find blooms from every season.

Take first light on any given Sunday. The street is always in a right old state. Broken bottles, bent-up aerials, pizza flyers everywhere.

You can sometimes hear it happening on a Saturday night – the drunks and the delivery boys, the crazies and the arguing couples, tinkling glass and car alarms, always damage being done. And yet I know that when I surface I'll find the place transformed and the market in full swing. It takes a lot of clearing up by the traders, but life just had to go on: people doing their best with all they had – which is why I wanted to stick around. I belonged here now, even if it did mean I had to do some clearing out of my own.

'Think what you're doing here, baby. It doesn't have to end like this.'

We kept a weather eye open for our landlord, but saw no sign of life next door. Nobody came, nobody went, and the light stayed on as it always had. People sometimes did that as a security measure when they went away for a while. That was how Pavlov saw it, and he had been the one who kept checking the street, waiting there at the window for the pest-control man to answer his emergency call out. None of us had asked what he went on to find in the pipes under the toilet, but he did pop back to his van for a container, and left looking cheerful enough. The guy had a head like an insect, all big bulging eyes and a tapering chin. I envied him, in some ways. The looks he could keep, but the man was clearly being paid for doing something he enjoyed, which meant never having to work for a living.

'Cisco, talk to us. We're a team, remember?'

Kenzo didn't have to worry about working for a living either, if we were to believe the picture that came out of The Fish Eye. We had logged on to his site with some trepidation, checked out the cams poised over the tanks, and found the strangest thing: the shop had become the tank, submerged from floor to ceiling. A veritable nail bar too, but not the kind I would dare to suggest to our florist and dealer. The walls had been strafed and the waterpipes fractured like the aquariums they fed, but at least Kenzo's stock made the most of the space created. What's more, every specimen seemed so much prettier, swimming freely around the shop. I hadn't been able to say the same for the shark. It had vacated the shattered aquarium at the back, and looked even more menacing when it came around for a close-up. Slim swore he saw a severed finger drift into the mix, one with hooks hanging off as if it was bait, but I had seen enough by then. Enough to know it was time to get out of our own fish tank. And that was exactly what I pledged to make happen when the week started over. All I needed was a cigarette lighter, an incendiary blast of hairspray and the six-figure sum zipped up inside my shoulder-bag.

'This show is over,' I announce now, squaring up to Slim and Pavlov over the barbecue I've built. The flames are on a lick, lighting up the boys' panic-stricken faces. 'How else are we going to move on?'

'With that kind of money,' says Slim, 'we can go anywhere you choose.'

The pair of them are hardly dressed for adventure, Slim in his obsolete dressing-gown and T-shirt, my brother in a fresh-pressed shirt and boxer shorts. Had I been wearing anything more respectable, I would have asked them both to look at themselves before making any travel plans.

'That money won't take us where we really want to be,' I say instead. 'Not when I know what we paid for it.'

'We didn't pay anything.' My brother edges round the barbecue. Stopping short when I threaten to toast the first packet. 'Cisco, we *earned* it, didn't we?'

'Pavlov, we paid for it with our privacy, our self-respect, our *sanity*, almost, too.'

'All that will come back to us,' he says, seeking support from Slim. 'It's over now.'

'Oh, really?' I invite them to look back at the house. 'Then why are we still online in there?'

The boys glance at one another, silently acknowledging my reason for wanting out. All this grief we went through because of the webcams, and we hadn't even shut them down. Being exhausted

and overwrought was no excuse. The server had an off switch –
it wasn't rocket science. The three of us knew damn well why we
were still going out live on *camplicity.com*, but the reason remained
unspoken. Until now.

'Because it's money for nothing,' Slim ventures uncomfortably,
but falls short of saying it's something we all enjoyed. 'People are
still paying to watch.'

'Plus there's nobody in the director's chair.' My brother shifts
from one foot to the other. 'We really are calling the shots.'

'You think so?' I wasn't impressed. 'It's too easy, Pavlov. People
put themselves on public display and claim to be in control? All that
guff about "doing it for the experience"? Who do they think they're
kidding? Living your life in public might make you a household
name. It can even bring you good money, until the next tenants
move in, but what about the experience you sacrifice? The one
that's really worth something?'

I focus on the fire, we all do. The flames are pulling back into
the charcoal, the burn beginning to build. Then I look down at
the money at my feet. Even with some stoking, I think, it's going
to take a long time to destroy all the bricks in the bag.

'The cams are just a temporary measure,' says Slim, sounding
certain here. Enthused, it seems, by a way to stop me from
cooking the loot. 'Your brother has that meeting with his editor
this morning. After all your hard work, Cisco, there could be a big
pay rise in it for him.'

'*Sparkle!* has just doubled the advertising rate for the agony
page,' Pavlov explains. 'That's all down to the popularity of your
male insight into relationships. By rights, you deserve any money
I make.'

'We can split it,' I say, and tighten my mouth to stop a smile.
'It's what teamwork is all about.'

'Speaking of which,' says Slim, and suddenly looks like he's
busting to get the words out, 'I think Misty and I may have got
somewhere at last.'

'The vault?'

Modestly, Slim recounts how he had just scaled the cliff from the beach to find a mansion at the summit that no other Misty had been into. He claims he had even gained access through a broken window without spilling her veins all over the place – a final challenge before the ultimate reward. 'I only paused the game to clear my head,' he says. 'I was coming through to tell you. I wanted to wake you with some good news, and look where I ended up.'

'Seriously?' I consider what this really means. 'There are bank account details for a *million* in that vault!'

'What are we doing out here?' Pavlov is already turning when he says this – prompted, I think, by the fact that I've just picked up the bag to circle the barbecue. 'Slim, the pause on that game only lasts a couple of minutes. After that, anyone could beat you to it.'

'Let's move,' I say, hustling my boyfriend back into the house. *'Go, Slim!'*

Misty is panting heavily when Slim resumes control of the joypad. He kick-starts the action, game on again, but it doesn't do much to recover her breathing. Still, at least there's no grizzly bear in the chamber with her, no weirdness of any kind, just a rusty vault with a wheel handle. This is our zone, after all.

'Oh, Slim!' I turn from the screen and plant a wet kiss on his cheek. 'I'm so proud of you.'

'Me too,' my brother agrees, but leaves it at that.

I notice Slim's hands are trembling. He swallows hard, glances at us in turn. 'We earned this reward, right?'

'Every penny,' I assure him.

Slim presents me with the joypad. 'You do it,' he says. 'You're better at this than me.'

'No way.'

'My trigger finger is still a bit tender.'

'This is your moment, Slim. You'll be fine.'

'Will you quit being so nice?' asks Pavlov. 'If you let Misty hang about in this game for much longer, she'll end up with an axe in her back. Now open up the vault and *show me the money!*'

He's right, but this isn't a game, not really. With a million at stake, there has to be a legion of competing players close behind. I have no idea how many, but I suspect a few might be confusing one world with another, ticking over like time bombs in front of their screens. I just wasn't prepared to draw any more into the open.

'Okay.' Slim takes a deep breath, instructs Misty to step forward. 'Wish me luck.'

This is it! I think. Another moment we've all been waiting for. Slim isn't actually behind this final move, however. As soon as he walked her across to the vault Misty went in alone, following a pre-programmed sequence. An oil-starved crank as she turns the wheel, then a clunk and the door swings open. All around, I imagine everyone logged on to our webcams straining to take a look. Even so, there's nothing they can do about it. No way to interact. This fortune belongs to us.

'Oh, my God!'

'Look at that!'

I face Slim. His eyes are wide open, stunned by what he sees.

'It's *empty!*'

'Someone's nicked it!' This is Pavlov's immediate conclusion. 'Look for blood. If Rose has been in here with a Misty of her own at least we know where to find her. We can be at the hospital in no time.'

'We're the first,' says Slim, barely moving his mouth. 'Otherwise the vault would've been open already.'

Pavlov jumps off the sofa, collects the jewel box the game came in. He snaps it open, extracts the instruction manual, and drops the box at his feet. 'We've been swindled,' he says, seething now. 'It states right here that the vault contains a code. You call up the hotline, confirm the numbers and crack open the Krug.'

I lean forward and retrieve the jewel box before my brother stands on it. There she is. Misty Ventura on the front cover: black boots, bicycle pants and bullet-clad bosoms. I know the guys were thrilled when I first brought her home, but looking at her now she seems like such an artifice. Even Slim seems reluctant to spend more time with her. But then I guess all games lose their magic when you're all played out.

'Nobody has been here,' he says again, and that resigned tone confirms what I'm beginning to realise myself. *The Money Shot* we have here is a pirate copy, after all. It may have granted Slim access to the online arena, just like all the other players, but only the official version could offer a prize for real.

'We haven't been swindled,' I say. 'We cheated ourselves.'

A silence thickens in the air. I find myself looking everywhere but at the screen.

'So that's it,' Slim says finally. He tosses the joypad on to the carpet. 'Goodbye, Misty Ventura. The ride stops here.'

'It wasn't such a waste of time,' I remind him. 'You mastered some difficult situations, and I certainly learned a lot watching you play her.'

The way Slim sighs I think his soul has just slipped out. He slumps back and gestures at the golden egg up there: the webcam with its solid green light. 'People must think I'm such a loser.'

'Who *cares* what they think?' I say. 'At least you sat down on this sofa to achieve something positive. Okay, so the software was dodgy, but it could've been worse. You might have wasted your days logged on to another webcam site, watching someone else screw up. What would that have earned? Apart from reassurance that your own sad, boring existence isn't quite as futile as you feared.' I lean back beside him, do the leg-patting thing I've picked up from my brother. 'Forget about the viewers, Slim. This is your life, and I know you'll put your heart and soul into whatever you choose to do next.'

Pavlov leaves the sofa and crosses in front of the screen. It's strange to see him half dressed, padding to the door in his shirt, pants and socks, but reassuring too. He looks more relaxed somehow, more natural. 'I should leave you both alone,' he says. 'If you need me I'll be in the toilet.'

I smile sympathetically, but he doesn't acknowledge. Instead he scowls at something behind me. I know exactly what the problem is before I even turn to read the ticker.

GO . . . FOR . . . IT . . . BUNKMUFFIN!!!

'Ignore it,' I say.

'Do what you have to do,' agrees Slim.

But Pavlov doesn't leave. Doesn't blink. Doesn't breathe. 'A wee was not what I had in mind,' he says finally. 'Entertaining Kenzo here on Saturday turned out to be good training. It showed me I could hold on, if I put my mind to it.'

'Good for you!' I beam at him, and Slim gets up to shake his hand.

'Congratulations, man. You tied the knot at last.'

I expect my brother to flinch when Slim clasps his palm, but Pavlov proves me wrong. I put this down to the experience of living in a public space. If it meant he was starting to relax around the people closest to him, then something good had come of all this. Even so, Pavlov doesn't stop glaring at the ticker, that message still rankling, as if challenging the author to stand up and be counted.

'Can I ask you something?' Slim takes a second to work up to the question. 'If you don't need to pee, what *is* your business with the toilet?'

This brings Pavlov back to us. 'Cisco is right about the webcams,' he says next. 'We don't need Cartier's subscribers. We don't need their money either. My life is worth more than that, and I'll tell you something else.' Pavlov takes this to the ticker now, no longer talking to us. 'You can stick your agony job. I should've quit when you stopped with the close-up pictures for my page!'

'*Pavlov!*'

'Stay out of this, Slim. I'm talking to my editor here. The one who thinks it's funny to give a veteran agony uncle more problems than he deserves.'

'You're being paranoid,' Slim insists. 'Anyone could be behind it.'

'Let's just say I can feel it in my waters. And even if I'm wrong he's probably watching, which is just as bad in my view.' Pavlov bats his hand at the ticker, and promptly declares that he doesn't care for a meeting with the man any more. Whatever he has in store, it'll be too close for comfort. 'Anyway,' he finishes, 'I've just resigned.'

'Are you sure?' I ask. 'I really don't mind helping out with your columns.'

'I appreciate the offer,' he says, 'but it's about time I reclaimed some dignity in my professional life as well. A teen agony uncle at thirty.' He grins at the idea. 'Who am I kidding?'

I groan, and slump back on the sofa. 'How many times do I have to say you're never too old for agony? If you're young at heart, that's all that matters.'

'What will you do,' asks Slim asks him, like he knows my outlook won't wash, 'until you're old enough to be credible again?'

Pavlov responds as if he's just been told his socks don't match his underpants. He looks to the floor, beginning to blush. 'I've been sharing emails with Coral about that,' he says shyly. 'Instead of payment for her consultancy work, she's asked me to come on board another Internet venture.'

'She wants you to work as a *stripper*?' Slim gasps. 'One step at a time, mate. Even I'm not that relaxed about my body.'

'Actually, it's going to be a house-cleaning agency you book online.' Pavlov has colour in his cheeks now for a very different reason. 'I'm pleased to say that Coral is finished with the stripping game.'

'No way,' I say, delighted by this news. 'My brother, joining a start-up.'

'And getting his leg over?' Slim lifts one eyebrow, then relaxes into something more heartfelt. 'Actually, I think you two could make that work.'

Pavlov is nodding, indifferent now to the silent tirade from the ticker. I wonder if he's making resolutions with himself. 'Give me

371

that moment in the bathroom,' he says next, backing for the door. 'I'll feel the same way too.'

'Good luck,' I call after him, and I know for sure what he has to do up there. It reminds me of my own unfinished business, so I climb off the sofa and face Slim. I want his full attention, which means finding his hands as well. 'I'm about to make myself very late for work,' I say.

Slim checks his watch, sees something other than the time. 'Cisco,' he says, 'your *job offer*! That talent scout is expecting an answer first thing.'

'I know,' I say, smiling now. 'And she'll know my decision when I don't show up.'

'You can't turn it down! All that travel she promised, the chance to go places and spot new faces. It's everything you always wanted.'

'I'm glad I had the weekend to think about it,' I tell him. 'It made me realise that everything I want right now is here, with you. Going places would be fun, but I'd sooner put some roots down first.'

'But this is a once-in-a-lifetime opportunity.'

I show him the shoulder-bag, dumped beside the sofa. 'So is that.'

I'm ready for Slim to power up into some kind of protest, but Pavlov must have hit the switch upstairs just then because the house seems to power down instead. With all the technology embedded in the fabric of the building, there isn't much to see. The little light crowning the webcam above the TV turns from green to red, while the tirade still racing across the ticker contracts to a dot. What really strikes me, however, is the peace it brings. All that time, I realise, we had been living with an electrical hum, a sound so slight but so constant that the three of us had mistaken it for silence. For a second Slim and I just look around, taking in our surroundings with a renewed sense of wonder, then coming full circle to the bag with a fortune stuffed inside it. I suggest to Slim that the barbecue will be white hot by now.

'If we see it through,' he says eventually, 'we should celebrate afterwards.'

Straight away, my thoughts set out for the cybercafe. 'I'm friendly with a bartender in town. I'm sure he'll give us a drink on the slate.'

'No need.' Slim reminds me of our little trip out to the bank. 'I believe I have twenty quid in a savings book somewhere.'

'So you have,' I say, impressed. 'You might've earned a little bit of interest on that as well. Enough to get my hair done, even.'

Slim swings the bag over his shoulder. 'Maybe you should let your roots grow,' he suggests. 'Start as you mean to go on.'

'It's an idea,' I tell him, thinking it would be easier to manage, going natural. 'Although it might look a bit cheap for a while.'

'You never know,' he says, and turns for the door, 'some people might say that's erotic.' If there's a glint in his eye, I don't see it, but I know where he's heading and I'm glad we're going together. 'Let's get this job done,' is how he finishes. 'Then we'll blow what we have on a decent bottle of champagne.'

We leave Misty on the screen with the credits scrolling. I'll dress before we go out for real, but for this I'm fine as I am. I might get cold to begin, but I know there's a quilted puffa waiting for me at the bottom of the bag. As for Slim, he looks hot to trot. The way he picks up the pace through the kitchen and into the yard, I think his ankle must be healing up nicely. Leading me by the hand now, he practically swaggers back to where this all started.

'Look at you,' I say. 'Anyone would think you got money to burn.'

spiri
of the
hare

in
folklore, mythology &
the artist's landscape

by

Karen Cater

Illustrated by Karen Cater

Edited by
Colin Cater

Hedingham Fair

www.hedinghamfair.co.uk

To Mum
who used to watch Hares on the
Sussex Downs in the 1930's & 40's

ACKNOWLEDGEMENTS

Thanks to;
Colin for all his hard work and forbearance

Those who have kindly allowed me to include their songs:
Ruth Price's Uncle Gus, Phil Colclough, Roger Watson, Seth Lakeman,
and not forgetting the sources of the older traditional songs.

Peter Rasmussen for help with the Triple Hare chapter.

Martin Gosling for permission to include his dance 'Tinners Rabbits'.

Leaf and Hugh - great life models!

Artists and craftspeople who made the objects in my collection,
many of which have appeared in still life illustrations here;
Waterloo Farm Pottery, Firedragon Pewter, Spirit of the Fens Leather, Stephen Smith,
Helen Brown, Carl Newman, Chloe Harford, Steve Cousins, Paul Jenkins & Caduceus.
Also the makers of the unidentified pieces
- sorry if I have forgotten your names, it's my age, you know.

Artists and authors who have contributed to the final chapter;
Tony Bates, Kit Berry, Seth Lakeman, Hannah Willow, Carl Newman & Wendy Andrew.

Everyone who has told me about legends, beliefs, charms, places, objects, stories
- so many things that have made this project so fascinating.

And all the hares on the airfield - you taught me so much.

Contents

Introduction

Way back in the spring of 1999, I was invited to take my artwork and Hedingham Fair stall to an East Anglian regional Pagan conference called 'Leaping Hare'. From early beginnings in 1997, I had already produced several hand-made greetings cards; lino-cut designs of The Green Man and other mystical images, but I thought it would be good to do something especially for the event. I set about researching reference material to do with Hares and was fascinated to discover mythology from all over the world, linking the Hare to Spring, Easter and the Moon. This formed the basis for my first Hare image – 'The Moon and the Hare', which has proved to be both popular and enduring, still selling well over a decade later both as a card and on T-shirts.

The next Christmas, my daughter Aly gave me a small silver Hare pendant, which I love and have worn ever since. Then in the spring, I was walking on the old airfield near my home, when I saw several hares chasing one another chaotically about the field called 'Black Patches' among the half grown wheat. Suddenly I was attracted by a group of two or three more hares approaching from the Plantation nearby to join in the sport. These were slightly lighter in colour, and they all

'The Moon and the Hare' an image incorporating ideas around Spring, Easter, and the mythological link with the Moon.

cavorted together for a while, gradually heading away from where I stood watching, until they disappeared over a rise in the land. I was mesmerised. These were the most

stunning wild creatures I had ever seen. I began regularly to walk that way in hope of spotting them again, but they were elusive and unpredictable, and though I frequently saw one or two hares sitting up, showing long black tipped ears, I was seldom rewarded with a sight like that again.

Local farmer John Lewis later told me how the field 'Black Patches' got its name - derived from the areas of darker soil in patches all around the field. To me this seemed more than a coincidence – as it was the also the best place to see hares, sometimes only visible by the black patches on their ears and tail.

As my interest deepened I became aware of other artists working with Hare imagery. It seemed that whenever I looked in a gallery or gift shop window there was always at least one hare staring back at me; a sculpture or painting or card. The Hare was working its way into my consciousness as I became intrigued by this enigmatic creature and sought to learn more, not only about the animal itself, but also about the mythology and folklore I had briefly encountered when first researching 'The Moon and the Hare'. A friend recommended a book - John Layard's 'The Lady and the Hare', an account of a series of dreams told to an analytical psychologist and his interpretation of the central theme of one of the dreams, a sacrificial hare. Someone else told me about 'Leaping Hare' by George Ewart Evans and David Thomson, a study of hares from the perspective of the countryman. Both books also included a great deal of folklore, mythology and superstition – I was hooked!

Starting in 2004 I had embarked on a project to learn the tree lore associated with the ancient Druid writing system 'Ogham', initially for a series of greetings cards though it eventually led me to publish the book 'Ogham Sketchbook'. I decided that as much of my learning as possible should be 'hands-on' working with the local trees; so I took increasingly regular walks to the Plantation and Airfield in search of particular trees. Of course I frequently saw the hares on these walks. They became part of my daily life, particularly in springtime when they are so active with the mating and breeding behaviour they are famous for, even during daylight, so they were much more in evidence at this time.

Some years there are masses of hares to be seen; at other times I might go for months without seeing a single one, and it was partly this unpredictability that lent them such magic. When I did see one, it felt like a particular blessing. Comparing notes, many friends agree there seems to be a cycle to hare populations (possibly due to farming practices or patterns in the weather). Numbers of hares seem to wax and wane like the cycles of the moon with which the Hare is associated. I also noted aspects of Hare behaviour which seemed to disagree with facts stated in books, but then I'm never surprised by this – I always prefer to check 'established facts' against my own experience whenever possible, natural cynic that I've become in my old age!

 As I began to study the mythology and folklore of hares more systematically, I was astonished at how vast the body of material was, both across extended time periods and geographically. It seemed to come from almost every continent and from the earliest dawn of human civilisation. It was almost overwhelming. If I was not to spend a lifetime just in research, I would have to be quite selective as to what to include in 'the Spirit of the Hare', as the book was to become titled. Although I had at first intended to show the whole range of world Hare mythology, to make it more accessible together in one illustrated book, this was clearly going to be impossible. I needed to remind myself that I am primarily an artist!

It helped that I had my own memories of Easter bunnies, brooches made of hare's feet, stories about witch-hares and a few bits of nursery rhymes and superstitions, I also knew several Hare songs, some I'd known since I was quite young. I'd been working with British folklore for many years and could relate personally to it. Finding so much more folklore, and on a subject that was already fascinating me was like opening Pandora's Box. To begin with I concentrated on Britain and Europe but gradually I discovered Oriental, American and African, and other more geographically distant stuff – absolutely wonderful. Some of the messages I was getting from these further flung stories were fairly straightforward, but others were pretty confusing at first, though once I had chance to digest them for a while, patterns started to emerge, shedding light onto ancient historical migrations as well as human development, both culturally and spiritually.

I decided to concentrate more on the Indo-European material which makes up the majority of this book, with only the odd foray into other civilizations' mythology where it sheds light upon a specific point in question. So I beg your forgiveness if I appear to gloss over some areas rather. This book is also my attempt to set out my personal voyage of discovery, as that is what I know best. There are other fine publications that

deal with the whole spectrum of world mythology of hares, and I commend them to you as further reading.

I have deliberately avoided the subject of field sports, except for a couple of hunting songs, and stories in which hunting features. This is something I know little about and don't particularly wish to be associated with. It is also dealt with extensively in other books on hares.

So here it is – my journey; the hares I came to know in my own landscape; the stories and beliefs from many countries and the history of human development and spiritual significances I have gleaned from them; even a bit of Jungian psychology; together with the art I have developed myself, and what it means to me. Enjoy...

CHAPTER I
HISTORY AND HABITAT

The Brown Hare

Lepus europaeus

The Brown Hare is the largest of British hares, measuring 24 - 28 inches long; the males (Jacks) being slightly larger than females (Jills). Their black tipped ears are approximately 4 inches long. The fur on the back is shaded brown, while the flanks and chest are more gingery; the under belly is white, as is the underside of the tail, the top of the tail is black. Their large golden eyes are prominently positioned on the sides of the head allowing the Hare to see both in front and behind. When running, the ears are usually held upright and the tail is held downwards to reveal the black upper side. Powerful hind legs enable rapid acceleration and running speeds of up to 45 mph; hares can also run for extended periods. The size of the heart and volume of blood, which delivers oxygen to the muscles super-efficiently, are relatively greater than that of other mammals. When pursued, the Brown Hare will change direction and zig-zag with remarkable agility to escape predators. Found in open country, farmland and chalk downs up to an elevation of 1,500ft, Brown Hares are also present on islands around the coast of Britain and north-west Ireland. Predators include fox and buzzard, which will take leverets, although adult hares can usually avoid them; agricultural machinery, dogs & man are the Hare's main enemies.

It is the Brown Hare which is common in East Anglia, that lives in the landscape surrounding my home, forming the basis of my study. There are however, two other types of Hare native to the British Isles and although they will not figure in this book beyond the mention of 'White Hares' in folklore and mythology, I will briefly describe them here:

The Blue Hare - *Lepus timidus scoticus*

Also known as the Mountain, Scottish or Alpine Hare, is resident in northern Britain moorland and mountain areas. Smaller than the Brown Hare at about 20 inches long, the summer coat is greyish, turning white in winter, the tail is entirely white. Considered to be a pest by highland gamekeepers, competing with grouse for food on moorland, and distracting the Retrievers, they interfere with sport.

The Irish Hare - *Lepus timidus hibernicus*

A sub-species of the Blue Hare, but now thought to be genetically distinct from the Scottish, and more closely related to the Hares found on the European mainland. 21ins long, russet in summer, lighter in winter occasionally with white patches, the entire tail is white, it is rarely seen during daylight. Irish Hares are common over most of Ireland, especially in the west.

The Names of the Hare

Old English - hara
High German - haso
Norse - heri
Germanic - hason, hazon

Country Names

Broom Cat, Furze Cat,
Stubble Stag, Stag of the Cabbages, the Stag with the Leathery Horns,
Shagger, Dew-hopper, Light-foot, Herb Cropper, Hide-with-the-lambs,
Bright eyes, Puss (derived from latin lepus?),
Mawkin, Maulkin, Watt,
Aunt Sarah, Owd Sally
Sally (hares are associated with willow =
Ogham name; Saille, pronounced 'sal-ya'),

I was fascinated to discover that the word for a path or gap in a hedge habitually used by a hare is called a 'smeuse', 'meuse', 'mewse', 'pad' or 'smile' as before I married Colin, my previous surname was Mewse.

Stubble Cat

Hares and Cats

Puss is a name given to a hare in songs and poems, and often by huntsmen, originating in the 17th century – a time when witches were universally believed in. It was thought that witches could turn into hares, and they were frequently associated with (pet) cats.

A slender cat can at times look a little like a hare (apart from the tail!)
Many of the country names for a hare use the word 'cat' as if it was an alternative.
Mawkin, mauken = hare, also sometimes used to describe a feral cat, or a vagrant or tramp.

I was told a story by my neighbour, Elizabeth, that when she was a little girl her father shot a hare and brought it home to be cooked for dinner. She took the Hare, wrapped it in a blanket, tucked it up inside her doll's pram with just its head showing above the coverlet, and wheeled it about as if it was a baby – until her father took it back for the pot!

This reminded me of when my own daughter as a small child, she wrapped our rather disgruntled and long-suffering tom-cat, Oscar, in a blanket and pushed him around in her pram, much to the amusement of our neighbours – but not of the cat!

Hares and Stags

Several country names for the Hare, 'Stubble Stag', 'Stag with the Leathery Horns', 'The Short Deer', reflect the fact that the appearance of a hare when running in a relaxed manner is very like a small deer, with erect ears resembling antlers.

I have noticed this myself when watching a roe deer jog across a field near my home, followed by a hare in exactly the same gait. The proportions and movements of deer and hare were remarkably similar.

The Names of the Hare in English

This poem is translated from the Middle English, and is thought to date from 13th century Shropshire. On its recital, the bad luck often associated with encountering the Hare is reversed and the hunter is believed to gain power over the Hare, which will deliver itself into his hands. As in many folk tales (i.e. Rumplestiltskin), knowing the name of one's adversary delivers him into your power.

The man that the Hare does meet
He will never that hare beat,
Except he lay down on the ground
That he bears in his hand
(Be it hunting staff or bow)
And bless him with his elbow.
And with sincere devotion
Utter this one prayer
In praise of the Hare –
Then will he better fare;
"The Hare, the Hare-kin,
Old Big-bum, Old Bouchart,
The Hare-ling, the frisky one,
Old Turpin*, the fast traveller,
The way-beater, the white-spotted one,
The lurker in ditches, the filthy beast,
Old Wimount, the coward,
The slink-away, the nibbler,
The evil-met, the white-livered,
The scutter, the fellow in the dew,
The grass-nibbler, Old Goibert,

The goes-crooked-home, the traitor,
The friendless one, the cat of the wood,
The wide-starer, the broom-cat,
The purblind one, the furze-cat,
The clumsy one, the west-looker,
The wall-eyed one, the looker to the side,
And also the hedge-frisker,
The stag of the stubble, long-eared,
The animal of the stubble, the springer,
The wild deer, the jumper,
The short deer, the lurker,
The wind-swift, the skulker,
The shagger, the squatter in the hedge,
The dew-beater, the dew-hopper,
The form-sitter, the grass-hopper,
The fidgety footed one, the sitter on the
ground,
The light-foot, the fern-sitter,
The stag of the cabbages, the cropper of
herbage,
The low creeper, the sitter-still,

The pin-tail, the turn-to-hills,
The get-up-quickly,
The one who makes you shudder,
The white-womb,
The hide-with-the-lambs,
The numbskull, the food mumbler,
The niggard, the flincher,
The one who makes people flee, the
covenant breaker,
The snuffler, the cropped head,
(His chief name is Scoundrel),
The stag with the leathery horns,
The deer that dwells in the corn,
The deer that all men scorns,
The animal that no-one dare name"
When you have all this said,
Then is the Hare's strength laid,
Then you might go forth
East, West, North and South,
Wherever a man will –
The man that has any skill.
Have now a good day, Sir Hare!
God let you so well fare
That you come to me dead,
Either in onion broth or just in bread!

Amen

*Turpin – rascal

HAVE NOW A GOOD DAY SIR HARE

"Creep hedge, crop thorn,
Little cow with leather horn."
C19 Riddle from the neighbourhood of Sheffield.

Rabbits

*It is easy to confuse
Rabbits and Hares,
especially when they
are a distance away.
Here are a few aids
to identification*

*Young (kits) born below ground with
eyes closed and no fur. At about three
weeks (below), they leave the burrow for
the first time and begin to graze.*

Short ears,
dark eyes,
grey back,
paler belly.

*Tail held up
when running,
white under-tail
signals alarm.
Short legs,
hopping motion.*

*Rabbits live
communally in
burrows. Warrens
consist of tunnels
with sleeping and
nursery chambers.*

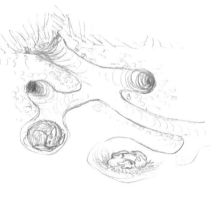

Hares

Hares often live in open fields, appearing solitary, they may be seen in the middle of fields on moonlit nights. Rabbits tend to stay nearer to the hedges for safety – quickly bolting for the cover of their burrows. When danger threatens, hares rely initially on remaining motionless to avoid detection, but if that fails, on speed and agility to escape.

Long black tipped ears, amber eyes, russet brown back, paler below.

Young (leverets) born above ground with eyes open, fully furred.

Tail held downwards when running showing black upper side. Long legs, stride loose and gangly.

Life Cycle of the Brown Hare

Brown hares' preferred environment is open farmland for which it is ideally adapted with long ears and large eyes to warn of danger, both from farm machinery and predators. They are common in most of agricultural England particularly East Anglia, but in the rolling grassland or wild moor of the South West the population is more sparse. In the late 1800s there was estimated to have been five times the present population, the decline due to many changes in farm-land use and management. Hares need tender grazing all year round, as they don't hibernate, nor do they carry appreciable fat stores to sustain them when food is hard to find. Fields are much larger now to allow for modern machinery, crops are less diverse, and there are fewer hedges with the accompanying undergrowth of grass and herbage, all of which contribute to poorer feeding conditions for hares.

It is usually stated that during the day hares rest in their 'form', an indentation scraped in the ground, or a place between the ridges in ploughed furrows. In this position, with ears laid back, they can hardly be seen, looking just like a lump of earth. Though hares feed occasionally during daylight, they are mostly nocturnal, becoming more active around sunset and dawn. During spring hares are often seen in fields where the young crops are still short, but once growth reaches eight to ten inches high it becomes difficult to see them unless they sit upright, with head and ears erect, showing above the level of the vegetation.

It is said that Hares will sit tight until danger is imminent, only bolting at the last moment, particularly if there is good cover, though in my experience, when cover from young crops is still short, hares will bolt fairly quickly when they perceive danger. It somehow seems that the hares have completely disappeared through the majority of the summer, until after the harvest, when their cover is removed and magically they soon reappear if food is plentiful.

The instinct to sit tight is present from birth; leverets behave in this manner to avoid detection. Adult hares can elude most enemies, but leverets are taken by owls, buzzards and most often foxes. If a hare survives to adulthood, it will probably live to three or four years, though some may live to twice that age. Weed killers and pesticides are another hazard as they may remove food plants or cause poisoning, particularly if sprayed directly onto the animal whilst sitting tight in its 'form'.

Hares tend to be reasonably solitary animals for much of the year. Though not gregarious, I often see several hares at a time on the Harefield close to my home, particularly in spring, spread across the field in loosely connected groups of two or three. When disturbed they will usually converge and run together to the scrubby waste ground at the other end of the field, or into the next field.

In the breeding season large numbers may congregate. This usually begins at the end of winter and though it can go on right through the summer, the height of the mating season is around late March. At this time hares indulge in chasing and jumping displays and 'boxing' in the fields – this behaviour is now thought to be the female fighting off the male's early advances, prior to acceptance of mating.

Leverets are born throughout the spring and summer, above ground in litters of two to four, fully furred, and with eyes already open. It is thought that soon after birth, to avoid loss of the entire litter from predators, the mother hare will distribute them around the nursery field, where they will hide alone in separate forms for most of the day. She will return to suckle them, individually in the early stages, but later calling them together, morning and evening. If you come across a young leveret all alone in an open field, don't assume it has been abandoned. It is perfectly normal for the leveret to spend the day on its own, the mother will be close by, unwilling to betray the position of her young.

In late summer, once fields have been harvested, it may take a while for the hares to return to the open field during daylight. There may be little to eat amongst the stubble at first, and if the field is ploughed immediately, nothing to eat at all. Their familiar cover is also gone. By winter, if the autumn-sown crops have sprouted the supply of food will call them back to their old feeding ground. Modern farming methods have changed the pattern of cereal growing to maximize yield, with ploughing as soon as the previous crop is harvested and autumn sowing, unlike the practice of past centuries of ploughing throughout winter and sowing in the spring.

Crops sown in autumn are sometimes unpalatable to hares by February, and though they provide good feeding during winter, unless there is also a supply of spring sown cereal, there may be a shortage of food at the very time it is most needed, the height of the breeding season. Stubble fields allowed to stand until later ploughing also enable hares to graze throughout the winter on weeds and tender young corn sprouting from seed spilt during harvest.

During the time I have been observing the hares near my home I have found that they seem to inhabit a more varied landscape than many written sources indicate. While they spend much of their time in the open fields, it is clear that the scrubby wasteland, the woods and the Plantation close by all form an important part of their daily lives as well. These habitats provide cover after the harvest, during inclement weather and when fleeing from disturbances. The mixed vegetation there also provides important sources of food (in winter when food is scarce, like the deer, they strip bark from the young trees to eat the tender inner flesh)

In the winter it is much easier to watch hares if there is a light covering of snow on the land, but if the temperature is below freezing and the snow is thick, the hares seem to take shelter in the bramble thickets nearby on the wasteland. All the books I have read state quite categorically that hares stay in the open all winter, either this is too simplistic or the hares round here are just soft!

Playing in the snow on
'Black Patches'

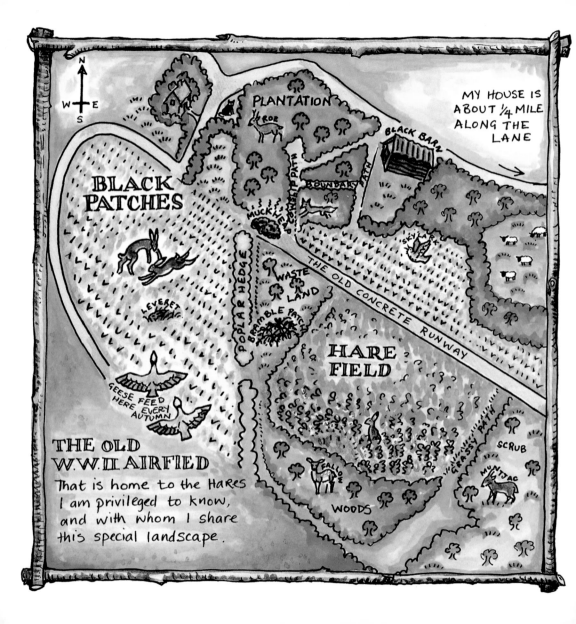

The Harefield Environment

The majority of my study takes place in the area around a large disused World War 2 airfield within half a mile of my home. The airfield itself is now largely arable farmland, the runways are mostly intact but have become paths between large fields where crops of wheat, barley, rape or beans are planted each year. Much of my study takes place on the largest field; I have called this 'the Harefield', which is also home to many skylarks that nest and sing there throughout the summer, and a grassy path separates it from a scrubby area to the east which is loosely planted with young trees. To the west is a field called 'Black Patches' (due to the nature of the soil there), this is ploughed and planted with various crops each year except for a smaller area, of about an acre to the northern end, which has been left fallow for several years. Between the Harefield and Black Patches is a wedge shaped strip of rough scrub, about 100 yards at its widest point, this I will call 'the Wasteland', with several huge bramble patches, some young trees and a hedge of hawthorn and white poplar acting as a windbreak on its western edge. Bounding the fields to the south is a strip of mixed woodland, some of which is mature, while other areas have been planted as recently as 20 years ago, giving shelter and cover in the underbrush. To the north there is 'the Plantation' of young trees of a similar age, comprising mostly oak, hawthorn, ash, rowan, birch and maple. Much of this area is undergrown with bramble thickets and provides habitat which also supports foxes, badgers and roe deer. The area around the airfield boasts a large population of deer; roe and fallow with a few solitary little muntjak, who can often be heard 'barking' at dusk, and the occasional visitation from a herd of red deer who roam for miles around the surrounding countryside.

This is an ideal environment to support a secure and expanding population of Hares, and I am privileged to be able to study them in such a place and so close to home!

TRACKS in the SNOW

I awoke to 5 inches of snow, and it was still falling gently. It is Imbolc; 2nd Februaury, so the theme for today is new lambs and snowdrops, but the gods were obviously having a laugh! The hare as trickster!

As soon as I'd cleared a track to the bird table and fed the poor starving things, I decided it would be a good time to visit the 'Harefield'.

I set off down the lane, well wrapped up against the cold. I had to pick my way pretty carefully, it was slippery on the road so I walked mostly on the verges where the snow was thickest and the footing safer. Under the snow the ground was still soft, obviously not at all frozen, hopefully that would make things easier, if a little squelchy!

As I turned into the Plantation it was as if no-one had been that way forever – virgin snow, or so I thought. There were no boot prints on the paths, and only vague indentations in the snow showing where vehicles had worn ruts in the surface below, but I soon started to notice the tracks of dozens of little feet criss-crossing the white blanket in front of me. I found it difficult to interpret them at first, some were tiny in regular paired patterns and they looked like the tracks of a small animal leaping in bounds over the snow – probably a squirrel. Then there were larger marks equidistant in an almost straight line – maybe a roe deer, possibly trotting. It was hard to make out clear detail as the edges of each footprint had been disturbed and blurred by the movement of the foot that made it, stepping in and then out of the snow. At one point I must have missed the fox that crossed the path in front of me and disappeared into the bushes by seconds, the tracks were so clear; perfect little dog-like pads but tiny, with the melt-water from hot toes still sitting in the minute claw marks. All around the stillness was deceptive, so quiet as the snow muffled all sound, but it was quite obvious that there were animals everywhere, I just couldn't see them! There were other tracks too; I couldn't make out what had made these at first. Irregular as if a few steps, then stop and look around, change direction, a few more steps. Under the overhanging brambles, out again. Some of the tracks showed all four feet in a square with a paw-print at each corner, as if the animal, about the size of a cat, had just stood still, then after that, the back feet had stepped pretty much where the front had been as it moved off again. Were the back feet long? Sometimes they looked as if they were, but sometimes they were small oval marks as if they were short — most confusing. It suddenly occurred to me that I might be following a hare!

I walked on along the boundary path, down the Cowslip Track and out onto the airfield's old runway. Through the binoculars I scanned the field, but could see no sign of hares, every time I spotted a dark shape that looked promising it turned out to be a lump of mud showing through the snow, as the field was still rough ploughed. I made my way along the runway and up to the gap in the hedge near the muckheap; still I could see many tracks, this time mostly the double slots of deer, and a clear one made by a fox coming round the end of the hedgerow, but not a creature anywhere to be seen — they were probably watching me from their hiding places and sniggering behind their paws. Who could blame them? Anyone out in this weather must be nuts! On 'Black Patches', among the early bean shoots, I could see a small flock of Fieldfares feeding; they were fluffed up to double their usual size against the chilly wind.

Between Black Patches and the ploughed Harefield, is a Poplar hedge, a rough footpath and a strip of scrubby ground, in the middle of which is a huge Bramble thicket. It was along the footpath I found more hare tracks coming from Black Patches, heading through the Poplar hedge, across my path and towards the thicket. I followed these tracks, treading carefully to avoid tripping on any bramble snares hidden under the snow, and skirting around the thicket, made my way back towards the old runway on the other side. This time there were no tracks at all — nothing. I found it quite difficult to keep my footing on the rough land, I was trying to pick a path between the first ploughed furrow and the scrub, and at one point I slid and fell sideways landing in a soft heap of snow-covered undergrowth, it felt like falling onto a pile of cushions!

But where had the hares gone to? The only place they could be was in the Bramble thicket, all the tracks led there and they certainly didn't come out the other side. This was a surprise, as all the books I'd read say that hares sit in their forms, out in the open fields even in the dead of winter. I can't speak for anywhere else, but here they seem to shelter in the Bramble thicket, and what a good place to shelter! To a hare it must be like a huge dome protected by a thatch of snow, and under the tangle of brambles it is probably dry, there may even be a small amount of food in the form of young shoots. Quite a cozy retreat, what better place to sit out the worst of the winter weather?

It was starting to snow heavily again, and I thought I had better get home before the forecast blizzard properly arrived. I retraced my steps from the airfield, walking alongside the tracks I had made earlier. A little way into the plantation among the trees, where the path was sheltered from much of the falling snow, I spotted something that made me laugh — there were tracks leading out of the undergrowth right up to one of my earlier boot prints, where a hare obviously investigated it thoroughly as the paw-prints were all around, but then, clearly not wishing to cross this strange smelling mark in the snow, she had turned round and gone straight back into the bushes!

*There were hare tracks
leading out of the
undergrowth right up to one
of my earlier boot prints.*

Legal Protection & Hunting

Hares are classed as Game, but as there is no closed season when shooting is not permitted, hares may be shot at any time of year, even when pregnant or feeding young, causing leverets to starve when their mother is killed. The Hunting Act 2004, prohibits all hunting of wild mammals with dogs in England and Wales. It also bans all hare coursing. The only other legal protection afforded to hares in Britain is the 'Hares Preservation Act' of 1892 prohibiting of the sale of hares between 1st March and 31st July. This applies to the sale of any hare, whether or not it was killed between these dates, therefore at this time even the sale of frozen hares is illegal. Originally designed to protect hares during the breeding season, this does nothing to stop their killing at this time.

Carved pub sign in High Garrett, about 2 miles from the Harefield.

The Innocent Hare

I learned this song from the repertoire of the Copper Family of Rottingdean, East Sussex. Some time around 1900, Jim Copper was given it by Mr Steyning Beard, Master of the Brookside Harriers – the local hunt, who always sung it to the accompaniment of much Punch after the Boxing Day meet

Sportsmen Arouse, the morning is clear, the larks are singing all in the air,
Sportsmen Arouse, the morning is clear, the larks are singing all in the air,
Go tell your sweet lover the hounds are out,
Go tell your sweet lover the hounds are out,
Saddle your horses, your saddles prepare,
We'll away to some covert to seek for a hare.

We searched the woods, the groves all round, the trial being over the game it is
Then up she springs, through brake she flies, *(repeat)*   found, *(repeat)*
Follow, follow the musical horn, sing follow hark forward the Innocent Hare.

The Huntsman blows a joyful sound, tally-ho my boys all over the Downs, *(repeat)*
From the woods to the valleys see how she creeps, *(repeat)*
Follow, follow the musical horn, sing follow hark forward the Innocent Hare.

All along the green turf she pants for breath, the huntsman he shouts out for death,
Relope, relope, retiring hare, *(repeat)*
Follow, follow the musical horn, sing follow hark forward the Innocent Hare.

This Hare has led us a noble run, success to sportsmen everyone, *(repeat)*
Such a chase she has led us for hours or more, *(repeat)*
Wine and beer we'll drink without fear, we'll drink a success to the Innocent Hare.

Strategy for Survival

It was said that hares, when returning to their daytime resting place, would do so by a circuitous route and take the last few steps backwards, then leap sideways a considerable distance into their form. This was thought to confuse tracks and disturb the scent trail

> "Tis instinct that directs the jealous hare
> to chuse her soft abode. With steps reversed,
> she forms the doubling maze; then, ere the morn
> peeps through the clouds, leaps to her close recess."

Hares whilst fleeing their pursuers have been known to:
- Hide under Juniper bushes as the strong smell masks the scent trail and confuses the hounds.
- Swim across rivers to hide in reed beds
- Jump onto a high wall to hide amongst the covering ivy.
- Hide amongst a flock of sheep to evade capture.

The Little Brown Sheep

This story from the Isle of Man tells of a helpful goblin – a *phynnodderee* – who offered to round up a shepherd's flock. When the shepherd, thinking it had taken a very long time, came to see what was happening, he was greeted by an exhausted helper who complained that it would all have been very much easier if it hadn't been for the antics of the 'little brown sheep' who had caused so much trouble. When the shepherd, not recognizing the description as any of his flock, looked to see which one he meant, it turned out to be a hare!

If caught in the headlamps on a country lane after dark, unlike most animals, who will run aside to escape the light, hares will run ahead of the vehicle, often for long distances, sometimes swerving slightly from side to side, seemingly unable to decide which way to go. This behaviour must have resulted in many hares being run down by motorists, but when you think of the hare's traditional escape strategy, it is not as illogical as it first seems. Hares have always relied on their fantastic speed to evade capture by predatory animals, and until the advent of motorised transport, this has been sufficient to usually ensure their safety, but until hares evolve an alternative strategy, they will always be at risk whenever straying onto modern roads.

"I was driving along this country lane and a rabbit jumped out and ran in front of me for at least half a mile!"...
"That was no rabbit, that was a hare"

The Red Spotted Handkerchief

Harold Jenner, a naturalist, tells a story of how he was taught by a poacher in Suffolk to pick up a brown hare sitting in a field. It only works in March or very early April, when they're a bit mad with the mating season, and there must be a cross wind, so the hare can't smell you. One person walks up very slowly as close as he can get to the hare, right in front of it, and puts a handkerchief down on a stalk so it blows in the wind, then he walks backwards right away again. Then the second person comes up quietly from behind and, because the hare is busy watching the handkerchief, he just grabs it and picks it up. But you've got to hold on tight!

from George Ewart Evans – 'Leaping Hare'

I have been watching the brown hares around here for years, and only once have I been able to get close to one, usually they bolt before you get much closer than 50ft. Once they know you're there, they don't hang about to see what you want!

feeding in the Beanfield

Midsummer's Eve, towards dusk, it was a warm, soft evening. I went for a walk along to the Airfield, past the Black Barn and the plantation and on to the old concrete runway, turning left at the muckheap and round the headland of the Harefield which this year was planted with beans. I reached the far side as the sun was sinking low, throwing long shadows in front of me as I went. I saw a hare, then another one, about three hundred yards ahead in the open, just off the edge of the path, they were browsing on the young tops of the bean plants, where the leaves are soft and tender. Not wishing to alarm them, I moved forwards as slowly and quietly as I could, I didn't imagine I'd get very close, hares are very timid, wary, and I was dressed in red trousers and a red T-shirt which must have stood out obviously against the green bushes all around me. Very slowly, careful not to make sudden movements or any unnecessary noise, edging closer...but I was downwind, they couldn't smell me from here, which helped. Amazingly they seemed to be totally oblivious of my presence, so engrossed were they in their feeding. As I got closer I wondered whether hares are aware of colour, maybe they're colourblind, these ones must have been, because I was now only ten yards away and they still didn't seem to have noticed me, which was doubly surprising as the position of their eyes enables hares to see all around them, and I was standing way out in the open, in full view, dressed all in red in a big green field and behind me a hedge of green trees! I stopped now and waited. One hare had loped off into the beans, no doubt in search of tastier bits, and was no longer visible, but the other hare was

actually moving towards me! Just here the beans are quite thin.
There was a semi-circular area about ten yards across, which
had been quite heavily grazed by hares and deer too; this is a
favourite place for Fallow deer to emerge from the surrounding
woodland – I'd often seen them here from the other side of
the field at dusk. The hare was browsing a single plant,
pulling the stalk down to nibble the tender top leaves, a
corner of a leaf poking out of the side of her mouth
as she chewed in a funny sideways motion. Moving
with languorous loping steps to the next, each
time she came closer to where I was standing.
I kept absolutely still, barely daring to
breathe,

she was only six feet away from me now and, as she stared right at me, I looked straight into her eye – a beautiful rich golden colour, with a darker rim, surprisingly deep and animated. This was a real wild creature, but one which revealed a true individuality. She was still totally relaxed and unaware of anything out of the ordinary and still seeming to perceive no threat.

She moved on again, further along the row and past where I stood, until in another minute she was downwind of me. Suddenly she stiffened, lifted her head slightly and tested the air, her eye glittered as she froze, and with a panic stricken look she pelted away into the cover of the beans. That was the last I saw of her.

Broad Bean
in flower

On finding a dead hare

I wasn't sure how to include this piece, as I thought it might seem a little macabre to some people, but it was such an important part of my journey and I learned so much about the anatomy and appearance of the Brown Hare from this encounter that I felt it must be included. I hope you can read this in the spirit it was written in my diary, of awe and wonder at the perfect design and beauty of this fine, magical creature.

I was driving along a country lane, not far from home, the morning was spring-like, but with a biting March wind that cuts through any warmth the sunshine could give. At the side of the road I saw the limp form of a creature stretched half on the grass with its head in the loose gravel at the side of the road. It had obviously been hit by a vehicle pretty recently and was quite dead. At first I wasn't sure what I was looking at, a small-ish hare or a rabbit? It was dusty from the roadside so the colour was not clear and the ears were not easily visible, so with the most obvious features obscured I would have to take a closer look, so I stopped the van and climbed out. It was a Hare.

I picked it up, wrapped it up, and took it home to draw. What struck me as I carried the hare in my arms to my studio was how like a cat it felt. I have grown up with cats and almost always had at least one cat as a pet. On one occasion, finding the body of my all-time favourite cat which had been hit by a car, I carried him back to bury in the garden, and he felt just like this, the same shape and weight in my arms, almost like a young sleeping baby, but cold.

I carefully laid the hare on the desk, having first spread out plenty of paper, as there was still blood oozing from its wounds, and began my study. It was a male, fairly small at only 21 inches from nose to tail. The poor thing had taken the impact full on the face, which had shattered his lower jaw, he also had a broken left femur and abrasions to the right shoulder, which had attracted the attentions of what was probably a crow or a magpie, that had eaten away some of the flesh there as well as the eyes. Apart from these injuries he was intact, so it would be possible to do detailed 'life' drawings and study the anatomy in a way that is far superior to that done from photographs.

The first thing I looked at was the feet. The back feet were massive with long separate toes jointed with proper little knuckles and a small pad on the tips just below very strong blackish claws. There was no central pad like on a cat or dog, but here the fur was coarse and dense and served the same

purpose, forming a mat which must give
good purchase on soft mud or
slippery ground, there were also
smaller mats of dense fur on
each toe pad, giving a
continuous furry sole. The front
feet were similar, but on a smaller
scale, about one third the size. The
back legs were sinewy up to the 'knee' joint with little noticeable flesh
below, but from the 'knee' to the hip joint the musculature was
pronounced, for strength to provide the acceleration that hares are
noted for. The pelvis and buttock area was quite square and larger
than I expected, giving rise no doubt to the name 'big-bum' in the
medieval 'Names of the Hare' poem. The tail, white on the underside
and black above, was a
good three inches
long. The spine
was long and
flexible, allowing
an extremely
elongated stride
at full speed
rather like a
cheetah. The rib
cage was deep and
broad, encasing the
lungs and heart which
are proportionally larger than
any other mammal, enabling the hare

♂ Brown Hare found at roadside
damage to face + right shoulder area
left back leg broken femur

Tib + Fib section
v. thin, no flesh
at all, just
skin, sinew +
bone

36

to run fast over long distances. The front legs, visible from the high 'elbow' joint were slender, straight and shorter than the back legs. The neck was short and the ears long and low, set towards the back of the head, which when relaxed, appear on the same level as the eyes, and lie along the back. The colouring of the ears was remarkable, soft olive and ochre, beautifully shading to sooty black at the tips and a patch on the outside edges, with white margins giving an effect rather like the subtle tones of plumage on the under-wing of a greenfinch. The face was damaged, but I could see that the fur on the nose covered the rounded tip right down to the long curved nostrils, so no damp waxy flesh like many animals have, though the hare's sense of smell is said to be good. The upper lip was split right through to the nostrils, creating completely separate 'cheeks', below which the grooved top teeth emerge from the grey gum looking like fused pairs of incisors, angled to meet at the tips, between which was a soft triangular pad. The lower jaw, having taken much of the impact of

beautifully delicate shading of fur on ears white, ochre-blonde and deep black, gives a similar effect to feathers of greenfinche's wing the collision, was badly damaged and the two lower teeth were displaced and broken, but seemed to be long, curved and thick with an almost square cross section, it appeared that there were no more teeth behind these for a distance. Despite the injuries, the basic shape of the skull was discernable, the upper portion was narrow and swept up and over towards the ears, with the eyes mounted prominently at the sides enabling 360 degree vision, useful for spotting predators, though the sockets were empty.

Thick black eyelashes

eyes positioned prominently at side of head - enables hare to see behind as well as in front

The coat, though complex in shading, was a mixture of three colours; nearest the pale skin was soft fluffy, downy, white fur shading to black at the tips along the back, through this grew the coarser 'guard' hairs, sandy coloured, coarser and straighter which emerged beyond the under-fur to lay over the top, providing the smooth surface of the pelt. The combination of the blackish under-coat and the sandy-brown top coat along the hare's back gave an over-all mid brown colour, with a slightly speckled appearance. On the flanks the under-coat shades to grey and together with the sandy-brown guard hairs gave a paler, cooler brown appearance. Across the shoulders, chest and along the edges of the white belly the under-coat shaded to a warm ginger, and the guard hairs, which were longest here, were also paler, giving a soft golden brown colour. The fur on the face was mostly mid brown with darker shading which appeared almost like stripes when viewed from the front, running from around the eyes, which were rimmed with white fur, down towards the nostrils and backwards to the base of the ears. Across the jowly cheeks was another stripe which joined the first to form a chevron pointing backwards, just below the base of the ear. The overall effect looked similar to the markings on the face of a tabby cat, though less pronounced.

The rest of the day was spent drawing and photographing the broken body of what had been such a beautiful animal.

Long guardhairs on Shoulders and round ribs

Shoulder

back

Thigh

I felt a sadness at the waste of life, but was really grateful for the chance to study him, but more than this the overwhelming feeling was a sort of reverence for the wonderful design of this most magical of creatures.

I prayed that his spirit was running in the land of the Great Hare.

How the Hare got his Split Lip

A tale from South Africa

The moon was sad; she had been watching the people on earth and saw that they were terribly afraid of dying, so she sent the Hare with a message for mankind- "just as I die and rise to life again, so you also shall die and rise to life again". But the Hare was inattentive and got it all wrong. When he reached the earth and delivered the message he said - "like the moon dies and does not rise to life again, so you also shall die and not rise to life again". Then the moon heard the wailing and lamentation of the people, and discovering the Hare's folly, was very angry. The moon struck the Hare with a hatchet, but the Hare moved quickly and instead of being killed, the hatchet slit his top lip, which is why to this day the Hare has a split lip. The spider, hearing that mankind was given the wrong message, tried to deliver it herself by spinning the message in her web. To this day spiders spin webs in peoples' houses to tell them of the moon's message, but no-one knows how to read it.

The top lip is split right up to the nostrils. Front teeth are paired and slant inwards, touching at tips

A story from the Native American Seneca people tells of a hare who habitually stole squash from the people. When caught and beaten by the tribe, he cried so piteously that the chief agreed to just split his lip so he could not steal squash again.

PART 2

FOLKLORE & MYTHOLOGY
of the HARE

Correspondences & Associations

Spring, Dawn, the East, Fire

Feminine, Fertility, Menstrual cycle

Moon, Light in the Darkness

Intuition, Enlightenment, Spirituality

Silver, Mercury

White, Snow, Self Sacrifice

Changeable, Unpredictable, Creative

Magic, Witches

Melancholy, Madness

Rebirth, Resurrection, Immortality, Rejuvenation

Subversive, Wild and Free

Gorse (Ogham tree alphabet - Onn, spring equinox)

Willow (Ogham - Saille, March 18th - April 14th, also cat)

CHAPTER 2

IN THE BEGINNING

Being and Becoming

Egyptian Hieroglyphs

Un (also wn), the Hieroglyph depicting a Hare, means to be, to become, becoming or to spring up. This is possibly due to the hare's habit of suddenly leaping up from a hidden form and racing away.

Un - to be, to become, to spring up.

In the Egyptian civilisation, this sudden appearance may have been interpreted as an instantaneous creation - from not being, to immediately being, as if by magic. When seeking a symbol to represent the idea of creation and 'becoming' for use in picture-writing, the Hare presented itself as an appropriate choice epitomizing a whole cycle of related ideas which also included; to open or an opening, an hour or a time, to transgress or overleap, and to spring up.

Though the 'Un' Hieroglyph depicts a hare, it is not the word for 'hare', according to modern scholars, that would sound as 'sh't' in the Egyptian language.

Hieroglyph of
Osiris Unnefer

Dawning of the Day

Osiris, also known as Osiris Unnefer (depicted with hares ears at the sides of his crown), the principal God of the Egyptians was called 'Prince of the unseen world'. He was believed to rule the heavens with, or as an aspect of Ra, the Sun God, presiding over the day, while Osiris presided over the night as the personification of the nocturnal moon. Osiris is thus a God of the underworld and of the dead. At different times he is both father to and son of Ra, so mirroring the cycles of day and night. Osiris and Ra are like two sides of the same coin. As the new day dawns Osiris may be seen to present the light of Ra, the Sun god, to the world. The hare-eared god is the bringer of light to the darkened world.

As Un, the Hare, can mean an hour, open, leaping or springing up. Nefer means beautiful, youth. It is used to denote the shining radiance of a god. So Un-nefer, by combining these ideas becomes the moment of the up-springing radiance of the young god; as this is the arrival of Ra, the Sun God, then this moment is the dawn, the 'becoming' of day.

Osiris Unnefer - 'king in heaven, great one upon earth, mighty sovereign in the nether world' - says 'I am Ra in his first risings' - from the Egyptian Book of the Dead.

The Great Hare of the Algonquin

In ancient times, before the Europeans came, all over North America, stories were told of the Great Hare, Manibozho or Michabo, who created the sun and the moon, and made the land from a grain of sand brought from the bottom of the primeval ocean. He was their principal god, and provided for the people by teaching them how to find food by means of the 'Medicine Hunt', a ceremony of ritual and dreaming by which the *Jossakeed*, a shamanic priest, is shown the location of game for the tribe to hunt. The Great Hare, father and guardian of the nation, was ruler of the winds, inventor of picture writing and of knitted nets to catch fish. He was said to dwell in the sky with his brother, the snow, though the oldest myths give his residence as 'in the east' from where he sends forth his 'luminaries' on their daily journeyings. This story finds echoes with the Egyptian tradition of the Hare God, Osiris, bringing the light of dawn as the sun rises in the east.

Song of the Spirit Dance

KEHARE KATZARU
Ruwerera, ruwerera.
Atius ruwerera.
Atius ruwerera,

SONG OF THE SPIRIT DANCE
Father-Sun, Father-Sun,
Look, yonder He comes,
Look, yonder He comes.

In this Pawnee ceremony; the dancers gather at sunset and dance all night until the morning star rises, singing verses to the Evening Star, the Stars of Heaven, Mother-Moon, Morning Star and Father-Sun. Whenever the dancers grow weary and begin to flag, a new verse is started, as long as the singing lasts, the dance will continue.

Heralds of the Dawn

The hare's habit of leaping up from a hidden resting place and racing away when disturbed may have been the inspiration for the Egyptian hieroglyphic 'Un', symbolized by a hare, representing ideas of becoming, opening and springing up. Could this appearance have been interpreted as an instantaneous creation – from not being to being as if by magic? So it is understandable that hares would also be associated with the Dawn, the up-springing light at the opening of the new day. Together with the song-birds of the dawn chorus, hares greet the appearance of the newly risen sun.

Opening of the way

Hare as the 'opener of the way' - a title given to Osiris
Dawn; the start of something new, maybe a journey or an adventure.

At the Begining of a New Month

A common custom throughout Britain which has regional variants is to say "Hares" as the last word before going to sleep on the last day of the month (one cycle of the moon), then, on waking; "Rabbits" as the first word spoken on the first day of the next month. The concept of bad luck (as 'Hares' often represent) is ended with the closing of the month. Good luck (hares now transmuted into the more innocuous 'Bunnies',) is brought in with the dawning of the new month. This transition takes place during the hours of darkness, including the magical witching hour, conveniently during sleep. It is also customary to turn over the coins in one's pocket on seeing the new moon. It is said this will end bad fortune, bringing in good, with the transition from one cycle to the next. Invoking the power of the moon which rules the metal silver, is also thought to influence financial matters through the association with silver coins making up much loose change people carry around.

When I was a child my mother didn't tell me anything about saying 'hares', but always told me to say "White rabbits" as the first words I spoke on the first of the month, whilst walking downstairs backwards. Luckily I always forgot or I might not be here to tell the tale – our stairs were rather steep!

The White Rabbit in 'Alice in Wonderland' heralds a whole new adventure.

Leap Year Day

It was Feb 29th, a mild afternoon, bright and clear, with skylarks singing above the Harefield. I hadn't seen the hares for months; it seems in winter that our hares just vanish. Maybe they simply stay hidden in the scrubby woodland that surrounds these fields. Walking along the runway eastwards, with my back to 'Black Patches', I spotted a big hare, right out in the open, in the middle of the field, with ears erect, sitting up half clear of the young crop of wheat, which still looks like grass. At last, they're back!

As I continued to walk, I kept an eye on the hare, but she soon started to move off to the far side of the field, disappearing over the slight rise in the land towards the trees in a fairly relaxed way. I thought that if I make my way right round the field I'll probably see her again. So when I got to the end of the field, where it gives way to rough scrub, I took to the grassy path that runs between them, and round the Harefield, down to the woods at the back. I caught a fleeting glimpse of a hare on the path about a hundred yards in front of me, but it disappeared into the long grass that edged the field.

I walked on down to the corner where a young Alder tree is growing. At this time of year it is smothered with long tassels of golden brown catkins on the

top half, and lower down, last year's cones
are still showing a wonderful deep
chocolate colour. At the roots is a
large flat topped stone with hare
droppings on top, small and black,
as if to mark the place clearly. Do
hares mark territory? Stopping
here to scan the field I
spotted another hare, only
twenty yards or so into
the wheat, this time
lying in her form,
squashed down with
flattened ears, trying
to avoid detection,
but not very
effectively,

as her rich sandy brown coat stood out against the young green corn very clearly. I think this may have been the one I saw on the path. I managed to get quite close to her, probably thirty yards, before she bolted off across the field, a chunky square body with tail down displaying its black upper surface and head held high showing long black-tipped ears, racing away towards the woods.

Suddenly three, four, five hares appeared from nowhere, and were charging around in a random and quite chaotic fashion. As the group careered about, they were gradually increasing the distance between us, heading away from where I was standing, until I could hardly see them on the far side of the field over near the runway. There didn't seem much point in staying here, so I retraced my steps past the Alder and back up the grassy path. Once I'd reached the runway I could see them again, still a distance away, but quite clearly. They were running around in circles, jumping and twisting over each other, then one would charge off in another direction, with the others following in hot pursuit, and it would all begin again.

I stood and watched for about ten minutes. The hares were clearly enjoying the bright sunlight and mild temperature after what must seem to them a very long winter, and a joy it was to see them again after so long. Then for some reason the five hares suddenly scattered in all directions and vanished. Spring was obviously in the air!

CHAPTER 3
THE HARE & THE MOON

The Hare's Link with the Moon

Since the earliest recorded history, in almost every ancient culture throughout the world, the Hare has been regarded as a mystical animal linked to the Moon. Many peoples have legends connecting the Hare and the Moon. The hare is frequently an attribute of lunar deities, and represents aspects of the moon in both mythology and legend, as shown with Osiris.

As the cycles of the moon rule the earth's waters and also influence the female reproductive cycle, so the Hare has become a symbol of fertility and is considered a feminine symbol. The fast-running hare often appears in myth as intermediary between the moon (deity) and earth (mankind)

Moon Goddesses

I n North America, the Great Spirit, creator and father of the nations, is seen as a Great Hare whose grandmother was the moon. A tale from the Pacific Island of Malekula describes 'Grandmother Moon' conceiving children by the god of light shining upon her, so they were later born through the portal of their mothers' wombs. 'Grandmother' or 'Old Woman' figures exist in several diverse mythologies, suggesting that long before Osiris and the Great Hare there had been an older female moon deity. Her shadow may later be seen in the Egyptian hare-headed goddess, Unnu-t, 'mistress of Unnu', the moon city. Holda (also known as Harke or Harfa) is an ancient Germanic Moon goddess who predates Frejya, to whom she bequeathed some of her attributes. She is sometimes depicted soaring across the sky attended by a train of torch bearing hares. Another Germanic Moon Goddess, Eostre, is Hare-eared, and appears with childrens' visiting customs at Easter. She is also associated with eggs. The Japanese moon goddess Gwatten is often shown holding a crescent moon as a bowl in which crouches a white hare. Everywhere there are moon-goddesses associated with hares.

FREYJA

'Once a warrior, very angry,
Seized his grandmother, and threw her
Up into the sky at midnight;
Right against the moon he threw her
Tis her body that you see there.'

- Longfellow, 'Hiawatha'

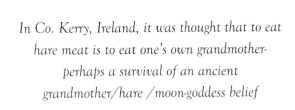

In Co. Kerry, Ireland, it was thought that to eat
hare meat is to eat one's own grandmother-
perhaps a survival of an ancient
grandmother/hare /moon-goddess belief

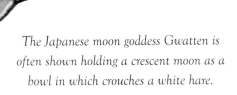

The Japanese moon goddess Gwatten is
often shown holding a crescent moon as a
bowl in which crouches a white hare.

Moonlight and Moon-shadows: light and shade

Nearly everyone is familiar with the appearance of the phases of the moon. Sometimes the moon is a thin crescent; sometimes a huge silver disk with strange markings; sometimes there is no moon visible at all. Unless the extended pattern is looked at systematically over a reasonably extended period, anyone could be forgiven for thinking the moon is quite unpredictable.

Moondial

Lunar Cycles

Scientifically, the light of the moon is merely reflected sunlight, as the moon produces no light of its own. The moon's phases are caused by the relative positions of sun, moon and earth as they revolve around one another. At the Full Moon the sun and moon are at opposite sides of the earth, so they are in an almost straight line (though if the line was completely straight, there would be a lunar eclipse, as the sunlight would then be blocked from reaching the surface of the moon by the earth in between). At Full Moon, as the sun rises in the east, the moon is setting in the west. At the end of the day, the sun will set in the west just as the moon rises in the east. On each day that follows, the moon rises about an hour later than the previous day. This shifts the relative positions, causing the illuminated area of the moon to appear to be reducing for several days (waning), and the moon to be high in the sky later during the night. You may also see the moon in the sky during the morning. About fourteen days after Full Moon, the moon will rise at nearly the same time as the sun, and in close to the same place in the east. It is not usually possible to see the moon from earth at this time, because the sunlight is so bright (very occasionally the moon's position moves directly between the earth and the sun, causing a solar eclipse). At this point in the cycle there appears to be no moon at all and this is called 'the Dark Moon'. It is halfway towards the next Full Moon. A day or two later a 'New Moon' is visible, a thin crescent, shortly after sunset, with both in the west. During the next few days the moon will appear to grow thicker (waxing) and may be seen in the sky during the afternoon. Eventually a twenty eight day cycle has been completed and the Full Moon can be seen again. Lunar cycles are usually said to start at the New Moon, ending just before the next New Moon.

The Hare in the Moon

The shadows on the face of the moon bear a strong resemblance to a hare in various ways. These are most clearly visible around the Full Moon, but can be seen for almost a fortnight from just after half-way through the waxing period of the moon's cycle until almost half-way through the waning period. As the moon passes its highest point in the sky a hare appears at full stretch leaping upwards and towards the right. But earlier in the night, either a sitting hare or the Hare that holds the Cosmic Egg may be seen. In Indian tradition, the Cosmic Egg was made by Shiva in a Hindu/Sanskrit creation myth. It cracked and expanded to form the universe, including sun, moon, earth and all the stars and planets.

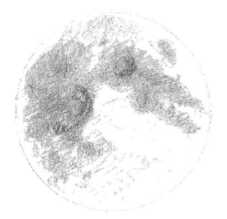

left: The Cosmic Egg
right: Leaping Hare

The Mark of the Hare

In many parts of the world, the shadows on the moon are known as 'The Mark of the Hare', particularly in China, Tibet, India, parts of Africa, Ceylon, Mexico and by many Native American peoples.

In a different version of the South African story 'How the Hare got his Split Lip', the Hare takes his revenge. When the Hare realised that the Moon had split his lip, he was so angry that he scratched the face of the Moon with his sharp claws, giving rise to the shadows that we can see on the full moon which appear in the shape of a hare.

Some legends appear very ancient, including that from Tezcucan, early Mexico. When the world was young, the sun and moon were equally bright. The gods did not think this was a good thing, so one of them took a hare and threw it at the moon, which made the hare-shaped shadows we see there and dimmed its radiance forever.

In Bedouin mythology the Sun and the Moon were sisters and walked side by side in the sky. One day they caught a hare and skinned it to cook, but while the hare was boiling in the pot, they quarrelled. The Sun picked up the hare's skin and threw it in the face of her sister the Moon. Angered by this, the Moon picked up the cooking pot and threw the contents over her sister the Sun. that is why the Sun is red and hot and the Moon has the shadow of the Hare on her face, and that is why they no longer walk side by side in the sky.

It may be that as hares are present in many countries, the perceived resemblance of the marks on the moon to a hare, as noted on different continents, may be nothing more than coincidence derived from common human experience. There is no way of telling, but in my more fanciful moments, I would like to think there was a point in pre-history when our distant ancestors saw the moon shadows as a hare, a mother creator-deity, and this belief travelled around the world with human migrations, surviving in different forms for many thousands of years.

The Buddha and the Hare

The Hare and the Moon feature widely in Buddhist stories from all over Asia. An Indian story describes how when the Buddha was a child he went alone into the forest to meditate, but he didn't take any food with him. After a long time he realised that he was desperately hungry, but still far from home with no food. All the animals took pity on him and brought him things to eat. Unfortunately, not knowing what human children eat they brought their own favourite foods. But the Buddha couldn't eat roots, leaves, grubs or insects. Eventually, the Hare came to him and said that if he would boil a pot of water, a meal would be provided. The Buddha did as he was told; he built a fire and set a pot of water to boil. Soon the water was bubbling and immediately the Hare jumped into the pot to make a hare stew! To reward the Hare's self-sacrifice, he was made immortal. Which is why to this day if you look at the Moon from that part of the world, it's not a face you will see – 'The Man in the Moon', rather the shadows look just like a hare!

In a Chinese version of the Buddhist story, three Fairy Sages turned themselves into pitiful old beggars and asked a fox, a monkey and a hare for food. The fox and monkey both had food to offer, but the hare had nothing to give, so he jumped into a fire and offered his own flesh as meat to feed the beggars. The Sages were so touched by this self-sacrifice that they gave him a place to live in the Moon Palace, and he became known as the Jade Hare (also known as the Jade Rabbit)

Jade amulets of Hares or Rabbits are common in China, and are often found as grave goods.

Moon Cakes and the Elixir of Life

In Oriental mythology from Japan, the Hare is depicted in the moon pounding rice with a pestle to make rice cakes. The Japanese words for full moon and for rice-pounding both sound like 'mochizuki' (note the similarity to Michabo, the Great Hare of the Algonquin). During the harvest festival, images with poems of the Hare in the Moon were printed in limited editions called 'Surimono' and were exchanged between family and friends much as Christmas cards are here. In China, the divine White Hare is thought to be the Moon Queen's servant, and lives in the moon, where it constantly pounds in a mortar the ingredients for the elixir of life. At the Moon festival ('Yue-Ping' – the 'Loaves of the Moon'), round cakes are exchanged representing the moon, stamped with an image of a hare sitting beneath a tree, just as chocolate eggs and bunnies are exchanged at the (moon) festival of Easter. As the hare mixes the 'Herb of Immortality' in the moon, this echoes the motif of eternal life, death and resurrection linked to the Lunar cycle, and it can be said that the vessel in which the elixir is pounded is in fact the crescent cup of the New Moon.

Messages of the Moon - Picture Writing

The Hare is thus rooted in ancient legends from all over the world, in many of them associated with the moon. So what is he doing there? Is the Hare the messenger bringing tidings and knowledge to mankind from the divine?

If, as the early Celtic Christians believed, the sun is the embodied face of God, hidden from mankind in the darkness of night, then the Hare in the moon represents the means by which the deity communicates with the people on the earth, he is the messenger; intuition, the unconscious channel by which divine knowledge - the sunlight reflected from the surface of the moon (the light in the darkness) – travels to us. This fleet-footed messenger brings tidings from the divine to mankind by way of dreams, flashes of inspiration; all personal, transient, easily lost or forgotten. By the invention of writing, whether pictures, symbols or script, these ideas are made permanent and available to those who can read and interpret them forever.

Many of the Gods associated with the Hare are said to have invented writing, either in the form of script or pictures. Hermes (Greek) who is also Mercury (Roman) are fleet footed messengers from the Gods, together with their precursor, Thoth (Egyptian) who is also linked to Unnu, the Egyptian moon city whose mistress Unnu-t is the Hare-headed goddess of opening

The Hare, messenger of the Moon, the channel bringing divine knowledge by means of intuition.

and uprising. They are all said to have invented writing. In the mythology of the north-east American nations, their creator-god, The Great Hare of the Algonquin, was also said to have invented picture writing.

Algonquin Picture Writing

Although the symbols convey simple concepts, by combining them, surprisingly complex ideas are conveyed. Communication can develop between distant people once the system is widely understood - it is easy to see why the people believed picture writing to be a gift from the Gods.

Egyptian Heiroglyphs

To enable abstract ideas to be conveyed, making communication far more versatile, Picture-writing gradually evolved into an alphabet capable of constructing words phonetically. The Egyptians used a combination of the two systems. Eventually the Greeks and Romans developed the writing styles we now use every day, but writing must have seemed like magic when it was first developed, truly a gift from the Gods!

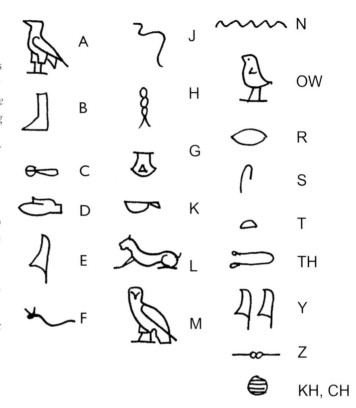

The Indian Sanskrit language shares a common root with Classical Greek and Latin, also with both Celtic and Germanic languages. This indicates truly ancient lineage back to their common source.

The Hare, the Elephants and the Moon Lake

An Indian story telling of Hare, the clever Messenger of the Moon.

On the banks of a great lake lived the King of Hares. One day, a herd of elephants came to the water to drink. But the elephants being so big did not notice the Hares, and many of them were trampled by the elephants' enormous feet. The Hare-King called his envoy, a very clever Hare, and said to him "As the elephants have now tasted the water of the lake, they will return again and utterly destroy our clan. You must go to the elephant leader and try to stop them killing us all." So, while he followed the trail of the elephants, the envoy thought carefully about how to carry out his task When he found the elephants he climbed onto a high rock and from there he called in a loud voice to their leader "I am an ambassador sent to you from the Moon and this is what the Gods say to you by my mouth – I live in a cool lake where dwell Hares whose king I am, I love them well, and I am known by men as the Cool-rayed, and Hare-marked. You have defiled my lake and slain my Hares; if you should do such a thing again I will show you my wrath." The Queen of the Elephants was stricken with fear and grief, and begged to be able to show her contrition for their terrible deeds. So the Hare-envoy led the herd to the banks of the lake and showed them the reflection of the moon in the water. There the Elephant-Queen bowed in awe of the Moon and vowed never to come there again. The King of the Hares saw what was done and honoured his envoy, and the Hares lived there in peace, calling the lake Chandrasaras (Moon-lake) forever after.

The Watcher of the Sky

'When the hare is awake he shuts his eyes, but when he sleeps his eyelids remain open though his eyes do not move' – Xenophon (430 – 354B.C.E. *Greek historian*)

'The moon is the watcher of the sky, that is to say she sleeps with her eyes open; so also does the hare' – De Gubernatis (1840 – 1913, *professor of Sanskrit, author of mythological studies*)

These quotations are somewhat confusing if taken literally in the physical sense, but if treated allegorically their meaning becomes perfectly clear. In this case the moon represents the 'light in the darkness' – intuition, the higher self, the spiritual. So the Hare, the inner being, has its eyes open to this higher consciousness, and as the Chinese believe, the 'Bright Eyes' of the Hare (as a sacrificial Hare in China is called), unlike any other creature, grow larger and brighter with age, i.e. with age, spiritual wisdom increases.

Although Richard Adams in his book 'Watership Down' was writing about a colony of rabbits, it is usually accepted that at times rabbit and Hare mythology is interchangeable. At the point at which the song 'Bright Eyes' is sung in the film 'Watership Down', Fiver, a clairvoyant and visionary, is following trance-like, an apparition in a dream, leading him to the whereabouts of the trapped and injured leader of the colony, Hazel. This dream sequence illustrates perfectly the combination of qualities associated with the Hare; that of intuition accepted with an openness of mind leading to a dawning illumination of otherwise inaccessible knowledge via a message from or connection with the Gods, or the other world, represented by the moon. It seems most unlikely that the use of such a song at this point in the film is mere coincidence.

Hare Watching

The Hare crouches in a form, her daytime resting place, from where she can keep watch, ready to run if danger threatens. Up on the field another hare watches from amongst the young green corn. As rooks and crows prepare to nest in the trees at the top of the hill, they keep a careful eye on the hare resting among the daisies – the 'day's eyes'- which open with the sun and close at night. The Classical Greeks first said that hares sleep with their eyes open, and this belief was enshrined in folklore.

The Archetype 'Hare'

'Who looks outside, sleeps. Who looks inside, wakes.' - C.G.Jung

Carl Jung (1875 –1961), the Swiss psychologist developed a system of analytical psychology based on his experiences of self analysis. During a lifetime of study he discovered that within the 'Collective Unconscious', made up from the experiences of all life since evolution began, 'Archetypes' exist; symbols which shape the way people relate to their world, available during sleep in the form of dreams, in order to make sense of present experience. This is a vastly simplified explanation of the concept (it took Jung a lifetime to explore and explain), but basically Archetypes frequently appear in mythology and represent models by which anyone can test their understanding of their own world and their place within it.

It seems that The Hare corresponds well to the notion of an Archetype as proposed by Jung, and represents a whole cycle of ideas based around the bringing of light - enlightenment. This may mean a flash of inspiration, like the cartoon lightbulb above the head of someone who has a bright idea, or possibly the 'light at the end of the tunnel' after a long quest for truth. We are said to 'see the light' when we finally understand a perplexing problem and are then 'enlightened'. The Buddha is said to have achieved 'Enlightenment' (with a capital 'E') or spiritual perfection. The light that Hare brings is understanding, inspiration and finally spiritual awareness.

The nature of the Archetype 'Hare' has had subtly different meanings to different civilizations and at different times in history, but the (re)appearance in popular consciousness of the Hare and its mythologies seems to me to have often heralded a significant step forward in the psychological evolution of humankind.

CHAPTER 4
FERTILITY, SPRING & EASTER

The Spring Goddess
Eostra, Eastra, Oestra, Ostara, Astrild

Eostra (Germanic), Oestra (Teutonic), Ostara (Anglo Saxon),
Astrild (Danish) - the goddess of Spring, Dawn & new life,
Hare-headed moon goddess.

Eostra , Oestra gives her name to Oestrogen, the female hormone which stimulates ovulation and therefore fertility. It is appropriate that her spring festival, Easter, is celebrated with eggs, often stained with natural dyes or painted in bright colours to be given as gifts, particularly to children, a custom that has survived to the present day (though chocolate brown seems to be the preferred colour these days!).

The Hare is traditionally sacred to Eostre / Ostara. There are almost certainly parallels with Astrild, (possibly an echo of Astarte, the ancient Phoenician goddess of fertility and sexuality, later called Aphrodite, when adopted by the Greeks). Astrild is the name by which the Danes knew Freyja, the Norse goddess who was attended by hares, bearing lighted torches to illuminate her path.

In the 8th century, the Northumbrian monk and historian, the Venerable Bede refers to Eostra in his 'De temporum ratione' (The Reckoning of Time). This explains among other things the Anglo-Saxon calendar and a method for the calculation of Easter. Bede describes Eostra as a goddess of the light of the rising sun, a young female dressed in a short tunic, wearing a hood with hare's ears, and carrying a round silver disk on which could be seen an image of the moon. A thousand years later, Jacob Grimm again described her (Ostara) as a divinity of the radiant dawn, the upspringing light, and a spectacle bringing joy and blessing.

In Germany, small stone altars, 'Easter-stones', dedicated to Ostara were decorated with garlands of flowers as part of the Easter games, when young people would dance around them by the light of bonfires. This practice, similar to English 'Maypole dancing' was finally ended at the demand of 19th century priests.

Easter
The Great Festival of Spring

According to Bede, the name Easter is derived from the Germanic Eostra April = 'Eostur-monath' or 'Ostermonath' – dawn-month, the beginning of the new cycle of life, springtime when the plants resurrect from their dormant state of winter sleep to become green and alive again.

The Calculation of Easter

From the early days of the Christian church, Easter, when Christ was believed to have risen from the dead, was observed at the time of the Jewish Passover (Pesach). To this day the date of Pesach may vary by anything up to a month. The Jewish calendar calculates Pesach as a week beginning on the 15th day of the month of Nisan, falling in either March or April (Julian calendar), but also depending on both lunar cycles and crop ripening. This caused great confusion, and while Bishops argued among themselves, ordinary Christians consulted their Jewish neighbours as to the date of Passover, and celebrated accordingly, some on the first day of Nisan whenever it was; some on the Sunday following. The First Council of Nicaea (325 C.E.*) said that the 'disorderly' state of the Jewish calendar (which did not coincide with astronomical events) was no basis on which to hold such an important Christian feast-day. Instructions were issued that the Alexandrian method, independent of the Jewish calendar, be adopted throughout the Christian world. Unfortunately, no details of this calculation were stipulated, so the method was disputed for several decades.

In Britain a totally different system was employed, developed by Irish missionaries who in typically Celtic fashion had incorporated an 84 year cycle of the moon! It took until the Synod of Whitby in 664 C.E. to bring Britain into line with the rest of Europe and unify the date of Easter.

However, confusion returned with the introduction of the Gregorian calendar across Europe (1582 - Britain finally complied in 1752). Although this is closer to the solar year, and was meant to standardise dates, the Eastern Orthodox churches continued to use the old system. So now there are two Easters, as much as 5 weeks apart. In the western world the method of calculating the date of Easter has coalesced. It is now celebrated on the first Sunday after the first Full moon, after the Spring Equinox – how Pagan is that!

*C.E. - common era, also known as A.D.

Spring Equinox

"Mad March Hares" box in the fields by the light of the Moon. Some say this is to compete with rivals for a mate, but now it is believed that the female will rebuff the male until she is ready to mate, while also giving her the opportunity to assess his strength and prowess. The Hare is thought to have been the original 'Easter Bunny', but rabbits live in burrows, while hares shelter in shallow scrapes in the ground in open fields. This may have given rise to the old belief that hares lay eggs, which hatch into leverets, mistaking ground nesting bird's eggs for the produce of the hares who share the same land; it's easy to see where the Easter egg originates! The resurrection theme of Easter also reflects the cyclical phases of the moon, which dies and rises again every month.

As Mad as a March Hare

During mating time in spring the erratic behaviour of hares, charging around, leaping and boxing in the moonlit fields has given rise to the expression 'Mad March Hare'. Some claim that 'Mad' does not necessarily mean 'crazy', but that there is an older English usage of the word 'Mad' meaning aggressive or fighting, hence the Mad March Hare is the Boxing Hare as seen in the mating season.

A Horse misused upon the road
Calls to heaven for human blood,
Each outcry of the hunted Hare
A fibre from the brain does tear.

William Blake – an extract from 'Auguries of Innocence'

Despite the explanation based on old English usage, it is nowadays considered that hares typify madness, lunacy and melancholy, and 'Lunatic' clearly derives from the erratic and unpredictable behaviour of the 'Moon-like'

Spring Equinox

21st March, dawn, full moon. I awoke at 5am and set off to the Harefield, I'd been planning this visit for ages. It was very cold with a biting SW wind. I arriving just as the sun began to rise, washing the dead grass at the side of the path up to the runway with a warm golden glow, and illuminating from below the broken cloud, like pink patchwork to the east. There was a thick bank of cloud to the west, so I couldn't see the moon as it set, which was a shame. There is a very special atmosphere about the time at which the sun and moon rise and set at the same moment. This was all the more perfect as it is the Spring Equinox, when the hours of dark and of daylight are exactly equal, standing at the threshold between the light and dark halves of the year, like a point of exquisite balance

Considering the date and the time of day I was hoping to see some activity from the hares, boxing would be fantastic! But as I scanned the field through my binoculars all I could see was a couple of Roe deer

Hare facing sunrise

grazing on the far side near the trees. Not a hare in sight. There were several skylarks singing already, and I had seen a green woodpecker flying through the trees as I came past the Black Barn, I could still hear its distant 'yaffle' from time to time.

My shadow stretched far behind me as I walked towards the rising sun, along the runway, then up the grassy path, clockwise around the Harefield. I spotted a shape far out in the middle of the field, a creamy golden colour, almost round with dark blackish stripes fanning out from the bottom. I couldn't make it out; it could be a carrier bag that had been blown there, but I'm not sure. As I continued along the muddy path, taking care not to slide into the puddles that filled the many dips in the track, I kept looking at this shape through the binoculars. Eventually, as the angle changed from which I was viewing it, I realized that I had been watching a hare sitting crouched in her form from head-on; the stripes were the markings on the side of her head and the ears lying along her back. By the time I was sideways-on it was clear that she was watching me just as closely! The golden colour was accentuated by the glow of the rising sun, which she was facing directly, and she had her back to the chill wind. The imagery moonset

and significance of her position, on this of all mornings, was magic. At the point of balance between dark and light, winter and summer, night and day, she had turned her back on the cold wind, the moon and the retreating darkness, and sat bathed in the golden glow of the rising sun, representing light, warmth and life.

I moved on along the southern, wooded side of the Harefield and was surprised to see a pair of rabbits at the edge of the cultivated land, nibbling at the young shoots of wheat growing there. It is quite unusual to see rabbits and hares in the same field, it is said that rabbits spoil the land – make it 'sour' – for hares, so they are seldom seen together. I could only think that there can't be many rabbits here as the hares are so plentiful, there have been times in the past few years when I've seen as many as a dozen hares at a time on these fields.

By now I had reached the place where I had seen the two Roes but there was no sign of them now, they had ambled off back into the cover of the trees. I spotted another hare, she was sitting in exactly the same position and orientation as the other, but from that angle I was looking at her from the side, with the clear golden light illuminating her face and chest as she crouched in her form, throwing a deep shadow behind her. As I watched she sat up a little, stretched like a cat, with fore-paws stretching out in front and her back arching, and began to groom. First she nibbled at the flank nearest to me, and then started to wash her face rubbing first one side then the other with her paws, and working down from chest to stomach, she curled her flexible

spine until she was almost round with just her ears sticking out.
I rounded the corner and saw the Roes again in the long grass of the wasteland between the Harefield and the Poplar hedge. They took fright as they saw me and bounded away with a flash of white fluffy rump signalling alarm. I followed but lost sight of them as I picked my way carefully through the pathless (apart from the narrow deer trod tracks), bramble strewn scrub. Here I found early Coltsfoot starting to emerge, little Dandelion-like flowers straining upwards on scaly stems, to reach the open air.
By now the bird population were in evidence everywhere I looked, mostly in pairs chasing each other around the trees, all except a solitary Yellowhammer practicing his "Little bit of bread and no cheeeeese" call to herald the summer, though it doesn't feel very summery this morning – I'm off home for a warm up and a hot cup of tea!

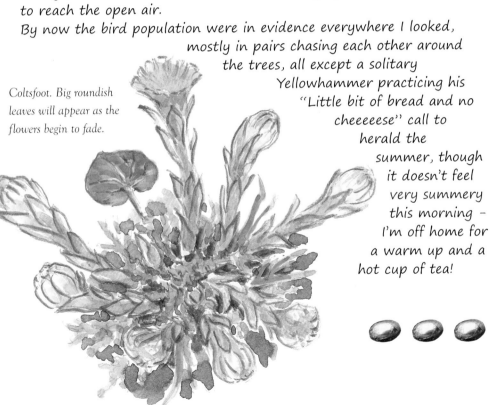

Coltsfoot. Big roundish leaves will appear as the flowers begin to fade.

The Two Magicians

From Peter Buchan's 'Ancient Ballads and Songs of the North of Scotland' 1828, the earliest recorded version of this ballad. I have adjusted some of the spellings to make it read more easily

The lady stands in her bower door, as straight as willow wand;
The blacksmith stood a little forebye, wi' hammer in his hand.

'Well may ye dress ye, lady fair, into your robes o' red;
Before the morn at this same time, I'll gain your maidenhead.'

'Awa, awa, ye coal-black smith, would ye do me the wrang
To think to gain my maidenhead that I have kept so lang!'

Then she has holden up her hand, and she swore by the mould,
'I wouldna be a blacksmith's wife for the full o' a chest o' gold.

'I'd rather I were dead and gone, and my body laid in grave,
Ere a rusty stock o' coal-black smith my maidenhead should have.'

But he has holden up his hand, and he swore by the mass,
'I'll cause ye be my light leman for the half o' that and less.'

*O bide, lady, bide, and aye he bade her bide;
The rusty smith your leman shall be, for a' your muckle pride.*

Then she became a turtle dove, to fly up in the air,
And he became another dove, and they flew pair and pair. *O bide, lady, bide...*

She turned herself into an eel, to swim into yon burn,
And he became a speckled trout, to give the eel a turn. *O bide, lady, bide...*

Then she became a duck, a duck, to puddle in a peel,
And he became a rose-combed drake, to give the duck a dreel. *O bide, lady, bide...*

She turned herself into a hare, to run upon yon hill,
And he became a good grey-hound, and boldly he did fill. *O bide, lady, bide...*

Then she became a gay grey mare, and stood in yonder slack,
And he became a gilt saddle, and sat upon her back.

Was she woe, he held her so, and still he bade her bide;
The rusty smith her leman was, for a' her muckle pride.

Then she became a het girdle, and he became a cake,
And a' the ways she turned herself, the blacksmith was her make. *Was she woe...*

She turned herself into a ship, to sail out over the flood;
He ca'ed a nail intill her tail, and syne the ship she stood. *Was she woe...*

Then she became a silken plaid, and stretched upon a bed,
And he became a green coverlet, and gained her maidenhead. *Was she woe...*

light leman – wanton lover
muckle – much
dreel – rough handling
het girdle – hot griddle
syne - then

The Two Magicians

A shape-shifting song describing the magical contest in which a 'Lady' attempts to avoid the unwanted advances of a 'Smith'. The blacksmith's power over metal by the transforming use of fire was thought to be essentially magical for thousands of years, and the term 'smith' was sometimes used to denote a magician, or, as in the case of the Anglo Saxon 'Wayland', a God. The lady in this case seems to be pretty proficient in the magical arts herself in that her shape-shifting includes animals (relatively simple) and a full rigged ship (a bit more ambitious), but how hard does she really try to escape? I mean, really – it seems she was more likely testing his ability to keep up with her, and the bed – well that was a bit of a give-away. It was as if she was saying – "OK, I'm ready now, you'll do". It all seems rather reminiscent of the 'boxing hares' scenario, where the female keeps the male at bay until she chooses the time for mating, and in the meantime, has the opportunity to assess his worthiness to be her partner.

Boxing Hares by the Light of the Full Moon

The Full Moon is pictured as concentric bands of blue and silver (moon colours) Celtic strap work surrounding the medieval "Triple Hare" design, which is often found, carved as a roof boss in churches on Dartmoor in Devon. The blue colours give a hazy, almost three dimensional appearance.

Eating Easter Hare

The Hare was considered a sacred animal by the ancient Britons, so eating hare meat was taboo, as Pliny and Caesar's 'Commentaries' both tell: "Hares, fowl and geese they think it unlawful to eat, but rear them for pleasure and amusement" - Caesar 54 BCE*. (In ancient Hebrew / Jewish tradition, the Hare was also taboo) Any taboo is almost invariably evidence of the survival of a shadow of former sacredness. Most taboos were subject to a single ceremonial exception, when the sacred nature of the object of the taboo created an event with a truly sacramental significance.

In Pomerania (on the Baltic coast) and also in parts of Germany - hares were hunted and caught to provide a public meal at Easter-tide.

In Leicestershire, Black Annis, a character of local legend, was a hag-witch who was said to eat children, and is thought to be a relic of the ancient British mother goddess Anu. She lived in the Dane Hills, just to the west of Leicester, at 'Black Annis's Bower' a cave she had gouged out of the rocks with her own claws, and was associated with the May-eve hare hunt (later Easter Monday). This Easter Monday Hare hunt was already recorded as ancient when described in town records in 1668 with the Mayor and 'his brethren' dressed in scarlet gowns. Though originally a real hare was hunted, by the middle of the 18th century this had been replaced by a scent trail of aniseed. Mounted huntsmen with dogs, cheered on by crowds of onlookers followed the trail around the countryside and back into the town, right up to the Mayor's door, where a feast was prepared for them. This municipal custom eventually degenerated into an annual holiday and Fair on Danes Hill and the Fosse Road.

Danes Hill and the Dane Hills are both situated to the west of Leicester City Centre.

*BCE - Before common era, also known as BC

The Easter Bunny and Easter eggs

Easter eggs were recorded as long ago as 1280. In southern Germany, children were told that it is the Hare that lays the Pasch eggs, and they built little nests in their gardens for the hare to lay their eggs in.

Since the 19th century in the Germanic regions of Europe, an old custom has frequently been recorded that toy hares together with eggs (painted hens' eggs or more recently chocolate) and Easter cards, usually depicting hares, have been given as gifts amongst family members. In England, this was common in the second half of the 20th century in my own experience, with the possible variation of cute fluffy rabbits being substituted for the hares. This may be a degenerate form suggested by Disney-esque style fashion of the 1950s. Chocolate eggs are well known Easter gifts, but chocolate 'bunnies' were also given then and are again available, as they seem to have experienced a resurgence of popularity recently and have been widely available in supermarkets in the last few years.

The Hare-child and Grandmother Moon

Across Eastern Europe there are several customs associated with the Easter period which include the egg and hare motifs. In Austria on Palm Sunday (the Sunday before Easter) catkins are brought to church and blessed, then taken home and kept outside the house until Easter Sunday. Then the first child to carry the catkins into the house at dawn (dawn/hare imagery) is rewarded with the first Easter egg. After church the children hunt for eggs which have been previously hidden in large numbers all over the garden. In the afternoon there is a ritual visit to the 'Grandmother' - either the children's actual grandmother or another older female substitute (remember the grandmother in the moon legends). The company processes, led by a child dressed in a cape with the head and ears of a hare (like the image of Eostra) carrying on his or her back a small water butt (water ; moon correspondence) filled with coloured eggs. When they arrive the party is treated to specially made cake like a flattish nest (hare's form?) filled with more coloured eggs. After tea a game is played by the children whereby the Hare-child gives the eggs in the butt to the other children, but this is not a fair distribution; with chasing and 'rough and tumble' as the result of the capricious whim of the Hare-child who may award as many or as few to whoever she chooses, favouritism rules! Afterwards there is another egg hunt in grandmother's garden. There is also an Easter children's game in which one holds a coloured, hard-boiled egg, while the other child tries to pierce it by stabbing at it with a silver coin, if the coin lodges in the egg, both are claimed by the attacker as a prize. Again the moon imagery of the silver disk is apparent.

Catkins

Easter Day

We awoke to a winter wonderland – thick snow, and still falling in big damp lumpy flakes, like clumps of cotton wool. By the time I went outside to feed the birds it must have been three inches thick. After breakfast Colin and I walked up the lane. Snow was still falling, but hadn't settled on the road, at least not until we got to the top of the hill where it must have been several degrees colder, and the snow was lying thickly everywhere.

Up on the Harefield, we were trying to keep from sliding around too much in the snow, which wasn't easy with soft mud and barely frozen puddles underneath it. Up here the snow was being blown by the keen biting wind which sent it in plumes like smoke across the surface of the land, to drift among the trees. We went clockwise round the field, and I didn't spot any hares until we were halfway down the grassy path (not that the grass was visible under the snow), then I saw one crouching in her form about a hundred yards away out in the middle of the field. I stepped off the path and walked along a tractor track between the furrows, towards where she was sitting, just to see how close I could get. At about twenty feet she took to her heels and bolted towards the trees. I continued on to where she had been, and looked for the tracks she had made as she fled, which were easy to find in the snow. Following them I was amazed at the length of each stride – the back and front paw marks were equidistant at a 'gallop', and the distance between one front paw mark and the next was at least eight feet!

Her remarkably flexible spine together with strong back leg muscles enabled her to propel herself at a speed of at least thirty miles an hour – and that obviously wasn't her top speed as she seemed to be irritated at being disturbed, but certainly not panic-stricken.

She had made her way into the trees at the back of the field, and I followed her tracks to where she had crossed the path, there I met Colin who had continued around the headland. At this point many other tracks could clearly be seen; more hares, some running, some with a more leisurely gait; others were of deer and fox, and the odd pheasant as well. A busy crossroads.

A pair of Roe deer appeared from among the trees further along the path and took off across the field, making for the plantation on the opposite side. We continued round the headland and then I followed a deer track across the wasteland, while Colin headed for the gap in the Poplar hedge. Suddenly he was beckoning wildly and calling me to see – there were hares on 'Black Patches'– lots of them!

A group of three hares were on the far side in the distance, and over to the right an odd one a bit closer and a pair who were boxing! This was the first time I had ever seen hares boxing in the wild – I was just so excited. I tried to take photos, but they were so far away and the snow both on the ground and also that still falling and blowing around just above the surface made it a 'white-out' through the view-finder. I pressed and prayed over and over again, but all I got was white.

So I just watched and enjoyed the spectacle.

They were two magnificent big brown hares, from this distance I couldn't see if they were exactly the same size, so I couldn't tell what sex they each were, but because the snow provided such a good contrast to the dark shapes of the hares they were clearly visible. They were both standing upright on long, muscled legs only inches apart, jabbing energetically at each other with front paws while craning their heads backwards to avoid the blows aimed by their opponent. A few frantic moments boxing, then a leap or two, a side-step, and back again to boxing. Sometimes one seemed to be about to overcome the other, but somehow that didn't seem to be the object. It appeared to be more ritualized than aggressive, neither was really trying to hurt the other, it was almost a dance.

The lone hare loped towards the boxing pair, seeming to be transfixed by their odd behaviour for a while, but then he tried to join in the fun, leaping about and copying the pair's antics. This wasn't appreciated by one of the couple who chased him away, so he ran a short distance, then slowly returned and tried again, only to be rebuffed and chased off once more. Time and again the lone hare tried to join the pair but to no avail, they just weren't having it.

They say these days that hares indulge in boxing when a female is not yet quite ready to accept the breeding advances of a male, keeping him at bay, whilst able to assess his strength and fitness. This would certainly fit with what I saw.

Just then a group of walkers appeared on the curved roadway on the far side of 'Black Patches', disturbing the other group of three hares nearest them, which ran towards the Poplar-hedge, crossing through it about 100 yards further down the row from where we were standing, across the wasteland to emerge onto the Harefield, where they sped out to the middle of what is a pretty large field. By the time I saw them they were right over the far side, in what was no more than a few seconds.

What caught my attention then was another hare that had appeared from the plantation. It loped out into the open space to join the boxing pair and the lone hare. The four hares started to circle each other then leap over one another manically, leaping and twisting over and over until they were so mixed up together that I could no longer keep track of which was which.

The walkers now disturbed the hare quartet, who took fright and raced off into the plantation, so we walked back along the Poplar hedge and past the muck heap. Then a vixen appeared, followed by a dog fox with obvious amorous intent; they flirted and played about in the field for a while. They were far too engrossed in each other to be aware of being watched, as all of a sudden – a full David Attenborough moment! The copulation only lasted briefly and they turned and trotted off together across the Cowslip path and into the cover of the plantation. I followed them to try and find their tracks, but saw no more of the foxes or the hares that day.

CHAPTER 5
FECUNDITY AND THE FEMININE
Allegory

In art and writing, fecundity and procreation are often represented allegorically by plants bearing prodigious numbers of seeds e.g. poppy or barley and by animals exhibiting rampant virility e.g. the bull, goat, rabbit and Hare. In a more value-charged (Christian) context the Hare signifies lasciviousness, luxury and laziness, but it is never consistently clear whether the Hare is considered to be generally moral or amoral. (Although this is a human construct and it may be unreasonable to apply it to animal behaviour, in symbolic terms critics often do so).

Moongazing Hare

In China it is believed that the Hare derives its existence from the vital essence of the moon, so is subject to its influence at all times. Some sources claim that conception occurs by the female hare licking the fur of the male, while others state that it is by gazing at the radiance of the full moon that the female becomes pregnant, eventually giving birth to leverets which are the children of the 'Light in the Darkness'

Classical Greek beliefs

The ancient Greeks held many beliefs about the miraculous fertility of hares, much of which appears to have survived into relatively modern times in the form of superstitions:

- The 'evil' breeding scent of hares lasts all year.
- Hares mate every month throughout the year.
- Females conceive without being impregnated by a male.
- Male hares bear young.
- Females conceive while still pregnant.
- Hares produce milk before the young are born.
- Hares' uterus contains nipples to feed young before birth.
- Leverets are born not all together, but at irregular intervals, at the mother's will.
- Herodotus claims that while the female is carrying young, some furred, others not, and some still forming, she conceives again.

Lack of detailed observation at this time would account for some of these misconceptions, but the claim that hares conceive whilst still pregnant is not as daft as it at sounds. 'Superfoetation' in hares is now held to be established fact, in which the pregnant female can be again fertilized, causing the simultaneous development of eggs of two different ovarian cycles within the genital tract. Both rabbits and hares will accept mating during pregnancy, but only the hare can conceive a second time.

Whatever the origin of these beliefs, the hare was seen as a divinely fertile creature, and as such became a symbol of sexual love and fecundity, often appearing in images together with Aphrodite, Eros, Cupids, Satyrs, and also in connection with Dionysus and the Maenads, all gods or mythical characters associated with sexual love and hedonistic behaviour.

Live hares, as well as images of hares on Vases, jewellery, decorated plates etc. were given as love tokens - wedding rings often bore images of hares in ancient Greece - sometimes depicting the hare alone, sometimes in compositions including cupids, or other mythological characters representing the particular form of love the giver wished to portray. There are several amphorae (wine jars) from around 500 B.C.E. decorated with images of mature male athletes presenting (usually naked) youths with hares. These have also been interpreted as depictions of the giving of love tokens, but in some of these cases it is possible that the focus of the gift may be the hare's swiftness, intended to celebrate the sporting prowess of the younger man. It is difficult to tell.

In Aeschylus's 'Agamemnon', an omen is seen of a heavily pregnant hare being eaten by two eagles, one black and one white. This scene takes place outside the palace as the army is preparing to set out for the attack on the city of Troy (represented by the hare), led by the princes Agamemnon and Menelaus (the eagles), and is taken to presage the success of the siege. The imagery continues as Artemis declares her anger at the eagles devouring the hare (sacred to her), indicating that she opposes the expedition. The Trojan War was occasioned by the abduction of Menelaus' wife, the beautiful Helen, by Paris, prince of Troy. Some sources say that Helen was granted to Paris as a reward for his giving of a golden apple to Aphrodite, in his judgement as the fairest of the Goddesses.

Artemis, the Archeress, whose symbol is the crescent moon

Hares on the Mountain

A well known 19th century country song in which the love or sex object is often represented as the hare. These are two versions of this suggestive song from totally opposite view-points, collected around the same time from places less than ten miles apart.

Young women they run like hares on the mountain,
Young women they run like hares on the mountain,
If I was a young man I'd soon go a-hunting
To my right fol de diddle dero, to my right fol de diddle dee.

Young women they sing like birds in the bushes,
Young women they sing like birds in the bushes,
If I was a young man I'd go and bang the bushes,
To my right fol de diddle dero, to my right fol de diddle dee.

Young women they swim like ducks in the water,
Young women they swim like ducks in the water,
If I was a young man I'd go and swim after,
To my right fol de diddle dero, to my right fol de diddle dee.

Collected by Cecil Sharp from Louie Hooper and Lucy White at Hambridge, Somerset 1903

Hares on the Mountain (2)

If all those young men were as rushes a-growing
Then all those pretty maidens will get scythes and go a-mowing.

If all those young men were as hares on the mountains
Then all those pretty maidens will get guns and go a-hunting.

If all those young men were as ducks in the water
Then all those pretty maidens would soon follow after.

Collected by Cecil Sharp from Mrs. Lock at Muchelney, Somerset 1904

Hares Changing Sex

There was a country belief that hares change sex, alternately becoming male or female in successive years. Otherwise it was thought that both male and female characteristics could appear together, so hares were thought to be hermaphrodite.

An apocryphal tale tells of the female hare sheltered from the flood on Noah's Ark, not able to tolerate the proximity of so many creatures, escaped, only to be drowned in the waters. God took pity on the plight of the Jack (male) hare, and made him capable of bearing young, so the species would not become extinct.

"A male hare was once found almost dead, whose belly being opened, there were three young ones alive taken out of its belly"

"He saw a hare which had stones and a yard, and yet was great with young"

- Edward Topsell - 'The History of Four Footed Beasts' 1607

Christian Art and Iconography

It has been suggested that in Christian art, particularly during the Renaissance, the Hare appears as a symbol of lust, with images of a white hare under the feet of the Virgin Mary denoting the triumph of purity over lust. I have read this statement in several books, and on numerous websites, but while I seem to have vague memories of such images, as yet I have failed to find a single example, despite extensive searching. I did find two pictures: one a woodcut by Albrecht Durer (1498) 'Holy Family with three Hares' in which Mary is seated on a manger, holding Jesus on her lap, Joseph stands behind, three small hares are playing around Mary's feet; the other an oil painting by

Titian (1530) 'Madonna and Child with St Catherine and a rabbit', St Catherine presents the child to Mary, who is seated on the ground while beside her sits a white rabbit or hare which she is holding under her right hand. So is the 'triumph over lust' a real image or merely another urban myth? Any evidence of this image will be gratefully received (– contact details at the back of the book).

My take on Mary 'Star of the Sea', seated in the crescent moon, nursing the Christ-child on her lap, with a hare beneath her foot.

Much of the iconography of Mary has been borrowed from earlier pagan sources; Mary, mother of Jesus, is frequently depicted seated in a crescent moon, nursing the Christ-child, leading some to argue that she is the inheritor of Isis, shown nursing Horus, and with whom she shares the title 'Stella Maris' - 'Star of the Sea'. Inanna and Hera can both claim earlier original ownership of another Marian title, 'Queen of Heaven', crowned with the stars. Could it be that Mary has evolved from an older Moon Goddess?

Irrespective of the Christian view of Hare symbolism and the triumph of purity over lust, in the countryside people knew what sex was for, and celebrated it in the symbolism of the Hare.

The Pledge

The masculine Oak tree, its acorns said to resemble the glans penis, and the haws (fruit) of the Hawthorn epitomise the fertility and fecundity of the male and female principles.

MAY

'March winds and April showers bring forth the May flowers' and the coming of Summer is marked with Maypoles and Queens of the May. The White Park cattle of Britain are an ancient breed. The bulls were chosen by Druids to be honoured in sacrifice to the Gods. Crowned with Mayflowers and decked with ribbons, the archetypal masculine symbol, ridden by the young maiden, represents a mix of imagery showing powerful virility subdued, at least superficially, by purity and innocence. But the underlying fertility symbolism is betrayed by the presence of the phallic Maypole and the fecund hare.

The Bonny Black Hare

A dirty little song, collected by George Gardiner in 1907 from Thomas Jones of Portsmouth
A somewhat re-written version was popularised by Martin Carthy in the 1970s.

One morning in autumn by the dawn of the day,
With me gun in good order I straight took my way,
To hunt for some game, to the woods I did steer,
To see if I could find my Bonny Black Hare

I met a young damsel, her eyes black as sloes
Her teeth white as ivory, her cheeks like the rose,
Her hair hung in ringlets on her shoulders bare,
"Sweet maid" I cried, "did you see my black hare?"

"This morning a-hunting I have been all round,
But my bonny black hair is not to be found."
The maid she then answered, and at him did stare,
"I never yet heard of – or saw – a black hare."

"I think you're deceitful, young maid" he did say,
"My bonny Black Hare I am told passed this way;
And if you have decoyed me, I vow and declare,
You shall go with me to hunt the bonny black hare."

"My gun's in good order, my balls are also,
And under your smock I was told she did go.
So delay me no longer, I cannot stop here,
One shot I will fire at your Bonny Black Hare."

His gun he then loaded, determined he was,
And instantly laid her down on the green grass;
His trigger he drew, his sight it was clear,
And he fired one shot at her Bonny Black Hare.

Her eyes they did twinkle and smiling did say:
"How often, dear sportsman, do you come this way?
There is few in this country can with you compare,
So fire once again at my Bonny Black Hare."

His gun he reloaded and fired once more,
She cried, "Draw your trigger and never give o'er.
Your powder and balls are so sweet I declare,
Keep shooting away at my Bonny Black Hare."

He said, "My dear maiden, my powder's all done,
My gun's out of order, I cannot ram home,
But meet me tomorrow, my darling so fair,
And I'll fire again at your Bonny Black Hare."

Childrens' Nursery Games

The natural consequence of all this fecundity and fertility is the procreation of children, so how does the hare figure then? In Swabia (Eastern Europe), children were told they were found in a hare's nest, much as English children are said to be found under a 'Gooseberry Bush', or Americans in a 'Cabbage Patch'. There are also nursery games which include much cuddling and the occasional tickle, providing amusement and an opportunity for closeness, that expresses sensuality experienced between mother and child, which though utterly innocent, may foreshadow other physical pleasures which the infant will not experience for years!

"Round about there
Sat a little hare,
The bow-wows came and chased him
Right up there!"

The child sits on the mother's lap and holds its hand open while the mother runs her finger in a circle round the flat palm then touches the centre (the hare), lastly making her fingers 'run' up the child's arm to tickle under the armpit.

Another version of the same game, collected in 1949 and said by the source to have been in the family for over a century, and originally learnt from north-country gypsies;

"Round about there
There lived a little hare,
That broke its heart with grief and care
To see the pastures all so bare,
And a little mouse ran right up there."

This game begins with the round and round gesture, and touching the palm of the hand, but then the mother gently tweaks thumb and all four fingers in turn, so it also bears many similarities to 'This little Piggy went to Market';

"Round about, round about,
Here sits the hare,
In the corner of the cornfield
And that's just there,
This little dog found her, (thumb)
This little dog ran her, (index finger)
This little dog caught her, (middle finger)
This little dog ate her, (ring finger)
 This little dog said 'give me a little bit please" (little finger)

CHAPTER 6

THE TRIPLE HARE

The Triple Hare design

The Triple Hare design consists of three hares running in an everlasting circle with their backs to its centre. Each hare appears to have two ears, but as these are shared between the three hares, only three ears are actually visible, forming a triangle. There is no other obvious common element to different examples of the design. Some are surrounded by decorative devices, particularly foliage; some form part of a larger design; others are completely unadorned. In Britain the Triple Hare is most often carved in wood or stone, but has been found as stained glass, tiles or plasterwork on ceilings and friezes. In other countries examples have also been found of silk textiles, painted fresco, ceramic decoration and cast or incised metalwork.

Where the Triple Hare has been Found

In Britain the Triple Hare is found in buildings dating from early medieval times onwards, particularly churches. Findings include a floor tile from Buckinghamshire (1300 CE), another tile in Chester Cathedral (1400 CE); roof bosses at St David's Cathedral, Wales, Selby Abbey, Yorkshire, Corfe Mullen, Dorset and Cothele Chapel, Cornwall (1480 CE) and secular plasterwork in Scarborough, Yorkshire. The largest cluster of Triple Hares are the roof bosses in West Devon churches, 17 in all, mostly in villages on and immediately to the north of Dartmoor. Many of these churches were enlarged or rebuilt during C15*.

A modern tile, made in traditional earthenware with a coloured slip picking out the three hares pattern. From my own kitchen, made by Waterloo Farm Pottery.

During the Sui and Tang dynasties (581-907CE), three rabbits or hares images were painted on the centre of the ceilings of many caves dug by Buddhist monks from the cliffs along the Daquan River at Mogao, near Dunhuang, China. Typically, the circle of rabbits or hares is surrounded by eight large lotus petals and forms the focal point of a large painted canopy covering the entire ceiling.

*C15 = 15th century

Origins of the Triple Hare

Extending their search beyond England, the Three Hares Project (Tom Greeves, Sue Andrew and Chris Chapman) has found examples in China, the Middle East and Western Europe, many of which predate any English finds. Discoveries include a C11 Hindu medallion, C13 Egyptian pottery, a C14 Mongol Empire southern Russian silver filigree box, the decoration on an early C14 bell in a Cistercian abbey in Trier, Germany, a painting on a C15 castle wall in Italy, a C16 Jewish synagogue ceiling and a medieval Jewish manuscript, a C18 Iberian figurine.

The earliest examples found so far, are painted on the ceilings of Buddhist cave temples dated C6, in Mogao near Dunhuang, China, and thought to be artists' representations of textile canopies, possibly based on woven silk originals. It is thought that if the Triple Hare motif originated there, it probably travelled , woven into silk fabric, with traders along the 'Silk Road' – the trade route by which silk and other commodities found their way from Chang'an (present-day Xi'an) in the east, through Central Asia, India, Persia, and eventually, westwards into Europe.

In 1453, Constantinople, capital of the Christian Byzantine Empire, finally fell to the Muslim Ottoman Turks, as long threatened. In anticipation of this a mass of scholars and artists fled westwards,

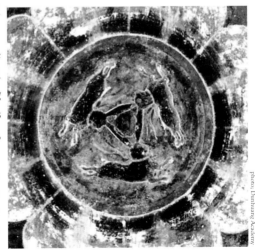

Thought to be one of the oldest of the Three Hares images, from Cave 407 at Mogao, Dunhuang. In this image the hares/rabbits are running in an anticlockwise direction, and have white scarves trailing from around their necks.

photo: Dunhuang Academy

carrying a wealth of Icons and relics into Western Europe. Trade in relics was immense, Bones of 'saints' or splinters of the 'True Cross' were often wrapped in costly silks and housed in reliquaries. Chinese silk was considered to be of the highest quality, and is known to have been used for this purpose, as well as for vestments, altar cloths, for decorating shrines and lining precious books. It is perfectly possible that the Triple Hare design, woven into silk fabric arrived in England between C12 and C14, becoming widely known by the C15.

Triple Hare Hunting on Dartmoor

I had read so much about, and been fascinated by, the Triple Hare design, but it was also confusing me somewhat. On a cold weekend in February, I set off for Dartmoor to see the Hares for myself.

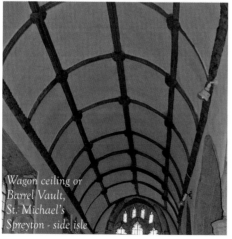

Wagon ceiling or Barrel Vault, St. Michael's Spreyton - side isle

Many of the churches in which Triple Hares appear are situated to the north and west of the moor, and were re-built in the mid 1400s, which was a time of prosperity despite the Wars of the Roses, partly due to a thriving tin-mining industry in the area. The churches I visited all had 'wagon ceilings' also called 'barrel vaults', which are made up of a series of semi-circular arches placed one after another and linked by beams along the length of the roof. At each intersection are carved wooden roof bosses, decoratively securing the joints, and displaying various devices including stylized foliage, human and animal figures and coats of arms.

Outside the first church I visited, St. Michael's at Spreyton, beside the lych-gate was a modern name-board painted with the Triple Hare design, but in this case the animals appeared quite clearly to be rabbits in a crouching position, sharing long ears, and surrounded by oak leaves and acorns. Inside there were two Triple Hare roof bosses, the first half-way down the side aisle, the second in the sanctuary ceiling in a central position flanked by bosses showing a Green Man and a complex foliage design.

Then at St Andrew's in Sampford Courtenay there were two roof bosses showing Triple Hares. The first was half-way down the chancel ceiling; the other in a central position in the sanctuary ceiling with several quite spectacular Green Men on the surrounding bosses.

My lino-cuts of Triple Hare and Green Man, Sampford Courtenay.

At Chagford parish church, the hares were wooden carved and painted in red and gold on a boss just inside the chancel immediately behind locked gates in the middle of the ceiling. Here the design had been reproduced on tapestry kneelers and cushions in several pews, appearing in a quilted wall-hanging depicting many aspects of the town, and was also available as a car-sticker in the shop. Chagford town has obviously adopted the Triple Hare, it appears in shop signs, house name-boards, and as decorative devices everywhere you look. A lady I spoke to in one of the shops told me that here it is known as 'Tinners Rabbits' and there is a 'Tinner's Fair' in the town to celebrate May-Day. Chagford was a major centre of the tin-mining industry covering a large area of the surrounding moor, and the miners were fed on rabbits bred for the purpose in a warren near the mines. There is a pub near Postbridge commemoratively called the 'Warren House', whose sign-board shows a Triple Hare.

St Pancras church at Widecombe-in-the-Moor boasts a collection of colourfully painted roof-bosses depicting foliate designs and Green Men, but here there are characters and emblems from chivalric tradition among the more usual biblical themes, while the Triple Hare, placed in the centre of the chancel ceiling is called the 'Hunt of Venus' and it is claimed to be a symbol of the Holy Trinity.

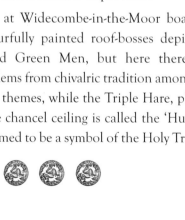

Chagford: Roof Boss in Parish Church, Kneeler, House sign, Shop sign; Roof Boss in St. Pancras, Widecombe-in-the-Moor.

Hunt of Venus – *from the manuscripts of Basilius Valentinus, also known as Basil Valentine, a 15th-century alchemist and the Canon of the Benedictine Priory of Sankt Peter in Erfurt. This illustration is possibly the source of the name used to describe the Triple Hare design in some Dartmoor churches. Here the Triple Hare motif forms part of a complex alchemical style design.*

After visiting the Dartmoor churches, I realized that the confusion I had initially felt was beginning to evaporate. It seemed to me that on Dartmoor the central position of the Triple Hare roof bosses was suggesting that there was indeed a common significance. Every church I visited had carvings of the Triple Hare in the middle of the chancel (choir) or sanctuary (the 'sacred place' where the altar is), which is where it would be expected to find the most important symbols. The fact that within these ceilings the Triple Hare design was placed in the most central area would suggest that it was intended to portray a central concept. I was beginning to accept the theory that Medieval Christians had adopted the Triple Hare as a symbol of the Holy Trinity. However it is still difficult to explain why these bosses had escaped the vandalism of Puritan Iconoclasts to whom all imagery was anathema, perhaps being part of the joints of the roof, they were loath to risk destroying the church's structural stability.

I started to dig a little deeper, and was rewarded by a discovery; between 1420 and 1458 the bishop of Exeter, in whose diocese Dartmoor is situated, was Edmund Lacy, a man with a reputation for piety and the working of miracles. There are records of an illuminated manuscript, a psalter (book of psalms), containing an image of the Triple Hare, being in the possession of the diocese of Exeter, and therefore in the bishop's library, at this time. This is interesting, as it implies that to be included in the decoration of a sacred book, the design already may have had some sort of Christian spiritual significance.

At this time the Dartmoor churches, in which the Triple Hare roof bosses appear, were being built or extended. If Bishop Lacy was seeking symbols to be incorporated into the decoration of the churches, representing various religious themes, it is quite credible that the strange little Triple Hare design in his psalter may have presented itself as a possible device when considering the concept of the Holy Trinity. After all, in several of the Dartmoor churches' guide books, this is exactly what it is claimed to be, leading me to wonder if it was on his instructions that the design was incorporated into the works.

What does the Triple Hare mean?

In many of the Dartmoor 'Hare' churches the design is often positioned close to a foliate head roof boss – the 'Green Man'. This has prompted some to suggest an explanation which, though highly plausible, is impossible to prove. It is accepted that the Hare was sacred to our forebears, connected in legend with the moon, ruler of the waters and the female cycle. In this interpretation the 'Three Hares' is said to represent the female aspect of divinity and the fertility of the animal world; just as the Green Man is thought to represent the male aspect of divinity and the fertility of the

Iddesleigh

Sampford Courtenay

**Dartmoor Forest
& National Park**

Newton St Cyres

S. Tawton

Spreyton

Cheriton Bishop

A30

Throwleigh

Chagford

Bridford

N. Bovey

A386

elly

Grimspound

Postbridge

Tavistock

Widecombe
in the Moor

Ilsington

Paignton

A38

world of vegetation. This interpretation also presents the Triple Hare as a sort of goddess motif, which has found acceptance by many modern pagans, particularly women.

Seen together with the Green Man as in many Dartmoor churches, is the Triple Hare, therefore, more a representation of divine balance? Could it also be that other 'roof boss' images held a particular spiritual significance – were the foliate heads (Green Men) intended to portray God's presence in the natural world – after all, Christians claim that God 'made man in his own likeness', so who is to say that the face was intended to be that of a man?

Images of Triple Hares and Green Men from Chagford, Sampford Courtenay and Spreyton, on or near Dartmoor, Devon.

An Archetype

Every observer brings to their understanding of the Triple Hare something of themselves. Over centuries and generations, the myriad shades of interpretation and the significances implied, add up to an immense and diverse body of meaning. But underpinning all this is still a fascination for the image as it stands alone, uninterpreted, as an artistic statement. For why else should it have caught the imagination of so many just now? And why do people constantly ask me "what does it mean?"

Carl Jung's concept of 'archetypes' teaches that each symbol holds within it a cycle of ideas which has developed over thousands of years. An 'archetype' image takes on a life of its own, and accrues to itself significances that generations of observers bestow upon it. A Bishop interprets the Three Hares as a symbol of the Holy Trinity. A medieval craftsman working to a brief but also in search of inspiration carves it individually into the churches in which he works, so that each roof boss is subtly different from any other. Later, worshippers experience a mystical response to the image, in part because of the 'holy place' they are in and partly due to their reverential mood at the time at which they see it. Later still, tourists visit the church in search of the image to which they give a different meaning, depending on their personal beliefs. Imperceptibly the image has become an archetype, representing subconsciously, layers of meaning that work on many levels, yet possibly still retaining some of the significance with which the image was imbued by its original creator, hundreds of years before and thousands of miles away in ancient China.

My design for a Triple Hare pewter pendant. As well as the three hares symbol, the imagery reflects three aspects of hare mythology; Harvest, the Moon and Dawn, which in turn represent the Physical, Mythological and Spiritual aspects of the hare. Three threes - a magical image.

Yin, the Feminine Principle

hen I found something that stopped me in my tracks! I was looking at a website - www.threehares.net - when I noticed a photograph of a shard of pottery from Egypt or Syria circa 1200. It showed the usual Triple Hare image, but each hare was a different colour, one red, one black and one blue, on a white background. The conventional artistic method of portraying the colour white when shown against a white background is to substitute the colour blue - it gives the impression of white in shadow. Although this piece of pottery was made several centuries later, it is possible that this convention was used by the artist who decorated it, as a representation of the older design originally found in ancient China.

The second of the twelve emblems of the Emperor of China, is Yin, represented by three Hares; the White Hare, an auspicious omen, signifies divinity; the Red Hare is a harbinger of peace and prosperity, denoting a virtuous ruler; the Black Hare brings greetings from the moon goddess, and promises good fortune and success. If this singular design had in fact originated in China as a symbol of 'Yin' and was woven into silk canopies to decorate holy shrines, perhaps that would also account for the central position of the painted images still visible in the earliest Buddhist cave paintings at Mogao. Was the Triple Hare originally an auspicious symbol representing peace and tranquillity? (I have since discovered that this view is shared by Guan Youhui, a retired researcher from the Dunhuang Academy, who spent 50 years studying the decorative patterns in the Mogao Caves). What is more exciting is that it is also linked to the feminine principle, which Yin is, and to the moon goddess, through the black hare, and finds echoes in present day interpretations of the Triple Hare as the female aspect of divinity, and sign of the Goddess.

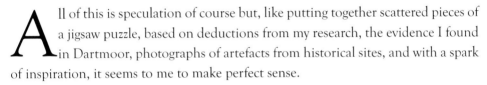

All of this is speculation of course but, like putting together scattered pieces of a jigsaw puzzle, based on deductions from my research, the evidence I found in Dartmoor, photographs of artefacts from historical sites, and with a spark of inspiration, it seems to me to make perfect sense.

It is clear that spiritual significance has been ascribed to the Triple Hare design by many countries, several religions and over hundreds of years. In fact it has been adopted by just about every civilisation and religion it has touched. This is still happening now - images of Hares have emerged in recent years in the imaginations of artists, and they clearly hold a sort of fascination and mystery which is beyond mere interest. For an image to become an archetype it must work on many levels, conscious and subconscious, visual and symbolic, and its meaning will evolve in response to the needs of generations of people, so in ancient China, the Triple Hare represents the divine feminine; in an age of Christian piety it becomes a symbol of the Holy Trinity; to tin miners who eat rabbit it is a badge of identity, the 'Tinners Rabbits'; and in an age of secular post-feminism, it is a symbol of the Goddess within, of the feminine principle, bringing the cycle round again. I can see no contradiction in this.

The Hares of Long Melford.

Not far from my home is the town of Long Melford, Suffolk, founded on money made from the wool trade and boasting two large Tudor Mansions and an imposing church. The rolling grasslands which supported the sheep surrounding the town may have been blessed with a large population of hares, providing sport for the wealthy and meat for the poacher, as the name of both the pub and a nearby road suggests.

'The Hare' public house and 'Harefield', Long Melford

Holy Trinity church, Long Melford, contains medieval stained glass attributed to the Norwich school dating from the late C15. As with many English churches, much of the stained glass was destroyed during the English Reformation (between 1530 and 1689), but glass from the highest windows survived and has now been repositioned in the main windows, as part of restoration works done in C19 and C20. Above the north door is the Trinity window, where restorers have grouped together images that may have Trinity connections; an angel holding a three-armed device on a shield, a 'Pieta' showing Mary crying tears in groups of three, below which is a small fragment clearly depicting a Triple Hare, the only known medieval example of the design in stained glass. It's unclear whether the roundel is a repositioned part of an undamaged window, though the fragmentary nature of the image tends to suggest it may be a shard saved from the smashed windows.

The three heads, with ears and the back of one hare are all that remain, but also interestingly, the roundel is completed with a sun ray fragment – if this is a restored shard, did the restorer know the significance of the sunrise within the mythology of hares, or was it fate that guided his hand? By what strange coincidence did this scrap of broken glass find its way back to such a prominent position in this window? Was it retrieved and saved at the time of the vandalism? Was it scooped up along with all the rest, or singled out for special attention, or happened upon centuries later by chance? Now it is in pride of place, the focus for many visitors, and with unseen feet the hares still chase around their circle in the golden rays of dawn. In the gift shop a postcard of the Triple Hare window can be bought to send out into the world; an icon again.

The Triple Hare window in Holy Trinity Church.

The Tinners Rabbits

But what of the 'Tinners Rabbits'? In her book 'The Outline of Dartmoor's Story' (1951), Lady Sayer suggests that Dartmoor tinners, by way of a thank-offering for their prosperity, financed the C15 church building work. As a result the tinners' emblem 'The Tinners rabbits' was carved in many churches. Whilst this is possible, it is more likely that among people attending the new churches were tin miners. It's well known that the Dartmoor tin miners ate farmed rabbits from the warrens on the moor. Perhaps, when they saw the Triple Hare, they might have thought it was an appropriate device to adopt for their own emblem. It appears that, as late as the mid 20th century, Lady Sayer was the first to make the written link between the Triple Hare symbol in the Dartmoor churches and the miners' 'Tinners Rabbits' emblem (incidentally, at around the same time, Lady Raglan first coined the name 'Green Man' to describe foliate heads). Folklore's a funny old thing. Walk round Chagford now and everyone knows what the 'Tinners Rabbits' is. You'll need a church guidebook to explain the link with the Holy Trinity!

'Tinners Rabbits' roofboss,
Sampford Courtenay

Tinners Rabbits – the Dance

The Border Morris side 'Grimspound Morris', named after a Bronze Age hut circle settlement on Dartmoor, close to the Golden Dagger mine, regularly perform a dance called 'Tinners Rabbits', written by their squire, Martin Gosling. It reflects much of the imagery in the Triple Hare motif, danced by groups of three, there are two figures in which three dancers link together and circle, much as the hares do in the 'Tinners Rabbits' sign; 'Three Star', in which each dancer grasps the wrist of the person in front, forming a triangle with their hands, and 'Rabbit Snares' in which the dancers are joined via a triangle of sticks. This dance has been widely adopted by Morris teams and may be seen danced at many folk and Morris festivals every summer throughout the country.

At Upton-upon-Severn Folk Festival 2005, as a thank-you for designing a T-shirt image for the Morris team "Stone the Crows", I was invited to join them for this dance (though their version has evolved a little since it was first written, and was to the tune 'Uncle Bernard's' in this case) and great fun it was too – thanks guys!

Stone the Crows

Tinners Rabbits – the Dance

For groups of three dancers, but three groups of three is the best magic!.
Sets are numbered 1 – 3 clockwise. Single stepping throughout (step, hop)

Fig.1. 1 Reels - Nos 2 & 3 step on the spot. No1 dances between them and does a figure of 8 around them, one and a half times, then back to place.

Chorus - *standing, facing centre, stick held two handed, all sticking forehand (right to left)* - 1 clashes with 2, then 2 with 3, then 3 with 1. One clash per beat, continue this circular pattern for 12 clashes, then three hits on ground, rising for next figure on last beat.

Fig.2. Three Star - A three man star; dancers grip left forearms and circle anti-clockwise.

Chorus...

Fig. 3. 2 Reels - Nos 1 & 3 step on the spot. No2 dances between them and does a figure of 8 around them, one and a half times, then back to place.

Chorus...

Fig. 4. Rabbit Snares - All turn left to face in a clockwise circle. Hold sticks in right hand turned inwards to form a triangle at waist height. Dance round.

Chorus...

Fig. 5. 3 Reels - Nos 1 & 2 step on the spot. No3 dances between them and does a figure of 8 around them, one and a half times, then back to place.

Chorus...

Fig. 6. Rounds - If 6 dancers (2 sets of 3) form a circle of 6, dance clockwise.

Circle and Star - If 9, three dancers (no1s of each set should be closest) do a Three Star while the rest circle around them in the opposite direction.

Lead off in single line.

the Tune - Scotch Polka

From the playing of Devon musician and Dartmoor Folk Festival founder Bob Cann

Grimspound Morris

Items from my collection; handbag by Spirit of the Fens Leather, Tiles by Aly Meuse, Iris Milward, toy by Dora designs.

CHAPTER 7
HARVEST LORE
Fertility and Fecundity of the Earth

The mother of Eostra, the Hare-headed goddess was Jord, the Earth, equivalent in Greek mythology to Demeter, the Earth Mother and corn goddess, known by the Romans as Ceres, who gives her name to the cultivated grains we call cereals.

As mankind made the transition from hunter gatherers to farmers, and established an annual round of crop growing, particularly corn – wheat, barley, oats etc – the new arable environment provided an increase of food and shelter, contributing both to growth in population, and increased frequency of sightings of hares by man. It takes only a small leap of imagination to see that new harvesting methods when combined with the Hare's natural timidity plus speed of escape when frightened could give rise to all sorts of associations in the minds of our ancestors.

Hares tend to sit still when first alarmed, hoping to avoid discovery. As danger draws nearer, the Hare prepares to escape, only running at the last moment.

This would often be seen as the harvesters progress across the field cutting the corn as they go. As farmers and labourers began to reap from around the edges towards the centre of the field, they also exploited hunting opportunities afforded by the escaping animals as they exploded out of the last patch of standing corn, scattering in all directions. Taking refuge in this way, Hares naturally became associated with the escaping spirit of the crop as they rushed out of it.

It is suggested that the origin of the association of hares with fire may be similar; accidentally burning crops or seasonal stubble burning for clearance would flush out Hares at the last moment, possibly singed by the advancing flames.

Fire & Disaster

It is thought that a hare running along the main street portends a fire in the village.

"on the day of the fire a hare was seen to run along one of the streets a few hours previous to the fire. Some who saw it expressed the hope that should the omen prove true, the fire would not occur at a factory or any other public works."

\- 1884 Rushden

"If in the Minster Close, a hare
Should for herself have made a lair,
Be sure before a week is down
A fire will rage within the town"

\- 1909 Peterborough

When fields of grain were cut with scythes, the Hares that were hiding there would often race out of the last patch to be cut. Eventually the running Hare came to be associated with the harvest as the life spirit escaping with the last sheaf to be cut. In some places customs grew up, conferring 'good luck' onto the man who cut the last sheaf, or by calling the last sheaf 'The Hare' and carrying it with great ceremony to the barn or farmhouse, where it would be kept in a place of honour until the following season when it was ploughed back into the field, or burned and its ashes scattered there to return fertility to the land.

The Hare As Corn Spirit

In Galloway, Scotland, there is a well documented custom – "Cutting the Hare" – as the last standing corn was called. When the rest of the crop has been cut, the last handful was left standing and this is the 'Hare'. The corn was divided into three parts and plaited, a knot was tied at the top and this pulled into two 'ears'.

The reapers then stood in a ring a short distance away and took turns in throwing their sickles at the 'Hare' attempting to cut it off below the knot. When the 'Hare' was finally cut, it was taken to the farmhouse where it was hung in a place of honour in the kitchen, usually over the door, for all to see. It was said that by doing this the corn spirit would ensure the fertility of the following year's crop.

Variations of this custom existed all over Europe. The last sheaf to be cut was called 'the Hare' in parts of the UK, Germany, France, Italy, Holland, Sweden and Norway, and the part played by the person who cuts 'the Hare' was also significant in different ways. Some areas held the cutting of the hare to be lucky, and the cutter was held aloft to bear his prize home in style, while in other places he was mocked or made to pay a forfeit – in Norway the one who 'kills the Hare' must give the other reapers 'Hare's blood' (brandy) to drink!

In Ireland the story of the hag who turned herself into a hare in order to steal milk from the cow was a common tale, and sometimes the sheaf was known as the hag or cailleach. It is possible that this association of the hag, as a creature known to steal food, with the cutting down of the last sheaf, represents the triumph of the human forces of agriculture over the chaotic or malevolent forces of nature in the shape of the hag.

In Wales there was a custom by which the men from the harvest field tried get the last sheaf into the house without it being wet by the women, who waited to waylay them with bowls of water. This may also represent the saving of the harvest from the chaotic forces of nature (interesting that the uncontrollable is represented as female) in the shape of rain and storms, always a concern at harvest time, even today.

AUGUST

At the end of August the barn is full, and Harvest Mice are feasting on ears of wheat as the last load is brought into the barn with great ceremony, pulled by heavy horses crowned with meadow flowers, and accompanied by a procession of jubilant harvesters celebrating the end of another year's toil. Held aloft for all to see, the final sheaf, 'the Hare', as it was called in some places, or in others, the 'Cern' or 'Corn Baby', was decorated with a corn dolly to house the spirit of the grain until next year. Later there would be a Harvest supper or 'Horkey', where the work of the harvesters would be rewarded with a feast of their own.

The Hare that Reaped all Ireland's Oats

*There is a family of stories from Ireland telling of a magical harvest,
in which the Hare as a symbol of fertility and of swiftness is celebrated.*

A farmer sowed oats to cover the whole of Ireland, and when the oats had ripened he was at a loss as to how to reap so much before it was spoiled. As he set out to reap, a Hare ran past, and thinking she would make a fine supper, the farmer threw his sickle at the Hare, and the point of the sickle stuck in her haunch, but she kept on running. She ran up and down the land, up and down, cutting the oats as she went, until by the end of the day, all the oats were cut and the farmer had a fine harvest.

Harvest Hare Hunting

Before the 2004 Hunting Act, hare hunting was both legal and common in agricultural areas after the harvest. In South Armagh, N Ireland, once the harvest was over, at the signal of a hunting horn blown, any farmers within earshot would bring their one or two beagles each, forming a pack, and go in search of a hare to chase on foot. Often hunt watchers would station themselves upon a hill where they could follow events, and were only too ready to cheer the Hare if she escaped. This arrangement has been called 'Chasing the Callyach; Callyach – a witch or a hare, as in the Scottish 'Cailleach' - a crone, whose day, 25th March, around the Spring Equinox, is also known as Lady Day and was also New Years Day until the Gregorian calendar was adopted in 1752. So an essentially post-harvest, and therefore autumn custom still has links to the Hare's corresponding imagery of magic, female, spring, new life (new year), bringing the whole cycle round again.

The Hills of Granemore

A song from South Armagh, N Ireland. I learned this song from Tony Small when we were
both in a band called 'The Wild Geese' in the 1970s, and have been singing it ever since.

On a fine summer's morning the horn it did blow,
To the green fields round Tassagh, where the huntsmen do go.
To meet the bold sportsmen from around Keady town,
For they love the sport better than the boys from Maydown.

And when we arrived they were all standing there,
So we took to the green fields in search of a hare.
We hadn't gone far when someone gave cheer,
Over hills and high meadows this 'puss' did appear.

When she got to the heather she tried them to shun,
But the dogs never missed one inch where she'd run.
They kept well paired when going over the hill,
For the hounds had set out the sweet hare for to kill.

With the dogs all abreast and the big mountain hare,
And the sweet charming music it rang through the air
Set fire the Black Bank for to try her once more,
For it was her last night round the hills of Granemore.

And as they trailed on to where the hare she did lie,
She sprang to her feet for to bid them "Goodbye",
Their music it ceased and the cry we could hear,
"Bad luck to the ones brought you Maydown dogs here"

"Last night as I lay quite content in my den,
Twas little I thought of the dogs or the men,
But when going home at the clear break of day
I could hear the loud horn and the tune it did play.

"And now that I am dying and the sport it is done,
No more through the green fields round Keady I'll run,
Nor feed in the glen on a cold winter's night,
Nor go home to my den while it's breaking daylight.

"I blame old MacMahon for bringing Coyle here,
He's been at the same caper for many's the year.
Every Saturday and Sunday he'll never give o'er
With a pack of strange dogs round the hills of Granemore."

After the Harvest

The evening was warm and still and the sun was getting low, birds were preparing to settle for the night, a flock of rooks passed high overhead making for their roosting site among the trees in the Broaks, an ancient wood half a mile away to the East. Colin and I found ourselves walking along the old runway, facing an almost setting sun, which burned our eyes as it began to sink down beyond 'Black Patches', beyond the trees in the distance, beyond the edge of the land. Standing in the gap in the Poplar hedge with our bare ankles threatened by the nettles which grew thickly all around the muck heap behind us, we scanned the field. Harvest had come and gone and now a green tractor was ploughing up the golden stubbly soil, turning the deep sod under and burying the remnants of the summer's barley, starting from the southern end of the field and making its way, five furrows at a time, up and over the slight rise in the land towards where we stood. It was time for the farmer to go home now, he raised the plough share and turned the motor off, leaving the green beast to rest the night alone at the end of the last row. The other half of the field would do for tomorrow.

Deciding it was time for us to go too, we started across the unploughed half of the field, diagonally along a path trampled in the barley straw towards the little lane where it joined the curving roadway which borders 'Black Patches'. To our right the barley stubble gave way to fallow land where last year had been a crop of rape, witnessed by the thin weedy rape plants growing among the grass and meadow flowers even now. As we walked, we put up a hare which appeared from nowhere — she had been hiding in her form no more than twenty yards ahead, directly in front of us, right on the path! She bolted towards the plantation, then hesitated for a moment to stand with black-tipped ears erect and looked right at us, before plunging into the undergrowth beneath the trees. Noting the place she had first appeared, I was determined to find her form if I possibly could, so we walked on and soon discovered a hare-sized indentation with bare earth at the bottom, on which I found a few hard black droppings and a tuft of white fur. Just by the side of the form was a stone, a pebble really, smooth and round and flat as if tumbled and roughly polished in a stream. It was pale grey, and on the upper side, markings like scratches, the colour of dried blood, in the shape of a letter 'H'. I picked these up and examined them, and feeling that a gift had been given to me, I silently thanked the hare and dropped them into my pocket.

By now the sky was alight with pink and turquoise fire as the sun began to slide below the horizon, and it was really time to be making tracks. We were halfway down the short lane leading back to the road when we heard a clamourous music – a flock of geese, hundreds strong was arriving in the field behind us. As we turned, a glance passed between us briefly as realisation dawned, immediately we both pelted back up to the entrance of the field we had just left. There we stood open-mouthed as skein after skein of Canada geese came tumbling out of the sky with feet outspread like water-skis and floated down to land, there to glean the spilled grain that had escaped the combine harvester. In the next few minutes more and more geese arrived, some were Greylags or Pinkfeet – I never could remember the difference – and many more Canadas with their long dark chocolate necks and creamy cheeks. There must have been thousands by now, congregated on the unploughed half of the field, and they were obviously pleased to meet up with the rest of the flock judging by the noise they were making, like hoards of old women gossiping at the tops of their voices! They seemed to be completely ignoring our presence though we were standing almost amongst them, so intent were they on greeting their companions and searching for their supper. I wondered how close we could approach before they would react, so I started to walk towards the middle of the flock. I never quite got close enough to touch one, but if I had reached up and jumped I'm sure I would very nearly have managed it as they took to the air again and again, wheeled around my head and landed a little further up the field. Eventually we thought we should leave the geese in peace to feed on the last of the grain before it was all ploughed in the next day, so we bade them farewell and returned home with an immense joy in our hearts.

CHAPTER 8

UPHEAVAL & SUBVERSION

Overthrowing the Goddess

Before the rise of the great monotheistic religions, there is much evidence of Mother Earth Goddess worship, including Babylonian Tiamat, Phoenician Astarte, Sumerian Innana, ancient Greek Gaia etc. This female deity may also be linked to the grandmother in the moon mythologies as widespread as North America, Africa, Asia and islands in the Pacific as seen in Chapter 3.

The first of the Father Gods, Marduk, supplanted his grandmother, Tiamat, who over several generations, was transformed from the great mother into a serpent; from the nurturing force of order into the personification of wicked Chaos; an image that has dogged religion ever since.

When writing the history of the Jewish people, Scribes included very few female figures in the Tanakh or Hebrew Scriptures; possibly because the patriarchal Jewish religion was in direct competition with Canaanite religion whose matriarchal Goddess was Astarte. The priests of the 'Jealous God' may have had good cause to warn His people to have nothing to do with their neighbours' beliefs, as the future of their political power depended upon it.

It is thought that in the older matriarchal society, both power and property were held by women. Social order was dictated and enforced by the matriarch or queen, who was answerable to her people as leader and provider. Over centuries, as the newer paternalistic religions developed, power was gradually wrested from them by men; kings and warlords.

As a woman in a post-feminist society, it is easy to fall into the trap of stereotyping this process, but it would be an over simplification to describe a rural idyll, with a beneficent mother figure, and a sun-drenched land of peace and plenty, obliterated by hoards of warlike men, hell-bent on rape and pillage. However, to fully replace one social order with another, the values of the previous society must be overturned. History shows us over and over again that the most effective method of achieving this is partly by force (the new order was certainly supported by advancing technology; iron weapons superseding bronze etc), but also by systematically discrediting previous values, by demonizing the sacred and trivializing the most fundamental core beliefs and standards, removing any way for those who have been overthrown to claim moral superiority. Having achieved this, the subjugated population, be they a colonized country or a social group, are rendered impotent (power-less, un-masculine!!!), and unable to fight back against a system they are not only helpless within, but do not even fully understand. The only way for them to survive is to toe the line and behave as is required by the new masters, retaining only the vestiges of lost power secretly within themselves.

Gradually over centuries, this paternalistic new order became just that. Law and order, logic and reason became the preserve of men, the basis of control of the new social order and the only concepts of any value. Anything associated with the essence of the old order – instinct, intuition, and changeability – was dismissed as the preserve of women, as such inferior, but more to the point condemned as chaotic, evil and uncontrollable. Any element that is uncontrollable must be suppressed lest it pose a real danger to the new authority.

These processes took a very long time indeed, and were not consistent throughout the world. By the time the Romans ruled in Britain, patriarchy had long been established in Rome, but the Celts still accorded women equality with men and in 59CE even had a Queen in eastern Britain, Boudicca, and she was about to rebel!

Boudicca

On the death of Prasutagus, his widow Boudicca took over the rule of the Iceni tribe in her own right. But her late husband had borrowed extensively from the financiers of Rome, and a new imperial administration decided to call in the loans. When Rome sent debt collectors to her court in Norwich, Boudicca claimed that the money had been a gift and refused to repay it. As punishment and to dissuade other British chieftains from following her example, Boudicca was flogged and her daughters raped. Understandably, Boudicca was furious, not only at the personal injury, but also because of the contempt with which Rome had treated the people of Britain. She declared war.

Boudicca - the red haired personification of Hecate, the black witch-goddess of death! "She was very tall, in appearance most terrifying, in the glance of her eye most fierce, and her voice was harsh. A great mass of tawny hair fell to her hips, around her neck she wore a large golden torc, and she wore a vari-coloured tunic, over which a thick mantle fastened with a brooch. This was her invariable attire" wrote Dio Cassius.

First she marched on Colchester with such speed and ferocity that her victory left the Romans stunned. The city was sacked and 20,000 killed. When the Roman legion at Lincoln marched to engage the Britons they were slaughtered too.

Next Boudicca laid waste London, then Verulamium (St. Albans). The inevitable final battle took place, some sources say at King's Cross, some at Towcester, however historians agree that Boudicca's army outnumbered the Romans by ten to one.

It is recorded that as a preparation for battle, Boudicca would attempt to divine the outcome by releasing a Hare, sacred to the Britons, from beneath her cloak and observing its movements. This she did now, invoking Andraste, patron goddess of the Iceni, a warrior goddess of victory whose name means 'invincible'. Her warriors, seeing the Roman soldiers hacking at the hare, trying to kill it as it fled past, hoped that contact with the creature would transfer its timid nature to them and thereby the Iceni's enemies would loose their courage.

However, emboldened by her superior numbers, Boudicca made a fatal mistake; she allowed herself to be tempted into fighting on the Romans' choice of terrain. This time the Roman army were prepared for the fight and disciplined training proved more than a match for Boudicca's enormous rabble. According to Roman historians, 80,000 Britons were killed that day and in the confusion their queen escaped, only to take her own life, together with her daughters, by means of poison.

According to Dio Cassius, Boudicca was mourned deeply by her people, who gave her a costly burial, but her doomed campaign has earned her the status of national hero and the personification of the spirit of the warrior Celt.

St. Melangell,
Patroness of Hares

Feast day 27th May

The story of Boudicca demonstrates the use of the Hare as a symbol by a woman of power. Six hundred years later the story of St. Melangell, another defiant woman, demonstrates that the feminine, in the guise of the Hare, was still not fully demonised, following the introduction of Christianity into Britain.

Melangell, also known as Monacella, was a princess who fled from Ireland to escape a political marriage. Sailing to North Wales, she settled in Pennant, near Llangynog, in the heart of the Berwyn Mountains, where she lived in quiet contemplation, as a hermit, during the mid 7th century. Her legend tells of Brychwel, Prince of Powys, who, while out hunting in the Tanat valley, put up a hare, which took off with his hounds giving chase. Eventually the hunt followed the hare to a thicket, where they found a young woman in an attitude of divine meditation and prayer with the hare lying at her feet, hiding under the hem of her gown. Melangell demanded that he left the hare unmolested, and so touched by this scene of piety was the prince that he granted the land to her and built for her 'Melangell's Sanctuary' to be a "perpetual asylum, refuge and defence". Here she founded a community of religious women, and became their abbess. Brychwel also promised that all her beloved hares would be safe from huntsmen throughout the valley.

After her death the sanctuary became a place of pilgrimage and a shrine to saint Melangell. To this day, in her honour, the hares in Melangell's valley are never hunted, and are called 'Melangell's little lambs'. This legend is recorded on a carved wooden screen in the church which was later built on the spot, parts of which date from the 12th century.

Melangell's shrine

I visited St. Melangell's church one sunny May afternoon, finding the surrounding fields full of young lambs, but the only sign of Melangell's little lambs – the hares – were carved in the church. I was fascinated by a series of stone carvings by Meical Watts which are displayed along the side wall just above the pews, beautifully depicting curled and running hares. In the chancel, behind the altar, is the shrine which had originally been built to house the saint's remains, but during the reformation it was dismantled and the stones were reused within the churchyard. Now it has been restored, reclaiming most of the original materials, and stands in its original location. On the day of my visit, between the pillars supporting Melangell's shrine was a collection of coloured cards with prayers and supplications written on them. I felt it was a most peaceful place, and could quite understand why Melangell settled here so long ago.

The circular churchyard was once a Bronze Age site and is ringed by ancient Yew trees thought to be over 2,000 years old. I wonder what Melangell found when she first came to the valley, the Yews would have been mature trees even then, she must have recognized an ancient sacred place. There is a stream running close to the church wall, and above the valley a waterfall, though I didn't see it. I only heard about it a couple of months later, but I would love to return and find it. Hermits often chose to live near water sources, partly for the practicalities of drinking and washing, but also because wells and springs were held to be sacred in their own right as a source of life and healing. Perhaps Melangell was the keeper of the spring that fed the waterfall, ministering to the needs of the community there.

Demonising the Hare

As new ideas, religions, customs etc. took over from old ways, many of the deities and sacred symbols of old became demonised, transformed into the devils of the new religion. By the late medieval period, the Hare, far from being the sacred symbol of the Goddess, had become associated with lasciviousness and sexual excess and castigated as the familiar of 'Witches'. Witches were considered by the Christian church to be the agents of Satan (a Judeo/Christian concept which appeared with the paternalistic monotheists), and by association the causes of all sorts of evil. So the uncontrollable element – the pagan, the feminine, the unpredictable – became represented by a symbol associated with the old order, the Hare; and appropriately the Hare is the very essence of 'Wild and Free'.

Part of the demonization of the Hare lay in its gradual association with bad luck. Some ideas are quite ancient, dating from the recently Christianised Roman Empire. It is recorded that when the Teutonic hordes were besieging Rome in 410CE, a hare ran towards the walls, pursued by the besieging army, and the Romans, taking this to be an evil omen, deserted the gates allowing the city to fall without a fight.

It was said that to dream of seeing a hare might mean you have enemies, or that a death or misfortune will come to your family.

In 'The Anatomy of Melancholy' 1621, Robert Burton writes that by eating the meat of a hare, the timorous nature of the Hare would transfer to the eater "Hare is a black meat, melancholy* and hard of digestion". Jonathan Swift, who suffered a mental illness, possibly Alzheimer's, writing in 1738, also calls Hare, a "melancholy meat", probably quoting Burton. As recently as 1926 it was said that no Norfolk labourer will take a hare as a gift, although they are very fond of rabbit.

*melancholy – literally 'black bile', one of the four cardinal humours (liquids), the ballance of which were thought to dictate a person's character and state of health, when excessive, black bile caused depression and sadness.

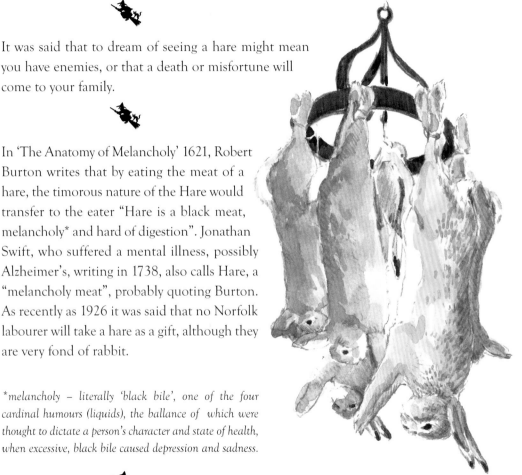

Hares and the Attack on Witches

Everyone has encountered the storybook stereotype of the witch as an ugly, toothless old woman with a wart on her nose, dressed in tattered black rags and a pointy hat, flying through the night air by moonlight on a broomstick, cackling as she goes, accompanied by her familiar, usually a scrawny black cat. She can call down curses on her enemies to cause sickness, or blight a farmer's crops. She preys on small children who stray too close to her meagre tumbledown hovel, and she

dances round a bubbling cauldron with others of her 'coven', chanting magic spells at their midnight meetings, called 'Sabbats'. To reach these meetings without being seen, she can change herself into a hare, and if she is injured as a hare, the same wounds will be visible on the old woman next morning.

What led to these beliefs and images of witches? It seems to me the expression of many superstitious beliefs and the product of the fevered imaginings of religious fanatics over centuries, and those who saw an opportunity to gain reputation, money or power by convincing people of the existence of these 'evil' beings. 'Witchcraft' had been declared a 'heresy', by the Inquisition and a clear popular link to devil-worship had become established in medieval times. This was mostly due to the 'confessions' extracted by zealous clerics, whose talents in extreme torture techniques were legendary; they were able to get their subjects to agree to anything they suggested just to make the pain stop. Witchcraft had become the preserve of Church courts to protect the Church socially and politically. After all, when religious reformers were laying claim to a personal relationship with God, what need was there for an established church with all its hierarchy?

Occasional manifestations of witch-hysteria had occurred throughout Europe since the Middle Ages, often directed as much towards men as women. As early as the twelfth century it was believed that women could change shape into the form of a Hare, and whilst transformed, they would steal milk from cows at night by sucking them dry. The demonization was progressing.

In northern European countries it is believed that a witch can fashion a supernatural creature and give it life in order to steal milk and dairy produce. This creature was often said to resemble a hare, and in Sweden was called 'mjolkhare' (milk-hare), though in Norway it is called 'trollkatt' (troll-cat); another instance of the interchangeable relationship between hares and cats.

"It has been a frequent complaint, from old times, as well as in the present, that certain hags in Wales, as well as in Ireland and Scotland, changed themselves into the shape of hares, that, sucking teats under this counterfeit form, they might stealthily rob other people's milk."

Giraldus Cambrensis Topographica Hibernica II xix. 1184

In Teutonic / Germanic tradition, by medieval times the ancient moon goddess Holda had evolved into Frau Holle, the lunar goddess of witches, riding across the winter sky on a white goose, later developing into the story-book character, Mother Goose.

Shape Shifting

As part of the propaganda aimed at discrediting witches, their enemies were able to make use of the ancient practice of shape-shifting and the many legends surrounding it. But what is shape-shifting and what are its origins?

In the ancient past, animal or animal-headed gods were worshipped by our distant ancestors. Tribal holy men practiced shamanic rites, trance-state journeyings into the Otherworld, communing with the divine, possibly under the influence of psychotropic drugs, Ergot and Mistletoe are both known to have been used in this way by the ancient Celts. The shaman may have sought to gain power over, or understanding of the nature of an animal, perhaps invoking its spirit for the success of a hunting expedition. Alternatively s/he might seek knowledge by taking on the attributes of another being; the bravery of the bear, the far sight of the eagle or the speed of the hare. During these excursions s/he may have dressed in the skin, skull, feathers etc. of the creature to feel closer to its spirit, to enhance the experience, to "get into the zone" in modern parlance. To the uninitiated, it would appear that the shaman had *become* the animal.

A shaman dressed in a deer skin, from a famous 20,000 year old French cave painting

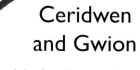

Ceridwen and Gwion

One of the best known shape-shifting legends is the tale of Ceridwen and Gwion from the Mabinogion. Ceridwen, the Welsh Crone Goddess, keeper of the Cauldron of Knowledge and Inspiration, laboured for a year and a day to brew a potion of knowledge and magic for her ugly son Afagddu. Setting Gwion her servant to stir the cauldron, she warned him not to taste the brew on pain of death, but when at last the cauldron boiled, three drops splashed out and scalded his thumb. To ease the pain Gwion put his thumb into his mouth to suck. Immediately he realized that the knowledge and magic intended for Afagddu had passed accidentally to him, and he knew that Ceridwen would kill him. So he changed into the shape of a hare and fled, but Ceridwen saw what happened and became a greyhound to pursue him. Gwion then became a fish, but was almost caught by Ceridwen as an otter, so he turned into to a small bird, but she chased him as a hawk. Eventually as a grain of corn, Gwion hid in the barn, but Ceridwen found him and, as a hen, devoured him. Soon Ceridwen magically bore a beautiful son but knowing it was Gwion cast him adrift on the river. Stuck in a salmon weir he was found by a king's son, who named him Taliesin, later the great bard and seer.

By the early seventeenth century the belief was almost universal throughout the British Isles that a witch could take on the shape of a hare at will in order to travel abroad undetected. Stories have been found in almost every county in England of witch-hares chased back to their home, where they are discovered tending an injury inflicted during the hunt.

A tale from Duddleswell, Sussex, collected in the 19th century, has a nice twist: When the hare leaped through the window of her cottage to escape the hounds, Dame Garson's voice was heard to shout "Ah me boys, you ain't got me yet!"

Meg Shilton from Catforth, Lancashire, was promised that she could live in a new cottage rent-free if she could beat the landowner's hounds and get there first, so she turned into a hare and raced them. Just as she arrived at the door, the black dog nearly caught her, and ever after she walked with a limp. But she never paid a penny in rent!

The Aldermaston witch, Maria Hale, whose powers flourished in the 1850s & 60s, was said to turn herself into a large brown hare and sit outside the public house to listen to all the local gossip.

The Easington Hare

A story from Easington in Co Durham, collected in the 1840s and claimed to have been related to the source by people who remembered the events themselves. Telling of a hare that always appeared when the local hunt was out, and led the hounds off the scent they had been following. This hare did not behave like normal hares, as it did not zig-zag back and forth, nor double back on itself, but led the hounds straight into the village, where it always disappeared, thus spoiling the days hunting. The master of the hounds was advised (interesting this – 'white' witchcraft to catch a witch) that the only way to catch the hare was to acquire a black hound that had been suckled at a woman's breast. This was duly done, and the next time the hunt went out, the black hound managed to keep up with the hare and chased it back to a cottage in the village, where it escaped through a hole in the door just as the hound caught it by the leg. When the master broke down the door they discovered the old woman inside, out of breath and sweating profusely, bandaging her leg to stop the blood which was pouring from a wound that clearly resembled a dog bite. She was left alone to cope as best she could, but having been discovered; she had lost her powers and was ostracized by the rest of the community. When she died, even though she had never been known to go to church, she was buried in consecrated ground in the churchyard. But this is not the end of the tale. It was said that she was sometimes seen in the shape of a sheep, rolling over and over on the churchyard wall. The source tells that she saw the ghostly sheep herself on one occasion.

To Kill a Witch-Hare

It is said that the only sure way to kill a witch-hare is to shoot it with a silver bullet, a silver coin, or a piece of silver with a cross marked on it. It is interesting that the use of silver is prescribed, the metal associated with the moon and therefore having power over the moon's creature, the hare. A tale from Wiltshire begins with the customary witch-hare hunt, but then the farmer asks advice from the rector, who tells him to load a gun with a silver sixpence and shoot the hare. This he does and the witch is found dead in her cottage with a silver bullet in her heart.

Another story from Cleveland, collected in 1891 tells how a farmer whose saplings were being destroyed by a hare sat up one night with his shotgun charged with bits of old silver buttons, and saw "a great foul old ram-cat of a heear". He fired at the hare and hit it, and it ran away shrieking. The next day an old woman who was already suspected of being a witch was laid up in bed suffering from many wounds which she claimed were the result of falling onto broken glass, but the farmer knew...

While working at Whitby Folk festival, one evening my daughter Aly and I drove up to the top of the dale. We saw a hare running down a track and stopped to watch as it disappeared into the heather. Remembering that strange noises sometimes attract hares, we sang the Eskdale Hare at the top of our voices as the full moon rose, but the hare didn't oblige!

The Eskdale Hare

I learned this song from Ruth Price (Hex, Witchmen), whose uncle Gus Gomersal wrote it.

The farmers cry 'Oh alas and alack'
For the hares are running in one big pack,
And the damage they've done is exceeding rare,
And they are led by a great white hare.

Chorus
Beware, beware, beware of the Eskdale Hare
Beware, beware, beware of the Eskdale Hare

Well they took their guns and they went on the hunt
But they never got a shot at the one in front,
And they tried every trick with gun and snare,
But they couldn't catch that great white hare.

Chorus
Yes, they tried every trick with gun and snare,
But they couldn't catch that great white hare,
Until they shook with dread and fear
For they knew that witchcraft was lurking near.

Chorus
Well the wise old sage knew what must be done;
"With a silver bullet you must load your gun,
And level it when the moon shines clear,
It's the only way to kill that hare"

Chorus
Well the gun was primed and levelled that night
And the bullet found its home in the pale moonlight,
And the sight they saw filled them all with dread,
For where the hare fell, a witch lay dead.

Chorus

Witch or Wise Woman?

In reality, a village 'Witch' is very likely to have been a Wise Woman, a healer providing services to the community. After the Dissolution of the English Monasteries (1530s), property that had previously been owned by the Church: abbey and monastic lands etc. became forfeit to the Crown to be afterwards sold to people whose wealth and influence grew, motivating much of the later conflict between Catholic, Anglican and Puritan. The 'craft of the wise' became increasingly misunderstood and demonized by the Church. It was independent women, often themselves property owners, the uncontrollable element in society who suffered most during the Witch Finder persecutions the mid 17th century (Matthew Hopkins etc). Fuelled by the political machinations of both church and state, owing far more to paranoia than the paranormal, a 'witch' could be anyone denounced by their neighbours for personal reasons, to settle a score or out of greed. If the 'witch trial' that followed was successful, both witch finder and accuser benefited from the division of the 'witches' property!

A woman living alone, perhaps a widow who had retained her husband's property, was not subject to the will of her 'natural' master – a man. She may have been strong-minded with outspoken views, or one who was unpopular or resented by her neighbours. She may have been literate, thirsty for knowledge for its own sake, and horror of horrors, owned a book or two! She may have been psychic or clairvoyant. She may have possessed skill in healing, and knowledge of herbs, a not unusual thing in the days before most country people could afford the doctor's fees. All the while she was able to help her community she would be respected, but when plague or fever strikes, woe betide the wise-woman whose remedies could not perform miracles. Bad weather resulting in a cereal crop diseased with the fungus ergot in several successive years caused widespread poisoning from mouldy bread, the symptoms of which included paranoia, convulsions and hallucinations, also sensations of tingling and crawling of the skin. All of these symptoms appear at various times in accounts of bewitchment from evidence given in witch trials all over the western world.

'Witchcraft' needed to be suppressed, to deal with public disorder issues during disease epidemics, to control independent women, but above all to distract the public from the real issues of power politics within the country, and particularly the Church.

The best way to suppress witchcraft was to discredit witches, by blaming them for all the community's misfortunes; sickness, bad weather, the natural death of a cow, anything - the crazier the accusation, the more power the witch was implied to have, and ignorant people misled by the ravings of puritanical clergymen believed there were witches everywhere.

In a well known engraving from a book said to have been written by Matthew Hopkins, two 'witches' recite the names of their 'imps', which include a black hare called 'Sack and Sugar'

The Witchcraft Trial of
Isobel Gowdie of Auldearne, Scotland

Spell to become a hare;
    "I shall go intil a hare,
with sorrow and sych and meikle care;
    and I shall go in the Devil's name
        Ay while I come home again."
Spell to revert from a hare;
    "Hare, hare, God send thee care.
    I am in a hare's likeness just now,
But I shall be in a woman's likeness even now."

Between 13th April and 27th May 1662 Isobel Gowdie appeared before the Presbyterian minister of Auldearn, a village near Nairn on the Moray Firth. This well known spell for shape-shifting into a hare was recited by Isobel during her trial. Without torture she freely confessed to witchcraft on four occasions, each time giving detailed and imaginatively descriptive accounts of events including her first encounter with 'the devil' together with a description of his physical attributes, meetings of her 'coven' (she was the first to be recorded using this term, a Highland word simply meaning 'a meeting'), the nick-names of many of the witches and of their familiars, the fashioning of 'Elf-arrows' with which to kill their enemies, various acts of mischief enacted by the coven, and the cruel beatings she and her fellow witches were subjected to by her 'lord' if they did not behave in the way he expected of them.

Much of what she recounted is remarkable in the descriptive details given, but she was a Highlander, steeped in the ancient storytelling tradition of the Highland people, and used many of the standard devices of this art-form to arrange and order information, a method of committing details to memory, and in the case of the description of the coven meeting, mirrored the court session she was attending at the time she was speaking. Other accounts she gave seemed to reflect imagery from traditional folk-tales and ballads or already well known witchcraft motifs that had appeared in the confessions of alleged witches for generations.

Though the belief that witches could transform themselves into hares had been held for centuries, this is the first occasion on which a spell for so doing had been recorded, and the style suggests that if Isobel herself had made the verse, she was a talented storyteller indeed in the best Bardic tradition (though the first line of the reversing spell appears two hundred years later as a charm to avert bad luck when meeting a hare, which suggests this may have been a commonly used phrase even then). The spell has not only survived the time since it was first written, but has captured the imagination of many a writer on witchcraft, folklore or wildlife since. However, as it has been written down and broadcast, traditionally it is believed that its efficacy will have been spent.

We do not know what happened to Isobel Gowdie. No record of a verdict or sentence exists. By this time Scottish courts were often acquitting alleged witches, particularly if they were paupers, as with no means of paying, the cost of their maintenance in custody was born by the Kirk via the poor-box. The judges had also become quite sophisticated in the assessing of evidence, and were no longer taken in by the earlier hysteria or by the unsubstantiated allegations of vengeful neighbours.

The End of the Witch Hysteria

After the restoration in 1660 of Charles II and the English monarchy, witchcraft hysteria suddenly subsided. In the mid 1660s, 4 Acts called collectively 'The Clarendon Code' were passed by the Cavalier Parliament, re-establishing the Anglican form of religion and banishing from public and political life anyone who would not accept the Anglican Creed. This was a clear attack on the Puritans and Presbyterians who had, among other things, been instrumental in the persecution of 'witches'. After this time the 'Squirearchy' became established, wealthy men who now owned much of the former monastic lands taken from the church during the Reformation. It was in the interests of the new gentry to maintain the new order, as much of their wealth depended upon it, so that cases of religious extremism, including allegations of witchcraft, began to be dismissed as ignorant superstition. It is also interesting to note that many Puritans and Presbyterians including those recently displaced emigrated to America throughout the seventeenth century, establishing settlements in 'New England' which included Salem, Massachusetts, where witch trial hysteria was to live on for some time afterwards.

But is that the whole story? At some level, the old regard in which the Hare was held, as a symbol of the Earth Mother Goddess, albeit in a degraded form, almost certainly survived down the ages. Just because Britain has been considered a Christian country for over a millennium it does not necessarily follow that all vestiges of earlier beliefs or images have been obliterated; Triple Hare and Green Man images certainly survived. Not all aspects of human life are dictated by the Church, nor were they throughout the past thousand years. Churches have often been satisfied with token Sunday observance, leaving the business of living largely unsupervised. Hearth and home, the preserve of women on the whole, have always held a measure of autonomy - a matriarchy in microcosm - uncontrolled by the squire, parson or state, a place where low magic can happen. To the authority figure in a paranoid community, the brewing of simples* for healing, the chanting of homely prayers, enchantments, to help ease the troubles of living, even the alchemy of the cooking pot, may appear to be potential threats to male power. It's a good job the men tend to keep out of the kitchen!

*simples - remedies made from one ingredient, i.e. chamomile tea, used as a mild sedative to aid sleep.

The Intuitive, Creative Woman

The intuitive, creative woman can access through altered states of consciousness a parallel 'otherworld' of knowledge, magic, spirit, call it what you will, that cannot be controlled on the physical plane. By visiting this otherworld she can escape from the physical and partake of experiences that may be spiritual or she can access wisdom that may be, as Jung believed, a form of collective consciousness made up of the sum of human experience, like a form of common memory. This may be in the form of dreams, visions, symbols (archetypes), or intuitive flashes of inspiration, where the answer to a predicament comes as if by magic; a message from the gods. This ability is not exclusively feminine, but 'manliness' is mainly expressed in physical terms and this form of behaviour in a man is usually considered fanciful. I believe that women have been behaving in this way at least since the time of the patriarchal 'conquest', and when considered in terms of the masculine establishment, it is definitely considered a form of subversion, as a small and secret form of power wielded by women seeking some kind of control over their own lives that they cannot always feel in their daily existence. (As a child I was frequently accused of 'day-dreaming'!) It is therefore understandable that as the post-feminist world tries to come to terms with the emerging order, the Hare, symbol of the subversion of masculine authority, wild and free, has been unconsciously adopted by many women, some of whom as Pagans are proud to call themselves 'Witches'.

For most of my life I have had issues with authority. For many years I worked as a technician in an art college, I loved my job as it allowed me a measure of autonomy, and to spend my working life in a creative environment was a privilege, but though most of my colleagues valued my contribution and considered me indispensable, some of my managers seemed to resent me. I could never understand why I was expected to abase myself to flatter the egos of my 'superiors'. The problem was that I felt my value within the structure to be of equal importance to everyone else's, whether manager or cleaner. If a person fulfils the role required of them, however humble, to the best of their ability, be that in the home, workplace or the wider community, then they represent an integral building block in the structure and are worthy of respect. (These views have recently been widely adopted in modern teamwork approaches to workplace management). Some might call this arrogance, but the attitude that rank demands deference for its own sake is, to me, equally arrogant. After all, we've all met incompetents who only achieve promotion by obsequious behaviour towards an egotistical boss. It is not arrogance to believe in equality of value, but respect. Respect for all beings. We all have a vital role in the web that binds us together, forming a pattern which supports each one of us. To remove one element would be to change the pattern, so everyone is as important as everyone else, both above and below. But suggest that to some people in authority and you are likely to meet with a hostile reaction, as it is usually seen as a threat to individual power.

So the Hare may be seen today as a symbol of subversion of the authority of the establishment, perhaps it is no coincidence that the Hare has become so important to me! Don't get me wrong, I have no problem with authority itself, but individuals in authority are so often tainted by insensitivity, self-importance and self-interest, paying scant regard to the real object of their role – that's where my problem lies.

CHAPTER 9
FOLKLORE

From Chapbooks to Urban Myths

From the development of the printing press in the mid sixteenth century, popular culture started to circulate widely in written form. Broadside ballad sheets were sold throughout the country by pedlars, often singers, musicians and story tellers, very cheaply at fairs and markets. Often these would be stuck to the walls of alehouses or in other public places, where those who could read translated to those who couldn't. Many of these contained antique stories, often mystical or heroic. However the new press also assisted the propagandist, many of the ideas supporting Puritanism were spread widely by this means, including the writings of John Lilburne (Levellers) and much anti witch propaganda with gruesome reports of witch trials, hangings and burnings.

An embryonic news service was emerging. Ballads often told gruesome stories of executions in gory detail, illustrated with woodcuts, together with (frequently invented) confessions and appeals to God for mercy, anything to titillate the public's insatiable appetite for sensational gossip. Chapbooks (literally cheap-books), originally a folded sheet forming a pamphlet, were beginning to appear by the early 1700s which could include songs, sermons, almanacs, jests, stories, Mummers Plays etc. Shape shifting stories of witches into hares may also have been popular. These legends spread throughout the land, reinforced by the repeated new versions produced

Ballad seller, an 18th century woodcut

to support the printer's business, much as the tabloid press of today operates. All this goes some way towards explaining the similarity in many regional folklorists' collected tales, and the common elements in apparently unconnected stories.

As the 18th century progressed, ideas initially coming from French philosophers, started to take hold, giving rise to the 'Enlightenment' in which science and reason began to take over from superstitious beliefs. 'Witchcraft' started to lose its capacity to frighten and demonise but continued to flourish as entertainment. Many stories of witches, including those in which they could shape shift into hares lived on in 'chapbooks', whose wide circulation in the countryside probably gave rise to the many variations of legends collected in the 19th and 20th centuries by academic folklorists, and published as 'traditional' folk tales in story books and learned journals to this day.

Folklore, as it became known, was not entirely dependent upon printed circulation. People still transformed circulated stories, songs etc, and made them their own, often giving them a local flavour, so the individual and the mass media interacted to produce the body of tales which the 'collectors' encountered, recorded and published, resulting in yet another turn of the same cycle. And the cycle still continues; only now the mass media has expanded to include all forms of electronic media, so the circulation has become broader and faster. However a look at many websites relating folkloristic stories will soon show that the individualisation of these tales still goes on.

Top Hats and Mad Hatters

Some Hare folklore seems to have a quite rational explanation and be of relatively recent origin

Hare fur was the main material used in the manufacture of hats during the 18th century, in fact so much was required that thousands of hare skins were imported from Russia. In the 1840s John Hetherington, a London clothier, designed the first top hat, which soon replaced the 'tricorne' in popularity across all social classes. This new fashion caused such a stir, that the first time it appeared in public, worn by its designer, women screamed and fainted. The sensibilities of delicate ladies were clearly offended by the possibly phallic connotations of such an apparition. The sensation was such that John Hetherington was eventually arrested and fined £50 for disturbing the peace, and a law was passed to forbid the wearing of top hats in public on the grounds that it scared timid people. Obviously this law did not last long as within a few years it was considered the height of fashion and everyone was wearing them.

The very best top hats worn by the upper classes were eventually made of felted beaver fur, while the majority of top hats were made from the more traditional 'Hare', and the more plentiful, and therefore cheaper, rabbit fur. The fur of both hare and rabbit was very soft and quite short, so to promote matting to form the felt of the body of the hat, it was treated by boiling in a vat of mercury nitrate. At that time every hat-maker would have a vat of this brew bubbling away in his workshop, so it was inevitable that he would constantly inhale the fumes. Modern medicine now knows that breathing in these vapours causes a form of poisoning, the symptoms of which include anxiety, excessive timidity, loss of self confidence, paranoia and the desire to remain unobserved. It can also cause neurological damage, displayed as confusion, distorted vision, hallucinations, disjointed speech, drooling, trembling, memory loss and psychotic behaviour; symptomatically similar to dementia.

By the 19th century "as mad as a hatter" was a phrase in popular use and Lewis Carroll drew on this imagery in his 'Alice's Adventures in Wonderland'. Here the 'Mad Tea Party' (often referred to as the 'Mad Hatter's Tea Party', though not called this by Carroll) was attended by the 'Hatter', a 'March Hare', and a dormouse, as well as a bemused Alice.

Fishermen dreaded seeing a hare when mending thier nets, it was said to bring incredibly bad luck.

Bad Luck at Sea

Fishermen dreaded seeing a hare when on their way to their boats or when mending nets, it was said to bring incredibly bad luck. On board a vessel, sailors will not speak the word 'hare', as it is said that if it is spoken, a great storm will sweep away the boat and all hands will be drowned.

This may be because it was believed that hares could be witches in disguise, and it is widely believed that witches can summon storms – 'whistling up a wind'.

Curse –
To wish a hare's foot
in a fisherman's creel
is to wish disaster upon
the voyage.

In 1937 a crew of fishermen from Wick, arriving at the fishing grounds of Stornaway, found to their dismay a hare's foot among their nets, apparently placed there by a rival crew, or for a joke. So great was their fear that they turned back to land and lost the whole season's income rather than risk the loss of life that they believed would result if they continued with the trip.

Mining Disaster

Seeing a hare whilst setting out from home, particularly to work in a mine or on a boat, is considered to foretell doom for all concerned, and people would often return home and stay there until another mealtime had passed before resuming their journey.

In West Cornish mining communities the appearance of a hare predicts a fatal accident. At Wheal Vor mine it was said that a white hare would appear in the engine house before a disaster. It was even considered disastrous to speak the word 'Hare' in the mine.

On a more practical note, at Portland, near Weymouth, Dorset, quarry workers would return home if they saw a rabbit on the way to work. It was believed that as the rabbits burrowed under the ground it created weak spots that might cave-in and cause accidents.

Diglake Fields by Phil Colclough

This song explores the relationship between the Hare and the disaster of 14 January 1895, at the Diglake colliery, Bignall Hill, near Audley in Staffordshire. The main subject is the contrast between the lives of the landowner, with her trivial pastimes, and that of the miners toiling in life threatening conditions to provide the wealth she takes for granted. The hunt for the white hare is an allegory of the lady's thoughtless cruelty, incapable as she is of comprehending the tragic consequences for others of her actions.

Cornish tin mine

Diglake Fields

The sun comes up on Diglake Fields; it wakes the milk-white Hare,
The lady calls the stable boy to saddle up her mare,
The hands that hold the reins are cold; the spurs are polished steel,
She'll take the mare without a care to race on Diglake Fields.

The sun goes down behind the town as miners start to rise
From their beds with sleepy heads to leave their anxious wives,
Off they'll go with never a look to cut the coal below,
Saying "hello night, farewell daylight, be careful how you go"

The horse's hooves on Diglake Fields throw water in the air,
Sometimes she's lost among the mist that gathers round the mare,
At her command is all this land and all the coal that's there,
In morning sun and at full run she saw the milk-white hare.

No sun will shine down in the mine, a thousand feet below,
Where hares don't run and days don't come and winds refuse to blow.
And by the cold dark rivers run, they stream in from the seams,
And men down there, who work with care, see water in their dreams.

No fear of fox, nor of greyhound, the hare can beat them all,
She can outrun the huntsman's gun and miners' dogs galore.
But now this lady races on to cut the wild hare down,
She dearly wants the milk-white fur to trim her dancing gown.

The coal is cleared down in the mine, cut by the morning shift,
The cutters call the firemen in to start another drift,
The shots are placed, men take their break, they pass the tea-can round,
Then all retire, the shots are fired, and sixty men are drowned.

In the night the fire burns bright, the band take up the tune,
The dance begins and heads they turn as she moves into the room.
Her face is flushed, her eyes they shine, they sparkle with the fire,
The gown that's cut above her breast is trimmed with milk-white fur.

Stories of Witch-Hares

Long before the end of C18, stories of 'Witch-Hares' would be recounted around firesides and in public houses during long dark evenings with the assurance that every word was true, this to add dramatic weight to the telling and to enhance the reputation of the teller.

The Hare Witches of Maxton

One day Harry Gilles, Laird of Littledean, near Melrose, was out hunting, in pursuit of a large brown hare, when suddenly the hounds stopped and would run no further. The laird grew angry shouting and beating the dogs, but they would not chase the hare. He feared that this was no ordinary hare, and swore that it must be one of the witches of nearby Maxton. No sooner had the words been spoken, than the hill was covered in hares. At this his anger flared so violently that he began to beat his hounds for refusing to chase the hares, but one suddenly took off in pursuit of a huge hare. He galloped after them, but by this time the greyhound had turned the hare, which was heading back directly towards the laird. As she tried to leap over the horse's neck, he managed to catch her by the front leg, but she struggled so violently that, in his attempt to kill her with his knife, he cut off the leg he was holding, and the hare escaped. Suddenly he was alone on the hill with one greyhound, and all the hares had vanished.

The next morning the laird was given an account of a woman in Maxton who had mysteriously lost an arm, and when he went to inspect the severed hare's limb, it had turned into a human arm! He went straight to the woman and compared her stump with the arm he held; it proved to be a perfect match. When confronted with his tale, the woman confessed to being the witch who had tormented the laird's hounds, and she was taken to the well and drowned the same day.

from Thomas Wilkie
1788-1838

The Zennor Witch

Once there was an old woman living near Zennor, Cornwall, who was said to be a powerful witch, and was treated with great respect by her neighbours out of fear. Her husband, however, did not believe in her magic, and was not afraid to give his opinion of the rumours to anyone who would listen.

One evening he came home to find there was no dinner prepared for him, and being hungry after a days work, began to shout at his wife, saying that if there was nothing to eat within half an hour, he would be the death of her. He taunted her that if she had such wonderful powers, why didn't she use them now?

The old woman put on her cloak and bonnet and her husband watched as she went out, but rounding the corner of the cottage, she disappeared, and in her place there stood a big brown hare. Off ran the hare towards the town, and the husband, somewhat shaken by what he had seen, sat down to wait for her return.

In less than half an hour the old woman returned with meat and tatties, all steaming hot and ready to eat, and her subdued husband ate his supper vowing never to cross his wife again. He kept the vow until the day of her death, which happened a little while later, and we are told that during the funeral procession to the churchyard, a big hare jumped up onto the coffin, frightening the bearers so that they dropped the corpse and fled.

Bowerman the Hunter

Bowerman was a jovial giant of a man who lived on the eastern side of Dartmoor, and he loved nothing more than hunting on the moor with his pack of strong hounds. All the people around those parts were afraid of a coven of witches who met in the wild places around Dartmoor to cast their spells, but Bowerman wasn't scared, and told everyone not to worry about a few old hags and their 'mumbo-jumbo'.

Then one day he was chasing a hare, with his hounds in full cry, and the hunt charging along a deep wooded valley when they came to a clearing and the hare ran straight through the circle of witches, crouching over a bubbling cauldron. Bowerman was galloping at full speed and only managed to avoid the group by jumping over them, but the hounds ran right amongst them and tumbled the witches into a heap on the ground. As they struggled to their feet they could hear Bowerman laughing as he rode off down the valley, and they swore they would have their revenge.

The witches knew that Bowerman would have to return that way, as the valley came to a dead end a little further on, and they hatched a plan and waited. Sure enough, a little while later the hunt retuned, having lost their quarry, trotting wearily back the way they had come. Then one of the witches turned herself into a huge hare and ran across their path. The hunt was on again, with the dogs chasing after the witch-hare, but Bowerman did not suspect mischief. They all raced on down the valley, round the rocks and out onto the open moor. They had a fine chase that day, but just as he thought his hounds were going to catch the hare, she led the pack onto a ridge and round behind a tor, right into the witch's trap. Caught unawares, Bowerman was helpless, as the witches chanted their petrification spell and changed him and his dogs to stone.

And to this day, there is a granite outcrop surrounded by boulders which looks just like a tall man and his pack of hounds, and on moonlit nights it is said that Bowerman's hunt can still be heard chasing across the moor around Hayne Down.

'Bowerman's Nose', a granite outcrop said to be Bowerman and his pack of hounds turned to stone by the witches of Dartmoor.

Stories of Bewitchings

Hares have often been associated with unfortunate experiences in love.

Anne Pierson of Goathland, North Yorkshire

The Squire had discovered his daughter's love for a farm labourer, but he had other plans for her and tried unsuccessfully to encourage her to direct her affections towards a rich neighbour. Eventually, in desperation, he secretly went to the cottage of the notorious witch Anne Pierson, to seek her help. She gave him a bottle, saying the contents would solve the squire's problem and told him to tip it into his daughter's supper that night. Next morning, instead of having lost interest in the boy as her father had expected, the girl's legs were found to be paralysed.

News spread of the plight of the Squire's daughter, and when her boyfriend heard of it, he knew that witchcraft was involved and went straight to a Wiseman, a curse lifter, to ask what could be done. The cure was simple; the girl's feet must be rubbed with a mixture of holy water and the blood of the witch who had cast the spell.

Late that night the farm boy waited outside Anne Pierson's cottage with a shotgun to catch her, as he knew she would emerge as a hare to travel across the moors on her secret business. Eventually a big grey hare appeared; he aimed and shot her on the back leg, which caused her to screech in pain and limp away under a hedge, leaving a trail of blood on the grass. The lad took out a clean handkerchief and wiping up a few drops of the blood; he ran to his true love's house and climbed in through her bedroom window. He took the bloody handkerchief, tipped a little holy water he had taken from the church in a vial onto it, and rubbed the girl's feet with the mixture. She immediately recovered the use of her legs, jumped out of bed, and flinging her arms around his neck, they eloped.

 Anne Pierson was not seen for several days, but when she finally ventured out again, her leg was swathed in blood-stained bandages.

John Bird and his Lover's Fetch*

A story recorded from the Sussex branch of an old Dorset family tells of a young man, John Bird of Batcombe, Dorset, who, in 1868, was convinced he was bewitched by a local young woman. She appeared to him every night in the shape of a hare and sat on the bottom of his bed, preventing him from sleeping. In desperation, to stop this persecution, he laid a scythe on the bedroom windowsill, as this was where she entered the room. The next morning, there was a trail of blood leading from the window to the cottage where this young woman lived. Having been discovered, she never troubled John with nocturnal visitations again.

The Hare-Swain

unusually this hare was a man

In Elton, Gloucestershire, a young man was in love with a girl whose father guarded her well to keep the would-be lovers apart. One Sunday morning, her father saw the lad walk past their house, as if on his way to church. Shortly after he spied a hare sitting watchfully outside the house. He fetched his gun and shot the hare, which ran off, bleeding from a wound on its haunch. Later the lad returned, but as he walked back past the house, he was limping badly.

a 'fetch' or 'bid' is a spirit double; it may appear as an animal or as a ghostly double of its originator.

The Slighted Lover's Curse

In the 1870s a Preston girl, slighted by her lover, made a charm of a hare's heart, stuck with pins, and buried it with invocations designed to call down torment upon the faithless man.

Cornish tradition says that a young girl who dies of a broken heart will return as a white hare to haunt her faithless lover. This may have originated with the legend of Pengersec, a story from West Cornwall based on events said to have occurred in medieval times.

The Legend of Lord Pengersec

The Cornish legend of Lord Pengersec is a close variant of the Lord Bateman ballads, which continued to circulate on broadside ballad sheets until the end of C19, and which tell of an English nobleman fighting, presumably in the Crusades, captured in battle, but then freed by a Turkish noble woman who has fallen in love with him and who eventually follows him to England. All usually ends happily. Pengersec is a much harsher version – he is unfaithful, and upon his return his deceit is revealed and through the actions of a white hare he and his family are destroyed.

Lord Pengersec, bored with peaceful life, went to an eastern country to find adventure, and soon met and fell in love with a princess who was the daughter of a desert ruler. Secretly he wooed her, and she gave him a sword that she told him would make him invincible. She wished to marry him and accompany him home to his own country, but as she was a princess, she hoped in vain. As a token they broke a ring between them and each kept half, and swearing undying love, Pengersec sailed home to the wife he had left behind. In less than a year, a ship sailed into the harbour, and ashore stepped the princess with a baby in her arms. She went to Pengersec's castle and confronted her lover, but he cruelly sent her away, saying he wanted nothing to do with her now he was back in Cornwall. She was distraught and cursed him, calling down on him misery, pain and destruction. During the argument that followed, Pengersec pushed her over the cliff to her death on the rocks below.

Pengersec was fond of excitement. His favourite pastime was hunting wolves, which were common in Cornwall at that time. He would often hunt alone all day, and a short time later he was in full chase on Tregonning Hill when, as darkness fell, a violent storm blew up. The thunder was so loud his hounds were yelping with terror and cowering around their master. Suddenly by the lightning's glare a white hare with eyes like burning coals was seen on the road ahead. The terrified hounds howled and Pengersec knew instantly that this was the ghost of his murdered mistress; his horse reared and threw him to the ground as the animals fled in fright. Next morning he was found half dead, still lying where his horse had thrown him, and as he was carried home he realized he had lost the wonderful sword and with it had fled all his courage. He remembered the princess's curse.

Years passed and Pengersec lost his wife but not before she had given birth to a son, Marec. Pengersec married another woman, but she turned out to be wicked and spiteful. She drove Pengersec's heir away with her jealous accusations and plotted to poison her husband, who finally met his end on another stormy night. Pengersec was riding by the sea shore returning from the port where he sought news of Marec when the white hare with burning eyes appeared, just as before, in a flash of lightning. The horse was so frightened that it galloped headlong into the sea, and neither horse nor rider was ever seen again.

Bad Luck on Meeting A Hare

Many of the omens and portents associated with the hare seem to be very old. Belief in the bad omen of hares was written about as far back as 1159 by John of Salisbury, and in 1180 by Nigel de Longchamps.

In most places, meeting a hare was a bad omen; though some claim it is only bad if the hare approaches from the left (sinister, evil), if it comes from the right (dexter, good) that's ok as long as it doesn't actually cross your path.

In some areas it is only unlucky to meet a white hare. Meeting a brown or black hare is considered lucky, and a wish should be made when it passes.

It is bad luck to meet a hare when going to work, particularly in a dangerous occupation e.g. mining or deep sea fishing; many will turn round and return home, not venturing out again until the next meal has been eaten

For a wedding party to encounter a hare, whilst going to or returning from the ceremony, is thought to be a very bad omen for the marriage.

If you meet a hare, to counter bad luck, spit over your left shoulder and say;

"Hare before, trouble behind; change ye, cross, and free me"

Or touch each shoulder with your forefinger and say;

"Hare, hare, God send thee care." (remember Isobel Gowdie?)

If a pregnant woman encountered a hare, it was believed that her child would be born with a hare lip. She could circumvent this by tearing her garment three times, or spitting on the ground and drawing a cross in the spittle. Or if she had stepped into a hare's nest, by placing 2 stones into it, the disaster could be averted.

A white hare was thought to be a ghost, or to be an omen of death. If a hare looked in at a cottage door it was thought that a death would follow there.

In Ireland, a hare caught on May morning is said to be a witch disguised, and should be stoned or burnt. A legend collected in Ireland in 1864 suggests it is considered particularly unfortunate for a farmer or his wife to encounter a hare on May morning, as it is said to take away the milk from the cows.

In both Ireland and the Isle of Man people would set fire to the gorse and heather to drive out the witch-hares.

In Wales a hare that is difficult to skin, or will not soften in cooking is said to be a 'bad old witch' with many sins to answer for.

Gorse

In northern England, it is considered unlucky to see a hare jump on a wall. Movement of hares is also associated with adverse changes in weather. To see hares moving from low ground to high ground promised heavy rain and floods.

In Scotland hares are said to take to the open country before a snowstorm.

Country Stories

The Gamekeepers Lie Sleeping

The unfortunate hare in this well known song, whilst displaying the ability to speak, a recognisable motif from folk legend, was unable to save herself. Collected by George Gardiner from Chas. Bull of Marchwood, Southampton, 1907, and Jas. Ray, a 21 year old gypsy, at Petersfield, Hants. 1908

I got a dog and a good dog too,
I has him in my keeping,
To catch those hares that run by night,
Whilst the gamekeepers lie sleeping.

My dogs and me went out one night
To learn some education,
Up jumps a hare and away she run,
Right into a large plantation.

She had not gone so very far
Before something stopped her running,
"Oh Aunt! Oh Aunt!" She loudly cried
"Stop a minute, your Uncle's coming!"

Then I took out my old penknife,
And quickly I did paunch her,
She turned out one of the female kind,
How glad am I, I caught her.

I picks her up and I smooth her down,
And I puts her in my keeping,
I says to my dog "it's time to be going,
Whilst the gamekeepers lie sleeping."

Away me and my dog did go,
Back into the town,
I takes this hare to a labouring man ,
And sells her for a crown.

We called into some public house,
And there we got quite mellow,
For we spent that crown and another one too,
Don't you think I'm a good-hearted fellow?

Payment for Coursing

From Swythamley, near Macclesfield, Cheshire, The 'Old Hag', farm is named after a legend that a 17th century witch who lived there would turn herself into a hare, and Farmer Wood from Frith Bottom, in return for a gratuity paid to her husband, would course her with his hounds, while her husband would 'watch the sport with interest'. It is not clear whether the witch knew about the men's arrangement.

The Poacher Hanged By A Hare

In Condover Park, Shropshire, a tale is told of a poacher who had caught a fine hare and was taking it home still alive, in his sack slung over his back for supper. He was just climbing over the park wall when he heard a voice coming from the sack crying "let me out, let me out!" In great alarm he tried to throw the sack away, but he got tangled up in the cord and at that moment he slipped and fell. As he fell, the cord wrapped around his neck and the hare in the sack fell on one side of the wall, leaving the poacher suspended on the other, where he hung, unable to free himself from the noose. Some say he died there, others say he was found by the gamekeeper and tried for poaching. Anyway, he never poached another hare!

The Christmas Hare

Written in 1964 by Roger Watson, whose grandmother told him the tale she heard in the 1920s
of a hare caught after a frantic drive from Hucknall to Mansfield one Christmas Eve.
A wonderful example of Urban legend evolving into a new folklore!
The tune is a version of 'God rest ye merry gentlemen'

It was one chilly Christmas Eve, as you shall quickly hear;
There was winter on the tree tops and the air was crisp and clear.
The bus set out from Hucknall, for Mansfield it was bound,
And steadily it made its way as the night was coming down.

It was down by Newstead Woodside as we were passing there,
From out behind a thicket ran a bonny brown hare;
Down the road she started and she set a cracking pace,
And the driver shouted "Tally Ho!" and after her gave chase.

Then he revved up his engine crying "hark, hark away";
The spirit of the chase it fairly carried him away;
As we swung along the road to the music of his horn
We thought that we would never live to see the Christmas morn.

Arms and legs were flying as we lurched around the bends;
Wives clung on to husbands, and friends clung on to friends.
The conductor rang his bell like mad but the driver took no heed,
Or else he took it for encouragement, for he quickened up his speed.

And in Newstead and in Annesley they stand and stare aghast,
As they hear a bus's engine and a hare comes running past.
Imagine their amazement as they wondered what was up
When the bus went flying past and left them standing at the stop.

Now she never looked behind her and she ran so straight and true,
But the chase was nearly over when East Kirkby came in view;
For, coming past the 'Badger Box' and up to Mutton Hill,
The hare began to tire – it was time to make the kill.

Then all at once the bus stopped dead and we all fell on the floor,
And looking out the window, hare and huntsman there we saw.
He held her by the ears, saying "isn't she a winner?
I've a wife and seven kids at home, and here's our Christmas dinner!"

The Road Runner

It was nearly midnight on a cold winter's evening. We'd just come from The Cock, a country pub where we had met a group of friends for a regular monthly session, to sing a few songs and play a few tunes; Colin on melodeon, the others on melodeons, concertinas, sometimes a fiddle, and maybe a bit of percussion from the spoons – that's me. We'd had a super night, the music and company was always good. We bade farewell to our friends, stowed the instruments inside the van, climbed in and were making our way home, hoping not to encounter too much ice on the back lanes. The heater had just about warmed up enough to stop us shivering and we were on a long stretch of single track road that winds its way through farms and fields. At this time of night it was unlikely we'd meet a car on such a quiet lane, and I would see the headlights long before they got close, so driving wasn't difficult and we were chatting about the evening's music.

Then all at once a big brown hare jumped out of the bushes at the side of the lane and started running in front of us down the middle of the road! I slowed down and stayed behind the hare, to give him chance to consider where to go. I thought that if he wasn't panicked, he was more likely to take off back into the bushes and let us past. He seemed to be running at a fairly relaxed speed, not really hurrying at all. Every so often he would veer slightly to one side, but just as we thought he was about to go off into a field, he seemed to change his mind and was back right in the middle of the road again. He ran on like this with us following a few yards behind for what seemed like ages, I looked at the speedometer and he was running at a steady 20mph with no obvious effort at all. By now we had driven nearly a mile since we had been joined by our fellow traveller, and there appeared to be no immediate sign of him forsaking our company. Colin and I were in fits of laughter, it was just such a ridiculous scenario, but there was nothing we could do to encourage him to leave us. The dimmed headlights were illuminating the road ahead for the hare as well as for us, and maybe this is what kept him running in front of the van, whatever the reason he ran on and on. Then on our right there appeared a five barred gate in the entrance to a ploughed field, it was standing wide open and the gap must have been well over six feet wide. The hare spotted it too and as suddenly as he had joined us, he was gone!

CHAPTER 10
CHARMS & HEALING

Healers

Until well into the 20th century, in the countryside, simple homely medicine was the preserve of the 'goodwife' of the household, a skill every woman was expected to learn, probably from her mother, in the days when doctors were both expensive and often ineffective. For more difficult cases, charms and healing, a more advanced form of the same skill, might be practiced by a Wisewoman, and may require quite advanced herbal knowledge or magical practices; divining, removal of curses etc. (much of which would now be recognised as forms of therapy or counselling). Though there are records of Cunning Men working in this way, on the whole they were more interested in the more 'magickal' aspects, leaving the day to day treatment of ailments to their female counterparts.

It is interesting to note that the more positive aspects of 'Good Luck' associated with Hare lore are reflected in the feminine, intuitive and maternal realm, hinting at possible links with the archetype in its subversive guise, and harking back to matriarchal origins.

Theatrical superstitions appear in this section, though at a time when acting was suppressed as a female activity, being considered unseemly for the fairer sex. Some more adventurous women who started to overcome this taboo were rewarded with condemnation and a reputation for loose morals, akin to prostitution. However acting is a profession which demands an intuitive approach and for the purposes of this chapter may be considered within the spectrum of masculine/feminine to be closer to the feminine character.

Good luck - Hare Charms

Protection

In Sussex where I was born, it was customary that a newborn baby's face would be brushed with a Hare's or Rabbit's foot to ward off evil. It would then be placed beneath the pillow to prevent misfortune occurring to the child.

The heart of a hare pierced with pins and buried in the foundations of a house protected those who dwelled there from evil influences or 'witching' A rabbit's or Hare's foot was carried as a good luck charm and to ward off witches, evil and bad luck.

Some actors would apply make-up with a hare's foot, kiss it for luck and rub it on their face and hands for luck on the opening night of a play.

When I was a child growing up in the 1960s, you could buy rabbits foot key-rings in Woolworths. They were small, white or speckled brownish grey, very soft and furry with little claws, and mounted where the leg would have been with a cylindrical metal cap attached to a short chain with the key-ring at the end. They were very cheap, but if you wanted a really posh one, in the dress shop further down the High Street (I knew they were posh because all the prices were in guineas!) you could buy a proper Hares foot brooch, bigger than the rabbits feet, a lovely rich brown, and mounted with a Marquisette studded cap and there was always a tiny ring on one of the toes with a sparkly stone, and to stop the brooch getting lost, a silver chain that looped from the mount to the pin and dangled down decoratively when it was worn. Lots of really old ladies wore them on their winter coats or hats, but you never see them now except in antique shops.

"Well, the Rabbit / Hare weren't lucky were he?"
- dry Sussex country wit!

In North America, the Montagnais and Naskapi people practiced a form of divination – scapulamancy, by which the bones of a sacrificed hare were thrown into a fire, eventually the scapular (shoulder blade) would be retrieved, and the scorch marks and cracks were interpreted by a holy man.

Healing and Remedies

Newborn babies were fed a concoction of hares brain reduced to a jelly if they were unsatisfied and restless after suckling. As recently as 1930 at Alscot in Warwickshire, it was customary for the lady of the manor to supply the hares head for the purpose.

The Romans believed that if a woman ate hare flesh for seven days it would make her beautiful.

Amulets made of the head of a hare were worn by the ancient Egyptians, and are still know to be used by some Arab women.

Hares' genitals were carried to avert barrenness, and used as an ingredient in aphrodisiacs and love potions.

An Anglo-Saxon draught to prevent oversleeping – hares brains in wine. The hare is said to never close its eyes from the moment of its birth (leverets are born with eyes open), it even sleeps with its eyes wide open, so the wakefulness of the hare would be transferred to the drinker.

My daughter, Aly, related to me an experience she had walking across a local field when she chanced upon a hare, sprawled on its side, fast asleep and snoring! She stood and watched it for several minutes and it never stirred, nor did it open its eyes.

So it's official – real hares sleep with their eyes shut – at least they do in Essex!

To prevent cramps and ameliorate the symptoms of rheumatism, carry a hare's foot.
"Gouty pains are alleviated by a hare's foot cut off from the living animal" – Pliny 77CE

The bone from a hare's foot *"mitigateth the crampe"* – Scott 1584

"I no sooner handled the foot but my belly begin to loose and to break wind" - Pepys 1665
- but it was believed that it would only work if the foot included the joint.

Healing charm from the Magical Spells of Marcellius Burdigalensis, a 4/5th century
Gallic medical scholar who wrote extensively on herbalism and folk-magic healing:

> Catch a live hare, pluck *5* hairs from its belly,
> then *release the hare bidding the disease go with it, reciting;*
> *"Fuge, fuge, lepuscule, et tecum aufer coli dolorem"*
> *("run, run, little hare, and carry with you this sad disorder")*

This seems to be a fairly standard type of sympathetic magic; the hare becomes a
scapegoat, to which the disease is believed to be transferred. By taking hairs from the
animal a magical link is established conferring power to the sufferer over the scapegoat,
which then escapes, taking the disease away with it. (Possession of a body part e.g.
hair, nail clippings etc. was considered to give the new owner power over the donor,
hence the practice of burning such things to avoid them accidentally
falling into the wrong hands.)

There is an older version of a common nursery rhyme which
bears a remarkable similarity to this ritual:

> *"One, two, three, four, five,*
> *I caught a hare alive,*
> *Six, seven, eight, nine, ten,*
> *I let her go again"*

William Cowper
(1731 – 1800) and his Pet Hares

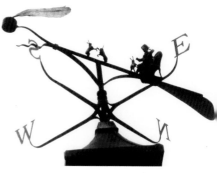

Cowper's hares in the Market Square, Olney

The poet William Cowper lived at Olney, Buckinghamshire, and suffered from what today would be diagnosed as manic-depression or Bi-polar syndrome, being treated for some time at Dr. Cotton's Home for Madmen in St Albans. In 1774, during one of the depressive periods in which he would shut himself away for months seeing virtually no-one, he was given a pet leveret which had been mistreated by the small children of a neighbour. Later he acquired two more, all three male, calling them 'Puss', 'Tiney' and 'Bess'. Cowper built for them separate houses to sleep in, but gave them freedom to roam about the house and garden by day. From his account of their behaviour, each had a distinct personality, Puss was affectionate and enjoyed being carried about and fussed, rather like a cat. Tiney would bite and did not accept this treatment, but was very playful and amusing. They would "be admitted into the parlour after supper, when the carpet afforded their feet a firm hold, they would frisk, and bound, and play a thousand gambols" All three hares were scrupulously clean in their habits and had no obvious odour or parasites. They ate a wide variety of vegetable foods preferring lettuce, dandelion, sow-thistle, wheat-straw, and musk-mallow but their staple diet was bread cut into small squares. The antics of these hares delighted Cowper who considered their company and the routine duties of caring for them a stabilising factor in his mental condition. Bess died shortly after reaching maturity, but Puss reached the age of nine and Tiney survived for almost twelve years. This account shows how the dark, melancholy sickness of a reclusive, literate, and highly creative man was transformed by the light of the hares' influence.

CHAPTER II
TEACHING

Hare Stories as Allegory

Agroup of legends and stories exists, from all over the world, in which the Hare is often described as a 'Trickster'; a word which often carries negative connotations in modern times. Though some of these stories display an element of cruelty, the Hare trickster is often just quick-witted, turning difficult situations to his own advantage. This can be achieved by eloquent or articulate persuasion, by reversing the logic, finding an unexpected, alternative interpretation or by the use of lateral thinking; another manifestation of the subversive, a combination of intelligent free thought and an unconventional disregard for rules. However, reading the stories closely there is frequently an altruistic motive in the Hare's actions hidden within them. It seems likely that the stories have been used as a means of education, particularly of children, in the manner of Biblical parables.

In some cases the message is obvious – don't behave in this way or it will be to your disadvantage. Some tales have comic value, others have clear allegorical significance, hidden messages likely to continue to be beneficial in providing guidance in a modern society.

The Hare & the Prickly-Backed Urchin (Hedgehog)

from the Brothers Grimm; Jakob 1785-1863 and Wilhelm Grimm 1786-1859,
German academics best known as collectors of folk- and fairy-tales first published 1807

One summer's morning, the sun was shining, the birds were singing, the blossoms were blooming and the entire world was happy, and the prickly-backed Urchin was happy too. He was standing by his door, sniffing the breeze and humming a little song to himself. He was thinking he'd go for a stroll to look at his turnip field. Well it wasn't really his turnip field, because it belonged to the farmer, but it was next to his house and he would nibble the turnip tops from time to time, so he called it his turnip field. He was strolling along the headland, when what should he see but a big old Hare coming along the other side.

Now the Hare was doing the same thing as the Urchin, and when the hare looked up, the urchin said "Mornin', how're ya doin'?"

But Hare rather fancied himself, and instead of saying "Good morning, how are you?" he looked down his nose at the Urchin and said in an accusing sort of a way, "What are you doing here in my field?" Well the prickly-backed Urchin was rather taken aback at this, but he replied quite politely "Just havin' a stroll round." "I should think you could find something better to do with your bandy legs than to come spying on me!" answered the Hare rudely.

Well the prickly-backed Urchin was used to a bit of teasing, because he was a lowly sort of a fellow, but he wasn't going to put up with anybody insulting his legs, he was quite proud of his legs, even if they were a little bit bandy. So he bristled himself up to the biggest size he could manage (which wasn't very impressive because he was quite a small urchin) and said to the Hare "you talk like you got legs somat' better'n me". The Hare laughed "I should think so!", "well I bet I cu'd show you a fing or two in a race" said Urchin. At this, Hare snorted "you must be joking, I'm famous for my speed, but if you're so keen, we'll have a race". "Not so fast" Urchin replied "I've got a fing or two to do first, be back 'ere in half an hour an then we'll see wot's wot"

So Urchin shot off home as fast as he could (which wasn't very fast as he really did have quite short bandy legs) and when he got to his cottage he called out "Wife! I've got somat' as you can help me wiv" and he told her the story of meeting the hare and how rude he had been, and then explained the plan he'd dreamed up to knock him down a peg or two. Well, Mrs. Urchin thought it would be a grin, so she followed her husband out to the bottom of the field and when they got there he told her, "You bop down in this 'ere furrow, and when that ol' hare comes a-runnin' up, you jump up and say 'Here I am!'"

So the prickly-backed Urchin went to meet the Hare. "Are you ready now?" asked Hare, "Aye, I is, come on then, one, two, free, GO!" and the pair bounded away down two parallel furrows, but of course Urchin stopped where he was, knowing his wife, who looked just like he did, would be at the bottom of the field to meet the Hare. Off went the hare at top speed, and he soon got to the bottom of the field, and thinking he would be there long before the Urchin, he was most surprised when up jumped his adversary shouting "Here I am!" Well the Hare thought it was a bit odd, but surely the Urchin couldn't beat him again, "Let's go again" hare cried and off he went back down the furrow. When he got to the other end, "Here I am!" shouted the Urchin, and wasn't even out of breath! Well the Hare was perplexed, but he would not be beaten by this bandy-legged upstart, after all he was a Hare!

Anyway, this kept on for half an hour or more, whenever Hare arrived at the end of the furrow, there was Urchin calling "Here I am!" so they ran again, and in the end Hare's heart gave out. So Mr. and Mrs. Urchin won the race.

Teaching that self-esteem tempered with self-knowledge can be a strength, but when allowed to become vanity and pride, destroys respect for others and may cause your downfall.

The Hare and the Tortoise

from Aesop, slave and story teller from ancient Greece 620 – 560BCE

Once upon a time there was a Hare who was so proud of how fast he could run that he was always boasting about his speed and agility. The Tortoise was so fed up with hearing him bragging, he decided to challenge him to a race, and though he didn't expect to win, at least it gave the other animals a chance to show Hare that not everyone was impressed by his proud boasting.

The Hare accepted the challenge, but although most of the animals were cheering the Tortoise, none really thought he could beat the Hare. The Hare and the Tortoise came to the starting line. "Ready, steady, GO!"

Off they both went as fast as they could run, and soon Hare was out of sight, but poor old Tortoise just plodded along, doing his best. Soon Hare looked back to see how far Tortoise was behind him. It was a warm day and Hare thought it would be alright to stop for a moment and sit down; he would be able to win the race easily even if he had a short nap. Hare settled down under a tree and started to doze, and soon he was fast asleep.

Tortoise kept walking, slowly and steadily, even though it was getting warmer, and he was starting to feel tired, he just kept going. After a while he had caught up with Hare, and as he passed, he smiled to himself as he heard the gentle snores coming from his sleeping opponent.

Japanese 'netsuke', a decorative carved toggle used to secure a purse hung from a kimono sash

Time passed and Tortoise eventually reached the finishing post, as he crossed the line all the animals cheered to see the humble creature beat the braggart. So loud was the commotion, that it woke the Hare. Quickly he roused himself, jumped up and bolted towards the finish, but too late, the Tortoise had beaten him. How humiliating!

After that he never bragged about his speed again, and he kept himself to himself ever after.

Teaching the same lesson as before, but also rewarding persistence and determination.

The Simple Minded Men Of Wilby

Attributed to the C12 Cistercian monk, Odo of Cheriton.

The villagers of Wilby in Norfolk, had forgotten to pay their rents until the day the money was due. To avoid further delay, they decided to tie the rent up in a bundle, put it in a satchel and give it to the fastest creature to deliver. Their choice of messenger was a hare, but when they told the hare where to deliver the money and let it go, it set off in completely the wrong direction!

Teaching that important duties should be taken seriously and given due attention. But if trusting another to carry them out, choose your representative wisely.

Rabbit or Hare wearing a 'scrip' or satchel. St Mary's Church, Beverley

The Story of the Man that went out Shooting

When I was a small child I was given a copy of 'Strewwelpeter' by Dr Heinrich Hoffmann (C19 German psychiatrist), an illustrated book of moral Victorian-style verses designed to encourage good manners and teach children the consequences of antisocial behaviour.
I loved this book, and it is one of my treasured possessions to this day.

This is the man that shoots the Hares;
This is the coat he always wears:
With game-bag, powder-horn and gun
He's going out to have some fun.
He finds it hard without a pair
Of spectacles to shoot the Hare.
The Hare sits snug in leaves and grass,
And laughs to see the green man pass

Now as the sun grew very hot,
And he a heavy gun had got,
He lay down underneath a tree
And went to sleep, as you may see
And while he slept like any top,
The little hare came hop,hop,hop,
Took gun and spectacles, and then
On her hind legs went off again.

The green man wakes and sees her place
The spectacles upon her face;
And now she's trying all she can
To shoot the sleepy green-coat man.
He cries and screams and runs away;
The Hare runs after him all day
And hears him call out everywhere;
Help! Fire! Help! The Hare! The Hare!

At last he stumbles at the well
Head over ears, and in he fell.
The hare stopped short, took aim, and hark!
Bang went the gun, - she missed her mark!
The poor man's wife was drinking up
Her coffee from her coffee cup;
The gun shot cup and saucer through;
"O dear!" she cried, "what shall I do?"

There lived close by the cottage there
The hare's own child, the little hare;
And while she stood upon her toes,
The coffee fell and burnt her nose.
"O dear!" she cried, with spoon in hand,
"Such fun I do not understand."

Illustrations from 'Struwwelpeter'

The White Hare of Oki

from Japan

The was once a Hare who lived on the Island of Oki. He had a yearning to visit the mainland, but the water was too wide for him to swim across, so he hit on a plan. All around the coast there were a great many crocodiles, so the Hare contrived an argument with one of them as to whether there were more Hares on Oki or crocodiles in the sea. To calculate the number of crocodiles, the Hare made them form a line, side by side across the straight, and ran across their backs, counting them as he went, but the last crocodile, realizing what Hare was doing, bit him, and pulled off all his fur. Later Hare was found by a group of brothers, who were travelling to the court to try for the princess's hand in marriage. Cruelly the older brothers laughed at the Hare and said that if he washed in the sea and dried himself in the wind, his fur would be sure to grow back. Hare did as they suggested, but the salt water and keen wind caused him great pain. Then the youngest brother took pity on him and bathed him in fresh water and dusted his skin with pollen, with which the fur grew back again, but now it was white. Hare travelled on with his new-found friend to the palace, where they learnt that the older brothers had all been rejected by the princess. But when she met the gentle youngest brother with his charming companion, she fell in love with him straight away. They were married and ruled the kingdom together, and the White Hare lived happily with them in the palace.

In this story guile is penalised but kindness is rewarded. The use of guile is only desirable provided that it is as much for the benefit of others as of oneself.

The Lion who tried to eat the Hare

from India

In a forest lived a fierce Lion who killed every animal he saw. One day the frightened animals met to try to find a way to deal with the problem. They decided amongst themselves to send one animal every day to feed to the Lion, which might stop quite so many being killed. Lion agreed as he only really needed one meal a day, and this arrangement would save him much effort.

When the turn of the Hare came, he concocted a plan to save all the animals, thinking that it is truly a brave creature who can stay calm in the face of great fear.

Hare came later than Lion's usual mealtime, who angrily asked why he had been kept waiting. Hare told a story of how he had been detained by another fierce Lion. Furious that he should have a rival, Lion demanded that Hare show him where the other Lion could be found. So Hare led him to a deep well, saying "look, here is the Lion". He roared, and seeing his reflection in the clear water and hearing the echoing of his own roar in the well, Lion jumped in to fight his adversary, but of course, he was drowned, and all the animals in the forest lived peacefully after that.

Hare uses his wits to protect others by the use of lateral thinking, ensuring that there is a place for everyone under the Moon / Sun – everyone benefits, except the tyrant.

The Lion Becomes the Hare's Horse

from Africa

The Lion and the man were brothers. The Hare wanted to be the man's brother, but the man said "No, I am the Lion's brother" Hare replied "the Lion is of no importance, he is my horse" When the Lion was told of Hare's boasting, he went straight to the Hare and confronted him. The Hare said what the man told him was a lie, and he wanted to go and tell the man so himself, but was too ill to walk, so the Lion offered to carry Hare to the man's hut. Off they went, but Hare soon asked Lion if he would wear a bridle, as it was hard for him to stay on Lion's back, because he was so ill. Lion agreed, but soon Hare complained that the flies were bothering him, could Lion give him a little stick to shoo them away with. So when Hare arrived at the man's hut he was riding on the Lion and hitting him with his stick, shouting "I told you the Lion is my horse!"

The power of mind over body is illustrated by the wit of the Hare overcoming the brute force or base instinct represented by the Lion.

The Hare put his own mother in the moon, and every night he would call "let down the rope"

The Man Kills the Hare's Mother

from Africa

The Hare and the man were friends. One day the Hare said to the man "let us kill our mothers, then we shall both be free", the man thought it would be good to be free, so he killed his own mother, but the Hare only pretended to the man that he had killed his mother, the knife he showed dripping with blood was really covered in red sap. The Hare put his own mother in the moon, and every night he would call "let down the rope" and his mother let the rope down for him to climb up to feed from her. When the man found out where the Hare's mother was, he tricked her into letting down the rope for him, then he climbed up and killed her and all her other little Hares except one. Next day the Hare came to find the rope dangling, climbed up and discovered what had happened from the surviving little Hare whereupon he determined to take revenge.

Next day the Hare told the man that he knew where to find food, saying if the man laid down in the road and closed his eyes, he'd throw food into the man's mouth. When the man did as he was told, the Hare put red-hot stones in his mouth, which killed him.

In this story Hare represents intuitive instinct, whose mother is spirit, the originator of intuition (we're back with the grandmother in the moon!). Man represents reason, and together they make up the three aspects of humanity. This parable is complex; when reason and instinct act together, a spiritual dimension is needed for a positive outcome. All three; reason, instinct and spirit are essential aspects of human nature. If any two of these three interact without the third, the result will be destructive. When Hare determines to take revenge, all reason is lost.

American Tales

When African slaves were transported to work in the cotton plantations in America, they brought with them their entire cultural heritage. A gradual evolution took place through which this became fused with aspects of the culture(s) of the land in which they found themselves. Elements of stories from Africa started to merge with American and European tales.

In 1881, Joel Chandler Harris, a white journalist and promoter of racial integration who had served an apprenticeship on a plantation in Georgia, published a book of the tales he had heard the black workers and their families telling there. 'Uncle Remus, His Songs and His Sayings: The Folk-Lore of the Old Plantation' was a collection of stories, songs and oral folklore supposedly narrated by a fictional kindly wise old ex-slave to children gathered around him, or to the little boy from the 'big house' on the plantation.

The central character in many of the tales is 'Br'er Rabbit' (the American 'Jack Rabbit' is biologically a hare), who constantly plays tricks on all the other animals, especially Br'er Fox (Brother Fox), and occasionally is outmanoeuvred by them. The Great Race is similar to both the Prickly backed Urchin and the Hare and the Tortoise, in which Br'er Turtle and Br'er Rabbit race once around the Old Plantation, but Br'er Turtle's sons hide along the way to give the appearance that he is keeping up with his opponent.

The best known story is.....

The Tar Baby

B r'er Fox was trying to think of a way to get his own back on Br'er Rabbit for all his tricks, so he went out into his shed and found a bucket of tar and some turpentine which he mixed together into a big glob that was stickier than honey and smellier than a whole bunch of skunks. Then he got an old straw hat, a comb for a mouth and a couple of buttons for eyes, and his masterpiece was ready - the 'Tar Baby'.

Br'er Rabbit was a crafty creature, but he was friendly too, always greeting anyone he met, especially strangers, so when he called out "good morning" to the Tar Baby and got no answer, he tried again. "I said good morning – how are you, stranger?" Still no answer. Well he was getting annoyed that the stranger just ignored him. "You're mighty stuck up, and if you don't say Howdy, I'm going to give you a smack" The Tar Baby just sat there, saying nothing, so Br'er Rabbit took a swing at him but his fist got stuck fast in the tar. "Let me go or I'll knock you again" said Br'er Rabbit, and tried to punch the Tar Baby with his other fist, but of course that got stuck too. By the time Br'er Rabbit had got both feet stuck as well, trying to kick the Tar Baby, and was completely helpless, Br'er Fox stepped out of the bushes where he had been hiding, watching the fun and trying not to laugh out loud.

For once Br'er Fox had Br'er Rabbit just where he wanted him, and was deciding what to do with him. He could cook him for dinner but he had no kindling to make a fire, he could hang him but he had no rope, he could drown him but there was no water nearby. Just then Br'er Rabbit spoke up "I don't care what you do to me, hang me, drown me, anything, but don't throw me into the briar patch"

Well Br'er Fox thought a bit, "If he really doesn't want me to throw him into the briar patch, then that's just what I'll do" and he picked up Br'er Rabbit and flung him as hard as he could right into the middle of the biggest, prickliest patch of briars he could find. Now the briars stuck to Br'er Rabbit, but they also stuck to the Tar Baby, and by wriggling a bit, Br'er Rabbit managed to get free, and off down the road he ran, shouting back to Br'er Fox "I told you not to throw me into the briar patch! Maybe next time you'll listen!" and with that he ran all the way home to clean the rest of the tar out of his fur.

The Bramble (Briar) patch on the Wasteland,
providing shelter from inclement weather. There is a
mewse in the poplar hedge opposite and the hares run
through from Black Patches straight into the thicket.

Here recognisable elements from both African and European tales are present. Br'er Rabbit's violent reaction to the Tar Baby would have been his downfall if he had not used his quick wits and tricked Br'er Fox into doing the one thing that could save him.

It is interesting that these stories were being collected from African Americans at the same time and in the same manner as the great European folklore collections were being made. In this case an educated white journalist and amateur anthropologist is collecting and publishing material from ex-slaves on his previous employer's plantation, continuing the tradition of publishing and circulating stories established centuries earlier, and in the process, ensuring continued survival and evolution of the material collected.

As the 20th century progressed, racial issues and the legacy of slavery developed increasingly strong political significance, particularly through the American Civil Rights Movement and the Anti-Apartheid Struggle. The Uncle Remus character became an unacceptable stereotype, and, grouped together with the 'Black and White Minstrels' and 'Gollywogs', was consigned to oblivion. By 1940 Br'er Rabbit had evolved into a more acceptable, non-racially charged character – making his debut with an animated film entitled 'The Wild Hare' - Bugs Bunny. Anyone familiar with Br'er Rabbit, who has spent half an hour watching Bugs Bunny's 'Looney Tunes' and 'Merrie Melodies' cartoon antics, will instantly recognise his provenance. The strength of the earlier stories remains and their usefulness in educating while entertaining young people should not be dismissed.

l to r; Br'er Rabbit, from the cover of an early book; and from a Walt Disney cartoon film; Bugs Bunny.

Items from my collection. Pot - Stephen Smith; jug - Helen Brown; pendant - Firedragon Pewter

CHAPTER 12
A NEW SPIRITUALITY
Elements of Hare Symbolism

The Pentacle of the Elemental Hare

The Pentacle or Pentangle is a five pointed star constructed from a single line which weaves in and out in the manner of Celtic knotwork, and represents eternity in its never ending pattern. Placed within a circle, itself another eternity symbol, the Pentacle signifies the five elements; Earth, Water, Fire, Air and Spirit which together make up the universe, physical and spiritual. This powerful and positive symbol is also the sign of humanity, being the geometric representation of the human form standing with outstretched arms and legs in a position of at the same time both strength and surrender; being made from but also subject to the elements.

The Pentacle of the Elemental Hare

It seems to me that the different aspects of the message of the archetype Hare, as I have come to understand it, correspond to the five elements, and may be illustrated by employing the Pentacle, which is also a mystical and magical symbol in its own right.

Element of Earth - Wild and Free

The adult Hare is the essence of wild and free, living in the open fields, running free as the wind upon the earth. Without home or clan, feeding where food is found; a hard life when conditions are harsh, but a life of the pure joy of living when winter is past and spring is in the air. I believe that the wild and free hare teaches us to beware of placing too much reliance on material possessions which may become a burden rather than a comfort if we hoard more than we really need.

*The Gift of the Earth Hare - **Freedom** - Running Wild and Free upon the Earth.*

Element of Water - the Feminine

The feminine Hare is changeable like the tides, fluid like water that cannot be held or restricted. I believe that if a lifestyle is causing detrimental effects on one's physical or emotional wellbeing, then a change may be needed. It may not be a fundamental change to completely remove the problem, as this approach often has unforeseen consequences that just cause another, just as difficult set of problems. Usually a change within oneself is more helpful, by trying to approach the situation with a different mindset, particularly if it involves seeing things from another person's perspective. Though I often try to do this, when I am tired or stressed it is not always easy! I am fortunate in that I have not had to take more drastic action for many years, and I firmly believe that if a relationship is worth having it is worth working at.

The feminine Hare is fertile, creative, she invites me to explore my own creativity, talents and psyche, as this is the route to self knowledge which in turn brings confidence, and will help me in the quest to try and become the best I can be. My route may not suit others, after all we are all different, and each person must find their own way to personal fulfilment. If something works for me, that's great, but the same thing may not work for you, so none of us should seek to impose our beliefs on others, that's bullying!

*The Gift of the Water Hare - **Life** - The waters of life bring fertility, flowing like the tides which are the realm of the Moon, the source of creativity.*

Element of Fire - Subversion

*The Gift of the Fire Hare – **Balance** - As fire burns away all that is dry and dead, it cleanses the way for renewal and redresses the balance.*

The subversive hare may be the 'Trickster', using quick wit and lateral thinking to sidestep a difficult situation, but I think there is a more serious role here that is helping me in my spiritual journey. Just as fire destroys the established order, the wild, subversive hare refuses to follow the herd. There are times when I feel bombarded by sources of frustration and restriction; conventions, fashion, the media - all telling me what I 'ought' to be or to do. By questioning these in favour of thinking independently, working out my individual values and standards I seek to live a fuller, more spiritual life - my own way of being. It is not necessary to accept everything we are told, in fact it can be unhelpful and positively destructive on a personal level to be limited by the expectations of others. As we are about to see, John Layard's 'Lady of the Hare', by trying too hard to live by the strict rules of her upbringing injured both her own and her daughter's emotional wellbeing. Once she began to trust her own instincts, their process of healing could begin.

Transformation Through Dreams

John Willoughby Layard (1891–1974), an English anthropologist and psychologist,
studied with, amongst others, the great analytical psychologist Carl Gustav Jung.
In the late 1940s he worked in the C.G. Jung Institute, Zurich.

In his book 'The Lady of the Hare', John Layard, a Jungian analytical psychologist, gives an account of a series of twenty-four dreams told to him over the course of several months by Mrs. Wright, the mother of a daughter, Margaret, both of whom had been emotionally repressed by a strict Presbyterian upbringing and the overbearing influence of various relatives and other figures of authority.

In her ninth dream, Mrs. Wright and Margaret were approaching a square house surrounded by snow. There were people standing around the gate, but mother and daughter walked up the drive alone. As they reached the house, the lady-owner told Margaret to fetch a drink for her, and they both went in through the front door, and were not seen again. Mrs. Wright went to the back of the house and into the kitchen, where there was a great light and everything was as white as it had been outside.

In the kitchen there were people standing watching her, and Mrs. Wright saw a white bowl with a little water, and a live hare in it. She was told she had to kill the hare, and a kitchen knife was lying by the bowl for this purpose. Terrified, she unwillingly started to cut into the hare, but was shaking so much she found the task extremely difficult. All the time the hare was sitting peacefully in the bowl, and did not seem to mind what was happening to it, in fact it continued to look straight at her with bright eyes and an expression of complete trust and satisfaction. Outside, though Mrs. Wright and her daughter had walked in the snow, they had left no footprints.

This dream, though neither John Layard nor his patient realised immediately, was the turning point in her treatment. When discussing the meaning of the dream afterwards, a sudden dawning of understanding in Mrs. Wright occurred, that she was trying too hard to be 'good' to satisfy others, and suppressing her own maternal instincts, to the detriment of her daughter.

Neither did John Layard immediately realise the significance of the hare, it was only some time later, when he had researched the symbolism surrounding the mythology of hares, that he realised just how important the central motif of the dream was.

The square house (representing the inner psyche) surrounded by snow, with a bright light and whiteness within (enlightenment dawning), being the scene of the sacrifice of the hare (agent of transformation), sitting in a white bowl (crescent moon), looking trustingly with bright eyes (willing sacrifice and spiritual awareness); these are all themes which constantly recur in hare mythology across time and on many continents. The consistency with which these motifs and interpretations appear is amazing, particularly so in this case, where, at the time, the provenance for them was not consciously known to either analyst or patient.

Element of Air - Messenger

Much as divine messengers, birds or bees have done in other mythologies, the messenger hare moves between the heavens and earth, bringing messages from the Gods, in this case the reflected light of the Moon. The messenger hare represents intuition, the means by which I find inspiration* for my art through meditation, dreams or the liminal space between sleeping and waking. For me, intuition brings flashes of inspiration as a message from the otherworld, allowing glimpses of supernatural or metaphysical images which equate with archetypal concepts. There are times when it feels as if I am also being guided and guarded by the messenger.

*The Gift of the Air Hare - **Light**.*
Air, the medium through which we
breath in the light of inspiration.

inspiration; interesting word, literally; breathing in, taking the air (or word or idea) into one's body, metaphorically making the abstract physical

Dreams and Archetypes

Much of Jung's writing deals with the use of 'Archetypes' in mythology and how ideas and concepts are communicated from the 'collective unconscious' (the repository of all life-experience available at a primeval level), via the subconscious, in the form of dreams and visions, to the conscious mind. As archetypes are symbols which work on many levels and hold within them a whole cycle of meaning and group of correspondences, when an archetype appears in a dream, it is because these meanings bear significance for the development of the dreamers' psyche; that is what the dreamer needs at this particular time, in order to grow spiritually or to advance in psychological maturity.

There are countless archetypes, many representing universal concepts, like 'mother', 'home' or 'hero', which speak to our inner psyche and provoke a profound response. Some are more specific, targeting particular aspects of human development, and often appearing as a motif in mythologies, appearing in different cultures and times, but always with the same message, e.g. Dragons or magical rings.

It has become increasingly apparent to me during my study that 'Hare' is such an archetype whose message encompasses concepts connected with spiritual fulfilment and enlightenment*this is demonstrated by the hare's achievement of immortality in the cultures of antiquity.

* enlightenment = this term carries a huge spectrum of meaning, much as the layers and levels of meaning held within an archetype. From the mere physical 'shedding of light upon' to more abstract concepts within this range, ideas which are interestingly expressed in terms of increasing light: from a fleeting 'spark of inspiration'; an 'illuminating' experience; to 'shed light on' a problem; 'the light at the end of the tunnel'; a 'guiding light' or 'beacon'; the 'light in the darkness'; 'dawning consciousness', to 'see the light'; until eventually at the other extreme, 'Enlightenment' (with a capital E), is a Buddhist concept meaning to merge with the Great Spirit, and to become absorbed within the universal divinity in perfection (though this is an aspiration which is very difficult to realise). All these different parallel concepts are present in varying degrees at different times within the mythology of the Hare.

Eureka!

Archetypes act like a bridge, operating by means of dreams and visions within the subconscious, to bring ideas and concepts from the collective unconscious into the waking world of consciousness.

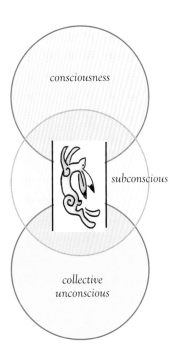

consciousness

subconscious

collective unconscious

Alchemy

Classical Greek Hermes (known as Mercury by the Romans, messenger of the Gods) is associated with the Hare, and was also said to have invented writing. By late medieval times, as Hermes Trismegistos (Hermes the thrice greatest), he was considered to be the fount of all magical knowledge. The 'hermetic' works were the basis of alchemy, an experimental science, the aim of which was the transformation of base material into the sublime – ostensibly, base metal into gold, but the ultimate goal was the spiritual transformation of human nature into the divine.

Maybe it is now time to re-establish this aim. Perhaps we all need a more spiritual dimension in our lives, and just possibly now the Hare, wild and free, as a mystical creature, feminine symbol and agent of enlightenment, has re-emerged to show us the way. Just as in the African legend, maybe the hare has come to reinforce the link with the spiritual grandmother in the moon.

Element of Spirit - Sacrifice

As the 'Lady of the Hare' discovered, the sacrificial Hare provided the transformation necessary to heal her mind and make her and her daughter whole. Legends of the Hare and the Moon have shown repeatedly that the willing self-sacrifice and giving up of physical self-centeredness by the Hare resulted in its translation into the moon and resulting immortality. Through this self sacrifice, it appears that a state of divine enlightenment may be achieved which can be equated with attaining 'Nirvana', as Buddhists believe, or entering into 'Paradise'. According to legend, the Hare has made and become the symbol of this transition, and from time to time returns to call people to reconnect with their spiritual side, bringing us a message of hope. Is this the message that re-emergence in popular consciousness of the Hare is now attempting to bring to those who can read it? It seems to me that people are being called to renounce self-centred and uncaring attitudes, and the overly materialistic approach to life which seeks happiness mainly through the acquisition of consumer goods and money. For many this only brings frustration and disappointment. As an alternative, I think we are being called to be open to the possibilities of a simpler, more spiritual existence that will bring the rewards of self fulfilment we have been seeking all along.

The Gift of the Spirit Hare – **Peace.**

After sacrifice comes fulfilment; peace and tranquillity.

The Hare's Sacrifice

This parable tells of the Buddha in one of his previous incarnations as a hare. The wise hare was teaching his three friends, the monkey, the jackal and the otter, that in order to live a good life, all beings should give alms, obey the law and observe holy days. "Tomorrow is a holy day, be sure that if a beggar passes by that you have something to give him to eat, and do not eat yourself until he has eaten his fill". So the three set out, and each found food to give a beggar, if one appeared. Hare decided to wait until the time came and not worry about finding food for himself, but then if food was required by a beggar, he would give his own body as a sacrifice. Then Sakka, the lord of all the Gods, perceiving the holiness of the Bodhisattva's* thoughts, decided to set a test for him; disguising himself as a Brahman (a travelling holy man), he set out to encounter the four animals. First he met the monkey, the jackal and the otter, each of whom offered the food they had, and the Brahman thanked them but refused to eat. Then, meeting the hare, said to him "Wise one, if I had something to eat I could fulfil my priestly duties". Delighted with this the hare said to Sakka "Brahman, you did well to come to me for food, for I will give my body that you may have meat to eat and can observe your holy duties, but as you may not kill, if you prepare a fire I will jump into it and give myself as a willing sacrifice." So the Brahman made a fire, and called the hare, who shook himself three times to remove any tiny creatures who might be hidden in his fur, that they should not be burned. Then he jumped into the fire, but the magical fire felt cold, and did not burn him. When the hare asked the meaning of this, Sakka revealed himself and, using essence squeezed from the mountain, painted hare's image on the face of the moon that he would be remembered forever for his sacrifice.

*Bodhisattva is the name given to a being who in a preparatory lifetime, already in a high state of spiritual advancement, will in a future incarnation develop into a Buddha (i.e. gain full Enlightenment).

WILD AND FREE, THE **EARTH HARE**
RUNS UPON THE LAND,
BRINGING THE GIFT OF **FREEDOM**

THE FEMININE **WATER HARE**, CHANGEABLE AS THE TIDES,
IS FERTILE AND CREATIVE.
SHE BRINGS THE GIFT OF **LIFE**

THE SUBVERSIVE **FIRE HARE** BURNS AWAY THE OLD
AND HERALDS THE NEW,
RETURNING THE GIFT OF **BALANCE**

MESSENGER OF THE GODS, THE **AIR HARE** TRAVERSES THE
HEAVENS TO BRING IN FLASHES OF INTUITION,
THE GIFT OF **LIGHT**.

THE ENLIGHTENED **SPIRIT HARE** HAS SACRIFICED HIMSELF
TO BRING US THE GIFT OF **PEACE**.

Ribbon of Stars

In Native American legend, the Great Hare is the creator of the earth, hero-saviour, father and guardian who transforms the animal nature of man. This last clearly refers to his being the agent of Enlightenment, a fitting function of a Hare-God. The Ribbon of Stars is the path which brings souls to the Spirit World and leads to union with the Great Hare.

The Pathway of the Hare

Enlightenment in Native American tradition

The native peoples around the Patawomeck (Potomac) river in Virginia, believed that the path to the afterlife led from the tops of the trees to the house of the Great Hare, where the sun rises. Here the spirit would live out a lifetime, to be reborn into the world again when that time was over.

The Dene Hareskins, a native people of North West Canada, worshipped a Moon god, also god of hunting, plenty and death, and therefore of the underworld, or spirit world. Legend tells of a member of the tribe who, by way of serpentine paths, travelled to the underworld of profound darkness, but escaped by throwing the head of a white hare into a fire, whereupon it became dawn, bringing light into the darkness.

Here are obvious parallels with Hare and Moon myths, with the allegorical transition from base nature to Enlightenment, by means of the light in the darkness. Dawn or moonlight illuminates the way or dawning consciousness brings the contents of the soul (the subconscious) into the light of day.

The Pathway of the Hare

During the past decade I have gradually come to the realisation that Hare is running ahead of us like a standard bearer, calling us to follow. The pathway we are invited to tread is the promise of peace. Every religion has held some of the same truths that Hare is telling us; Put less store in the self-obsessed ways of the world. Come to know your spiritual self. Be true to yourself. The key to peace and contentment (heaven to some) is within you. Respect and help each other. Some of these messages are explained further in Ch 13 while exploring the imagery of my own artwork.

How have I come to this place? Partly through my study of folklore and mythology, but much more so by observation of the mystical phenomenon that 'Hare' has come to represent. Since the turn of the 21st century, increasing numbers of visual artists, painters, sculptors and photographers have begun to produce images of hares, both figurative life-like animals and more stylised allegorical images; maybe

Items from my collection. Made by Carl Newman, Chloe Harford, Waterloo Farm Pottery, Paul Jenkins and Steve Cousins (Buggs Bunny from Kelloggs)

sculptures, photographs or paintings reproduced as prints and greetings cards, and sold in galleries and high street shops. These have provoked a very positive response among many people, fascinated by this elusive, charismatic and mysterious creature. Creative writers are also using hares in their work, either as the main focus of a piece, or to convey an idea linked to hare imagery in mythology. When I am working on the Hedingham Fair stall in folk festival craft fairs, I am constantly asked by customers what the hare is all about, what does it mean?

Previous Hare Incarnations

It seems to me that the Hare has been a significant cultural and spiritual icon on many occasions throughout history, and often it heralds a breakthrough in human development. At the dawn of consciousness, when people first began to rationalise existence, the 'how did we get here?' question, they formed creation myths which have endured in some form to the present day. It is surprising how many, as we have seen in previous chapters, have as their central character the Hare, either as the Grandmother in the Moon, or as the Creator God. As people started to communicate their ideas in writing, it was the Hare deity who was said to have invented (picture) writing. In the 5th century BCE, Hare and Moon stories appear in the teachings of one of the world's major spiritual leaders, the Buddha. In 1st century Britain, Boudicca's sacred Hare symbolised the resistance of the native people of Britain to Imperial Rome. The period of religious and political upheaval (approximately 1530-1660 in Britain) that begins in late medieval Europe with the Renaissance and runs through the Reformation, sees the Triple Hare appearing in church architecture at its beginning and the shape-shifting of witches into hares as a subversive theme towards its end. Eventually it settles into the philosophical movement interestingly named 'The Enlightenment', leading to the 'Age of Reason', when advances in science began to overturn the belief that many unexplained or inexplicable occurrences were the work of God or the Devil.

In more recent times there have been fairly comprehensive swings in Western belief patterns towards secularism and consumerism, and as the decline in organised religion has led to an almost total loss of its authority, churches are much less capable of giving guidance or challenging the worst excesses of human behaviour. Perhaps it is not surprising that once again the Hare symbol has re-emerged into human consciousness in order to redress the balance.

I believe that what we are witnessing now would at a personal level be like the archetype appearing increasingly clearly in dreams. Hare has progressed from the collective unconscious, and is emerging from the subconscious, the artists' realm, into the waking consciousness of the world at large. Hare is calling to more and more people, and they are beginning to take notice. But Hare is really the Icon for a movement that has been developing for several decades.

In some ways much has been achieved already; the Suffragettes, Feminism, post-feminism, and equal opportunities legislation have all made progress in the re-balancing of the gender issue, and perhaps the Pagan movement has also helped to rehabilitate the Goddess! Tolerance is beginning to replace prejudice in some areas of society and recent trends towards a simpler life, living in harmony with our environment are showing us that there are alternative lifestyle choices out there. It also seems that there have been related social phenomena in the recent past, concerned with other aspects of reawakening spiritual consciousness...

The Green Man

In the 1940s, during a period of academic interest in folklore and mysticism which began at the end of the 19th century with the early collectors and the publication of works like 'The Golden Bough' by James Frazer and later 'The White Goddess' by Robert Graves, Lady Raglan coined the term 'The Green Man' to describe foliate heads carved in medieval English and European churches and cathedrals. By the end of the 20th century interest in 'The Green Man' had developed to such an extent that artwork and books on the subject were very common. Festivals and events sprang up everywhere with the Green Man as their central theme, and the majority of the population had some understanding of the significance of, or at least some awareness of, this icon. It was summed up in the sub-title of William Anderson's book; 'Green Man - The Archetype of our Oneness with the Earth'. It is my belief that this Green Man era was synchronous with a wider movement of ecological awareness, leading to interest in conservation, organics, environmental and green issues generally, to the point where it has now filtered through even to big business and international politics. In some cases commercial gain has been the motive of establishing 'green credentials', but the effect on a substantial proportion of the population has been to generate genuine concern for the planet, and a sea-change in their behaviour in line with the new attitudes engendered by the Green Man. It is also interesting to note that the response to what had become a catastrophic period of waste and pollution was heralded by an archetype, and not a moment too soon!

In my own Artwork

Many years ago I awoke one morning with an image of the Green Man in my head. This signalled a whole new direction for my art, as until then I had mostly been working with images of folk customs and dance, but now native British mysticism started to impact upon my consciousness. While working with Green Men I discovered a whole world of imagery opening up to me, ancient British mythology, Neolithic burial chambers, stone circles, holy wells etc. and it was while I was wandering about in the woods, plantation and the old airfield near my home researching the Tree lore surrounding the Druidic Ogham script that hares leapt, quite literally, into my life.

Once hares have found their way into your head, it's impossible to ignore them - you start to see them everywhere you go, they creep into your dreams and your work, they stare out at you from gallery windows and card shop displays, they lurk in fields beside roads you have travelled frequently without ever having seen them before, they make you take notice, they just won't go away. Yes I suppose they have become a bit of an obsession - well I wouldn't be writing this book if they weren't!

*Ogham
Tree Wheel*

So, having spent the last dozen chapters examining the mystical, historical and archetypal meanings of 'Hare', it is now time to examine the meaning they have brought to certain pieces of my art. In the last bit of this book, I would like to explore the Spirit of the Hare as it relates to my work and to the work of several other artist friends who have worked with Hare imagery.

CHAPTER 13
THE SPIRIT OF THE HARE

Channelling Hares

For much of the last decade I have been working with Hare imagery. Often a dream or a vision that comes to me in that liminal space between sleeping and waking will provide the basis for a design. Alternatively, I may have been thinking about a particular aspect of Hare mythology and an image relating to this will come to me during a meditation. It seems that these visions appear in my consciousness in a similar way to how Jung describes archetypes filtering through from the collective unconscious during dreams. Dreams take place within the subconscious, while meditation operates at its threshold, and allows conscious memory to work far more efficiently, so I can usually recall images from a meditation in sharp detail, giving clues to the deeper meaning of the design. These visionary images work in several layers or levels of meaning, much as archetypes do, there may be an obvious literal meaning, but there will be symbols, associations and correspondences as well and people often say to me that the more they look, the more there is to see in my art (which is great - I must be doing something right!). Sometimes it takes me a while to decipher all the elements, even after the artwork is completed, I will suddenly notice another meaning I'd missed before. So remembering as much detail as possible is very important; I don't want to scramble the message by missing a vital bit!

Spirals

Spirals appear in the work of many Hare artists, and in 2004, quite early in my work with hare imagery, I developed the 'Moongazing Hare' design, which came to me in a meditation. This incorporated two spirals; the first leading down from the eye of the Hare, towards the haunch or belly, and formed from a twisted skein of black and red threads. The imagery represents the life-force (red thread is a life-force symbol) derived as the Chinese believed, from gazing at the moon, entering the hare's being via the eye and flowing down to the belly, the womb, resulting in the pregnancy that would in time produce leverets, which are the children of the 'Light in the Darkness' (the moon). Surrounding the full moon is a stream of gold and rainbow colours in the shape of a figure of 8, the symbol for infinity, eternity, alternately running clockwise (sunwise or deosil) and anti-clockwise (widdershins). Within this stream are shown spirits gathering as the developing leverets in readiness for birth into the physical realm. In the complete version of the Wiccan Rede, instructions are given to perform the circle dance; "deosil by the waxing moon", and "widdershins when the moon doth wane", which of course means the change of direction is made at the full moon, as illustrated. Spirals may appear as the double helix, DNA, the building blocks of life, which hold the code for all life and reproduction, and this reflects the fecundity aspect of hare symbolism.

Secondly, the spiral is a coil, emanating from the centre, tightly bound up, but with the potential when released to explode into life, just as the Hare leaps up from its form and symbolically 'becomes', bringing with it the dawn, spring, and all beginnings.

Thirdly, the spiral Labyrinth can be seen as a puzzle, a convoluted path to walk, twisting and turning, making choices, guessing which route to follow, until we finally arrive at the centre, achieving the open space within the maze, to receive our reward; the light which had been obscured by the high walls; Enlightenment, another gift of the Hare from ancient mythology, and the goal of every lifetime.

When artists portray hares, it is no surprise that spirals frequently figure in their work; it may be a device to give the impression of energy, vigour and the power of pent up speed, but the symbolism is so rich, and so ancient, that one can only wonder at how right and perfect it appears to be in this context.

Labyrinth at Rocky Valley, near Tintagel, Cornwall.

The Hare and the Pool of Dreams

This is another channelled image, but one that came as I emerged from sleep one summer morning in 2008 after I had been contemplating ideas around the 'Messenger of the Moon' and 'Enlightenment' aspects of Hare mythology. The hare descending from the moon is the messenger bringing the light of intuition, which is indirectly perceived as a reflection by the hare who seeks Enlightenment by staring into the water.

The moon-hare can be seen leaping from the left side; the intuitive, feminine, and magical side (Latin; left = sinister), towards the right; the physical, corporeal, logical side, representing the transition from the collective unconscious (or otherworld), via the subconscious, into the conscious waking world of sensual perception. Originally appearing as the shadows of the moon, seen by many as a hare, the metaphysical moon-hare becomes more solid as it incarnates before the seeking hare, who is 'scrying'; a divining technique used by clairvoyants to access visions by staring into a dark mirror or a bowl or pool of water. The pool, representing the channel through which the visions brought from the moon (the light in the darkness) are perceived, is the 'Pool of Dreams' into which drop the seeds of oblivion shed by the poppy heads, hinting at a narcotic source of inspiration popular with many Victorian visionary artists and writers. Surrounding the pool, the waters of life (which are rippled with the triple spiral, the Triskele, another life symbol) feed the tall corn, the fruits of contemplation, which is food for the soul.

The spirals on the hares represent the labyrinthine path of spiritual seeking and the life-force which is present in the message from the moon. I have been told that the ethereal forms of the hares, almost shorthand or skeletal representations, bear a remarkable resemblance to ancient aboriginal paintings of spirit animals thought to be used in shamanic journeying, and found in cave paintings from several continents.

The Hare and the Pool of Dreams

Visions and Inspiration are often encountered in that unguarded liminal state between waking and sleeping when glimpses from the other world are able to slip through, unbidden, into our consciousness like reflections in the waters of life. The shadows upon the face of the moon are in many cultures thought to be the image of the mystical Hare, messenger of the Gods, traversing between the world of mortals and of spirits bestowing, through dreams and intuition, deep truths and wisdom. These are the fruits of contemplation which feed our souls.

The Dawning Light

It is interesting to think of the obscured light, suddenly revealed at the centre of the labyrinth, as a dawning. I have found it fascinating to examine the mixture of allegorical and literal imagery incorporated in this concept of the Hare as a symbol of spiritual fulfilment or enlightenment. If the marks on the moon are a hare, then the Hare lives in the moon, and is its messenger. The moon is the light in the darkness of night; the darkness represents our basic aloneness, underneath our public face, everyone is searching for a hand to hold to help them survive. Perhaps we must eventually accept that no-one can entirely rely upon another person to pull them through, though it is important to remember that we can and do help one another to find the light. In the end though, what we need most is within ourselves. Ultimately, we must get to know, understand and love ourself. This is the process of personal exploration and maturing that Jung calls 'Individuation'. It is a manifestation of progress towards spiritual fulfilment; a step along the road to Enlightenment.

The Hare is the agent of the change in thought and understanding that the light bestows to bring about this individuation. As sunlight is reflected from the moon's surface onto the dark benighted side of the earth, so the light the Hare brings us comes from the source of life and warmth to the isolated seeker in the dark.

When light dawns upon the land in the morning, it is not the light that has moved; it is the movement of the earth that causes the light to dawn. The light was always there, it is only the observer's position that has changed. When the Hare brings a psychological dawn, it is because a change has taken place within ourself, so that now we may see the light – we become enlightened.

We speak of Mother Earth , we are *of* the earth, we *are* the earth. The sun shines on the far side of the earth when we are in the dark, it is the other side of ourselves that we need to find. If we can access the hidden side of our own psyche, truly accepting

all that we are (not just the comfortable bits), the light dawns and we become whole. Light and shade, complete. The journey of exploration of our own psyche is part of the road to Enlightenment. It is like a route-map to the spiritual plane. That is not to say that self-seeking in the selfish sense is the object, for paradoxically, the clearer the light becomes, the less individuality is defined. Once some degree of individuation is achieved then we can try to help others towards the light. However, moving the earth is not easy, but by allowing it to move in its natural way - and it happens all on its own - tomorrow always comes with the dawn.

The Winged Hare

It appears that we do not make the journey alone. I have always felt that whatever help is needed to make each small step on this journey, it is there, available to me if I only know how to look for it. Sometimes the words of a song that has been haunting me or a passage in a book will jump off the page and grab me – "so THAT'S what it meant!" is my usual response when reading something that explains a puzzling dream or a sequence of events, the significance of which I had completely missed. I may overhear a conversation, or meet someone who tells me about a place I seem to need to visit, the possibilities are endless, but by opening myself to these possibilities and being as responsive as I can, progress can sometimes be astonishing.

It feels at times as if there is something guiding me, like a sign post pointing the way. The concept of a guardian angel, guarding and guiding, is now accepted in a wider world than the Catholic primary school environment in which my spirituality was first kindled, with 'Angel Magic' a regular topic at many Mind, Body and Spirit events throughout the country, bringing even atheists into contact with this 'new' power. But what is an angel?

The word 'angel' simply means 'messenger', and an angel is usually thought to be an androgynous figure with supernatural beauty and big wings.

As I know from my own experience, archetypal concepts from the otherworld are received by artists as symbols, visually representing ideas which are both abstract and complicated by layers of meaning. It is a bit like trying to describe accurately in words a flavour or a texture, the only way it can be approximated is by using "it's like....but not quite" or like the letters that make up a word, giving clues to the meaning of the word, but each letter alone is almost meaningless. So visionary images can communicate to different individuals some of their content, but only so far as the individual's personal experience allows. This is the realm of correspondences and

To the ancients the appearance of a
rainbow after a storm signified the presence of a benign
deity. In different civilisations it was a link or a bridge spanning the
divide between the heavens and earth. By the use of a prism it can be shown that
the colours of the rainbow are the constituents of pure white light. Here the messenger of the
Gods, the Winged Hare, carries this symbol of enlightenment to the world below.

symbolism. Interestingly, when presented with such an image, even those who have little understanding of the archetypal message(s) it contains, can often be fascinated by the image itself, as if they know at a deep level that there is a message there if they can only see it.

Back to angels - Flight enables existence in two elements, on earth and in the air. Travel between land and sky implies the possibility of exchanges from one element to the other, the transfer of knowledge or the bringing of messages between the dwellers in the sky, the Gods, and mortals upon the earth. Just as bees and birds are in different mythologies thought to be messengers of the gods, winged figures have appeared in art (and writing) for millennia.

By portraying a winged character, divinely beautiful so obviously not entirely human, and delivering a message, the concept of the transmission of divine knowledge to humankind is hopefully understood. Unfortunately, it appears that these visionary images are often taken quite literally by those who misunderstand the creative process. It is sometimes difficult to see past the individual letters to the true meaning of the word!

When I first made the images that appear in this book, I was only aware of some of the significances written here, it took many months to uncover the rest, and I have no doubt that more will occur to me in time. As more designs are added to my portfolio I learn more about myself, and about life, the universe and everything. It is a fascinating journey, and I hope that my experiences have been of interest (and maybe even of some help) to whoever reads them.

But now, I would like to introduce to you some other artists and authors I have met on my journey...

CHAPTER 14
ARTISTS and FRIENDS

Over the last decade or so, I have been privileged to meet many artists working with Hare imagery, many of whom have become my friends. Some are painters or sculptors, some write books or songs, some make exquisite jewellery. For some the Hare is their principle inspiration, others are fascinated by folklore or local legends where hares appear by chance, but always whenever a hare appears, there is magic present.

She will look upon you and steal your soul away

While writing this book, I couldn't resist the opportunity to include some of these special people and their work within its pages. So I asked them to contribute an image, song or story and to tell something of the reason they work with hares and what hares mean to them. I couldn't wait to see what they would write, and it was enthralling stuff, especially when a theme seemed to be developing - just how many of them had close encounters with hares that left them deeply affected in some way, much as I had myself in the Beanfield.

So this is what they wrote.....

Tony Bates

Lincolnshire photographer, specialising in Wildlife, Landscape and Astrophotography.
Tony sells his images as cards and prints, and whenever we meet, we swap Hare-watching stories.

Frost dancer, dew hopper, dyke jumper, ditch leaper, corn stag, quick scut, wintail, puss, the malkin; just a few names for the Hare, our countryside's most enigmatic and magical creature, steeped in folklore and superstition: a mysterious animal to most people, who only get to see one fleetingly as they go about their busy daily lives.

I've lost count of the hours I've spent watching Hares, I know I never come home disappointed from a Hare watching trip, maybe no photos, but seeing and entering their world is reward enough.

It was after my first really close encounter with a wild Hare, as I sat along a hedgerow bordering an arable field, one wandered up to within a few feet of me. I looked into that startling hypnotic, some say spooky, amber eye and found a connection with a truly wild creature. I knew this was the animal I wanted to spend more time with than any other; watching, learning about and from. To date it has been a fantastic journey witnessing many facets of their lives.

Watching Hares has led to many other memorable wildlife encounters as I have sat quietly; a Stoat, frenetically searching a hedgerow in short bursts of activity, or a Fox sitting quietly surveying the scene from the shade of an oak tree. Maybe the quiet calls of a Bullfinch, Goldcrest or Coal tit, or most recently a pair of Long tailed tits nest building, watching them collect lichens from a nearby Ash tree was fascinating.

The Hare links me to many wonderful wildlife moments in our beautiful English countryside and enriches my life, so may it always grace our lives with its presence, the magical mystical Brown Hare.

Frosted Whiskers
By Tony Bates

www.tonybates-outside-in.co.uk
Tel. 01778 425137

Kit Berry

Author of the Stonewylde series of books

I met Kit at a Halloween festival where she was launching her third book in the series 'Solstice at Stonewylde'. I was selling my 'Ogham Sketchbook', and we swapped books, each dedicating to the other with 'Bright Blessings'.

Stonewylde is a secret place that exists in the fertile landscape of imagination and dreams. It's a beautiful Dorset estate hidden deep in rural England. The community lives simply, in close harmony with the Earth and the seasons.

An enclosed sanctuary where nature is protected from modern exploitation, Stonewylde is a place of standing stones and earth energy, an idyllic refuge from the stresses of contemporary life; somewhere that feeds your soul and nurtures your spirit.

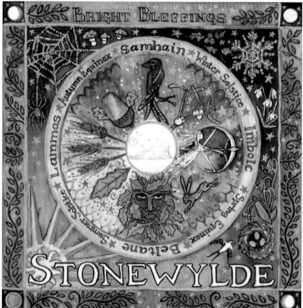

Here Sylvie, the moongazy girl, dances with the hares around the standing stone on top of the hill singing to the full moon "She is rising, she is rising, the silver one is coming, bringing her bright blessings to us all."

But all is not quite as it seems, there's another side to Stonewylde where brutality is rife...

To find out more -

www.stonewylde.com

Stonewylde Wheel of the Year © Helixtree

The Golden Hare

The hare is said to be a creature of transformation, and I'm living proof that this is true. Several years ago I was a school-teacher living in Dorset, and life was hard as a single mum with three teenage boys. I'd recently lost my mother after a long struggle with cancer. I was in a state of limbo; my life was directionless and barren, full of sadness.

One sunny summer's day I was walking alone in local woods I'd been to many times before. Sunlight filtered through the high beech canopy, dappling the thick undergrowth where birds flittered and squirrels rustled. High overhead a buzzard mewed, mingling with the cries of gulls from the sea nearby. It was a beautiful, drowsy afternoon and I had the green woodland to myself.

I turned a corner and there, in a pool of sunlight on the path before me, sat a great golden creature. I thought at first it was a fox, but then I saw the ears and realised I was looking at a hare. A shaft of sun fell like a spotlight, picking out the gold glints in its fur. It had massive ears, pink-veined and dark-tipped. Its eyes were lozenges of pure amber. Nose and whiskers twitching, the hare looked me straight in the eye. I froze, unable to breathe, terrified of scaring it away.

But the great golden hare seemed unconcerned. It crouched, ears upright, gazing at me. Something passed between us and I wanted to cry, so magical was the moment. I felt honoured, blessed. After a good couple of minutes – which felt like forever - the hare turned and slowly loped off, huge hind legs giving it a lolloping gait. It disappeared into the undergrowth and I took a deep breath, profoundly moved by such a strange experience.

The encounter both changed me and charged me. I became interested in local wildlife and folklore. I walked every day and saw nature with new eyes. I discovered the pagan path – or rather remembered it, for everything I learned seemed so familiar and right. And eventually, I began to write. Three years later Stonewylde was conceived and today I'm a full time author, happily married and living in a transformed and magical world. The hare changed my life forever.

242

Seth Lakeman

English folk singer, songwriter, and multi-instrumentalist, who mostly plays fiddle and tenor guitar.
His songs are inspired by the stories and legends of Seth's birthplace and home of Dartmoor, and he
attempts to capture the spirit and atmosphere of the wilderness of the moor.

In 2006 he was nominated for the prestigious Mercury Music Prize.

His single "The White Hare" (released October 2006) reached no 47 in the UK charts

The Seth Lakeman band playing at Bromyard folk festival September 2009 - great gig guys!

The White Hare

by Seth Lakeman from 'Freedom Fields' CD
A West-country legend that tells of a witch who takes the form of a hare and goes out looking for prey at night, if she catches your eye, she steals your soul away.

I heard her in the valley,
I heard her in the dead of night,
The warning of a white hare,
Her eyes burning bright.

Careful you don't catch her
Or give her right of way,
She will look upon you
And steal your soul away

For the white hare is calling
She's dancing in the night,
She'll be out till the morning light

Out upon the heather
A shadow came onto me,
Her hair was hanging over,
Her face I could not see.

She ran behind the rocks,
I heard the hounds cry
The image of a woman
Her head she held up high

For the white hare is calling
She's dancing in the night,
She'll be out till the morning
With her eyes burning bright
The white hare is calling you.

If you go a-hunting,
Calling out your prey,
If you see a fair maid
With hair an ashen grey.

Careful you don't catch her,
Give her right of way,
For she will look upon you,
Steal your soul away.

www.myspace.com/sethlakeman
www.sethlakeman.co.uk

Hannah Willow

Lovely Hannah, who makes the most amazing Hare jewellery.

I am an artist and jewellery maker living in the Wiltshire countryside, surrounded by hills and ancient places, carved white hill horses and rings of standing stones. My inspiration comes from the land, wild and free places, stories and folklore, poetry, myth and legend. I strive to capture the hidden knowledge held within the landscape and spark rememberings that will connect us back to our deepest roots and the hidden memory of this land.

Hare features strongly in the landscape in which I live, and is often present when I walk out across the land, running ahead of me, darting across frosted white ploughed fields and hiding in the long shadows of the summer meadows.

Since I was a child, I have had a love and fascination for Hares. I was inspired by the artwork of Kit Williams to research and learn about the folklore and mystery of hares and it is an animal that is deeply attached to the roots of our land and our psyche, embracing the wild freedom of the open fields and yet also the small hidden mysteries that call us to look within. Hare inspires and calls me to paint and create, endeavouring to bring out the magic of the unknown, the secrets of land and sky, ancestral memory, and deep connection to our past. I paint and create hares in the night sky landscape, lit by a pale Moon that illuminates the trickster hare, lights his path across the fields and back into the elusive land of our dreams.

above left - the beautiful Hare Tree pendant made by Hannah which Colin gave me for my birthday.
left - 'The Hidden Songs', which appeared on the cover of the Earth Pathways Diary 2010
above - 'Lunasadgh'

to contact Hannah -
www.hannahwillow.com

Carl Newman

Photographer and sculptor
I met Carl many years ago when I visited him in his beautiful
old Suffolk cottage surrounded by fields alive with hares. It
was spring and we watched newly hatched bluetits via a web-
cam he had set up in a nest in the garden, while discussing
which of his amazing sculptures Hedingham Fair would stock.

The Hare population has been dwindling within the UK for various reasons and I have been in the fortunate position of residing in their last stronghold of East Anglia.

For many years they have intrigued and fascinated me, steeped in mystery and folklore, their connection with the moon phase and being a symbol of fertility are well documented.It is this connection that appeals to me, the link between death and birth and the symbol of spring. Whilst watching Hares, particularly in spring, I feel honoured to be able to view their behaviour and characteristics. Hares lend themselves to the medium of sculpture, it is a joy to replicate and exaggerate the long ears, huge alert eyes and muscle bound legs. The term 'Stag of the Stubble' is incredibly appropriate when you witness the antics and hierarchy in the fields.

The whole life cycle of the hare is interesting and fraught with problems. When looking out on to a frozen snow covered field you have to feel for the small crouched animal that remains motionless and half sunken in the freezing conditions, they are to be watched the whole year through as a gauge of our land.

On many occasions I have had Hares within ten feet of me whilst sitting with a camera on a particularly active spring morning. The local fields have a fairly healthy population and one field held a head of fifteen hares all vying for a partner, a very heavy dew the night before had left the field soaking wet and the Hares were spraying the dew into the dawn light as they chased the females and boxed like I had never seen before, a vision I shall never forget.

Being able to watch any wildlife behaviour at close range is a privilege but with hares being so timid and cautious towards humans it makes the experience far more exciting and magical, it feels you are entering their world.

www.carlnewman.co.uk

opposite left - 'Who's there?'
above - Leaping Hare pewter brooch
right - a slightly dewy hare

Wendy Andrew

Artist, author and illustrator of 'Luna Moon Hare'

When I met Wendy it seemed that we had so much in common; all the concerns of the creative artist, trying to make a living, while having to live in the real world; trying to find the time and space to truly connect with the spirit that drives and inspires us; and still being everything else we have to be in the rest of the world around us. I felt I'd found a sister!

*left - Hare Dreaming
far right - Luna at
Samhain (From
Luna Moon Hare)*

I have always found the hare alluring and enigmatic. She runs through the timeless realms of myth and dances through the veils between reality and imaginings. It seems to me that she is calling us to remember... remember the ancient ways, remember the natural rhythms of life, remember to care. Whenever I see a hare it feels like a real blessing! She is stunningly beautiful, graceful and powerful. I always think of the hare as female. She seems to embody the female spirit of the land... intuitive, wild and free. She communes with the moon and understands her mysterious ways.

She somehow seems to touch my inner being like a key to my secret self.

Hare's song

Touch me I am your key,
I am forever in your soul.
Turn me and be free,
Let wildness make you whole.

In silhouette within the moon
I call to you to meet me there.
I dance to an ancient tune
Come dance with me for I am HARE!

www.paintingdreams.co.uk

The hare has been a source of inspiration for many of my paintings. Her extraordinary body can appear sometimes muscular and sinewy and sometimes soft and cuddly. Her big, all-seeing eyes are always such a joy to describe in paint.

In 'Luna Moon Hare', the hare represents the life force of the turning seasons.

It seems to me that the hare carries a vitally important message for this time. It may be embedded in our subconscious memory of ancient stories or wrapped in the allure of this beautiful creature. But on whatever level she speaks to us, I feel we would do well to listen!

Epilogue

During the writing of this book I have been on an amazing journey of discovery which is still continuing. I have found folklore and mythology from all over the world and from the dawn of time; I have met some lovely people, artists and writers who feel much as I do about the magical hare; I have learned a bit about Jungian psychology; and I have developed my own spirituality a little further. I have produced a lot of images, some of which I present for sale on our Hedingham Fair stall, where I meet more lovely people who sometimes tell me about other Hare stories and legends and with whom I have had some fascinating conversations. I am so lucky to know you all! But before I finish, let me tell you of another encounter, this time with a leveret, nearly fully grown, that I had just before the harvest this year.

The Young Hare

It was early evening around Lammas time, the wheat was not yet cut and I was walking along the poplar hedge at the side of Black Patches, the light was just beginning to fade. Back in the summer there had been signs of leverets in the middle of the field, so I wasn't surprised to see a group of three young hares in the grass on the headland about ten yards ahead. I stopped to watch and leaned on my stick to ease my aching back. They hadn't seen me at first and were playing together, just loping about and chilling out. Then one leveret straightened up and looked in my direction, the others hopped slowly into the undergrowth through the hedge and away, but the first was obviously more adventurous than his siblings and started to move through the standing crop towards me. Immediately in front of me was a semi-circle grazed by the deer living around the plantation, which acted as a natural amphitheatre, and the leveret appeared through the curtain of wheat to my right. He stood for a second looking straight at me considering for a moment, then seemed to decide that I was not a threat, and worth a closer look. Moving a step or two down-stage he sat, and we gazed at one another for what seemed at least five minutes. His fur was a sooty shade of warm brown, the markings on face and ears still indistinct, though hints of the black tips had started to show. His eyes a softer amber than the sharp glittering adult hue, and as he held my gaze I began to feel that he was delivering a message, which went something like this...

For all your learning of folklore and mythology, for all your imagery and archetype, remember this; in your mind I may be a symbol of many things, but these are human things of which I know nothing. What I know is the wind in my face as I run, the taste of dew on spring grass, the exhiliration of leaping and boxing and the bitter cold of the midnight fields. I am real, I am young, I have my whole life to live. Let me live in peace and we will meet again on my land when you least expect me.

BIBLIOGRAPHY

The Hare, Jill Mason

The Leaping Hare, George Ewart Evans & David Thomson

The Lady of the Hare, John Layard

Hare, Simon Carnell

Wildlife of Moor and Mountain, Ian Niall

Mountain Hares, A. Watson & R. Hewson

A General History of Quadrupeds, Thomas Bewick & S. Hodgson

The Encyclopedia of Superstitions, Christina Hole

Penguin Guide to the Superstitions of Britain and Ireland, Steve Roud

IBM Dictionary of Superstitions, Iona Opie & Moira Tatem

Black Cats and Chimney Sweeps, Past Times

A Penny for the Ploughboys, Colin Cater

Folklore Journal December 1892

A Dictionary of British Folk Tales, Katharine M. Briggs

Everyman's book of English Folk Tales, Sybil Marshall

The Folklore of Hertfordshire, Doris Jones-Baker

Folklore Myths and Legends of Britain, Readers Digest

The Lore of the Land, Jennifer Westwood & Jacqueline Simpson

Traditions & Hearthside Stories of West Cornwall, W. Bottrell

The Witches of North Yorkshire, Michael Wray

Weather Lore, Richard Inwards

Ogham Sketchbook, Karen Cater

Pagan Pathways, Pete Jennings

The Lunar Almanac, Rosemary Ellen Guiley

The Moon Myth and Image, Jules Cashford
The Golden Bough, J.G. Frazer
The White Goddess, Robert Graves
The Great Scottish Witch Hunt, P.G. Maxwell Stuart
An Egyptian Hieroglyphic Dictionary, E.A. Wallis Budge
The Indians' Book, Natalie Curtis
Strewwelpeter, Dr. Heinrich Hoffmann
The Popular Ballads of England and Scotland, F.J. Child
The Idiom of the People, James Reeves
Constant Lovers, Hammond & Gardiner
Marrowbones, Hammond & Gardiner
Folksongs Sung in Ulster, Robin Morton
Everyman's Book of British Ballads, Roy Palmer

INDEX of STORIES and SONGS

Stories

Songs

INDEX

258

Index of Deities

Many of the illustrations in this book are available
as greetings cards, mounted prints or T-shirts.
Some of the ceramic, pewter and leather items
in the paintings also appear for sale in
Hedingham Fair's catalogue.

For a free illustrated catalogue:
www.hedinghamfair.co.uk
e-mail; info@hedinghamfair.co.uk
Tel. 01787 462731

260

also by the same author

The Ogham Sketchbook

The Ogham Tree Alphabet is the only native British writing system, devised over 2000 years ago by Celtic Druids, and carved using simple notches onto wood or stone. Not only is it an alphabet, but also a calendar and zodiac, with each tree or shrub representing a lunar month, a solstice or equinox. Around these has grown up an extensive mythology of historical and religious stories, of the uses of each tree for craftwork and medicine, and a divinatory system similar to the Tarot.

Working for many years as an artist, Karen Cater has revealed searching insights into Britain's native culture: its customs, folklore, mythology, mysticism and traditions. Discovering the Ogham, Karen was enthralled. How could such mysteries be encoded in the land itself, in its flora and fauna? She set out to produce a series of designs based on each Ogham symbol, and working in harmony with her landscape she made a pilgrimage to each tree, finding most of them within a short distance of her home. With mind and spirit open, she kept a diary of her experiences. Her unique magical journey unfolds through this book.

Experience the changing and enriching process that the trees bestowed, gaining knowledge both into the world of long ago and into living peacefully in the modern world.

available from www.hedinghamfair.co.uk
ISBN 978-0-9556475-0-5
www.hedinghamfair.co.uk